The Blackmail Club

A Jack McCall Mystery

by

DAVID BISHOP

TELEMACHUS PRESS

Cover Designed by Telemachus Press, LLC

Cover Art:
Copyright © shutterstock/US Capitol Congress House Representatives Senate Night Reflections Washington DC/28532185/Bill Perry
Copyright © shutterstock/Sexy Woman's Legs/47123824/Nejron Photo

Published by Telemachus Press, LLC
http://www.telemachuspress.com

Visit the author website:
http://www.davidbishopbooks.com

ISBN# 978-1-937698-77-5 (eBook)
ISBN# 978-1-937698-78-2 (paperback)

Version 2012.01.17

Printed in the United States of America

10 9 8 7 6 5 4 3 2 1

Novels by David Bishop

For current information on new releases visit:
www.davidbishopbooks.com

Current Titles:

The Beholder

Who Murdered Garson Talmadge

The Woman

The Third Coincidence

2012 Releases:

The Blackmail Club   February, 2012

The Original Alibi   Summer, 2012

Future Titles:

Empty Promises

Murder by Choice

The Red Hat Murders

The Schroeder Protocol

To be notified when each of the above titles are available,
send your email address to:
david@davidbishopbooks.com

For more information on books and characters visit:
www.davidbishopbooks.com

Each forthcoming novel will have a new list of titles and dates.

Dedication

This novel is dedicated to my loyal readers. It is for your enjoyment that I write. The Blackmail Club is also dedicated to my first son, Todd David Bishop. And to all my other relatives and loved ones whose faith in me was critical to my surviving the early writing years, including my sister, Diane Kilby, and the love of my life, Jody. And no thanks could be complete without remembering my unselfish and talented editors: Kim Mellen, John Logan, Jamie Wilson, Jerry Summers, and the talented and sincere people at Telemachus Press who have done so much to further the success of my novels.

The Blackmail Club

A Jack McCall Mystery

PROLOGUE

DR. CHRISTOPHER ANDUJAR was swimming in a sea of fear, confusion, and hopelessness. His life had unraveled.

As a psychiatrist he understood the gloom of depression, the danger. But his detached clinical knowledge made no difference. He was lost. Swamped by the very forces he had controlled just a few days before—or thought that he had. His prayers had gone unanswered and nothing any longer seemed worth the effort.

Suddenly his hand jerked and the air ripened with gun stink.

His head recoiled, then flopped forward, a softened thump on the desktop, his cheek wrinkling against the drag of the blotter. His hand, still cradling the gun, made his final sound, a thud on the mahogany desk, his finger, protruding through the trigger housing, pointed at the ceiling.

A lifetime of accumulated ink stains, and one stubborn spot of mustard, disappeared as the green felt pad sopped red.

Then the door to his study clicked shut.

CHAPTER 1

THE OFFICIAL RECORD stated Jack McCall's wife, Rachel, had been dead four months, but for Jack it had been the kind of time you couldn't find on a watch or a calendar.

He also knew it was time to get back to work. His friend and father figure, Dr. Christopher Andujar was dead. The police had closed the case with the label, suicide. But Chris's widow, Sarah, believed her husband had been blackmailed prior to taking his own life, and that made the blackmailer a murderer, or so she said.

After Jack and Rachel had closed a government case known as The Third Coincidence, he resigned from the CIA and she left the FBI. They remained in Washington, D.C. and, after their honeymoon, opened McCall Investigations, partnering with Nora Burke, a former DC homicide detective. A few months later, Rachel had been killed and Jack traveled throughout Europe and the Middle East trying to ascertain if his wife's death might be blowback from his counterintelligence work. Finding no linkage, he had flown home from Egypt. His first order of business would be getting to the bottom of the death of Chris Andujar.

Jack felt that had he been less self-absorbed, he might have saved Christopher. He couldn't undo the death of his friend, but, by God, he was determined to find out who killed Chris or what drove him to kill himself. It would be far less than Jack owed the man, but it was all he could do, and he would not rest until it was done.

After unpacking, he called Sergeant Suggs, the DC homicide detective who had handled the inquiry into Chris's death. Suggs wasn't in. Jack left a message, made a drink and sat down at his piano. After trying several tunes, all of which sounded like the woman-gone blues he pulled the cover down over the keys. He stood at the window watching the light rain which had been falling off and on most of the day. Then his cell phone rang; he recognized Nora Burke's voice.

"Hi, Jack, welcome back."

"It's good to be home. I'm unpacked and raring to go. Have you heard from Sarah? We need her take on the death of her husband. It's a reasonable place to start."

"I set it up for Tuesday. That'll give you tonight to get settled at home and tomorrow to get re-acquainted with your office. You do remember where we are?" she asked, "eighth floor?" I deserved the remark. I hadn't been to the office even once since Rachel died. After a polite laugh, she went on. "I told Sarah we'd be at her home around noon. She said you knew how to get there. You want me to call Sergeant Suggs?"

"I've already left a message for him. I briefly met the man once so it's probably a good idea I touch base with him."

Jack poured two more fingers of Maker's Mark and headed upstairs while listening to Nora bring him current on a few minor matters MI, the acronym she had given McCall Investigations, had going.

At the top of the stairs he paused to read a framed engraving he had brought back from Europe. The passage was from *A Tale of Two Cities*, and it summarized the last year of his life.

It was the best of times, it was the worst of times. It was the season of Light, it was the season of Darkness. It was the spring of Hope, it was the winter of Despair.

Just when he thought Nora was winding down, she said, "There's another matter. You have an appointment Monday at four in the afternoon."

"I don't really want us taking on anything else. Chris's death gets our full attention. This one's personal."

"Let me call you back on my cell. I've got a date so I need to get out of here. We can talk while I'm driving home. Okay?" Jack grunted. Then Nora said, "Sometimes calls get dropped in the underground parking so it'll be after I get up on the street."

With the drink in hand, Jack stepped out onto the small patio off the second-story bedroom where he and Rachel used to sit and watch the Potomac River. He ignored the soft hypnotic rain falling from a sky flexing between dim and dark.

Some nights, when the wind was just right, the sounds from Georgetown drifted close enough to be heard, but not tonight, not in the damp air. He leaned on the wet rail and listened to the gentle sounds of leaves swaying in an easy wind, periodically punctured by the deep songs of distant frogs.

He had lived so many places during the past twenty years of foreign intelligence service, but he was beginning to consider Washington, D.C., home. It was a beautiful city, at least on the surface. A closer look revealed a city in which some people had way too much power, arrogant and corrupting power, while most struggled to sustain economic equilibrium. The seat of the most powerful government in the world, and yet a city that each year was looking more and more like a fortress.

After a few minutes he heard the cooing voices of a couple walking on the far side of the street. The woman reached beyond their umbrella to point at the lights twinkling off the river. The very lights Rachel always said made the river seem alive.

The man tilted back the umbrella. The couple kissed, giggled, and moved on leaving Jack with his memories and diluting whiskey. Then his phone rang again, and Nora picked back up with what she had been saying.

"The Monday appointment at four, you're interviewing Max Logan. Now before you say anything, there's a story to this. You'll be getting me out of a hole. One I dug for myself."

"Tell me."

"You remember my ex-homicide partner, Frank Wade? Well, before me, Max Logan had been Frank's partner. When Max retired, Frank tapped me."

"How does that get me an appointment to interview Max?" Jack asked as he went inside, pulling the sliding door closed and wandering back downstairs.

"I run into Max here and there, sometimes he stops by the office to say hi. He tried being retired, but had no real hobbies. He works some as a security guard and doesn't like it. He wants back in the game, part time. I kept telling Max I had nothing, that maybe when you got back and things got cooking. Listen, I dug the hole and I can get myself out of it, but Max is a first-rate detective. Frank always said he could read the streets like a child reads a popup book. And Max is a good guy. The job never corrupted him or jaded him. I know we don't need him, but if we ever do need someone, well, Max would be a good choice. The man knows everybody in this town, and is well liked."

"Sold. Four o'clock, tomorrow. Oops, I got an incoming, its Suggs. I'll talk to you later." Jack switched lines. "Jack McCall."

"McCall, this is Sergeant Suggs, DC homicide. You called me."

"Thank you for returning my call, Sergeant Suggs. We met briefly last year when—"

"I remember, The Third Coincidence case. The one that made you a bit of a legend in this town, but then legends around here are a dime a dozen. What do you need? And it better be important. This is Sunday, a day of rest if you haven't heard?"

"I'd like to talk with you about the death of Dr. Christopher Andujar."

"McCall, I was sorry to read of the death of your wife some months back. But let's get something straight. I don't like you private guys poking into my cases."

Jack was about to tell the violent crime's detective where he could shove his attitude when he heard Suggs exhale. "Ah, screw it," he said. "The Andujar case is closed. Whatdaya wanna know?" The detective's voice sounded weary.

"Thank you, Sergeant. I was very close to Chris Andujar. I'm going to see his widow on Tuesday. She's asking for my help."

"With what? It's over!"

"Not in her mind, Sergeant. Whatever it is, I'll be better equipped to help if you'll give me a rundown on the death of her husband ... Please."

Suggs's voice came right out of the freezer. "The bullet entered Dr. Andujar's head from close range. The medical examiner found powder stippling around the wound and the star-like pattern which results from a close shot into the cranium. He was holding his own gun with his smudged fingerprints, and powder traces were found on his hand. There was nothing suggesting burglary and there were no signs of forced entry or foul play."

No longer sounding weary, Suggs had charged through his summary like a telephone solicitor racing through a say-this-when-they-say-that script. After the detective took a deep breath, he closed with, "It was a suicide. Open and shut. End of story."

Jack heard the dial tone. "Asshole!" he screamed at the silent phone. Somehow that seemed more adult than hammering the innocent phone against its cradle.

CHAPTER 2

AT FOUR MONDAY afternoon, Nora leaned into Jack's office. "Max Logan's in the lobby. He and I have talked plenty, so I'll leave you boys to bond. I'll watch the front."

Jack walked out to see a fireplug of a man in his sixties with a full head of salt and pepper hair and a hint of a pot belly. He had a broad nose and busy eyes. He rose without effort and stood around six feet tall, several inches shorter than Jack.

"Mr. McCall, I'm Max Logan. Thank you for seeing me."

"My pleasure, Mr. Logan. Would you like some coffee or tea, maybe a bottle of water?"

"A bottle of water, if you will. Except for a morning cup, I'm off me coffee. A large dose of water during the day, chased by a wee taste of the Irish curse at night. That's the secret."

"Sounds like a recipe for eternal life. I'm Jack. Will Max be okay?"

"It's me name, so that'll do just fine." He settled into a chair and pointed toward Rachel's picture on the credenza behind Jack. "Your wife?"

Jack nodded. "Rachel died a little more than four months ago. Hit and run. Unsolved."

"Any witnesses?"

"A couple, but they only remembered a white van, like a million others in the city. No markings. The person behind the wheel wore a white baseball cap. They couldn't even say if the driver was a man or woman."

Max shook his head. "I understand the sadness in your eyes when you said her name. My wife died six years ago."

"What was her name?"

"Colleen. Her maiden name, O'Grady. I called her Etain, an ancient Irish word that means 'Goddess who married a mortal.'" Max's face took on a sorrowful look. "We got married late, but we had twenty wonderful years together before the cancer took her."

"I'm sorry for your loss," Jack said, quietly wishing he had gotten twenty years with Rachel. They talked a while about Max's thirty years with the DC police department, the last fifteen in homicide. Then Jack asked, "Did Nora speak with you about our not needing anyone now?"

"Yes. I still wanted us to meet. Hopefully reach an understanding. I can handle whatever help you might be needing, whenever you bump up against a situation."

"That could happen, Max. We're looking into something right now on which there could be something, but no guarantee. It's loose, but the best I can do at the moment."

"I appreciate your candor. When you call, I'll be here."

They shook hands, and Jack stayed near Max. "When you turn on the blarney, you have the lilt common to South Ireland, yet certain words suggest the lowlands of Scotland. Which is it?"

Max raised his eyebrows. "You've a good ear, Jack. My pa and his family were from a small town in Scotland on the north shore of the Firth of Forth. Both my ma and my wife were born in County Cork, Ireland. So I'm a mutt, I 'spose."

He chuckled. "My folks moved to Chicago when I was very young. Ma insisted we speak English, so I was always hearing Pa with a Scottish accent, and Ma with her Irish brogue. Truth being, I'm not often sure which I'm using when."

"Americans find the Irish and Scottish accents charming," Jack said. "That's probably why you selectively turn it on."

"Aye, you've found me out. Nora told me a leprechaun couldn't sneak past ya at midnight."

Nora leaned in to put an end to Jack's and Max's spreading of the blarney. "Suggs is on the phone." She pointed like Uncle Sam on a recruiting poster. "He wants you."

Jack walked back around his desk, gave Max a signal to wait, and picked up his phone. Nora loitered in the doorway. "Hello, Sergeant Suggs. What can I do for you?"

"Forty minutes ago my partner and I pulled a call. City Sanitation found the ripe body of a man shot and left in a trash dumpster. Smells like at least two, maybe three-day leftovers. The dumpster's behind your high-rise."

The detective bit off his next words. "Chief Mandrake asks that you come to the scene."

"This would seem a routine homicide, Sergeant. How did Police Chief Mandrake even know about it?"

"He was with the chief of detectives when the call came in. Chief Mandrake said, 'Hey, that's the building Jack McCall's in. Get him down there. Maybe he knows something.' So are you coming McCall?"

"How does this connect to me?"

"I'm getting to that." Jack heard Suggs take a hard breath before continuing. "The victim had no ID on him, but he had a cigarette pack rolled up in his t-shirt sleeve with a matchbook slid inside the pack's cellophane wrapper. Your name and address were written inside. I ain't got all day to chat, McCall, you coming or what? It makes me no never mind."

"Be right there." Jack hung up and looked at Max. "You know Sergeant Paul Suggs?"

"A long time. We teamed on homicides for a lot a years."

"How can I get the chip off his shoulder?"

Max grinned. "Paul Suggs is Wyatt Earp caught in a time warp. He resents the movement to coddle-the-bad-guys, but he's determined to get his thirty-year pension, shouldn't have long to go."

"How do I get closer to him?"

"Don't take his shit. Don't let him get you angry, but don't be intimidated. Kid with him some, but not about the squeak in his shoe."

"Squeak?"

"Yeah. He's worn the same kinda black soft-soled shoes like, forever. The left one squeaks, always has. His walk must have something to do with it, 'cause it don't stop when he gets a new pair. He can't hear the squeak. His ears just don't pick it up. The guys have razzed him to the point where it's like picking at a scab."

"I'm headed down there. Wanna tag along?"

"Sure. I was hoping you'd ask. Be good to see Pauli again."

"Okay, Max. Let's not keep the good Sergeant waiting. The man has a corpse with our name on it."

CHAPTER 3

THE LATE AFTERNOON sky, smeared with illumination from the rotating lights atop the police cars, cast the alley in an eerie, reddish-grayish-yellowish hue.

As Jack and Max approached the scene, some local youths, with their caps turned backwards, sat along the top of a block wall at the back of the alley like fans in a first row of bleacher seats. One of them hollered, "Where's the CSI babes?" They all giggled.

A uniformed officer stopped the two men. Max pointed, "There's Pauli."

Twenty yards away, Sergeant Suggs stood pushing down one side of his shirt collar that poked out the way collars do when one side lacks a stay. He moved toward them, unfastened his collar button, the erect side relaxed. Then he yanked loose the knot in his gray knit tie, the kind with a square bottom that was popular a few decades back.

"I'm pleased to see you again, Sergeant."

"What's pleasing about it, McCall? I got your nose in my case."

"You called me, Sergeant."

"You trying to fuck with me, McCall? Cause that'd come in real handy. I need someone in my life to give a ration of shit on days that turn sour. Make that every damn day."

Suggs's chin hinged along the deep lines that creased down from the corners of his mouth. He feigned a jab at Max's mid-section. "Hey, Max man, you good-for-nothing mick, I thought you retired."

"I'm working some with this lad." Max stepped closer. "Don't bust his chops. Jack's one of the good guys." Then he stepped back. "So, whatdaya got?"

The gruff cop shrugged. "A John Doe." He jerked his head toward the dumpster and led them on a path that avoided the portions of the search grid the technicians had not yet completed. Two flashbulbs sparked on their right.

"We bagged two shell casings from a thirty-eight, down there," Suggs motioned, "near the wall of the building at the far end of the dumpster. I need you guys to ID the vic."

The two men leaned forward taking care not to touch the dumpster. Jack had never seen the blunt-nosed corpse, and he said so. Max shook his head, neither had he.

"A good soldier," Max said, "never knows just when the Lord will be giving him passage to Fiddlers' Green."

Suggs, who stood about five-ten, raised his chunky body onto his toes and looked over the edge of the dumpster. "Come on, guys. This fellow was headin' for your office. Take another look."

Max took out a packet of menthol-flavored lozenges. They each took one.

"Sergeant, the body is on top of the trash," Jack said. "Janitors come at night, so it's a stretch to conclude this fella was coming to see us late on Friday after the janitors had finished. But if he was, he never got to us and wasn't expected. We don't know him."

The unfortunate stranger had a Popeye tattoo on his right bicep. His t-shirt was dark enough that in the smorgasbord lighting, even with a flashlight, Jack couldn't decide between black, dark brown, or navy blue. He guessed the victim's age as somewhere in his sixties.

"The janitor service did come Friday night," Suggs said. "We checked. That supports him being killed sometime between late Friday and now. My nose votes for Friday." He gestured toward the victim's legs. "That smaller torn bag is home garbage, some cheap bastard dumping where he works to save a nickel."

The putrefied food stuffs inside the dumpster had attracted a regiment of busy ants which ignored the crime scene tape to trail over the lip of the dumpster.

"The body likely stayed the way it went down until the refuse workers threw back the lid and found him a little more than an hour ago," Suggs reasoned.

"Looks as if he climbed into the dumpster before being shot," Jack said. "You agree?"

"Yah, you betcha. The first shot got 'im in the ticker," Suggs said poking Jack in the chest, with a finger crowned with a chewed nail.

"That was the kill shot, all right," Jack said. "Then after he dropped below the top of the dumpster, the shooter added the head shot to clinch it."

A middle-aged woman walked purposely toward the dumpster. Jack recognized her from the news: Mildred Rutledge, doctor of Forensic Pathology and DC's medical examiner. She was not attractive enough to intimidate other women, yet shapely enough to draw a man's eyes.

Jack watched her small, deft hand gestures as she spoke. "I'm going in for a closer look. I don't want the body moved until I've made a preliminary check for lividity and rigor." She moved away from the ants, slipped on an impervious coverall, gloves and boots that fit over her shoes, then leaned on a co-worker while tugging her shoe covers tight. The co-worker also helped her into the dumpster.

After climbing out, she talked with Suggs. He jerked his head toward Jack. She looked over, nodded, and brushed back her windblown brown hair. When she came over, she grasped Max's forearms and they shared the look of old friends not expecting to see each other.

She moved her pink tongue over her red upper lip. "Mr. McCall, you understand my comments will be preliminary." She leaned on Max to pull off the boots covering her shoes. "There are procedures we will not be able to perform until the body is out of that box."

Her manner didn't acknowledge the pungent fumes that continued to attack Jack's nose and eyes, but she did take one of Max's lozenges. Jack took a second one. The three of them moved to the upwind end of the dumpster.

"The belly is already distended," she began. "This bloated condition normally follows both the earlier rigor mortis and the later flaccidity. There are blisters on the skin and the lips are puffed. Fluid is leaking from his ears, and there are fly larvae in his mouth." Dr. Rutledge pushed down on the top of her small flashlight and pointed the beam. "You can see that maggots have been eating the skin, and look, look at his neck. Spiders have already arrived to feast on the maggots. All this suggests the victim has been dead more than two days. Naturally, all this can be altered by stuff like the weather and the bacteria and bugs indigenous to a dumpster in an alley."

"Thank you, Doctor. Any release of information will come from your office or the police department, not McCall Investigations."

She reached inside her blouse to reposition a bra strap that had slipped toward the crown of her shoulder. "Now if you'll excuse me."

Jack walked up to Paul Suggs. "May I see the matchbook?"

Suggs led Jack to the closed trunk of one of the squad cars and handed him a clear evidence bag. The opened matchbook was trapped inside with Jack's name and address hand-printed in block letters. He turned over the evidence bag. The back of the bright red matchbook cover was embossed with gold foil in the outline of a woman's legs sitting crossed over the name Donny's Gentlemen's Club.

Jack wondered if this reference to Donny Andujar meant anything more than the victim frequented his club, but he said nothing. Then Jack glanced at Suggs. "Anything else?"

"He had a ballpoint pen clipped in the neck of his t-shirt. The ink appears to match the writing of your name. We'll confirm that later. Did you have a Friday afternoon appointment, a no show?"

Jack shook his head. "No appointments, Sergeant. I told you. We do not know this guy."

Suggs shrugged. "If this was a heist, the robber could've made him get in the dumpster to intimidate him. But robbers rarely shoot unless the person resists, which wasn't likely once the vic got into the dumpster."

"Could the victim have been shot and then put in the dumpster?" Jack asked.

"Could, but if you're the shooter, why shoot and lift?"

"Maybe he was shot somewhere else and dumped here?"

They both looked up when the evidence team turned on their Klieg lights to brighten the crime scene as twilight matured toward darkness.

"Maybe," Suggs allowed, "but that don't explain the shell casings next to the dumpster. Of course, if the casings don't match up with the slugs or we don't find the slugs in the vic or the dumpster, then your 'maybe' gets stronger."

Max, who had lingered near the dumpster, came over to join them. "My two cents," he said, "this here's a killing. Not a robbery."

Suggs's pudgy face wobbled slightly while he nodded, listening to Max.

"It's time for us to get out of your hair, Sergeant," Jack said. "Please give my appreciation to Chief Mandrake, and I'd like to be kept informed, including the victim's identity."

"I'll pass on your request to the chief. But don't forget," Suggs said, flipping his wrist back and forth between them, "communication is a two-way street. If you find out who this guy is or why he was heading your way, let me know. Deal?"

"Deal."

"Listen, McCall, Max says you're okay, but I don't like nobody using politics to nose into my cases."

"Which part of Minnesota do you come from, Sergeant?"

"Little town, north of the Twin Cities, you never heard of it. Been here most of my life. You could still tell, huh?"

"Yah, you betcha."

Suggs's face took on an unpracticed smile. "The Norwegian farm still slips out."

"Listen, Sergeant, I don't blame you for getting pissed when people play politics in police matters. I imagine it happens a lot in this town. I didn't know anything about this until you called me, so you know there were no politics played from my end."

"Let's leave it at that." Suggs said, before following Jack under the yellow tape and outside the crime scene. Then the detective touched Max on his arm. "When we were doing this together, you were pretty good at reading the scene. What did you see?"

While Suggs wedged an unlit half-smoked cigar into the corner of his mouth, Max glanced at Jack who nodded his approval.

"The victim was left-handed," Max answered. "My guess is he was a night janitor, maybe with this building's janitorial service. Then again, if he was heading for McCall's office he likely worked for a different service."

"I picked up on the left-handed part," Suggs said. "His skin appeared lighter on top of his right wrist, which also had less hair. Most people wear their watch on their weaker arm. And the cigarette pack was rolled up in his right t-shirt sleeve. But how did you get 'works nights as a janitor'?"

"His head hair is all matted and gnarled from wearing the stocking cap that's half-stuffed in his back pocket. Despite the death pale of his skin, it looked to me like he had a tan when he died. That suggests he's outside a lot during the day, so he either had a day job outside or worked nights. A day job outside is likely inconsistent with the stocking cap. A day job inside isn't a great fit with his tan."

Jack grinned.

"The soles of his shoes," Max continued with a twinkle in his eye, "went to the soul of the matter. They support the idea he did janitor work and confirm he was left-handed, and that all jibes with his cap and tan."

"Oh!" Suggs said as his eyes reshaped into saucers.

"When you go back, look at his left shoe. The sole is worn thin at and just above the toe. That won't happen from walking. The top of his shoe above the worn area is heavily discolored. The top of the right shoe has a similar discoloration, but much less than his left. Your lab experts will likely find the discoloration is floor-cleaning solution. When janitors run their big machines on a hard-surface floor, they often keep a scouring pad with them. They use it under their toe to scrub off the stubborn black marks caused by the heels on some shoes." Max demonstrated. "The old-timers call it Fred-Astaireing the floor. Most janitors do it with their stronger and better coordinated leg. In this case the victim's left."

Sergeant Suggs continued chewing his cold cigar while listening.

Jack could see that Max was enjoying demonstrating he still had the eye for the details of a crime scene and a feel for how it all fit together. He was clearly showing off, probably mostly for him, but Suggs had asked.

Max shrugged. "Take care, Pauli."

Suggs nodded while pointing his cold soggy cigar toward Max. "You can still kick ass, Maxman."

The wind slapped at Jack and Max when they turned the corner of the building. Ugly clouds were crowding the sky and the air smelled damp. Max flipped up the collar on his jacket.

"I thought this was spring," Jack said, watching a little whirlwind lift leaves and odd pieces of paper from the sidewalk.

"The season's in the seam. The weather's a coin flip every day."

Jack leaned against the wall in the elevator. "Now tell me what else you saw."

The elevator stopped at the floor below MI. Two people got in. Instead of answering Jack's question, Max told him the story behind the word *blarney*: "It began when the Irish Lord of Blarney Castle would dazzle the Queen of England with colorful double-talk rather than obey her royal edicts. The queen came to refer to the lord's reports as blarney."

Back in Jack's office Max took the last swig from the water bottle he'd left on the desk before answering. "The vic wore silk socks and had gold-capped teeth. Not what you'd expect for a janitor, unless he owned the business and it was successful. Then again, maybe he had another source of income, maybe criminal, could be that's what brought him to an early end."

Jack pinched his nose and blew out trying to dispel the memory of the stench he'd brought back from the crime scene. "The victim had been under heavy stress for some weeks prior to his death."

"Cause?" Max asked.

"The creases in his belt showed he had it cinched two notches tighter than normal, so he had recently changed his eating habits."

"You got a wee touch of the observer in ya too."

"You saw more than I did. Great work, Max."

"Thanks, Jack. It's parta convincin' ya to take me on."

"When we get something requiring more manpower, I just hope you're still available."

Jack walked Max to the door, and then told Nora about the corpse in the dumpster. They decided that whoever the dead guy was it looked like he planned to contact MI, but the killer got to him before he could. They would remember the matchbook, but, at least for now, had no reason to connect Donny Andujar to this killing.

CHAPTER 4

NORA BURKE'S SHADOW twisting and ducking against her window shade grew faint in the rising sun. Then her shadow left and did not return.

It was Tuesday morning, and the blackmailer had learned that Nora's landlord, who lived next door in the corner house, was away on a spring cruise. Nora had the property all to herself. The house on the other side was thirty yards away with the space divided by a dense, shoulder-high hedge.

The clank of her garage door startled him. He eased down his binoculars and watched her raising the top on her Mustang convertible, and then backing out of the driveway. Her brake lights winked as she stopped before accelerating down the street.

Jack went out to pick up his morning paper, and saw Roy, a ten-year-old boy who lived next door with his divorced mother. Roy came over to say Hi.

"You're big, Mr. McCall."

Jack mussed Roy's straight-cut blonde bangs. "I never planned to be. It just happened. I haven't seen you for a while. How are you? And how's your mom?"

"I'm fine, so's my mom. She always is, 'cept when she hollers at me."

Jack had met Roy and his mother, Janet Parker, the morning they moved in. Roy had kept throwing his foam football into Jack's backyard until Janet came out and told her son to stop. She had worn one of those loose-fitting house dresses that would drape the same on a telephone pole or an exotic dancer. A gust of wind had blown the fabric tight against her, revealing she definitely was not any kind of pole. She had a nice smile and lively eyes.

During the year before his marriage to Rachel, Jack had spent many evenings with Roy and Janet, barbequing and watching family movies. He was very fond of Roy. When the boy spent weekends with his mother's parents or had a sleepover at a friend's house, Jack and Janet would have their own sleepover.

"How big are you, Mr. McCall?"

"I'm six-foot-two and I weigh two-hundred-ten pounds."

"Gee, I hope I'm big when I grow up."

"Is your dad tall?"

"Don't got a dad. Got a grandpa though," Roy said with one eye squinted because of the morning sun.

"Is he big?"

"Grandpa's way shorter'n you. He's my mom's daddy," Roy said. "Seems like I oughta have my own dad though, don't you think, Mr. McCall?"

"Some youngsters do. Some don't. You see a lot of your grandpa?"

"Yeah. Grandpa was a policeman in Baltimore 'til he got too old. His name's Elroy, Grandpa Elroy, so's mine. Only mine's just Elroy. But I go by Roy. You like Roy better than Elroy, Mr. McCall?"

Jack had seen Grandpa Elroy. The man wasn't tall, but he was built like a garage beer fridge. Jack settled his hand on the curve between the boy's neck and his shoulder. "I like you and Roy's a fine name."

The boy held up his metal dump truck and asked Jack if later on he wanted to go across the street and haul some dirt.

"I can't today, Roy."

The boy hung his head, the hand holding the dump truck dangling at his side. "Gee whiz. It's no fun alone."

"Where'd you learn to say gee whiz? I used to say that when I was your age."

"My grandpa says it a lot."

"Roy, a lady I work with is coming by to pick me up. I came out front to wait for her. But tell you what, one of these Saturdays, real soon, if your mother says okay, I'll call my friend who owns a company that has lots of dump trucks. We'll go over and take a ride on one of the real big ones, okay?"

"Gee whiz, really, Mr. McCall?"

"Really, Roy. If it's okay with your mother."

"She'll say okay. I'll be really nice to her so she'll let me. 'Sides, she likes you a bunch, Mr. McCall. She told me so."

"I like her too, Roy. She's a fine lady."

"I gotta go, Mr. McCall. My mom's looking for me."

Jack watched the youngster run toward his house and saw his mother standing on the front porch in a dark pantsuit, heels, and a scoop-necked white blouse.

"Come on, Roy. You need to get ready for school and I can't be late for work." Janet waved, Jack waved back. She put her thumb to her ear and her little finger in front of her mouth and lip synced the words, "Call me." Then she followed her son inside.

Jack tossed the paper inside the front door and sat on his front step to wait for Nora. After a while his attention drifted to a line of ants busily carrying bits of something in a precision march across his porch and down into the lawn which, with the help of the coming spring, was struggling to recover its color. A second row of ants carrying nothing hurried back the other way, toward him. The two rows passing like tiny dark sedans speeding along a miniature two-lane road.

Jack's mind drifted to thoughts of his own father, a career navy man who, like the ants, had always been in a hurry. His strongest boyhood senses of his father were the man's aftershave and the hard touch of his stiff white naval uniform.

It had been Dr. Chris Andujar who had helped Jack realize that his own twenty-plus-years special ops and counterterrorism career had likely been a result of his father's frequent litany on the subject of duty. As a teen, Jack realized his parents' marriage had never been a good one. The year after Jack left for college, his mother divorced his father and moved to Chicago. She had promised to stay a part of Jack's life, but she had not kept that promise.

When his father died ten years ago, Jack felt surprise, but not grief. Chris Andujar had told him, "On an emotional level men expect their fathers to live forever, so men are always surprised when their fathers die. And the sons are left with the thoughts of the things fate had left unsaid."

A car horn blew. Jack looked toward the street to see Nora behind the steering wheel of her Mustang convertible. The air was on the cool side, so she had the soft top up. He climbed in.

"You didn't see me?" She ran her fingernails along her leg, scratching through her black capris.

"Sorry. I was lost in thought."

At the corner Jack looked in the side-view mirror and saw Roy, wearing his school backpack, just standing at the edge of the road watching as they drove away. Jack stuck his hand out the window and waved. Roy waved back.

The blackmailer spoke into his cell phone. "What's happening with McCall?"

"He just got picked up by some fox in a Mustang convertible. They split."

"You still on 'em?"

"Being on her tail would be nice, but I'm on 'em both."

The caller hung up, got out of his car across from Nora's home and, dressed as a workman carrying a toolbox, ducked through the bushes along the side of her house. After fiddling with the appropriate pick and tension tool, he freed the lock on her front door and stepped inside Nora's duplex.

After a quick look around, he chose two spots to secret small FM transmitters. He put the first one atop the valance box over the bedroom window, and the second, using two-way tape, under the edge of the couch near the living room phone. Each of the transmitters had been previously configured to wirelessly transfer to the CD of a voice-activated recorder he would hide among the rip-rap sized boulders that bordered the side of the property.

CHAPTER 5

JACK WATCHED NORA'S legs as she worked the pedals. She had small feet with red painted toenails revealed by her open-toed black pumps. In a lot of ways she reminded him of Rachel. Nora's shoulder-length hair was strawberry-blond, Rachel's black. That was certainly different, but not much else. At five-eight Nora was shorter by an inch, and, like Rachel, she had a body that made clothes come alive.

Nora turned onto MacArthur Boulevard and asked, "Do you figure Dr. Andujar for a suicide?"

Jack shook his head. "Some people get tired, just tired of dealing with whatever, and they quit on life, I don't figure that for Chris."

They drove quietly for a few miles before he said anything more. "Nice shoes. New?"

"Just yesterday, I didn't really need them, but what's a woman to do?"

"Don't buy them."

"Men just don't understand."

"Don't understand what?"

"A woman shopping for clothes."

"Men's clothes are fashionable, too."

"Oh, please. Take a look at those old movies you enjoy watching. Men are wearing the same clothes today that they wore in 1945. Maybe fewer hats, but that's the only real change. Lapels going from wide to narrow and back again, and the comings and goings of pleats and cuffs in trousers don't exactly constitute changes in fashion."

"Sounds practical to me," Jack replied, knowing it was a weak defense.

"I like your shirt," she said. "Denim looks rugged on a tall man with a trim waistline, well, reasonably trim."

Jack scowled but didn't say anything. He had just this morning been forced to back off a notch when cinching his belt.

"The blue matches your eyes and goes nicely with your khaki pants. I'm glad you took my advice to stop wearing suits and ties."

"We're going to a friend's home."

As they drove on the Key Bridge over the Potomac, Nora brought up an old subject: a grand opening for McCall Investigations. Nora and Rachel had intended to go over the final plans for MI's open house the day Rachel was run down after she pushed Nora into the clear. The open house was forgotten, Rachel was buried, and Jack went off to Europe and the Middle East.

"I'm aiming for Friday," Nora said. "The invitations are addressed. Just give me the okay."

"Keep the pressure on, right?"

"Seems like a good plan."

He looked out over the river at the bluish-gray sky, smeared with clouds stretched thin and long like hand-pulled taffy. Then turned and looked at Nora. "MI's already been open for nearly five months."

Nora steered into the right lane as she approached the Virginia side of the river. "Rach told me you don't like big gatherings, but it'll be good for business."

"It's been nearly five months," he repeated, shaking his head in a slow arc.

"I don't mean to sound matter-of-fact about it, but your leaving town was in all the followup articles on Rachel's death. We need DC to know Jack McCall is back and ready for business. Where do I turn?"

"You know how to get on George Mason, toward the Virginia Hospital?"

"Sure."

"Go like that. A few blocks past the hospital we'll turn left on Patrick Henry Drive."

When Nora downshifted on the off-ramp and then reapplied the gas, Jack noticed she pressed the accelerator with her red toes down, while holding her toes up when applying the brake.

"Jack. The open house. While you were gone, I took a few missing persons cases and some background-checking work. It hardly kept me busy and now that you're back ..." Her words trailed off, then she closed her argument. "Your name is juice, and we need it to establish MI as the firm to call when someone needs a private investigator."

"Let me think about it. Okay?"

"I need to know tomorrow morning—early. Any later and I'll have to cancel the caterer and reprint the invitations. Now, tell me about the events preceding Andujar's supposed suicide."

He took in a long breath and let it out slowly before beginning. "Sarah called two days before Rachel was killed, begging me to come for Sunday dinner and talk with Chris. She said,

'He's very moody and he won't tell me anything. I'm worried sick. He'll always talk to you.' After Rachel was run down, I forgot all about Chris and my promise to go for dinner. Maybe he'd still be alive if I had just ... I need to find out what really happened."

CHAPTER 6

THE FRESHLY-PAINTED white picket fence around Sarah Andujar's home simulated fresh recruits standing at attention as Jack and Nora approached the house. Folded towels and bed sheets hung patiently on the porch rail, waiting to cover the more delicate plants in the event of another cool spring night.

Jack heard the clunk of the deadbolt before seeing Sarah's pruned complexion peeking through the crack of the door. She inhaled through her first words, "Oh, Jack!" And exhaled through the finish, "I am so glad to see you." Her cheeks were more sallow than he remembered, her eyes more haggard and cavernous, but crow's feet still danced around her eyes when she smiled.

Sarah hid her small hand inside Jack's while leading her two guests though her home. For Jack, the Andujar home had always held the comfortable feeling of an old, favored sweater, but not today. Today it looked perfect, spotlessly clean, everything in its place, precisely in its place.

"I made berry-flavored herbal sun tea," Sarah said, pointing toward a pitcher on the table in her screened sun porch. "I think you'll like it." She had also put out a platter with cold-cut sandwiches on little triangles of white bread trimmed of their crusts.

Jack turned to Sarah. "Forgive me for not coming to dinner that Sunday. Maybe—"

She reached up and touched her fingers to his lips to stop him.

Jack had seen her expression on the faces of wives and mothers of men lost under his command in covert operations. A look of pride and despair tossed like a salad in the empty place where their once happy hearts had beaten.

"There is no need to apologize," she said, moving her hand from his face. "I had no idea Christopher had—," her eyes welled. "And please accept my condolences. I remember your wife, Rachel, as a lovely and caring person." The old woman hugged Jack.

"Ms. Andujar," Nora said, "I'm picking up the most wonderful fragrance from your garden."

"Thank you. That would be my early-season lilacs and the cucumber magnolia."

They all sat around the small table in the sunroom. Jack and Nora each took one of the small sandwiches and a napkin. Sarah reached in and straightened the stack of napkins.

"Nora. Is that short for Eleanor?"

"Yes. My mother was a huge fan of Eleanor Roosevelt. I never felt the name fit me so I eventually dropped it. Please call me Nora."

"I will, if you will call me Sarah."

The old woman sat still for a few moments staring at the flower pattern on the patio chair that framed her thin legs which she kept close together. Then she told Jack and Nora about her stressful experience with Sergeant Suggs when he had come to interview her. While she spoke, a breeze tinkled the wind chimes hanging at the fringe of her patio. She didn't seem to hear them.

Sarah's lips moved as if she were considering but rejecting words. Then she spoke. "Christopher was murdered. Forgive me. I should be clear. I understand that technically my husband took his own life, but because someone was blackmailing him, though I cannot imagine over what. To my way of thinking, that makes the blackmailer a murderer."

Jack put his hand on Sarah's arm, his fingers circling to meet just above her wrist. "Whom have you told about your blackmail suspicions?"

"Only you. I could not bring myself to tell that coarse Sergeant Suggs."

Sarah leaned forward and took a sandwich. Jack waited while she chewed, then watched as what she had swallowed worked its way down her withered throat. Then he asked, "What makes you think Chris was being blackmailed?"

Sarah pinched her eyes shut, then blotted her mouth with a handkerchief curled over the tip of her index finger. "When I first met Christopher, I believed he had hung the moon just for me." She dabbed the corners of her eyes. "I am sorry. You were asking?"

"Why do you think blackmail?" Nora said repeating Jack's question.

Sarah took Nora's hand in her left and reached over to hold Jack's in her right. The skin on her hands was mottled. "He was a healthy, successful doctor. He planned to retire next year. We were both so looking forward to spending our twilight years traveling. Then it all changed somehow. Two months before ... that day, my husband had told me that in addition to paying off our home he had accumulated a quarter of a million dollars in his safety-deposit box. I never told the police because I didn't know how he had gotten that much cash."

"Did you ever see a blackmail note," Jack asked, "or overhear a phone call from the blackmailer?"

"No, but what other explanation could there be?" She used the fingers on her other right hand to fiddle with her wedding ring. "I went to the bank the day after that horrid Sergeant came to my home. The box was empty. That's when I knew, knew for certain. That was why Christopher had been so moody. He had no more money to give the blackmailer, so he—" She shuddered, and then regained control. "I considered calling the sergeant, but did not. He probably would have accused my husband of losing the money gambling or running around in some inappropriate manner. I am afraid Sergeant Suggs has become very jaded from all the unsavory characters with whom he has dealt."

Jack heard a noise and looked up to see a young man with a thin face step through the kitchen door. He wore sunglasses and sported a neck hickey.

"Donny Boy," Sarah said after putting her hand to her mouth, "shame on you for neglecting your old mother."

The young man's smile barely wrinkled a face smooth as polished glass. His mother made introductions.

Jack had never met the son, and Chris had rarely spoken of him. Donny looked to be in his late thirties. He wore an open-necked green shirt, a big silver-buckled belt on designer jeans, and square toed snakeskin boots.

Donny leaned in and gave his mother a serviceable hug and took a seat. He reeked of cologne. Sarah poured him a glass of tea, and then used a fresh napkin to absorb the drop lingering on the ledge of the spout.

Donny eyes moved like lottery balls before the pick. "How do you know my mother?"

"I knew your father for many years. I've been out of the country and wanted to pay my respects."

The young man wagged his finger. "Wait a minute, Jack McCall. I remember my father talking about you. You're the super-spook who caught that dude last year who had bumped off some bigwigs in the government?"

"Donny Boy, mind your manners. These people are my friends."

"Yes, Mother," he said in a tone about a buck short on sincerity.

Jack nodded politely. "Yes. I headed up that investigation."

After Jack answered Donny's questions about The Third Coincidence case, the young man downed his tea and stood.

"I gotta run, Mom. I just came by to return the shawl you left in my car after Dad's funeral. I put it on the cedar chest at the foot of your bed."

He winked at Nora before snapping his business card onto the table next to her. "In case you ever want a career change."

Nora turned her head from Sarah and gave Donny a look that would stop a dog in heat.

Sarah spoke toward her son's back as he stepped up from the sun porch. "I love you. Come back soon."

"I promise, Mom," drifted back over his shoulder as he moved out of sight.

"Excuse us," Sarah's face flushed, "a mother and her son, one of life's eternal struggles."

Sarah got up and straightened Donny's chair. Then opened a drawer in a side table and handed Jack a large manila envelope, the kind held closed by a short red string wrapped around a dime-sized hard paper disk.

"This statement contains everything I can tell you that might be of help. If you need anything further, I will provide whatever you ask. As for the bank box, I considered it my husband's. He knew I would never open it before ... this. The identification of the bank box is on my statement. Christopher and I were on the signature card at the bank."

"Not Donny?" Nora asked, rotating only her eyes toward Sarah.

"No!" Then after a deep breath Sarah looked at Jack. "Is that a concern?"

"We're just gathering information."

"I apologize if I upset you," Nora said. "Jack knew your husband. I didn't. Tell me about his work?"

"Christopher was a psychiatrist in private practice. His office is ... was on Massachusetts Avenue, NW. Jack has been there. He specialized in sexual dysfunctions." She blushed. "A few of his patients were wealthy kleptomaniacs, but he referred most of *those* to his friend, Dr. Phillip Radnor. I think they saw some kind of connection between those two miscreant behaviors. They met once a week to work on a technical paper of some sort." She paused. "Christopher paid the office rent semiannually. The lease expires in a few more days. The exact date is in there," she gestured toward the envelope. "The key is also there."

"Did you tell your son about our coming today?" Nora asked.

"I have not spoken with Donny since we discussed your coming by today."

Jack took Sarah's hand. "We've read all the newspaper accounts and we'll get a copy of the police reports, but tell us about your ... finding Chris."

"I got up that morning. Took a shower. I'm an early riser. Then made myself a tea and took a cup of coffee in to Christopher. My normal routine, I would wake Christopher most mornings. His bed had not been slept in. I found him in his office, the gun still in his hand." She stopped to wipe her eyes and cheeks. "I called the police."

"What did the two of you do the night before?" Nora asked.

"I had book club, a friend picked me up. Christopher stayed home. He said he was going to work some and watch some sports thing on television."

Nora sipped her tea before asking, "Do you know if anyone was going to come by to see him, or perhaps meet him for dinner somewhere?"

"I made him a cold meat loaf sandwich on rye with catsup, one of his favorites, and an apple waldorf salad before I left." She glanced at Jack. "You know my husband was a quiet man. For him that was a great evening." Jack nodded his head slightly, adding a small smile.

"Did you look in on him when you got home?" Jack asked.

"No."

Nora raised her eyebrows. "Why not?"

"The study door was shut. After decades, a woman gets to know a man's rhythms. When he shut the door he meant, 'I don't wish to be disturbed.' So I didn't. I made a cup of tea with honey and went up to bed to begin reading next month's mystery book club selection."

"You said a friend picked you up for book club, so you wouldn't have seen his car in the underground lot." Jack said. "Can you be certain Chris was home when you got home?"

"Oh, yes. He was here."

"How do you know?" asked Nora.

"I could see the light under the door. Christopher would keep a horribly messy desk, but never leave a light on, a quirky combination for certain. The light was on; he was in the study."

"We know Chris died in the apartment in DC," Jack said gently. "But this was his home. Could Nora look around inside while you and I visit out here?"

Sarah smiled at Nora. "You go right in, dear. Look wherever you wish."

"Thank you." Nora scooted back her chair, taking care to push it in level with the table. "Did your husband keep an appointment book at home? Oh, and do you have a safe?"

"We do not have a safe. The police took his appointment book. Chief Mandrake brought it back personally after Suggs closed the case. You'll find it in the study on the desk."

"Did you discuss the case with Chief Mandrake?" Jack asked. "Perhaps tell him about your belief that Chris had been blackmailed?"

"Oh, Nora," Sarah called out just as the younger woman stepped inside. "I unlocked the file cabinet and removed the password on his laptop. You take it, dear. I have no use for it. It may help you."

Sarah turned back to Jack. "I did not discuss the case with the chief. We had some iced tea and talked about the good old days. Before the chief's wife died several years ago—the four of us had some grand times. It seems so long ..." She stopped talking and her face went blank as if a light had flickered off behind her eyes.

"May I have some more of that grand iced tea," Jack asked, "and another of your little sandwiches?"

"Certainly," she said. "Let me pour." She made no move for the pitcher, but jiggled her head, as if her wiring had shorted, then stared out toward her rose garden.

"I'm terribly ignorant about flowers," Jack said. "Will you show me your garden?"

"I would like that. The roses are my pride and joy."

The garden's brick walkway had been set directly into the soil. Sarah held Jack's arm while stooping to pick up a rose petal wedged between two of the bricks. "It is such a challenge to keep all of this looking just so," she said. Her yard was as immaculate as the home had been inside. The stars of her garden were four rows of alternating white, pink, red, and yellow roses.

"That bright red one near the middle I took from my mother's garden after she died ten years ago. She was eighty-one and had remained a lady in the regal sense of the word, right to the end. Christopher gave me all the other roses."

The air was filled with the sound of the bees busily darting about the vines that climbed trellises along the side of the detached garage. The blossoms they visited reminded Jack of the lilacs his mother had grown when he was young. After a while the brick walkway circled around to bring them back to the roses.

"Christopher worked the soil to keep it aerated and treated the roses to control the aphids. I come out here sometimes and sit in that garden chair," she pointed, "near our roses and remember him."

"Your roses are beautiful."

"You're a sweet man, Jack, just like my Christopher." She absentmindedly reached up and touched the wrinkles in her cheek as if they were play buttons for her memories.

When they were again seated, Jack asked about Chris's friends.

"I listed them on the statement I gave you." She patted the envelope on the table. "I included a brief history of his relationship with each and their addresses and phone numbers—the ones I know about." She sniffled and dabbed her nose with her hanky. "Because of his work, Christopher often socialized without me. Those friends should be in his laptop."

"One thing I do know," Jack said. "We'll never have a client who is better organized or more cooperative."

Nora came out the back door. "You have a beautiful home, Sarah. I love your Early American furniture and your Persian rugs in the study and hallway."

"Thank you, dear. Do you have any questions?"

Nora cleared her throat after briefly looking down. "I noticed your husband had a bedroom apart from yours." She raised her eyes and looked directly at Sarah. "Why?"

"My husband snored loudly and often worked late, so he used the bedroom downstairs near his study, and I the one upstairs on the opposite side. We had the same arrangement in our three-bedroom DC apartment, which also had two downstairs bedrooms, one he used as a study, I used the one upstairs."

"Do you still have the apartment?"

"No. After Sergeant Suggs concluded suicide, the police released their hold—or whatever they call it—on the apartment. The manager had a new tenant waiting. I called Goodwill to donate the furniture."

"How do we contact your son?" Jack asked.

"Donny's information is on my statement, including his cell number. The best place to catch him is at his disgraceful Gentlemen's Club, although I cannot imagine a gentleman going there. Christopher and I desperately tried to stop him from opening that loathsome place. It's on M Street, just west of Foggy Bottom."

Jack stepped in close and held Sarah's frail shoulders. "You won't hear from us for a few days while we get organized. Call us if you think of anything else or just wanna talk. Okay?"

She circled his arm with her own, grasping it as one might a steadying pole on a bus. "You both have been so kind."

Sarah escorted them to the side door from her sun porch. After touching the knob she let her hand slide off and turned back. "Nora, a few minutes ago I was less than forthright. You deserve the truth." She stepped closer. "While Christopher did snore and work late, we did not—" She looked away, toward her rose garden. "We were no longer romantic with each other. I am afraid Christopher found me a bit prudish, probably with cause. I will go to my grave regretting I failed to deal with it. I am sorry I lied to you."

"I know that wasn't easy." Nora smiled. "Thank you for your honesty."

Jack put his hand in front of Nora just before they stepped beyond the cover of Sarah's house—more a slowing than a stop. She paused while he looked left and right. It was an old habit born during a covert operation when, had it not been for a young Kurdish fighter, Jack would have walked right into the beginning of a firefight between Kurdish forces and Saddam Hussein's Republican Guard. Since then he had habitually looked both ways when he came to corners. Street corners, corners of houses, store aisles, it didn't matter. Before stepping into the open, he looked.

A dark coupe was parked at the curb several houses to their right. The startled driver exhaled a large gray billow of cigar smoke against the side window, gunned his engine, and sped away before the smoke cleared enough for Jack to get a good look.

In the street where that car had been parked, Jack found a spent wooden match snapped in two, a habit suggestive of an older driver, one not concerned with fashion.

CHAPTER 7

JACK WAS SITTING at his desk early Wednesday morning reading newspaper stories that largely sounded like the ones he read every day: politicians blaming the other party rather than solving the nation's problems, or politicians entangled in some kind of personal scandal.

He gladly put the paper aside when he heard the front door opening. He got up and looked out to see DC's chief of police, the lanky Harry Mandrake. The chief's eyebrows were bushy and set farther apart than his eyes. Jack could not recall ever seeing anyone else with that particular facial feature.

"Hello, Chief."

"I thought you might be an early riser," Mandrake said. "Can we talk?"

Jack motioned for him to come on back to his office. "How do you take your coffee?"

"Black's fine."

While Jack poured, the chief settled into one of the oxblood leather chairs and lifted off his service cap. "I ran into Nora at the supermarket last night. She mentioned you had picked up a case that was going to keep you two pretty busy and so you were looking for a part-time receptionist. I'd like to talk with you about the position."

Jack lowered his cup. "We're flattered, Chief, but at the risk of sounding indelicate, aren't you a bit old for that job? And you'd have to take a pay cut—a big one."

The chief's laugh echoed about Jack's office.

"Well, if you're turning me down, how 'bout my goddaughter, Mary Lou Sanchez? She's a law student at Georgetown with one year to go. Clean cut and presentable. After graduation she'll pursue a law enforcement career, maybe the DA's office or even the FBI. She wants to follow in her papa's footsteps. Her daddy, Tino Sanchez, was my partner all my years as a detective. When I became chief of police, I made him chief of detectives. Tino was killed in the line of duty."

The chief leaned forward resting his forearms on his knees, turning his hat on the ends of his fingers. "I guess I sort of adopted Mary Lou. Her life's been rough since she lost her daddy. She's a good kid, works hard and holds top grades at Georgetown. She would need you to work around her class schedule."

"If she's right, no problem."

The chief's cell phone rang. Jack started to get up, but the chief motioned him to stay. "Tell the mayor I'll stop by on my way to the station." The chief flipped his phone shut and turned back toward Jack. "I haven't made up my mind how I feel about these damn cells. They're supposed to be progress but I'm not so sure I always want to be connected." He looked at his watch. "Christ, the day's running away on me."

"Have Mary Lou stop by. I'll be here all day."

The chief gulped the last of his coffee and left the empty cup on the corner of Jack's desk. "I appreciate your agreeing to see her. Whether you hire her or not is your call."

"It'll be my pleasure to meet Mary Lou." Jack rose to walk the chief out, then asked, "Where's her momma?"

"She died giving birth to Mary Lou. You don't think that happens anymore, but it does." He started to say something else, but his mouth closed on the first word. Then he restarted, "She just bled out. Tino was all the family Mary Lou had until the job took him. Now she has none."

"Except for you," Jack said, his hand clasping the chief's shoulder.

"I promised her papa," he said, twirling his hat another half a turn. "I'm glad you're back to work. It'll be good for you."

Jack smiled and accompanied the chief to the elevators. After Mandrake stepped inside one, Nora stepped out of another. She wore an above-the-knee black skirt, a black blouse, black high-heeled shoes, and a blazer the color of yellow mustard, which sounds ugly but looked great.

"And a good morning to you, Eleanor."

She smiled and punched Jack on the arm. "That's the last time I want to hear that from you, mister." When he turned to open the office door, she slapped him on the butt. "My name is Nora."

Jack wondered if his growing infatuation with his partner was because her body and style of dress reminded him of Rachel. Yesterday he had lingered near her long enough to breathe in her fragrance before walking away.

"How 'bout I get us some coffee," she said, "and then we can talk about the Andujar case?"

"I've got a cup," he said. "I'll get you one. But we've got something else first. Chief Mandrake asked that we interview his goddaughter, Mary Lou Sanchez, for our receptionist."

"I've met Mary Lou. She's a cutie and talks mature for her age."

"I told the chief to have her come by this afternoon. I'm ready to hire her unless she flat turns us off. What do you think?"

"I agree."

Nora followed Jack into their case room and sat on the same side of the conference table, leaving a chair between them.

"Give me your impressions on this Andujar case," Jack asked, "then we'll come up with a plan."

"Sarah must be the honorary grandmother of all the neat freaks in the world. I kept trying to find a towel hanging crooked on a rack or a book out of kilter on a shelf."

Jack laughed. "I've always suspected that Sarah had a secret side, something like an elder leader of the flower children of the sixties, but for as long as I've known her she has been exaggeratedly proper. She's going through a difficult period right now and being overly fussy may bring her some comfort. It'll pass."

Nora raised her eyebrows. "I know she's special to you, but I sensed a hard broad lurking somewhere inside that sweet, old frail lady." She opened her notebook. "I jotted down the titles of a couple of the books that were on the shelf in the study: *Perversions of Infidelity*, and *The Symbolism of Sexual Mutilation*."

"They probably belonged to Chris; his practice was sexual difficulties."

"That's true."

"I guess the bottom line is," Nora said, "if you want us to help her as a freebie, its okay with me."

"Chris Andujar did more for me than I could ever repay. I've gotta understand his death."

Nora leaned toward Jack, the light reflecting off her nylon-covered knee. "Where do we start?"

Jack took a deep breath. "Donny Boy's a jerk; I just hope he isn't mixed up in it somehow. It'd break his momma's heart."

"Remember his comment about Sarah's shawl?" Nora said. "Donny hadn't seen his mother since the funeral. Her son came by to size us up, and Sarah said she hadn't told her son we were coming." Nora slouched forward in her chair and crossed her arms, pushing her black bra and its mounded contents into sight. "Maybe he got a call from Smokehead in the coupe."

"Smokehead had to have been tailing us," Jack said. "If he was tailing Donny he would've split when Donny left, and we'd have never seen him. But as you say, he might have called Donny to tell him we were at his mothers."

Nora sat her coffee cup down, the red crescent from her lips still kissing the rim. "Let's talk with Chris's former receptionist and his psychiatrist buddy, Radnor."

Jack got up and wrote *Radnor* and *Receptionist* on the white board on the wall of their case room. Then he wrote Donny Andujar above those two.

"What else?"

Nora pushed a runaway strand of her strawberry-blonde hair away from her eyes. "I'll go through Chris's appointment book, and then attack his laptop. Maybe I can find a few more strings we can pull."

"I'm going to ask Sarah again if she told her son about our visit," Jack said. "Then I'll meet her at the bank to make certain Chris didn't add someone else to the signature card for the box. And I'll try to get Chris's medical doctor to talk. We need to eliminate the possibility he had some serious health condition that made him choose suicide. I'd like you to call Suggs over at Metro to find out the status of any insurance policies on Chris's life. We could ask Sarah, but I'd rather not. Now, how should we proceed with Donny Boy?"

Nora swiveled the extra chair between them a half turn, kicked off her heels, and put her legs into that seat, her toes pointing toward Jack, her skirt inching up her thighs. "We need to learn more about his doings," she said. "We could tail him, but we've got a problem. He knows us both by sight."

"We need somebody Donny doesn't know," Jack said. "That sounds like Max Logan, assuming Donny doesn't know Max."

Nora's calf muscles lengthened when she got up and dented her well-shaped butt against the edge of the table. "I'll call and ask him to come by as soon as possible."

CHAPTER 8

MAX CAME INTO MI mid-afternoon, Nora buzzed Jack to alert him before sending Max back. Jack motioned him to a chair and jumped right into why they'd ask Max to come in.

"Did Nora talk to you about the help we need?"

"She told me you're needin' some tailin' done."

"That's right. You interested?"

"Yes, sir, I can do your job and would be glad for it. Truth is, I miss havin' me nose in the wind."

"We want this fella tailed round the clock." While Jack talked, he pulled two bottles of water from the half fridge in the corner behind his desk. "The job includes you putting together a team, and keeping it going until I say stop."

"Can do, and I'll be startin' and stoppin' when you say. We do need to talk pay a mite. I'll have to give up being a security guard. It's a flavorless job, but it buys me needies."

"We'll pay you thirty an hour and guarantee the number of hours needed to cover what you made as a security guard. We might work you more. We'll pay the men you pick twenty an hour, without a minimum. You okay with that?"

Max screwed the cap off his water bottle. "A more'n fair offer, Jack. I'm aware it's a temporary job, but I should be telling ya I take it with the intent of convincing ya to retain me permanent."

"That could happen, Max, but I don't promise. At the moment we have but one case." Jack leaned forward and handed him an information sheet.

"Life has few promises," Max replied. "I'll take what I earn, no more." He held up the page Jack had given him. "Is this the donkey you want me to pin a tail on?"

"Yes. Donkey—Donny Andujar."

"I know the lad by sight, but he has no shine on me. I know his club. It's fancier than most, but when you lift the lid, it's no different from the rougher stripper joints."

"Do you need a camera with zoom and night vision?"

"Takin' pitchers is me hobby." He raised his hand and clicked the button on a phantom camera. "I have one, and I can pass it along to my lads as we change shifts." After a pause, he said, "Art Tyson, a local PI—Nora knows him—tried to hire me to be one of his camera-slingers. But to paraphrase your American West, 'a man's gotta decide which brand he'll ride for.' For me," he shook his head, "it'll not be Tyson's outfit. I'm ready to start anytime."

"Now would be good. Thanks for riding for our brand." Jack winked. "Welcome to MI."

"Good to be with you."

Jack took another twenty minutes to bring Max up to speed on the case; what little they knew and that at this point they had no clues or intuitions.

After he walked Max out, he told Nora the terms under which Max would be working and that he has started immediately. In turn, Nora told Jack that Mary Lou Sanchez had come by while he was talking with Max. That she had hired Mary Lou and she would be starting tomorrow morning. Nora and Mary Lou would work out their schedules so that one of them was always at the office.

Jack stood shrouded by the afternoon shadows, at the grave of his dead wife, Rachel. "I'm sorry I haven't come to see you, Rach. I've been traveling, trying to learn if there was a connection between your death and my past work for the government. I found none. Nora caught up with me in Egypt to say that Chris Andujar was dead. The police have ruled suicide, but Sarah thinks Chris had been blackmailed and that's why he took his life. We've meet with Sarah and have nothing so far that confirms either explanation of his death. But I swear to you I will find the answers."

After a while a breeze brought aromas that made him remember Luigi's, Rachel's favorite restaurant, but Luigi's was miles away. He touched the chiseled granite, letting his fingers ride the cold grooves of each letter.

Rachel McCall, beloved bride of Jack McCall

The choice of bride, rather than wife, had been unusual, but after so short a time together, bride had seemed right.

The stone showed her age to be forty-three, four years younger than Jack.

He had survived hell many times on the world's declared and secret battlefields. He had seen so much he could only explain through a belief in God. Had an angry God orchestrated Rachel's death to punish him for some of his past covert activities? He could not accept that the God he believed in would do so.

For the second time, Jack let his fingers trace the curves of his love's name, and then he walked into the lengthening eastward shadows.

After dinner, a long walk, and a whiskey neat, Jack poured another and called Nora at home.

"Did I wake you?"

"No. I got back from a jog about two hours ago, and just got out of a candlelit soaking tub. It was heavenly. Is the Andujar case playing with your mind?"

"Yeah. Kinda. You had any more thoughts?"

"You know we have no proof that the quarter mil was ever in the bank."

"I can't see any reason Chris would lie to his wife about that?"

"I agree. So, let's assume for now that the money did exist," Nora said. "But Chris could've spent it lots of ways other than blackmail or, maybe no cash and no blackmail. Either way, Metro may have gotten it right—your friend put himself down without outside influence."

"They found no suicide note," Jack said while rinsing out his glass over the sink.

"That's unusual," Nora said, "but not probative."

CHAPTER 9

JACK'S ALARM WENT off at six. He had suffered through another night of late drinks, old movies, and little sleep. He remembered watching Humphrey Bogart's great portrayal of Sam Spade in the classic, *The Maltese Falcon*, and wished real cases were so easy and as filled with colorful characters.

He sat on the edge of the bed dry-scrubbing his face with the palms of his hands, then went into the bathroom and brushed and flossed. That took the flannel out of his mouth, but did nothing for the pattern of red lines in his eyes that resembled something printed from an Internet mapping site.

In the kitchen he recapped last night's whiskey bottle, and poured a cup of black coffee. The coffee pot timer had come on before the alarm clock went off. God bless automation. For a while he sat in the kitchen drinking coffee and fooling around with the crossword puzzle in the morning paper. After a second cup he picked up the cordless phone and called Sarah Andujar.

"I can meet you at the bank in an hour," she said. "I am on the other line with Christopher's medical doctor. I am going to try to add you in on the call. We do this sometimes in my book club. If I mess it up, I'll call back."

He waited until Sarah came back on the line. "Jack, are you still there?"

"Yes."

"We're on the line with Christopher's physician. Doctor, thank you for answering my questions, I will hang up now and let you and Mr. McCall talk."

When Jack got off the phone, he had learned something he had expected and something he had not.

Jack had left the bank and was turning right onto Twenty-first to get back to MI when his cell rang. It was Nora. She had arranged a meeting with Chris Andujar's psychiatrist buddy, Dr. Radnor, and had spoken to Chris's former receptionist, Agnes Fuller.

"Fuller told me," Nora said. "'I've put that sadness behind me. The police declared his death a suicide, so I don't have to talk to you, and I won't.' Frankly, her attitude caught me by surprise, and I didn't handle it very well. She stonewalled me, after having told Sarah she'd help any way she could. I'm going to call that woman back and find out why she's playing both ends against the middle."

"Why don't you hold that thought until after we talk with Radnor?"

"If you say so. How'd it go at the bank with Sarah?"

"The signature card for the box showed only Chris and Sarah. She had signed to gain entry only once, the day after Metro declared Chris's death a suicide."

"What was in the box?"

"Empty. Where are you?"

"In the office."

Five minutes later Jack pulled into MI's underground parking and saw Nora waiting next to his parking space. She opened the passenger's door and leaned in, her breasts and white bra showing.

"I thought I'd meet you down here. We need to be at Dr. Radnor's at one, and I need a favor. It's on the way." She got in carefully so as not to spill her coffee, then put her hand on his forearm.

He turned, letting the car idle. "What?"

"First, Mary Lou Sanchez started this morning, she's up there now. Second, seeing you have a knack for rubbing Suggs the wrong way, I took him to breakfast to try a woman's approach."

"What did you learn from Sergeant Charm?"

"Don't wear open-toed pumps the morning after it rains."

"Huh?"

"I stepped into a puddle getting out of my car at the restaurant. After I left Suggs, I had to go home to change my shoes and pantyhose." She turned her legs sideways, pushed her toes against the floorboard, and slid her camelhair skirt several inches up her thighs. "You men don't care what we gals have to go through to keep our legs looking good."

Sam Spade would have said, "The dame has great gams." But Jack said, "Suggs. Chris. Give."

"Okay, okay. Lower your flag, mister. Chris Andujar was killed by a thirty-eight. The gun was registered to him. The shot entered at his right temple and exited the other side. The trajectory was consistent with a self-inflicted wound. His fingerprints were smudged; forensics figured that resulted from the gun sliding down his finger as his arm collapsed."

Nora paused to finish her coffee. "The ME reported Chris had been dead about twelve hours when Sarah found him. Like you said about the bank, it's all jibing with her story."

"Did Suggs find anything that hinted at foul play? And what about life insurance?"

"Nada on anything suspicious."

"Nada?"

"It means nothing, and sounds better than what Suggs said."

"Which was?" Jack asked, starting to put the car in reverse.

She put her hand on his shoulder. "Don't leave yet. His exact words: 'Damn it. I told McCall there was no foul play. Tell him to go fuck himself.' It took me ten minutes to mellow him out enough so he'd talk about the insurance."

"And?"

"The Andujars had carried term life when they were younger, but the premiums kept increasing as they aged, so when Donny got older they let it expire. Now it's your turn, what did Chris's physician tell you?"

"His health was fine. The shocker was that Chris had listed *me* as the person to be contacted if his condition ever prevented him from making decisions about his treatment. That's what let the doc feel okay about talking with me."

"Not Sarah?"

"She was listed third."

"Donny second?"

"Nope. Me, then his psych buddy, Radnor, then Sarah. Donny was not listed at all."

After finally getting around to asking the favor, Nora got out of Jack's car and walked over to her own. She wanted him to follow her while she dropped off her Mustang to get new brake linings.

Ten minutes later, Jack watched Nora's hips pivot as she walked toward the office at the brake shop. Her small waist and legs reminded him of Lauren Bacall, the actress who had married Humphrey Bogart. When she came out of the office, and walked toward him he noticed she had larger and more active breasts than Bacall—but then bra technology had come a long way since Bacall's days as a vamp.

CHAPTER 10

DR. PHILLIP RADNOR'S office was in a high-rise building on NW Rhode Island Avenue between Scott Circle and
Connecticut Avenue. Inside the suite a receptionist with busy
eyes and a saggy body leaned against the wall behind her desk,
talking on the phone. She used the hand not wrapped around
the phone to point toward the lobby chairs. Jack and Nora
took a seat.

Dr. Radnor was a large man, not tall and powerful, but
short and, the polite word, rotund.

"Mr. McCall?"

"Thank you for seeing us, Dr. Radnor. This is my partner,
Nora Burke."

The psychiatrist nodded and led them into his office
which was furnished with a desk, the anticipated couch, and
two occasional chairs on an area rug near the window. Jack
and Nora sat there.

Several hunting and golfing photos hung on the side wall.
In one of the golf pictures Radnor stood with Chris, Troy
Engels, a CIA deputy Jack knew, and Chief Mandrake.

Nora opened a scratch pad. She kept most of her notes in
her Palm Pilot, but she had told Jack she believed people were
more comfortable talking without technology.

"Doctor, you were listed after me as the person to be contacted in the event Chris needed others to make decisions about his care. Why us? Why not his wife and son?"

Radnor put his hands flat on his desk blotter. Then brought them together and separated his palms leaving his fingers touching like flexing tent posts. After lowering his hands, he spoke.

"Chris thought very highly of you, Mr. McCall. To say he loved you as a man loves a son would not be a stretch. I'm sure it was no secret to you that he saw his own son Donny as a huge disappointment. As for Sarah, she was ten or twelve years older than Chris. Maybe he figured she'd die before he would need someone to make any acute-care decisions for him."

"What made Chris depressed and suicidal?"

Radnor ran his hand back over his shaggy crew cut.

"Mr. McCall, your question presumes Chris suffered from depression. Frankly, I agree. One cannot contemplate, let alone carry out suicide without being depressed. Admitting some failure on my part, I saw nothing that indicated he was suffering anything near that level of depression."

"Doctor, we understand the two of you had been collaborating on some research project, and that you were also treating him for his own problem. What problem was that?"

"Chris and I had been friends since school. His death stunned me. I miss him. We were coauthoring a highly technical research paper. In laymen's terms, our hypothesis holds that some relationship exists between kleptomania by the very wealthy and sexual dysfunction among that same group. While very few of our total patients who suffered from a sexual dysfunction also suffered from kleptomania, a high percentage of the wealthy who suffered from kleptomania also struggled with aberrant sexual behavior."

Jack found it an interesting aside, but Radnor had evaded the question.

Nora crossed her legs, letting her black high heel slip off the back of her suspended foot. "Doctor, for which of those conditions did you treat Chris Andujar?"

"I'm sorry, Ms. Burke. I told Sarah I would cooperate any way I could, but I must respect patient-doctor constraints."

"Doctor," Jack pleaded with hands spread, "Chris is dead. His wife asked you to talk with us. You know I was his primary designee to be consulted for his care. Please. Work with us."

"Yes, Chris is dead, but my other patients may not want their treatment conditions to become public even after they die. I'm sorry, Mr. McCall, there is nothing further I can say."

"A court could rule otherwise upon a petition from his wife."

"I would then be free to tell you what you want to know—what I would be happy to tell you if I could do so without compromising my reputation. Then again, seeing the police have ruled his death a suicide, a court might see such a petition as an unnecessary fishing expedition into a doctor's files. No, Mr. McCall, we're into areas where I must assume if Chris had wanted you to know, he would have told you himself."

"He did tell me Dr. Radnor. Chris had come to the realization he was bisexual and he hoped that with your help he could get free of it."

Radnor moistened his lips and tilted back his chair. "Chris guarded that secret, but seeing he told you I see no reason not to answer your question. He was desperate to rid himself of his gay side. He knew it would devastate his antediluvian wife, and destroy his already fragile relationship with his son."

"How promiscuous was he?" Nora asked.

"From what Chris told me, he had only one gay lover. And before you ask, Ms. Burke, he would not identify him." The doctor stood. "I must ask you to excuse me." He moved toward the door.

Jack stood. "Was Chris making progress?"

"He was not, to both Chris's and my disappointment. Now, I really must get on with my day. Goodbye, Mr. McCall, Ms. Burke."

After they got back in the car, Nora turned toward Jack, "Where the hell did that gay bit come from? Why didn't you tell me Chris was gay?"

"It was a guess."

"The Red Sox winning the World Series is a guess. That was more than a guess. Give."

"Chris always came across as a man's man, never effeminate, yet in the service there were persistent rumors. I made a presumptive statement figuring if anyone knew for certain, it would be Dr. Radnor."

CHAPTER 11

A MIDDLE-AGED frumpish looking woman with jowls drooping as if her mouth were saving quarters, started toward Jack when he pulled into his underground parking space after dropping Nora off to pick up her Mustang.

Despite the dim light, the woman wore rose-colored sunglasses. She carried a pink sweater laying over one arm and hand while keeping her other hand in sight. He guessed her age at forty-five, but she wore a hairstyle and carried her purse in a way that conspired to make her look older.

He lowered his window.

She moved close, her flabby chin resting on her collarbone. "Mister McCall. I'm Agnes Fuller, Christopher Andujar's former receptionist." The gap between her front teeth caused a slight whistle when she said *Andujar's*.

"Shall we go up to my office, Ms. Fuller?"

She glanced both directions. "Let's talk here." She walked around the car, opened the passenger-side door and, ignoring the constraints of her sack dress, stepped in like a man—one leg followed by the other.

"Why all this secrecy, Ms. Fuller?" Jack asked, twisting on the seat to face her.

The makeup clogging the pores of her forehead and cheeks crusted in the deeper ravines venturing out from her nose and mouth. She took in a slow breath while her eyes kept moving like a bird in an unfamiliar cage.

"I'm being watched, Mr. McCall, some big ugly guy I saw outside my new job yesterday morning, I saw again at lunch." She ran her hands over the sweater on her lap as if smoothing invisible wrinkles. Then she changed the subject. "I apologize for being uncooperative when Nora Burke called from your office. I think my phone may be bugged."

"Don't worry about it. Ms. Burke is very understanding."

Ms. Fuller pulled a strand of her hair across her cheek. "Last night I didn't sleep a wink. This morning I knew I had to help. I owe it to Chris—Dr. Andujar." Her lower lip quivered.

"Take a deep breath, Ms. Fuller. I'll arrange for someone to check your house for listening devices."

She smiled without separating her lips. "Thank you. Dr. Andujar was a wonderful man and a fine doctor. His patients loved him. He helped a great many people. I started with him two years after he opened his practice. When his wife retired I became his office manager as well as receptionist. The last few weeks, before his death he was a changed man. Nervous. Fidgety." Her face contorted. "He started drinking more coffee than ever. And he started smoking again after having quit for five years."

One of her hands found the other. "The next thing I knew, he was dead."

"Dr. Andujar specialized in sexual dysfunctions. I take that to mean he had patients who pursued and engaged in sexual behavior outside the norm. Did he engage in any of that himself?"

Her lips twitched, as if she were receiving a coded message through her dark amalgam dental fillings. The message
must have told her to keep talking because she did.

"You know, before I took that job I could have defined
sexual behavior outside the norm, but not after working with
Dr. Andujar. But, no, gosh, no, no way could the doctor and
certainly not Sarah be involved in any of that stuff."

She blotted her eyes with the pads of her fingertips; the
way a woman does to avoid smearing her makeup, and then
returned to her pattern of hurried speech. "When Sarah was
the office manager, she was hard on people. But like I said,
the doctor and his wife were as straight as Ozzie and Harriet
Nelson. Not that some of his patients didn't try coming onto
him, they even hit on me. It was no dull job. I can tell you
that. Dr. Andujar even helped me shed some of my own silly
inhibitions."

She was talking a mile a minute and skipping through
random thoughts. Unsure what she might say next, Jack
decided to let her ramble.

"Mr. McCall, I've been wracking my brain, and I can't
imagine why he would take his own life. But I can tell you
he was frantic toward the end. Maybe if he found out he had
terminal cancer or something. It would have been like him to
not tell me about that." Her hands continually pierced the air
with darting gestures. "But Sarah said his physician told her
Dr. Andujar was in good health. Why did he … kill himself?"

"A few minutes ago you described Sarah as 'hard on people.' What did you mean?"

"Don't get me wrong. Sarah is a lady. A real lady. But
when you're around her all the time, well, sometimes she
shows a different side."

"Like what?"

"She would speak harshly to our computer repairman, even the young hunk who delivered our bottled water. Stuff like that. When she belittled her husband, I was embarrassed for him."

"Anything else?"

For the first time, Fuller spoke in a normal cadence. "Did he really kill himself?"

"I plan to find out, Ms. Fuller."

"Call me Agnes, please. Sarah is lucky to have you as a friend." Agnes turned toward the door, causing a loud leather screech, then twisted back with a note in her hand. "Here is my address and phone numbers. After Chris's death I was unemployed for a long time. I recently got a job as a secretary at the State Department. I've been there about two weeks. Please don't contact me until we find out who is following me. I don't want whoever it is to know I've spoken to you."

She pulled the door handle.

Jack reached for her arm. "Do you live alone?"

"Yes. I have a boyfriend, but he works most nights until pretty late. Why do you ask?"

"Tomorrow night at six-thirty, a repairman will come to your home. He'll tell you he has come to repair your dishwasher. He will find and remove any surveillance equipment in your home. His name will be on his shirt, Drummond."

Her voice rose and the cadence of her speech again quickened. "I'm scared. Terrified is more like it"

Jack gripped her forearm, held firm, and smiled. "Let's find out if you're being watched. The man who will come is an expert. No one will think he is anything but a repairman. Do you have a neighbor you're friendly with?"

"Yes. Why?"

"Find a way to tell your neighbor you're having trouble with your dishwasher. Put a rack on your drainboard and put in a few clean, wet dishes. Let it be known you're expecting a repairman. It'll be fine. Just do it like that."

"Okay, Mr. McCall. Sarah says you're the best. Send your repairman. I'll be alone."

Jack watched Agnes Fuller head for the elevator to go up to the ground floor. From the back she looked like two hundred pounds of cashews sewn into a one hundred-pound sack. He rushed up the parking ramp in time to see her cross Pennsylvania Avenue, walk one block farther away, and get into a dark coupe like the one that had abruptly driven away from Sarah Andujar's home. At that distance he could not clearly see the man or read the license plate.

As he walked back down the ramp, Nora pulled into the underground lot driving her Mustang with the new brakes. Going up in the elevator Nora reminded him about Mary Lou Sanchez. "She started work this morning. And don't forget our open house Friday. I need you here no later than six."

"We're going to do that?"

"I told you to get back to me the next morning after we went to Sarah's. You didn't, so I kept moving it forward. Friday. Six. Be here."

Mary Lou Sanchez looked to be about five-seven and not a pound more than a hundred and ten, with short black hair fashioned in a boyish cut. She hopped to her feet.

"Hello, Mary Lou," Jack said. "Welcome to MI." After a brief chat, they left Mary Lou at the receptionist desk and headed back toward their case room. Nora stopped off at the kitchen and picked up two cans of ginger ale. She closed the door and slid one can across the table.

Jack popped the top, took a drink, and told Nora about the unexpected visit from Agnes Fuller. As he finished, he heard Chief Mandrake's voice and headed up front to find him realigning a crooked chair in the lobby.

"Hi, Chief. I hope you're planning to come to our open house on Friday."

"Wouldn't miss it. I just came by to take Mary Lou home after her first day. I'm sure she's told you she has a big test Monday morning, so she won't be able to attend."

"I've got to pound the books," Mary Lou said, with a shrug. "I wish I could come, from what Nora's told me it'll be a blast."

"We'll miss you," Jack said, "but of course we understand."

The chief stepped closer. "Have you identified the stranger in the dumpster?"

"We're not trying. We have no client or case involving him. Naturally, we're curious. Have your guys found anything?"

The chief shook his head while helping his goddaughter with her coat. "The victim has no fingerprints on file with us. We're waiting for an answer from the FBI fingerprint center. I'll have Sergeant Suggs call you as soon as we hear. Of course, that will be confidential."

Jack waved off the comment. "Anything you ever discuss with us will be confidential unless you tell us it is not." Then Jack turned to Mary Lou. "Good first day. I understand you are coming in for a few hours Monday afternoon, after your test. I'll see you then. Good luck on your exam."

Jack locked the front door and rejoined Nora in the case room. She started talking before he sat down. "Here's a spreadsheet of Dr. Andujar's appointments for the past year." She pushed it into the table space between them. "His laptop referred to his patients only by file numbers."

"Wasn't there a legend matching the patients' names with those numbers?"

"Negative. And don't forget our open house Friday night."

"You've already reminded me, several times."

"But you haven't responded. I need you here by six."

"I won't forget our open house."

Nora smiled, "by six."

"Yes, by six, Friday. Satisfied? Now let's get back to work. Maybe Agnes Fuller knows the codes. I'll call her after Drummy debugs her house."

Nora answered the ringing phone and held it out. "It's Max."

"My team's not fully assembled," Max said into Jack's ear, "but I've activated the stakeout. Donny Andujar came out once about an hour ago to walk an older, sophisticated-looking man to his car. I didn't recognize him, but I got a picture."

The rest of Jack and Nora's week was filled with gathering copies of the police reports and the medical examiner's autopsy protocol, digging through Chris's laptop, contacting the people in his address book, and speaking to the Andujars' neighbors in Arlington and in the apartment building they had rented in DC. All necessary steps. All wasted time. They also came up with a few new ideas.

CHAPTER 12

JACK ARRIVED AT MI's open house promptly at six to see Nora in a clingy blue dress brought to life by the blossoms and narrows of her body. To the extent a woman's appearance was currency, Nora's scoop-necked dress flashed a healthy portion of her bankroll.

"It's midnight azure," she said. But, as was true for many men, Jack's color vocabulary only included light blue and dark blue.

"Is Max coming?"

"No," Nora said. "He hasn't filled his crew yet so he's on the Donny stakeout."

"That's a shame," Jack said. "He's a character. I like him."

Police Chief Mandrake arrived a few minutes later. He had brought along Patrick Molloy, the mayor of DC. Nora greeted them at the door and called to Jack. "Come meet Mayor Molloy."

After twenty years as a covert operative for the U.S. intelligence community, Jack was more chameleon than peacock, but he obeyed Nora's summons. The mayor had a build like Santa Claus, including the squishy, red-veined nose. Time had furrowed his forehead but not touched his greenish-gray eyes or their youthful-looking lids. The politician's acumen spoke for itself. He was a two-term Irish mayor in DC, not Boston.

Jack shook hands with the mayor, and asked, "Join me in a Scotch, straight, on shaved ice with a twist of lemon?" Nora had somehow learned that was Molloy's favorite drink. When His Honor nodded, Jack steered him in a wide turn toward the bartender set up in their conference room.

"You go schmooze with your other guests, Jack. I'll get our drinks." Molloy headed for the bar with two other guests carrying empty glasses trailing in his wake.

Most of the guests not elbowing near the bar were gathering at the rear of their eighteen-hundred-square-foot office. Rachel and Nora had furnished the back area with cherry wood tables and overstuffed seating to give the feel of a living room.

"Thanks for bringing Mayor Molloy," Jack said to Chief Mandrake. "We had invited him but got no confirmation from his office. I owe you one."

"I'll hold your IOU," Mandrake said, while grinning from under bushy eyebrows that gave the impression caterpillars were nesting on his forehead.

"It's my guess you know everyone here, Chief, so I'll leave you to mingle. The bar is to your left and hors d'oeuvres are near the back wall. Enjoy."

Mayor Molloy handed Jack a scotch and water, then headed across the room toward two congressmen whose synchronized wattles indicated an intense verbal battle was underway.

Eric Dunn, the writer of the nationally syndicated column *Dunn in D.C.*, strolled over with a cold Corona in his left hand, and what Chris Andujar used to call a shit-eating grin on his face. "Remember me?" he asked.

Jack hadn't been sure the journalist would come after he had used Dunn's name to suggest that anyone, even Dunn himself, could be a killer. That was during The Third Coincidence case Jack had handled the prior year while still employed by the government.

"I hope you're not still angry at me?" Jack asked.

"I was really ticked at the time, but the next week eleven more newspapers picked up my column and two political talk shows invited me on as a guest. All of which graduated you to hero status."

While spearing a Swedish meatball, Jack watched Art Tyson, a man with brown eyes surrounded by dirty whites. He had a face like one of those karate guys who impressed others by trying to break cement blocks with his forehead, and kept losing. Jack glanced at the bartender who held up three fingers; it was Tyson's third double. The bulky Tyson walked away from the bar in his rumpled light-blue seersucker, with his fresh drink in hand, and went face up with Mayor Molloy. A moment later, the mayor was shaking his head no—an emphatic no.

Jack walked over to Nora. "What's the skinny on your friend Tyson?"

"Arthur Tyson is no friend of mine." Her mouth twisted as if she had bitten into something bitter. "He quit the force a few years back after having been suspended several times for either drinking on the job or the use of excessive force. Now he's a PI specializing in cases involving cheating husbands." Her upper lip rose like she wanted say yuck. "The story is, not all his compensation is monetary. The man's an ape."

Art Tyson leaned into the bar and ordered another. Jack was close enough this time to hear him say double scotch rocks; he was also close enough to tell Tyson's suit reeked of cigar smoke. When he turned, his shirt, between its struggling buttons, gave the other guests more than a subtle peek at his belly hair. He stumbled and nearly fell on his way over to corner Troy Engels, one of the CIA's introverted and amoral geniuses. Engels had been the deputy director in charge of some of Jack's quiet ops.

Tyson's behavior was drawing stares. Jack had put down his drink and moved toward Tyson when Chief Mandrake stepped close. "Let me. I know how to handle Arthur Tyson."

Mandrake gently gripped the gruff man's elbow. "Mr. Engels, please excuse Arthur. I need his opinion on something." The chief's hand dented Tyson's doughy back as he began moving him toward the door.

"Welcome to our noble profession, Mr. McCall," Tyson said in a loud voice gurgling with phlegm. "Call me. I'll tip you off to the ins and outs of being a DC snoop-dick."

"My driver will take Mr. Tyson home," Mandrake said. "He'll come back tomorrow for his car."

The chief again nudged Tyson toward the door. The man's head flopped to one side spilling liquid from the corner of his mouth. Tyson swiped at it with the back of his hand.

Jack knew that Sam Spade would have just jammed Tyson's hat on his head and booted him out the door. In Sam's day these things had been simpler.

Nora was standing beside Jack when Mandrake finally got Tyson out of their office. Jack breathed in the fresh scent from her silky hair. "Keep mingling, Senor," she said before surreptitiously squeezing his tush and walking away. She looked back and smiled.

Jack forced his eyes off Nora's butt and strolled over to the hawk-nosed Troy Engels standing alone near the window. For a moment the two men stood quietly watching the river of cars flowing past the building.

"You miss the ops in my department?" Engels asked.

"No."

"Some people do deserve to die, Jack. You must believe that the world would be better off today had someone taken out Adolph Hitler or Saddam Hussein before those monsters destroyed their countries and damaged the rest of the world."

"I agree in concept, but the rub is who gets to choose the targets and the qualifying infractions?"

"Nothing's perfect, Jack."

The top dogs in the intelligence community who were opposed to Engels's department called him the director of assassinations. Jack had spent many long, lonely nights thinking about Engels's department and his own past role in their missions. He wanted to respond to this man who worked the buttons on most of the agency's black ops, but this was neither the time nor the place.

"I'm sorry you had to deal with Tyson," is all Jack said. "I should not have let him in."

"P-p-please k-keep him away, J-j-jack."

The spittle from Engels's "p" hit Jack's lips—scotch. He casually wiped his fingers across his lips. He had never before heard Engels stutter.

The last of the guests left two hours later; the catering service soon thereafter. Jack and Nora were alone.

She came to him. "Why don't you come home with me? I make a great omelette."

"Thanks, but I'm whipped. These kinds of events aren't easy for me. You did a great job setting it all up and keeping things moving smoothly all night. But I think I need to head home. I'm hoping Saturday will be a sleep-in morning; I'll talk to you sometime tomorrow."

She hugged him and went out the door.

Jack flipped off the lights and looked around his empty office. His eyes finding the faint light wafting over from a few lit offices in the building across the street.

He grabbed a half-full liter of Maker's Mark by the throat, took a long swig, and collapsed onto the couch in his office. It had been raining on and off since about noon, just as it had the night he and Rachel had finished furnishing the office.

That night he had taken a seat on this same leather couch, waiting while Rachel put the finishing touches on her own office. Instead, she had surprised him by changing into a short, tight dress, nylons and red heels.

He looked up and in his mind saw her leaning against his doorway, just as she had that night. Her lips curved into a delightfully wicked smile.

"Time for us to christen the place," she had said, holding up a bottle of Dom Perignon, the wet from the ice bucket dripping off its bottom.

His memory watched her hips as she came toward him, and the desire revisited his core. She handed him the bottle and set the glasses on the table that fronted the couch, her wide stance stretching her black dress taut across her thighs.

Jack's hands twitched as his mind relived tearing at the foil and twisting the wire to expose the cork. His eyes saw what they had seen that night.

Rachel's arms had moved to the back of her neck where her dress fastened. It slipped around her hips and dropped to the floor. She again stood before him wearing only the red heels and a black teddy. A low growl escaped him. She had always had the uncanny ability to make him feel like no woman ever had, like she had been molded especially for him.

At that moment, the cork had come free. The champagne had frothed over the neck and ran down its glass shape. Rachel took the bottle from his hand and licked the foam, her tongue darting into the bottle.

"Now that we're married, you don't have any objection to my seducing you in our office, do you, Mr. McCall?" Her words echoed in his mind.

"None whatsoever, Mrs. McCall," Jack said out loud, recalling his own words.

Jack's mind let him hear the snaps pop free as Rachel reached down and freed the crotch of her teddy.

After they had finished what Rachel often called *Good and Plenty*, they had sat without concern for the rest of the world, drank champagne, and watched the late rain dance within the ambient light of the night.

Jack turned his focus to the raindrops beating a silent rhythm against the pane, each drop joining with others to form ribbons and race to the sill. He felt Rachel leaning into him again, the tufts of her hair, still moist from their passion, settling against his neck.

The memory was so sensual that Jack reached up and touched the spot.

CHAPTER 13

THE NEXT MORNING, Jack's neck felt spray-starched, a leftover from sleeping with his head on the arm of his office couch. He went home and slept two more hours. Then, after a light lunch, he called Agnes Fuller to report that the man following her the last few days was involved in the security clearance for her State department job.

"Thank you so much, Mr. McCall. Last night, after Mr. Drummond told me there were no listening devices or cameras in my home, I slept like a baby. He said you wanted to talk with me further. I'm off today. If you don't mind doing it on a Saturday, I can be in your office in two hours. Say four-thirty?"

"That would be fine. Come upstairs this time."

At four that afternoon, Jack arrived at MI to find Nora already there.

"I got so busy getting ready for the party last night," she said, "I forgot to tell you that I checked Donny Andujar's liquor and business licenses. He's the only owner of record. On his application he put down the money for his club came from gambling winnings that he claimed he reported as income. I called a friend at the Tax and Revenue Office. It checks. He covered his story."

Before they could discuss much of anything further, Agnes Fuller walked in; she was a few minutes early. Jack led her back to their conference room, took a seat directly across from her, and cut right to the chase.

"Sarah believes Chris was being blackmailed," he said. "We think she's right. It's also possible that a few of Chris's patients may have also been blackmailed. Do you know his patient codes?"

Fuller looked back and forth between Jack and Nora, her loose jowls swinging slightly. "The codes were only kept inside the patients' jackets and in Dr. Andujar's head."

"That'd be just like Chris," Jack said. "He had a phenomenal memory."

"He did, didn't he?" Fuller nodded.

Fuller was quickly able to put names with a half a dozen of Chris's patient codes, those who had appointments the last few days before his death. Then she pursed her lips and shook her head.

"Who picked you up in the dark coupe after you and I spoke in the parking garage?" Jack asked.

"My boyfriend, Arthur Tyson, he's a local PI. Artie says he knows both of you."

Jack forgot his sore neck and snapped his head toward Nora. After wincing, he said, "Please tell Arthur we said hello."

The city had a zillion dark-colored coupes, so Jack couldn't conclude Tyson had been the driver outside of Sarah Andujar's house. But then he couldn't conclude he hadn't.

Agnes Fuller left.

Five minutes later Chief Mandrake came in. "I just cruised through your underground parking garage to be sure Tyson had picked up his car and I saw your car. I decided to come up and let you know we've identified the man in the dumpster: Benjamin Haviland, a federal fugitive who, during the late 60s and early 70s, demonstrated for every cause that needed someone to carry another sign. The Feds had nothing on the guy since '72. Sergeant Suggs tossed his apartment; he found nothing other than clothes and a high school track medal for winning the hundred-yard dash. He lived ready to run at any moment."

"Not much to leave behind at the end of a life," Nora said.

Five minutes after Chief Mandrake left, Max Logan came in.

"This is more visitors than we get on weekdays," Jack said to Nora.

"Here's the photo of the stranger I saw with Donny Andujar in the lot at his club." Max dropped the picture on the table.

Nora picked it up and immediately said, "Jack, this guy was here last night, at our open house."

Max perked up. "You know him, boss?"

"Meet Troy Engels, Deputy Director of the Central Intelligence Agency. But what's he doing with a pimply faced wannabe gangster like Donny Andujar?"

"Any guesses, boss?"

"No reliable ones."

"What else has been happening at Donny's club?" Nora asked.

"Boring! I've been singing Irish ballads just to stay awake. Donny shows up around noon, then leaves for the night sometime between dinner and closing time. Last night, it got a bit more interesting. Around six, he comes out with one of his ladies wearing a short skirt and a pair of them mid-thigh patent leather boots. The two of 'em got into his Porsche, and after five minutes of what looked like an argument, they drove off. I followed. A Porsche is a pretty easy car to keep your eye on in traffic."

Max used his hands to demonstrate a turn, and then continued. "Twenty minutes later he pulled up outside the Lord & Taylor store out on Western Avenue. The doll goes in. He waited in his car. I waited in mine. Fifty-five minutes later she comes out. Wow, what a change. I wasn't sure it was the same dish till she got back in Donny's Porsche."

"How had she changed?" asked Nora.

"She's all dolled up, fresh as a spring morn, including a new do. She had on a plaid above-the-knee skirt and a green blazer, with one of them phony family crests on the pocket. She'd gone from a lap dancer to a good-looking fox like you in under an hour. My apology," he added, his hands outstretched like a revivalist, "if that didn't come out like the compliment I intended."

"You can call me a fox anytime, Max." Nora smiled.

"Donny took off with me still playing shadow, and after a while he turned into the parking for the Loews Hotel on L'Enfant Plaza SW. He and the babe got out and went inside the hotel. Neither Donny nor the doll knew me from nobody so I followed on foot.

"They got off the elevator at the twelfth floor and the doll goes in one of the rooms. Donny returned to the elevator alone and took it down. By then I'm all curious so I hunkered down in the lounge area outside the elevators on twelve. I called my relief guy and told him I'd broken off the tail. I told him to hustle over to Donny's house to see if he went home."

"Had he?" Jack asked.

"Nope. My guy found him parked back in a reserved spot at his club."

"So what happened at the hotel?" Nora asked.

"Two hours passed with nothing going on. Then the door opens and a man comes out. He had to have been in the room when we got there. The doll followed him into the hall wearing nothing but her blazer. The little lass put her arms behind his neck and hopped up and wrapped her legs around his waist. He planted a two-handed grip on her butt. Then he put her down and walked backwards for a bit so he could watch her lean forward and jiggle in her single-breasted; that's the blazer, not the doll."

Max winked. "She wagged a crooked finger beckoning the guy back, but he shook his head. She went back inside, and he started walking toward me."

"Did you get a picture?"

"Sure. Took the picture through a hole in the newspaper I was holding because, this time, I knew the bloke."

"I've never heard a more colorful report on a stakeout, Max," Nora said, "but who the hell was he?"

After a final pause for drama, Max said, "You've met him, boss. The Honorable Patrick Molloy, Mayor of the great District of Columbia." Max slid the picture across the table.

CHAPTER 14

AFTER A QUICK Monday morning stop at a chiropractor to get his neck jerked into alignment, Jack called an old friend. "Hello, Carol. It's Jack McCall. I need a favor."

"Well, Jack. What's it been, a couple of years? How's it hanging?"

Carol had always talked more like one of the guys than one of the guys.

Jack and Carol Sebring had dated about five years ago. After going out several times they'd agreed to end their relationship and remain friends.

"Congratulations on your promotion to Special Deputy Assistant to the Director. I wouldn't be surprised if one day you become America's first female FBI director."

"The promotion was nearly three years ago, Jack. I got the flowers you sent then. They were beautiful and thoughtful. Now cut to the chase."

Carol had also always been a bottom-line person.

"A few days ago the body of one of your old fugitives, Benjamin Haviland, showed up in the dumpster behind my building. I'd like a look at his file."

"The identification of Haviland's body came up briefly in one of my meetings yesterday. Don't expect much. Until we identified the prints sent over by Metro, his file had been in the Bureau's equivalent of the post office dead letter section."

"Would four work for you?"

"I'll clear you with security. Ask for me."

A black Cadillac Escalade with heavily tinted windows followed Jack around a second corner. The car seemed sinister, but DC had many black Escalades. He parked on D Street and walked down Tenth toward the FBI entrance near Pennsylvania Avenue. After stepping inside he looked through the window as the Escalade drove by, its dark windows denying a view of the driver. He wondered if this had been a coincidence, or his imagination on overdrive. He thought not. Just a feeling, but he had come to trust *those* feelings.

Carol Sebring still hadn't gotten her nose straightened from taking a punch from a suspect. With the broken beak she had knocked out the perp. with a left-right combination. The slightly crooked nose gave her face character and added an invisible message: Don't fuck with me; I'm tougher than I look. Carol was a sexual powder keg. Jack had not met her husband, but he smiled in a moment of compassion and envy.

She escorted Jack to a small private room. "These files are hard copies from the old days. Take whatever notes you wish, but don't remove anything."

He nodded. "I appreciate you setting this up. Now, how have you been?"

"Wonderful. As you know, I got married to Cary Scott, so we have no problems with monogrammed linens." She laughed the laugh that follows a line used before. "Around here I still use my maiden name." She touched his arm. "I was saddened to hear of Rachel's death. I knew her from her time with the Bureau. She was a fine agent and an even better person."

"Thank you. I'm pleased you're happy. You deserve it."

She opened the door to leave.

Jack pulled out the chair. Then he twisted back toward the door. His neck was still tender, but since leaving his chiropractor there was no more sharp pain. "Carol." She stopped. "Did you mean to leave these other two files on, ah," he looked at the names: "Anson and Jensen?"

"Read Haviland first. You'll see the connection. If you need me, dial 322. It rings on my desk."

In the mid-60s, Benjamin Haviland had been active at every major demonstration in America. In the early 70s, along with a Carl Anson and Joan Jensen, he graduated to the big time as a prime suspect in the robbery and demolition of an unoccupied National Guard armory. The FBI estimated the street value of the stolen weapons and ammunition at $2 million.

The files included pictures of all three from their hippie days. The backs of the pictures carried the same notations: "Received, with a date stamp of four years ago. Source, San Francisco Police Department, originally taken at a mid-60s demonstration." Even after allowing for the impact of the years and the work of the maggots, Jack could easily tell that Haviland and the dumpster man were one and the same.

He punched in Carol's extension. "Did the FBI provide copies of these three files to Metro PD?"

"Their request was for Haviland," she explained, "came in through normal channels. After they read Haviland, if they want Anson and Jensen they'll put in another request. Then again, there's no particular reason for Metro to assume three hippies from the sixties have kept in touch."

Carol walked him through a deciphering of the transmittal sheets in each of the files. The notations told him the forty-plus-year-old pictures of the three fugitives had come in from Frisco four years ago. Then nothing until DC Metro requested Haviland's file.

Jack was back in his car by seven-thirty with his stomach reminding him he hadn't eaten since breakfast. He pulled in behind a diner and went in for a burger and a piece of coconut-cream pie.

When he came out, a parked green van sat in the space beside his car; the front seat was unoccupied. After he opened his driver's side door, the mid-door of the van opened from the inside. Then he felt a jab in the back, a jab he knew, a gun jab.

"Don't turn around, McCall!"

They knew his name so this was no random robbery, and they didn't intend to kill him. If they had, they could have simply put two slugs in his head without bothering to get out of their van.

"What do you want?"

A deep voice came from above his head. "Careful and slow, put your hands behind your back. Now!" The assailant punctuated his command with another jab of the gun barrel. Harder.

The space between his car and the van lacked the room for a countermove. He heard the cold, hard click of handcuffs, and then felt the active hands of a frisk. A strong punch in the side of his lower back slammed him against his car, his knee denting the side panel. Then a hand came around from behind and grabbed a fistful of his shirt, and a wad of skin.

He looked down. The hand was the size of a rump roast, a white guy's hand. No watch. No rings. No tattoos. But he did have hairy arms and dirty fingernails.

Jack felt the warmth of the man's throaty whisper against the back of his head, and smelled fetid breath sneaking below his collar. "Straighten up and walk," the voice commanded. From the location of the voice, Jack estimated the man to be at least four inches taller than him, which would put the guy around six-six. Then the hand gave him a healthy push in the direction of the alley off to one side of the lot. As he twisted from the push, he saw the hood of a black Escalade, the inside dome light illuminating its tinted windshield. The next push put the dark Cadillac out of view. Then he heard a car door close. He thought it was the Escalade because car doors sound tighter than the doors on vans.

The talker held the short chain between the cuffs higher than Jack's arms would comfortably tolerate, so he walked on the balls of his feet to slacken the pressure. From their footsteps he figured his greeting party had three members. Maybe four if whoever got out of the Escalade was involved.

When they got into the alley, Jack took a hard downward blow to the side of his head. He stayed up for a moment, and then dropped to one knee. He was immediately yanked back onto his feet.

"Get up," said one of the men from behind. "I thought you was a tough PI. Like on T.V." The remark was followed by enough laughter to confirm there were two men behind plus the one he could see in front. The two behind were close. He sensed they were the size of port-a-potties.

He felt a warm trickle of blood slaloming through his hair, racing down his forehead toward his left eye. He shook his head convulsively, the blood worm turned toward his temple.

The jagged stub of a broken bulb stuck out above one of the doors in the brick building; a dank trough gutter streamed down the center of the alley.

A strong jerk on the handcuffs made him pull up like a saddle horse without so much as a whoa from the guy playing jockey.

This is where it'll happen.

The front thug had a huge belly, even larger shoulders and a bull neck. Jack imagined a fleshy face with deep-set eyes, but he couldn't know. Dumbo wore a ski mask. When all you can see of a face are the eyes, it's amazing how much they can tell about what is going on inside the person. Dumbo's eyes filled with a here-comes-hell look. Then he tried to drive his massive fist into Jack's navel. The fist didn't fit, but in trying, it pushed out nearly all Jack's air.

One of Dumbo's support staff from behind jerked Jack's head up by his hair, his mouth impulsively working like a gold-fish orphaned to the front lawn.

The thug paused to straighten his mask, spit, and hitch up his pants. Three more rapid blows were delivered to Jack's face before the puncher returned to his belly. Determined not to cry out, Jack bit down on his tongue. The blows continued, too many to count. Jack bit harder. His body had begun to collapse under its own weight when the next punch, up into his breadbasket, momentarily lifted him off his feet.

A mushy, acidic mess rose from the back of Jack's throat, and somewhere in that slop his tongue found a strand of unchewed coconut. On the reswallow, it didn't taste like pie. Pie wasn't bitter. Pie didn't burn. At least it hadn't the first time down.

Somewhere during the sea of blows, Jack's feet quit trying to keep him upright. This made the two in the back work harder to hold him up. He nearly blacked out. Maybe he actually had for a few moments now and again. He dropped onto his knees; they let him. One of them came around front to grab his shirt and lift him back up onto his feet. The lifter stood as tall as a grizzly, but had hairless arms.

Dumbo was tiring, his punches weakening. Or perhaps Jack's senses had simply dulled sufficiently to register the blows lower on his private Richter scale. Jack longed to get in at least one blow, a blow one of them would remember.

Through blurred, swollen eyes Jack saw the now heavy-breathing puncher rear back for that little something extra. The resistance provided by being held from behind gave Jack the leverage he needed. As the front-pounder stepped forward to deliver his next sledgehammer fist, Jack raised his leg and drove the flat of his foot into the brute's kneecap.

Dumbo screamed and folded like a circus tent. A minute later the behemoth was back on his feet.

Jack tried to smile, but his face refused.

The pachyderm shook his head as if he were shooing flies, flipped open a switchblade and with a decided limp moved forward.

"Stop," came a voice from somewhere near. "Only a beating."

So there is a fourth.

When the commander stepped out from the shadows along the wall, Jack's handlers took off the handcuffs letting him free fall into the alley's foul-smelling center trough. He rolled over onto his side, propping himself up on his elbow. The effort caused his head to flop to one side like a rag dog, dipping his ear into the drain water.

The squaretoed boot of the one who'd emerged from the dark shadows pierced the light to deliver the final blow just above Jack's belt. His elbow failed him. He went down. Face first.

Hairless arms, protruding from a sleeveless denim jacket, reached down and grabbed a wad of Jack's hair. His head and shoulders came off the wet pavement, a mixture of blood and gutter water dripping from the end of his nose. Jack tasted the part trailing into his mouth. His attempt to spit failed. He tilted his head. The rancid mixture ran out.

"Drop the Andujar case or next time we'll hand you your pecker in a paper bag."

CHAPTER 15

SOUNDS AND SHADOWY images crawled into Jack's consciousness. Then a bright square appeared above him, darting in and out like a UFO using cloud cover to obfuscate its movements.

One eye—the left, he thought, began working on shapes as his vision fought the fog; then the second eye joined the effort. The bright square became a fluorescent ceiling light. The shadow turned into a large doughy doctor in scrubs moving back and forth between Jack and the light. The doc leaned close, his cheeks sagging like soft sacks of pudding.

Then Jack heard Nora's voice. He felt her lips and damp cheek gently touching beside his sore eye. When she stepped back, he saw that there were no wires connecting him to machines and none of his limbs dangled in traction—both good signs.

"Hello, Partner," he said. "If you're kissing it to make it feel better, I hurt all over."

She leaned down and softly kissed his cut lips, then next to his other eye.

"I'm going to have to get beaten up more often."

"And in more interesting places," Nora said.

He tried to smile, but his lips were split and swollen.

The doctor leaned back in, shined a light in Jack's eyes and led him through the doctor game: follow the moving finger.

The doc stood tall, his pudding-sack cheeks receding, then summarized his findings: "A few bruised ribs, no broken bones." He sprinkled his cheerful soliloquy with words like hematomas, contusions, abrasions, and sprains. "You'll be fine, Mr. McCall. We'll keep you here for a day or two for observation. You've suffered a mild concussion. Said plainly, your body has taken a hell of a licking but everything's kept on ticking. You're a lucky man." He hung the chart on the foot of the bed and walked out.

That's easy for you to say. You didn't take the beating.

Nora told him an anonymous call to the police had brought them to the alley. Sergeant Suggs then called her and she arrived just before the ambulance left to bring him to the hospital.

"Your keys were on the ground beside the driver's door," she said. "I drove your car here. It's in visitor parking. Suggs had one of the officers follow in my car. Your Beretta wasn't taken; it's still hidden up under the dashboard."

Jack managed to ask, "How did Suggs get the word?"

"I'm guessing he has a flag on your name in the department computer. That'd get him notified of anything that involved you."

"As Max would say, oh, tis grand to be loved."

Sergeant Suggs came in an hour later. Jack told him everything he could remember except for the guy with squaretoed boots offering to bag his pecker if he didn't get off the Andujar case. No one is beaten up to get them to stay off a case of suicide. Had he told Suggs about the threat, Metro might well reopen their inquiry into the death of Chris Andujar. If they did that, Suggs would get anal and order Jack to back off the case.

Suggs hoped Jack might be able to connect his beating with the murder of the dumpster man, as Benny Haviland had come to be known around the station. When Jack couldn't, Suggs left.

Jack turned his head on the pillow to face Nora. "I've got a note from my doctor, so I won't be at work tomorrow." His lips cracked when he tried to laugh. It hurt, but laughing with Nora felt good.

A nurse stuck her head in through the doorway. "You need your sleep, Mr. McCall. You can have more visitors tomorrow—which won't be long. It's pretty late now."

Nora left and the nurse came back in to give him two sleeping pills which he held under his tongue while drinking the water. The nurse had left a bedside urinal. Jack had never used one and he told himself he wasn't going to start tonight. He worked his way to the edge of the bed and stood; blood draining from his head made him dizzy. He held the foot rail until his vision cleared. His eyeballs felt gritty but worked well enough for him to find the bathroom. After flushing he glanced in the mirror. He touched his sore face, pursed his lips, and ran his tongue around inside his mouth, checking for damage, somehow he still had all his teeth. This personal checkup was less professional than the doctor's had been, but he knew it would give him the straight dope. He had no stitches in his face, but other than that what he saw resembled a meatloaf after being kneaded to fit the pan.

With the room light off, he could see the moon duck in behind a passing cloud. Under normal conditions it would have been relaxing to watch while falling asleep, but Jack had to make a visit before he could rest.

CHAPTER 16

JACK LEFT THE hospital after midnight wearing his still gutter-wet pants and dank smelling sport coat over the hospital's tie-back gown. He had been able to get his feet into his shoes, but they remained untied.

The pain was traveling fast as he slowly worked his way across the dimly lit main room in Donny's Gentlemen's Club. The hurt moved through him with the speed of a hamster in a wheel cage, one flash finishing and another rising to take its place. The marines had taught him more than the fundamentals of fighting and then the Special Forces honed it to a sharp point. He wasn't fooling himself, he had lost a step just as old shortstops do, but he was still a man that smart people didn't piss off, and he was pissed off now and not just at Dumbo and his cohorts. He had let himself be vulnerable in the parking lot; he knew better and pledged not to let it happen again. He also knew he would recover. Not tonight. Not tomorrow. But he could already feel his body fighting to regain itself. Until then, his visit to see Donny would be about proving the adage that it was better to give than receive.

When he reached the bar, he eased his reliance on the cane and tried to find a comfortable position. There was none.

The bartender, a woman wearing an unbuttoned leather vest open over her tanned bare chest, looked at him like he was a used car she wouldn't want to test drive.

He loosened his jaw. "Donny Andujar, tell him Jack McCall's here."

Overhead and floor level spotlights illuminated three stages featuring well-coordinated women. The girls were shapely, but you could see just as much shape in any downtown restaurant at lunchtime. What brought these girls attention was not what they had, but their willingness to show what they had.

The place was crowded with a lot of men and a few women. Some men wore clothing that said they donned hard hats by day, while others wore loosened, but still-knotted ties around their necks. There were college men, and men with long hair, men with grey hair, and men with no hair. Some of the men had fat faces, or sad faces. Some sat quietly. Some hooted and hollered. There were faces with mustaches, with beards, and clean shaven.

Donny Andujar appeared in a doorway at the far end of the big room. He parted his lips just enough to insert a dark, thin cigarette. He flashed a rictus that barely wrinkled his face, and started toward Jack sided by a man with arms like draft kegs dangling from his shoulders. The steroid junky was trying to walk soldier straight, but his gimpy right leg gave him away, *Dumbo from the alley.*

Donny took a long puff, then stepped beside Jack and crushed his newly lit brown in a bar ashtray. "Hello, McCall." Smoke leaked out as he spoke.

"Donny, some guys worked me over. It was connected to what I'm doing for your mother. Can we go somewhere and talk?"

Donny jabbed his head toward the back, then told his bodyguard to help Jack. The man was massive enough that Jack could have ridden him like Sabu of the Jungle rode elephants. The bodyguard raised one arm, his shirt revealing a tattoo of a red bird with wings spread, diving below his belt.

When they got to Donny's office, Jack paused to lean against the doorway. The big one followed Donny inside. A minute or two later Jack stepped in leaving the office door open. Donny motioned for his man to close it. When the thug passed by on his way back from closing the door, Jack drew a sap from his coat pocket and slammed it against the back of the behemoth's head. Dumbo went down. Jack grimaced from the extra hurt, but felt good for having delivered it.

Jack had brought the six-inch, leather-wrapped sap from the glove box of his car. He had bought the weapon, popular in the 20s and 30s, as memorabilia from Sam Spade's era. Saps had fallen out of favor in modern times but Jack had found it useful on more than one occasion.

Next, in a jerky move, Jack pulled his Beretta, ordered Donny to the far side of the room, and eased his backside against the edge of Donny's veneer-covered desk.

"Lock the door Donny and drag Dumbo onto the tile portion of the floor." After Donny had done that, Jack instructed Donny to set a straight-back chair over the downed man's upper right arm, and to put another chair a few feet from Dumbo's head. He then had Donny set a third chair six feet on the other side of his downed bodyguard, turn it backwards and straddle sit it.

Pain coursed through Jack as he sat in the chair nearest Dumbo's head. He placed the tip of his cane against the downed bodyguard's neck and looked around the room. A black safe silently stood against the wall behind the desk. The room was carpeted except for the tile strip from the door to the desk which sat just beyond where Dumbo lay. Recessed into one wall were nine television screens arrayed in three rows of three. The upper three showed the club's stages, the middle row watched the crowds sitting at those stages, and the bottom three sets focused on the front door, the bar, and a panorama of the full room. The bottom screens would have allowed Donny to see Jack come in and approach the bar. Donny's office had no windows and only the door through which they had entered.

"You may not know this, McCall, I once thought about becoming a cop."

"And I thought about becoming a priest, so after you answer my questions, I'll pray for your sorry ass."

"And here I thought you were a friend of the family."

"Enough with the small talk, Donny. Here's the deal. You've got a choice and it's not between good and better. There are things you're going to tell me right now or I call the police here from your office. You and this guy," Jack gestured toward the floor, "are wearing the same shoes you wore in the alley. My DNA will be on his fists and traces from my shirt will be on your boot. You'll be charged with assault and battery. That'll be enough to shut down this little tits and ass palace."

Donny eyeballed Jack with an air of defiance, "I don't know—"

Jack slammed his cane against the side of the desk, the reverberating bass from the big room's music masking the noise. He returned the cane to the neck of the man on the floor and rested his other hand on Donny's phone, which he had moved to the corner of the desk.

Jack's voice crawled out from a deep well. "Truth is, I'd enjoy seeing you in jail and out of this business; your mother would too, so no games. Do we understand each other?"

Jack couldn't risk letting Donny use his computer. Jack would have to get too close to be sure Donny wouldn't use the time to email for help. He gestured toward a file cabinet with his semi-automatic Beretta, "Use that old typewriter to write out your confession for assaulting me. Include the identity of Dumbo here and the other two scum suckers who helped you."

"Now listen, McCall, I'm just a guy trying to get a piece of the action."

Donny was doing his best to sound seasoned, but Jack could detect fear nibbling the edges of his words. "If you figure you're owed something," he said, "we can talk, but I'll be damned if I'm gonna write that down."

"No sweat, Donny. If you'd rather I call the police now, than you to have to gamble on what I'll do with your confession, well ..." Jack let his words trail off and picked up the phone.

After a bit more grousing, Donny moved the typewriter to his desktop and started typing. When he finished, Jack had Donny read the confession aloud, sign it, push it across the desk, and get back in his chair.

"Who's Ben Haviland?"

Donny gave a wide-eyed blank look. "Who?"

"Ben Haviland," Jack repeated, with enough enunciation to get his split lips bleeding again. "Come on, Donny. They found his body with one of your matchbooks in his sleeve."

Donny raised his eyebrows and shook his head in short, quick jerks. "I got no clue." After pausing, he corrected himself. "There's old Bennie. I never knew his last name. Every couple of months he shampoos our carpets. He works for Clark's Janitorial. Jesus Christ, McCall, our matchbooks are all over the bar and the tables. All over town, anybody could have one."

"Why did you kill your father?"

"What? I didn't kill him. I loved him, even though ..." He fell silent, his lower lip quivering.

"Even though what, Donny? Spill it! Even though what?"

"Promise me you'll keep it a secret," he whined. "Not tell Mom."

"You're in no position to bargain. Tell me or tell the cops. I will promise that if you come clean, I'll do what I think is best for your mother."

Dumbo moaned, his head moving the cane. Jack reached down and reintroduced his sap to the back of the brute's head. In his condition Jack couldn't put a full effort into the swing, but it was enough. Dumbo went back to quiet and Jack reset the cane against the bodyguard's neck.

"Sorry for the interruption." Jack felt blood leaking from his split lip. He swiped at it with the back of his hand. "You were saying?"

Donny sat stone still. His head down. His knuckles white from squeezing his thighs. "Dad was a f-fag. A queer. All right?" As he spoke, a silent tear snaked through his stubble.

"What makes you think your dad was gay?"

"I just know. All right. I know." Donny groaned.

"Let's have it."

"For years Mom went to Baltimore every other weekend to visit her old-maid sister. When she was gone, Dad would meet someone. It was always a man. The same man." He angrily swiped at a new tear. "I followed him. Okay. I saw him with his butt-fucking pal."

Donny's entire body wriggled.

"And you felt humiliated."

"Go to hell, McCall."

"Give."

"Damn you. Yes. I was humiliated. All right? You satisfied? I was humiliated. Okay?"

He started to stand. Jack wagged his gun. Donny sat back down.

"Is that why you killed him?"

"I already told you. I didn't kill him."

"Which one of your goons did it for you?"

"He killed himself. The cops said so." With a pleading gesture, he added, "Christ, McCall, even Mom agrees."

"I want you to give your mother the money you black-mailed from your father."

"What? Mom told me yesterday she thought that Dad had been blackmailed. If that's true, I swear it wasn't me."

Jack raised his cane and pointed it at Donny. "Why did you have me beaten?"

"I had to get you off the case. I couldn't let everyone find out that my old man was a fag." He looked down. "I'd be a laughing stock in my own club."

Perspiration rose from Donny's pores like the early bub-bles in boiling water. Jack could smell the sweat.

"You stupid putz, we had begun to think maybe your mother had it wrong. That it might have been a straight sui-cide. Nobody beats up anybody to keep them off a case of sui-cide. When you attacked me, you convinced me to stay on the case. Along with that, it's too big a coincidence that the dead Ben Haviland also did work for you. You may be big in booze and boobs, but you're a sorry excuse for a gangster."

"You won't have any more trouble from me." He sounded like an adolescent whose maturity and backbone hadn't caught up with his years. "Please don't tell about my dad."

"We're not done here." Jack took a deep breath, biting down hard to get through a jolt of pain from his bruised ribs. "How did you know we would be at your mother's last Sunday?"

"I just stopped by—"

"Don't slip back into bad habits."

"Art Tyson. He—he told me. Okay. He stopped to see my mother. She must've told him."

"Bullshit," Jack roared, then grimaced. "Your mother tolerated Tyson when your father was alive. I doubt she'd let him in the house now, and your mother swore she had not told anyone. Now who do you figure I believe you or your mother?"

Donny mopped his brow with the flat of his hand. "It was Engels. Okay? Troy Engles." Donny wiped his wet hand across his shirt front. "Engels stopped at the club."

Jack raised his hand like a traffic cop. "Stop." Then he sapped Dumbo again. The man hadn't moved, but Donny recoiled as if he had taken the blow himself. "Engels is an expert who deals in international espionage. Why would he bother doing favors for a punk gangster barely out of pimples?"

Donny's face turned white. "Engels was Dad's lover … I got pictures." He took a deep, hard swallow. "Engels keeps me informed of anything he runs across that affects me."

"So you were blackmailing Engels. How does he learn of things that affect you?"

"Engels is tight with Art Tyson." He clasped his hands to illustrate. "They played poker every month with my dad. The other regulars were Chief Mandrake and Mayor Molloy. They all lived near each other in the old days when they were young. From what I hear that newspaper columnist Eric Dunn, who's in solid with the mayor, has taken over Dad's chair. Engels told me Dunn has agreed not to print anything he hears at the poker games without an okay from the others."

If Tyson and Engels are poker pals, why did Engels con me at our open house about not wanting to be near Tyson?

"I'm getting tired, Donny. And thanks to you, I hurt. What little patience I had, is gone. Tell me the rest. What about Tyson? The chief? And the story behind your escorting one of your girls to rendezvous with the mayor?"

Donny's face registered shock. "Mayor Molloy protects me because he's bumping uglies with Jena Moves, my hottest lap dancer."

"Yeah, and?"

"Tyson has sessions with Jena, too, but he arranges his own. Jena told me she and Tyson sometimes do a threesome with some old ugly broad. I don't know her name. That fat fuck Tyson is always horny. He beats his dick like it owes him money." Donny squinted and shuddered. "Far as I know Dunn and Mandrake are straight. Christ, McCall, that's all I know. That's all of it."

"For now I'll hold your confession and won't tell your mother about your father being gay. But if I learn that you've held out, I'll be back."

"Whatever you say, Mr. McCall."

"A couple more things."

Donny's forced smile faded. "What the fuck else do you want?" he asked, sagging deep in his chair.

"Treat your mother with the respect she deserves. You might just find out she's a great lady."

"Yeah, yeah, I know. Like everybody else, you think my mother's Opie's Aunt Bea from Mayberry. None of you know the real Sarah Beth Andujar."

Jack's leg had gone to sleep. He shifted in the hard chair and stretched it out straight. "I wanna talk to Jena Moves. Give me her address, phone number, and real name."

"Her real name is Phoebe Ziegler. You can see why I had to change it. No man wants a Phoebe on his lap." He offered a weak chuckle.

Jack leaned down and laid another egg on Dumbo's noggin, then squinted at Donny.

"I don't know anything else," Donny said, his arms stretched out in front of him.

"Open that safe."

Donny jerked hard on the back of his chair. "I told you I didn't blackmail my father."

"If I thought you did, I'd turn your ass over to the cops right now. Open that safe and give me the pictures of Engels and your dad."

"Super spy comes in from the cold," Donny said with dripping sarcasm. "I read you inherited millions from your old man, but you're still just like the rest of us. You can never get enough scratch. Now you're going to blackmail Engels."

"Think what you will," Jack said, ignoring the increasing drumbeat in his head.

Jack would need to follow Donny to the safe, so he needed an alarm in case the pachyderm woke. After standing, Jack told Donny to put the two chairs they had been sitting on across his man's legs; one above the knee of one leg and the second below the knee of the other. If the man moved, the chairs would shift on the hard surface floor.

"Get on the floor and open the safe from a seating position."

As soon as the safe door cleared the latch, Jack barked, "Scoot back."

Jack's could no longer separate the bass from the treble in the music pushing through the walls from the main room. When he started toward the safe, his senses told him he was walking in foot-sucking mud. He shook his head and the second and third images of Donny disappeared. When he got to the safe and looked in, he saw neither a gun nor an alarm button.

"Get up. Put the pictures on your desk, along with two one-hundred-dollar bills."

"Anything else I can do, Mr. McCall?"

"I should also punch your lights out, but I won't." Then he smacked Donny in the jaw, the punk landing on the bed-long leather couch against the wall. "Like hell, I won't." Jack wasn't sure which of them it hurt worse, but he knew which of them felt good about it.

He picked up the photos, and acted out the final scene of Sap meets Dumbo before going out through the door.

Like medieval jousters, the oncoming traffic kept thrust-ing lances of light to complicate Jack's struggle to stay on the right half of the road. He parked in the hospital lot near Twenty-second and "I" Streets. Donny's two hundred went to reward a janitor for getting him back inside and up to his room without being seen.

He kicked off his shoes and put his dirty clothes back in the small closet, then took the sleeping pills he'd saved from earlier and crawled into bed.

Later today Jack would have visitors. He figured Max would come by and he wanted to know why the fella Max had tailing Donny hadn't helped him in the alley.

CHAPTER 17

THE MORNING LIGHT poured through Jack's hospital window and with its warmth came the realization that Donny could not have shaken down CIA Deputy Director Troy Engels over the intimate pictures of himself with Chris Andujar. Engels would have handled Donny like an experienced nanny handles an unruly child.

Nora came through the hospital door wearing a black blouse and her everything-is-going-to-be-better-today attitude. Her smile made him feel like a newborn colt, which was quite an accomplishment given his body felt like an old nag on the way to the glue factory. When she leaned down in her scoop-necked blouse to kiss him on the forehead, the colt had the feelings of a stallion.

"Did you get some rest?" she asked.

"They gave me sleeping pills last night. When I took them, they put me right out."

It was the truth constructed to work as a lie for Jack wasn't ready to hear her admonitions for having snuck out of the hospital to confront Donny.

"Max and one of his guys took your car to your home. They left it in the driveway."

"Good. What's happening on Andujar?"

"I finished going through Chris's laptop. Fuller was straight with us. There's no legend of the patient codes."

Max came in. "Thanks for taking care of my car," Jack said when he looked up at Max who wasn't wearing a scoop-necked blouse and didn't lean forward to kiss him on the forehead.

Max nodded. "Yellow isn't your best color, boss, particularly when you wear it with all those shades of bruise."

"Thanks, Max. I'll try to keep in mind next time someone wants to redo my skin tones."

Max turned serious and reported that nothing out of the ordinary had happened at Donny's last night until some hunched-over man limped in around one. "The old scruffer limped out about an hour later. I didn't even bother taking his picture." Max turned his face away from Nora and winked. "An hour after scruffer left, Donny came out beside one of his bouncers. The big one was limping and kept rubbing his head like he'd taken a bad fall. The two of them were shouting, then the big guy squeezed into the Porsche and Donny drove him home. I followed."

Jack turned his head away from Nora and winked back at the crafty Irish-Scottish breed. Then he asked, "Had Donny left his club earlier?"

"At first we didn't think so, but he must have. When I came on duty the man I relieved told me that earlier some big musclebound guy with a flat nose came out, got the van, and pulled it up tight to the club's side door. The open door blocked my man's view, but he could tell three more people got in. At the time he figured they were driving home a couple of drunks. They've done that a time or two before. It looked routine. My man took two zoomers. I looked at 'em, but nothing much showed because of that damn door."

Max shook his head. "That same van came back around ten-thirty, and Donny, his limping bodyguard, and a big nasty looking biker got out. They all went back into the club. The driver, another steroid experiment gone amuck, joined them inside after he parked the van. That's when I reasoned it was that group, not drunks, who left earlier. No two ways about it, we missed that, boss. Sorry."

"It couldn't be helped. Let me change the subject. Didn't you tell me you once worked as a guard at the building where Chris Andujar had his office?"

"Yeah."

"Do you know which janitor service the building used?"

"Clark's Janitorial. I walked past their van every time I made my rounds."

So the dead Benny Haviland had access to both Chris's office and his son's club.

"Max, stop by that building tonight and find somebody who works for Clark's. See if you can find out what other buildings they clean."

"You got it."

The door opened and the nurse walked in to chase off Nora and Max.

What Jack had heard about hospitals was true. You couldn't get any rest. If they weren't poking you, feeding you, running tests, or doing therapy, the doctor was coming in on rounds. To prove the thesis, the doctor walked in just as the nurse walked out. After doing enough to justify billing the insurance company, the doctor said, "You can go home at six if you promise to take it easy the next couple of days."

The doc left; Max and Nora came back in. Then Sarah Andujar walked in. She had her coat buttoned all the way up, a black scarf wrapped around her neck trailing back over her shoulder. She took Jack's hand. "I could not bear it if my asking you to look into what happened to my Christopher was the cause of your being beaten."

"It was a random mugging, Sarah, that's all, just some thugs out for kicks. Lucky me, eh, but I'm fine, really. They're turning me loose at the end of the day, so I'm on the mend."

Sarah shook her head slowly. "I can't imagine anyone doing such a horrid thing."

After a while, Nora stepped closer. "Max and I need to get going. I'll be back at six to drive you home."

Jack watched the automated door close over the space where he had last seen Nora.

Sarah stepped closer. "I need to leave too, and you need your rest." She held her scarf in place and leaned in. "I worry about you, you big lug. I love you like you were my own son." She kissed his forehead and left.

When Jack left the room at six he planned to check outside the door for a sign reading, THIS PATIENT NEEDS FOREHEAD KISSES. He eased himself into a semi-sitting position. It felt good as long as he didn't let the back of his head touch the headboard.

The beating had given him more reason to suspect Donny, but in the end he doubted the punk had the moxie for blackmail and murder.

He dialed Nora's cell phone on his and headed for the bathroom. "Where are you?" he asked when she came on the line.

"I stopped at my place. They just delivered a new bed. I got it on trial."

"Give me some personal comments on Tyson, Molloy, Mandrake, and Eric Dunn."

"Tyson's divorced. In my mind, he's worse than some of the guys he arrested. Mayor Molloy and his wife are strong Catholics. Rumor is neither will break the church's dogma on marriage for life. The chief's a widower. His wife died of cancer, oh, six, seven years ago. Other than to say hello, I don't know Eric Dunn. Why?"

"I'll explain later." Jack dragged his palm across his cheek. He'd need to find a way to shave before Nora arrived at six.

"In an hour," Nora said, "I'm meeting again with Agnes Fuller. She says she's been thinking back on the last few weeks and she thinks she may be able to match a few more names with Chris's patient codes. Bye for now."

"Wait! I haven't had a chance to give you the lowdown on what happened last night."

"You know who worked you over?"

"It was three goons from Donny's club—probably bouncers. Donny was there too."

"That little punk ass! Why didn't you tell Sergeant Suggs?"

"I don't want Sergeant Anal back in the middle of the Andujar case. He called it suicide and closed his file. Now it's ours."

CHAPTER 18

A MAN WEARING olive green pants; a baseball style cap, and a light tan jacket emblazoned with the water company's logo opened Jack's water meter near the curb. He looked down at the gauge, appeared to make a note of the reading, slid the lid over until it clunked back into place, and continued down the sidewalk until he was beside Jack's brown Concorde parked in his driveway. He walked slowly around the car, looking as one might at a car that had a for-sale sign in its window, then ducked between the car and the hedge next to the driveway. From the crouching position he removed a wrapped package from inside his jacket and shimmied his way under Jack's car.

An hour after Sarah left Jack's hospital room, Mary Lou Sanchez came in with the energy of a hummingbird. "Nora okayed my coming to see you. She's watching the office." Her smile drooped into concern. "How are you doing, Jack?"

"I'm fine, Mary Lou. A hundred years from now I'll never know this happened."

Her laugh raised his spirits. Then she kissed him on the forehead.

There has to be a sign out there.

"Lean forward," she said. "I'll fluff your pillows."

Pillow puffing wasn't in her job description, but what the hell. Jack leaned and Mary Lou fluffed.

"I'd like to hear more about your father."

She pulled a chair close so Jack could see her without having to move his head.

"My dad, Tino Sanchez, was a cop all his life; he loved it." Her eyes seemed to sparkle when she spoke his name. "He and my godfather, I call Chief Mandrake, Uncle Harry, but for real, he's my godfather. He and my dad were more like brothers than friends. Daddy told me once that Mom had some serious hots for Uncle Harry when she first met the two of them. Uncle Harry was already married, so the four of them became close friends. My mom and dad up and got married six months before I was born." She raised her eyebrows. "We all know how that goes. My mother died giving birth to me. Uncle Harry lost his wife a few years back, and then I lost Daddy. Uncle Harry has been like a second father."

She slipped off a locket that hung around her neck and opened it.

"This is my daddy and my mama." On each of their pictures she had a small tuft of hair. "Daddy gave me the locket with Momma's hair when I was a little girl. I swiped Daddy's hairs out of his brush after he was murdered."

"You look like your mother."

She opened her eyes wide and took in a big breath, the way one does to hold back the impulse to cry. "Uncle Harry says that too." Her tone turned wistful. "I loved them both very much. You know, all my friends take their parents for granted. They don't know how lucky they are to have them." She closed the locket, paused to hold it tight and then slipped it back over her head to again cradle against her chest.

"If it hadn't been for Uncle Harry, I don't know what would have happened," Mary Lou said. "He moved me right into his home, took me to his church, and helped me get a scholarship through the Police Officers Association. He's been fab—oh, that means just great. After he retires next summer, he's going to take me on vacation with him. He's promised to tell me a lot more stories about my mom. I keep asking him now, but he insists that we'll have more time then to really sit and talk. I can hardly wait." She flushed. "Uh, when I interviewed for the position Nora said it would be okay if I took that time off next summer."

"No problem. Which church do you go to?"

"Daddy and I always went to Uncle Harry's church." Her smile disappeared and she looked down. "Now, Uncle Harry and I go to Saint Thomas Apostle over on Woodley Road."

Jack furrowed his brow. "How come you changed churches?"

"That's a long story."

"I didn't mean to pry."

She brought her hand to her mouth. "Oh, that's okay. I just hadn't thought about it for a long time." She put her hand down. "I had gone to Father Michaels, the priest at our old church, for counseling after Daddy died." She rubbed her hands together as if they were cold. "Father Michaels ... well ... he fondled me."

"Jeez, Mary Lou, I'm sorry." Jack could think of nothing else to say out loud. *Bastard.*

"When I told Uncle Harry he got madder than I've ever seen him. He went high up in the church, but nothing ever happened."

Her eyes narrowed. "The church transferred Father Michaels to a Boston parish."

"Bad deal." *Son of a bitch.*

"Yeah, it was a bad deal all right." She clenched her hands in her lap and looked away. "There's been so much of that kind of stuff in the papers. This will sound just horrid, but it's reassuring to know I'm not the only person that kind of thing has happened to."

"I didn't mean to bring up bad memories."

"Heck. You didn't know Jack. It's no problem." Her gaze moved to the wall above Jack's head.

"So where are you and your Uncle Harry going on vacation next summer?"

She sat forward and again became animated. "Vanuatu. It's an island in the South Pacific. He's vacationed there every year since his wife died. He rents a beautiful home right on the ocean. I've seen pictures. The weather is super. He's going to teach me to deep-sea fish. I'm going to teach him to play golf—although I'm not all that good. It'll be a really cool vacation."

"I bet it will. You bring back lots of pictures, and be sure you're strapped down while your deep-sea fishing. We don't want some big marlin pulling you out of the boat."

She grinned. "Uncle Harry says those fish are really big, but don't worry. I'm tough." She pushed up the sleeve on her jersey and flexed her bicep.

After sitting quietly for a moment, she asked Jack about being a federal agent. He told her what he knew about the career opportunities in the CIA and military intelligence, and the lifestyle that came with it. Then he reached for her hand.

"Do you really want a career in law enforcement? You aren't just doing it out of respect for your dad or loyalty to your Uncle Harry?"

"Oh, no." She made a dismissive gesture. "I've wanted it since before Daddy died. It's a career that can make a difference." She stiffened her shoulders. "Someone has to protect and serve." She sighed. "That sounded corny, didn't it?"

"A little, maybe," Jack answered, "but it's true. There are a lot of good people ... and some bad ones. You must learn to discern between the two. There will be times when people's lives, even your own, may depend on your ability to do just that."

She stood up. "Along with Uncle Harry, will you help me learn how to tell the difference?"

"Sure." Jack nodded. "You know, with what you've gone through you're an amazing young lady."

She blushed. "I'd better get back or Nora will kill me." She kissed his forehead again and left.

Is this an age thing? Do women start kissing foreheads when a man gets to a certain age?

Jack smiled wistfully. All of us hope to make a real difference in someone's life. Chief Mandrake had been there when Mary Lou needed him. It looked like the relationship had been good for both of them.

CHAPTER 19

THE BLACKMAILER CASUALLY walked along the side street that fronted Nora's small rental house. When no one was in sight he ducked through the trees and swapped the CD from the recorder for a new one. He checked to be sure the coast was clear and walked back to the old car he had left parked around the corner.

The wind was blustery and, being across from a park, strangers in the neighborhood were commonplace. And most people were so self-absorbed that they rarely focused on much outside themselves and their own activities.

Twenty-five minutes later he pulled into a rental storage garage and turned off the pinging engine. From there he walked two blocks and got into the car he owned in his own name. When there were no cars or pedestrians coming, he placed his hat on the seat beside him and pulled off the mustache he had attached with spirit gum.

After driving home, he pulled into his garage and touched the remote closer. After opening the driver's door to turn on the car's dome light, he plugged a CD player into his cigarette lighter and leaned back to listen to Nora Burke's private conversations. At first, all he heard was her singing along with some music. She had a pleasant voice. Then she got a call from Jack McCall. He listened to them reason out that Chris had been blackmailed and likely had been murdered, although they conceded he might have killed himself as a result of being blackmailed.

McCall also told her it had been Donny Andujar who had him beaten him and threatened him to stay off the Andujar case. The blackmailer slammed the flat of his hand hard against the steering wheel, "You stupid punk." No one could hear him inside his car, inside his garage. "McCall is the only thing standing in my way."

He went inside his house and fed the CD into his shredder, poured a glass of wine, and sat down to plan his next move.

Jack's internal stiffness meter registered high as he inched his hindquarter down to the front seat of Nora's Mustang, a small price for leaving the hospital.

At the corner he got a full view of a building under construction he had only seen a part of from his hospital window. Its steel girders rising like a skeleton against the gray six-o'clock sky.

From the side-view mirror he watched a White Chevy Lumina pull from the curb to move in two cars behind Nora's Mustang. The Lumina dutifully followed when she turned onto M Street toward Georgetown.

"Let's go for a drive," he said. "Get some air."

"The doctor's order was, 'bed for thirty-six hours.'"

"I need to move around some," he said with a dash of petulance. "My God, they even made me ride out in a damn wheelchair."

"And just where do you want to go?"

"Turn right here. Quick. Quick! You'll miss it."

Nora jerked her wheel hard and held it firmly while her tires fought to hold to the lane nearest the curb. "Okay," she said, "I'm on Twenty-ninth Street. Miss what?"

"I thought we might mosey over to Chris's office," Jack said, keeping his eye on the mirror. "We can take this up to P Street, then right a few blocks, go around Dupont Circle and we'll be on Massachusetts near his building. You've still got the key Sarah gave us, don't you?"

"Mosey?" she repeated with a smirk. "Does that go with the yep you say sometimes?"

"Yep. It do. I picked up mosey from Max. I watch film noir. He watches westerns. We share slang from the genres. Here, I'll use them both in the same sentence. Yep, let's mosey over to Chris's office. Did you know the circles were put in DC's main arterial streets to slow opposing armies?"

"Yep, I surely do know about the circles. And yep, I've still got the key. But nope, we're not stopping anywhere. We're a headin' fer your spread, podner."

"Come on. The building has an elevator. Go along with me here. Then you can drop me at home and I'll do whatever you say. We have to go to Chris's office. The lease will be up tomorrow, and we need to see his office before they clear it out."

Like all great salespeople, he had first created interest, followed by a sense of urgency.

Nora frowned. "Then you'll do whatever I tell you tonight and tomorrow?"

"Whatever you say, little lady."

They laughed as she reined in her Mustang and rounded Dupont Circle. Two minutes later, Nora pulled into the lot of a seven-story brick building. Jack watched the Lumina drive on by.

Nora turned off the engine and reached into her purse. When she brought her hand out it held Jack's Beretta. "I took it from under your dashboard this morning," she said, "before Max drove your car to your house. Don't you think you oughta be packing in case the two thugs in the Lumina follow us inside?" She grinned. "You didn't think I saw them?"

He shook his head. "You're smarter than the town's new school marm."

She gently squeezed his thigh. "I'm gonna havta palaver with Max about this here westernizing of your lingo."

Nora held open the building door. Jack labored to keep up with her chattering heels as they crossed the marble floor. Coming out of the elevator she slipped her arm under his and tried to help support his weight.

Chris's office felt cool and smelled musty. It didn't appear anyone had been in it for some time. "Looks like the janitors never came back," he said.

"I spoke to Sarah yesterday," Nora said while flipping on the overhead lights. "The building manager is meeting the Goodwill truck at nine in the morning. She told them they could have it all."

Like doctors' offices across America, a little double-pan- eled sliding glass window loomed like a sentry between the empty waiting room and the inner office. Four three-drawer lateral file cabinets obediently stood in the area normally accessible to only the doctor and his medical staff.

The first three cabinets were empty. In the last one Jack found a single file folder laying flat on the bottom of the low- est drawer. On its flap were the handwritten initials: "TS." The initials had been written hard and deep, and underlined three times, but the folder was empty. TS could've stood for Tino Sanchez, Mary Lou's dead father. Could he have been one of Chris's patients? Then again, the initials could refer to anyone with those initials, including Tom Sawyer, or even inanimate subjects like Time Slips.

Jack picked up a paper clip from the top of the cabinet and shook it inside a loose fist, before throwing it against the window. He put his hand against his ribs and stood still until the pain let go of him. "Damn. I wish we had gotten this case before these files went to Dr. Radnor."

Chris's private office looked to be about fifteen feet by twenty feet. His desk sat at the far end away from the door. The area nearer the door where he met with patients had two occasional chairs, a coffee table, and a couch. The shutters in the patient area were angled to show the Canterbury Hotel across the street while a patient stood, but to avoid it being a distraction after a patient had sat or lain down.

The office had the aura of having died with Chris, the furniture holding their posts in sleepless vigil. A small closet held a man's wool coat. On the shelf, a wool hat, stuffed with a muffler, sat on its crown. Nora lifted an umbrella that leaned into the corner.

"There's nothing inside the umbrella," she said, "the coat, the muffler or the hat band."

Stale-smelling cigarette butts crowded the ashtray on Chris's desk, a few bent and stubbed out after only a puff or two. A swelled butt, once soggy from floating in stagnant coffee, was stuck to the bottom of a foam cup, stained brown.

"The anti smoking ads should have this picture," Nora said.

Jack sat at Chris's desk and went through the drawers while Nora did the same to what had been Ms. Fuller's receptionist desk. Except for two Bic lighters and a nearly full carton of unfiltered Camel cigarettes, the contents were not much different from what Jack would find going through his own desk. He pulled out the center pencil drawer and put it on top of the desk. Then he stacked the other drawers in alternating directions on top of the belly drawer. Nothing had been taped on the outsides of the drawers. He also wanted to look into the drawer holes, but he couldn't bend low enough to see into the lowest slots.

When Nora came back into Chris's office, Jack asked, "Will you come over here and check inside while I've got the drawers out?"

"Sure." She came over, looked inside, and shook her head. "That was hard for you, wasn't it? Asking for help, I mean."

He mumbled something on the way over to the couch where he sat with his back to the end with one leg stretched out across the cushions. She looked over and smiled.

"Did I ever thank you for dropping me off when I got the new brakes put on my car?"

"Yes. Yes, you did." His face flushed a bit. "Thank you for helping with the desk."

"Glad to do it, podner." She slid the drawers back in before holding up a photo of Sarah and Donny when Donny was a teen. In her other hand was a picture of Chris with Tyson, Engels, Mandrake, and Molloy.

"Goodwill will toss these and just keep the frames."

"What are you suggesting?" he asked.

"We can take them to Sarah." She pried up the little metal stays and removed the pictures from the frames. "There's nothing behind the pictures. You ready to split?"

Jack saw no tail car when they pulled out of the lot. "Let's take the pictures out to Sarah now. It'll only take an hour to drive there and back. Hand me your cell phone. I'll let her know we're coming."

Nora shook her head. "No way, José, our bargain was we go to Chris's office and then I'm the boss through tomorrow. You can call Sarah in the morning from home to tell her we'll give her these pictures the next time we see her. That's it, ponder. Live with it."

Jack frowned. "Yes Warden."

They laughed. He wouldn't admit it but he was quite sore by the time Nora pulled up in front of his house.

"Give me your car key," she said. "I'll pull your Concorde into the garage."

"Don't bother. Thanks for driving me home."

Nora insisted on walking Jack into the house and up to his room. Then she went down to the kitchen and brought up a pitcher of water and a glass.

"You sure you don't want me to pull your car into your garage?" she asked, while handing him the remote for the television that sat on top his dresser. "It's no problem."

"I can do it tomorrow. It'll give me a chance to move around a little."

CHAPTER 20

JACK WATCHED THE early sun give chase to the retreating night before heading downstairs to the kitchen. He stopped at the mirror on the wall at the landing halfway down. The face he saw more resembled a swath of Black Watch plaid, than the face he had worn before meeting Dumbo in the alley. The look wasn't pretty, and he knew that as the beating further ripened it would get even less pretty.

The coffee pot was finishing its cycle of hisses and gurgles so Jack wandered outside to get the morning paper. Halfway down the driveway, he saw Roy Parker, the ten-year-old boy who lived next store with his divorced mother, Janet. The boy came over to him.

"What happened to you, Mr. McCall?"

"A few bad men beat me up, Roy."

"Does it hurt?"

"Yes. Do you remember when you broke your finger last year?" The boy nodded. "Well, I'm just trying to be strong like you were then."

"There must have been a bunch of 'em to take you on."

Jack smiled and mussed Roy's hair. When Jack turned, he saw Roy's mother, Janet, on her porch. They waived. Inside, he poured another cup of coffee and went upstairs to the small desk in his bedroom and called Sarah.

"Andujar residence, Sarah Andujar speaking."

"Sarah. Jack. We stopped by Chris's office last night."

"Do we need to meet?"

"No. I just called to let you know we brought back a couple of things we figured you'd want to keep."

"What?"

"Personal photogra—"

"Throw them out! I don't want the damn things. None of them!" After a pause, she said, "I'm so sorry, Jack. I still react unpredictably sometimes when I'm unexpectedly reminded of Christopher. I apologize. It's just, well, I have plenty of family photos, and the study is already filled with pictures of Chris and his pals. You'll think me silly, but I'd rather not change the house at all from how it was with him ... not yet ... anyway."

Jack stood, taking care not to audibly moan, and switched the phone to his other hand so he could open the French door to the outside deck off the master bedroom. "It's I who should apologize. I brought it up out of nowhere."

"Oh my, I forgot to ask, are you home from the hospital?"

"They let me out late yesterday." The outside air coming in through the screen felt cool on his battered face.

"I'm so glad you're doing better."

"I'll go back to the office tomorrow."

"You men try too hard to be macho. Nora's a levelheaded young woman. You should listen to her."

Sarah's advice had been good, but Jack knew he would disregard it. The tendrils of the investigation were wrapping around his mind and the parts weren't fitting together the way he had hoped. He had to get back to work.

CHAPTER 21

AT NOON JACK'S doorbell rang. It took him a few extra minutes to get downstairs but it ended up being worth it. Young Roy's mother, Janet Parker, stood on his porch holding a tray of food.

"May I put this in your kitchen?"

"Absolutely you may. What is it?"

"Some Minestrone and home-baked bread."

He opened the door and Janet edged by. As she passed, he could smell the hot soup and her perfume. He also noticed her white shorts and tight cranberry top with spaghetti straps.

"How are you feeling?"

"I'm doing okay. This was very thoughtful, but you didn't have to go to the trouble."

"I know. That's what makes it fun. I haven't seen you since, well, since before Rachel died. I only talked with her a couple of times, but she was very nice. I'm sorry for your loss."

It was nice of her to say, but Jack would prefer that everyone just stop reminding him of Rachel, talking about her hurt. It brought back her last smile, their last lovemaking, her last laugh. Their never-to-be-filled plans and the unanswerable: Had he gone to lunch with Rachel and Nora that day might he have saved her? Of course, it was irrational, there had been no reason for him to have suspected she was in any danger, but feelings of helplessness are rash not reasonable.

He smiled thinly. "Thank you."

She hugged him gently, taking care not to squeeze anywhere.

"What are you doing home on a weekday?" he asked.

"Took a half personal day. They give us several each year. I've had a bunch of errands backing up on me so I decided to bring you some lunch and then get caught up. I got lucky; today's a nice sunny spring day."

Jack leaned his cane against the side of the refrigerator and walked toward the table slow enough to minimize a noticeable limp. "Will you join me?"

"What kind of a message would it send if I wouldn't eat my own soup? Sit down; it'll just take a minute to put a little more heat in the soup and slice the bread. Roy told me you were beaten up. Give me the adult version. Where do you keep your bowls?"

He pointed to the cabinet right of the sink, then gave her the same story he had given Sarah about a random attack.

She looked over her shoulder. "My father's taking Roy fishing tomorrow." She smiled. "He'll bring him back the next morning, could be like old times."

Jack thought her rear had moved a little more than would have resulted from the motion of slicing bread.

"Janet, I'm having trouble just walking. I'm not ready."

"You'll heal." She poured the soup into two bowls.

He smiled. "Rachel's only been gone a little more than four months. I just don't know ..."

She turned to face him. "That's part of the healing too. There's no hurry." She placed the soup in front of him, a spoon on a napkin beside the bowl.

They ate in quiet until she said, "That was nice of you a few days ago to offer to take Roy for a ride in a dump truck. He's still at an age where dirt is fascinating. He's really excited about going."

"Roy's doing me the favor. I enjoy his company."

Janet had a pleasant smile that reached up to involve her eyes. She also had nice legs which she kept crossed, sitting sideways. "I'm barbequing some steaks tonight for Roy and me, along with some corn on the cob. Roy loves corn. If you're up to joining us, call me by five and I'll marinate an extra steak. If you don't feel up to it there's enough soup and bread here for another meal." Her spoon clanked into her empty bowl. "I told Roy I'd pick him up at school so I'd better get a move on or I'll never finish my errands." Jack started to get up. "No." She put her hand on his shoulder. "You stay right there. I can find my own way out."

She looked back over her shoulder, turning just far enough to offer an excellent profile of God's generosity. "If you need anything, I'm just next door."

"Why don't you take my Concorde? Roy loves to ride in it. When you get back just leave it at your place, I'll bring it home after the barbeque tonight."

"Then you're coming?"

"I'll call if I'm not. Okay?"

"Speaking of your car, are you trying to sell it?"

"No." Jack raised his eyebrows. "What made you think so?"

"Yesterday, when I briefly stopped home during my lunch break, I saw the water guy read your meter. Then he stopped and looked at your car. He looked it over pretty good because I saw him stand up like he had been looking underneath. I figured you had a for-sale sign in the window."

"Nope. It's not for sale. I'm sure I'll see you tonight. I just want to wait a while to be sure I don't stiffen up too much."

He hadn't wanted to tell her that he needed permission from his temporary warden.

She picked up the keys to Jack's car. "Thanks. Roy'll be surprised and pleased."

When she closed the door, Jack got up and went to the window to watch her fanny as she walked down the driveway, unlocked his car, stepped inside and shut the driver's door.

An instant later what she had said washed over him in a torrent. He flung open the kitchen door and staggered out onto the small side porch, "Janet!" He grabbing at the rail for support. "Janet. Stop!"

She was looking down to insert the key into the ignition.

"Janet! Janet! Don't! Stop!"

She looked up.

He stumbled on the single step and sprawled down onto the driveway.

She got out of the car, ran to him and bent down. "Are you all right?"

"I'm okay." He said from the ground. "Did the meter man read your meter too?"

"Shit, Jack, who the hell cares? Are you hurt?"

"Help me get up." She did. He sat on the step. She stood in front of him with her hands on her hips. Her legs shoulder width apart.

"Tell me," he repeated, "what about your meter? Did the guy read your meter too?"

"No. My meter gets read early in the month. Wait a minute. That's odd. Why wouldn't they read both our meters at the same time?"

"Did you recognize him?" Jack asked, rubbing his leg.

"He's the meter guy. What's to recognize? I wouldn't know any of them if they stood at my door. Damn it, Jack, you scared me half to death, and nearly broke your neck falling off the porch, and all you want to do is talk about the frigging meter man."

"Forget about my falling. I may be being paranoid, but I want you to do exactly what I am about to tell you. Understood?"

The expression on Janet's face told him she was thoroughly confused, but that he had her full attention.

He took his car key from her hand, her fingers white from the grip.

"Inside the kitchen door, there's an override button that opens the garage. Inside the garage there's a flat yellow board on wheels. It's a size you could lay on."

"My dad had one to work on his cars."

"That's it. Bring it out here, also the flashlight that's on the workbench."

She started to speak. Jack put up his hand.

"Just do it. We'll talk afterwards."

She opened the garage and brought the scooter bed and the flashlight.

"Lean it against the porch rail."

She did.

"Now, I need you to go home. Go in the back bedroom, and stay there. Now, the hard part, do not look out your windows. In fact, pull your drapes and stay back from the glass."

"You're scaring the begebees out of me." A moment later her expression changed and she put her hand to her mouth. "Oh, my God. You think—don't you?"

"I'm probably just an ex-spook being melodramatic. Don't worry. Just do exactly what I told you."

"Jack. Don't lie to me. If that's what you're thinking, call the cops. You can't—"

"Janet. Okay, that's what I'm thinking. I'm probably wrong, but I want to err on the side of caution. But, yes I can. I've defused lots of bombs." *Actually, only one. And it was a long time ago.* "It's time to stop talking. Go home and do what I told you. Oh, first step inside and get me my cell phone. It's on the kitchen table. I may need to call you to do something else."

Like move further away and take the neighborhood with you.

She handed him the phone. Her face crowded with fright.

"Go on now. I'll get started as soon as I watch your fanny get inside your front door. It may be the last thing I ever see, so swing it girl."

She started to protest, but he put his hand his up, turned her toward her house and swatted her on the backside. "Go on," he said. "I'll call you as soon as I can."

Janet walked toward her house, stopping every few steps to nervously look back over her shoulder.

Jack grabbed the porch rail and pulled himself up. First he tested the flashlight. It worked. He held the railing while he did a few partial squats, slowly rotated his arms, and twisted his upper body trying to improve his range of motion.

This job's made for a guy in my condition. I'll be laying down the whole time.

It took him a couple of minutes to move to the Concorde, ease down onto the scooter bed, and roll as far as he could under the car. It was a tight fit, but eventually he got near where he wanted to be—below the driver's seat—and turned on the flashlight. Everything looked right.

Maybe it was just what Janet thought, some guy who digs Concordes.

Then he saw it: A block of C-4 plastic bonded explosive.

Okay. Decision time. Do I do this or do I call someone? The police have a bomb squad, but that means an open investigation. The only case we're working is Andujar so Metro could reopen their investigation, shoving MI to the sidelines. I could call the CIA or the Defense Department. They would handle it for me, but they would be required to advise the locals and that takes me back to square one.

The block looked like a U.S. military issue M118 demolition charge, but he had seen some composition four plastic explosive made in Iran that looked very similar. In any event it had a kill range adequate to get Jack off the Andujar case, off everything. Not to mention destroying his car and part of his house, but it wasn't enough to reach Janet Parker and his other neighbors.

If old enemies did kill Rachel, this might be their work, but this isn't the time for those thoughts. Clear your mind. Focus.

The malleable C-4 had been shaped around the steel frame using an adhesive backing like what comes standard on the M118. He gently felt the surface of the putty like explosive. The end had been shaped into a cone pointing toward the driver's area of the car.

Whoever did this, knew how to direct the explosive thrust.

If he remembered his training on explosives, this size blast would generate about seven-hundred tons of air pressure per square inch, as contrasted with normal air pressure of fifteen pounds psi.

Focus.

He slowly raised and lowered his arm so the flashlight would allow him to see all the sides and the top of the C-4. He had to find the detonator.

There it is.

An M8 blasting cap had been inserted into the block. An electrical detonator cord trailed off toward the front of the car.

It was a basic setup designed to trigger the explosion by shock energy when the ignition key started the car. The detonator, a smaller explosive, breaks apart the compound chemicals of the C-4 and the resulting gases come under very high pressure and expand rapidly.

They fucking explode. That's what they do.

A further inspection revealed no secondary detonation device or other booby traps. Jack took a moment to look out from under the car to be sure Janet had not come back or that the mailman or someone else was not approaching the property.

He took a deep breath and pulled the detonator free.

Absent the heat or shock energy of a detonation, C-4 is so stable that it will not explode if burned, cut, or even if a bullet is fired into it.

Jack stored the C-4 in a combustibles safe in his garage, returned to his car, held his breath and turned the ignition key.

After wiping his forehead and letting his heart rate ease some, he called Janet to assure her that the danger had passed. When she stopped crying, he made her promise not to discuss the incident with anyone.

"You can take the Concorde now," he said. "It's safe."

"No offense," she replied, "but I'll drive my own car, thank you."

CHAPTER 22

MAX CALLED AN hour later. Jack, who had gotten back into bed after dealing with the bomb, eased his legs around to sit on the edge.

"Hey, boss, how ya doing?"

"I'm doing Jim Dandy, Max. A wee bit of a headache, but by the morrow the sun will be shining on the trail before me and the wind will be nudging me onward. Now, what do you have, you phony Irishman?"

"It kinda hurts me, boss, when you poke fun at one side of me heritage."

"Is this when I'm supposed to apologize?"

"Now'll do just fine."

"I'm sorry, Max. May your ancestors forgive me and return to enjoy the grand pubs in Fiddler's Green. How's that?"

"A grand and moving tribute my boy, if ever one's been given, showing both your repentance and respect for those of my clan who came this way afore me. Now if you're done, I'll tell you what I got."

Jack flinched from the tightness that came with grinning. "I'm done, Max."

"Last night I stopped by Dr. Andujar's building."

"Tell me."

"I gave Nora the names and addresses of three other buildings cleaned by Clark's Janitorial. My contact told me Clark's supervisor stops by Friday nights about ten. I could go back then and tail the supervisor to identify more of their buildings."

"Hold off on that. Instead, find out who owns Clark's Janitorial and get a picture."

"You got it."

Jack stretched his sorest leg. "You be careful, Max. This bastard has no qualms about killing. Benny Haviland worked for that janitor service and now he's on a slab in the morgue."

"I'll ID the owners today. The picture'll follow. Boss, could Haviland have used his janitor keys to get the black-mailer into Chris Andujar's office? That could've been how he learned whatever he used to blackmail your friend."

"That's one possibility. But what else would've been in Chris's office?"

"Files on his patients," Max said.

"That's another possibility. Maybe Chris wasn't black-mailed, but learned that some of his patients were being blackmailed."

"Your friend could've been murdered just to keep him from spoiling the game."

"That possibility gets complicated because Chris kept track of the patients in his files and his computer only by code numbers. No names."

"Could your friend have been in on it? I know you don't want to hear that."

"There's still a lot more questions than answers, Max."

"You keep taking it easy, boss."

"You know you can call me Jack?"

"I know."

Before hanging up, Jack told Max about the C-4. "Keep mum about this. We don't need your old pal Sergeant Suggs horning in. But you stay on your toes, Max. The blackmailer knows we're looking for his trail. This thing with my car shows he's raised the stakes."

"That he has, but you appear to be the target, not me."

Jack hung up and called Nora. He told her the same thing he told Max. When she asked why he suspected something was wrong with his car, he told her about Janet Parker bringing lunch and about her seeing someone at his car.

"Give me your gut, Jack. Is this Andujar or your past intelligence work for the government?"

"Andujar. That's a guess, but I think it's a good one."

"Based on?"

"While I was in Europe and the Middle East, I talked to people who would have known or at least heard rumors if Rachel's death was revenge against me for my intelligence work. If the terrorists had wanted to take me out, they had much better chances while I was over there."

"Okay," Nora said, "that makes sense. It also makes Rachel's death look like a straight accident. But this attempt on you may still be someone trying to settle an old score."

"It's not likely. In any event, we can't be distracted." He listened to his partner take a deep breath before he said, "Max told me he spoke to you. Did any of the other buildings cleaned by Clark's Janitorial make a connection?"

"I was checking the addresses when you called. I'm almost done."

"Go ahead. I'll wait."

He watched the wind froth up whitecaps on the Potomac until Nora came back on the line.

"One of the buildings is where Radnor does his shrinking. There's no connection on the other two. Other than defusing bombs, have you been taking it easy like I told you?"

"Nobody likes a smart aleck, Warden Nora. My neighbor, Janet Parker, invited me over later for a barbequed steak dinner. Will you parole me in the custody of her and her son?"

"First, homemade soup and bread, now dinner. Is she young?"

"Young enough to have a ten-year-old son."

"Is she pretty?"

"Yeah, mighty pretty actually. I'm just looking for a juicy hunk of meat."

"That's exactly what concerns me. I'll parole you in the boy's custody," she said.

"I'm going to be more careful in the future about bargaining away control."

"Quit whining. I'm letting you out of jail in the morning."

"I can hardly wait." Jack said.

"If you call me after you get back from the barbeque, I'll slip into one of my special warden outfits and come visit your cell."

Nora hung up.

The suggestive remark had caught Jack unprepared. He had watched Nora walk, inhaled her fragrance, and looked at her rising breasts when she leaned forward. She had touched his arm and his leg, even squeezed his behind during the open house, but this was the first time either of them had openly spoken of their attraction.

CHAPTER 23

JACK'S FACE REMAINED an angry rainbow of black, bluish-purple, and varying shades of yellow. On the brighter side, Hannibal's Army, which had been stomping through his head, had moved on leaving behind a single foot-soldier in hobnail boots.

He had enjoyed the barbeque with Janet and Roy. She had offered to stop by and get him some breakfast, but it would have to be early. He had declined, saying he hoped to sleep in.

Despite that intention he had wakened early, and hadn't been comfortable enough to get back to sleep. At seven he got up and with the help of the banister got downstairs. The coffee pot lifted like a gym weight. Still, relying mostly on pigheadedness, he got through his normal morning routine.

At nine-fifteen, he walked into MI and found Nora in their case room sitting on the edge of the table, her skirt at half mast on her thigh, her legs crossed. She smiled and handed him a cup of hot chocolate. "A parting gift from the Warden," she said.

He tipped the cup and took a drink before they settled down to work without either of them mentioning her suggestive comment from the night before.

"Any progress?"

"Agnes Fuller has been able to put names with only five of Andujar's patients. I contacted all five by phone and told them the same thing: Your name came up in one of our investigations. We would like to speak with you in person. They all knew of his death but none of them had heard anything about him being blackmailed. They praised him as a shrink and refused to disclose why they'd been seeing him."

"Did you ask them if they'd been blackmailed?"

"No," Nora said. "I wanted to read their stress level without that and I didn't want them clamming up. I then went to see each of them."

Jack watched her slide out of her shoes, recross her legs, and wiggle her red-painted toes.

"The body language and demeanor," she went on, "of two of the five strongly suggested they were holding something back. I met the first one, Allison Trowbridge, in the living room of her penthouse apartment. Her father, Dean Trowbridge, is some big shot in banking or politics. She avoided looking at me and kept rubbing her open palms on the thighs of her pants.

"The fourth one I met with was Dorothy Wingate, the big boss at the *Washington Times*. A meeting regarding almost anything shouldn't rattle this woman, but, like Allison Trowbridge, something had tightened her screws. At least ten times she repeated the phrase: 'I know nothing that could help you.' These folks both have financial clout and political muscle. If we try to see them again, we can expect pressure from some direction. I recommend we leave them alone until we've got something that might shake their tree."

Jack nodded. "Anything else?"

"This morning, the reporter Eric Dunn called saying he needed to see you, alone. He wouldn't say why but he said it was urgent. You two seemed to hit off when he came to our open house, so I went ahead and set it up. He'll be here at four."

It was five after four when Jack limped out to greet Eric Dunn. "Hey suspect," Jack said, "how are you?"

After a full-body laugh, Dunn used the back of his thumbnail to stroke one side of his mustache.

"I'm fine." He followed Jack into his office. "But I can't say that about you." He shook his head. "You should have been a newspaperman. Unhappy customers use our thoughtfully crafted words to line their birdcages or wipe their asses. They don't beat us up. You know who did it?"

"No."

It was late enough for a beer, so Jack excused himself and got three. On the way back he delivered one to Nora. "I like your new hairdo," he told her.

"I was hoping you would."

Back in Jack's office, Eric wrapped his hand around one of the Coronas and followed a long pull with a long ahhhhhh. "I've heard you met with President Schroeder," he said, "after you got back to the States a week or so ago."

"The word meeting implies too much."

"The story is he's using you as a consultant on Middle East policy."

"The president and I have been friends for over twenty years, and friends chat from time to time. Eric, is this why you came by?"

"No. I'm not trying to learn your secrets. I'm here to reveal someone else's."

"Go on."

"Rumor is you're looking into the death of Dr. Christopher Andujar for his widow who believes her husband was being blackmailed prior to his death. I might have something."

Jack gulped his Corona and leaned forward gingerly, placing his forearms on his knees. "I'm listening."

"You and I need to agree on something first."

"I don't like backroom deals, Eric. Never have."

"What I'm here to tell you, I've agreed not to print in my column. You have to agree not to disclose it unless you find the story is a lie—okay?"

"That's very open-ended."

"I'm a journalist. I have to protect my sources."

"I have no secrets from my partner. If you tell me, it includes Nora. Her word is at least as good as mine."

"That's your risk, Jack. But I'm telling you if it gets out MI's rep could be destroyed." He ran his index finger through the condensation on the side of the clear beer bottle. "That's the kind of influence I'm talking about here." He blotted his wet finger on the fabric of his slacks.

I'm not sure I can trust this guy, but he came with something and he could be an excellent source of information in the future. "Okay," Jack said, "but I also need a commitment from you."

"What?" Dunn asked, obviously surprised.

"You must agree to keep confidential everything we discuss in this meeting. That means not to print it or talk about it with anyone, including at your poker games with Mayor Molloy, Chief Mandrake and the others. Will you agree to that?"

Like two boys making an imaginary blood oath, they extended their beer bottles and clinked the necks to seal their pact.

"I learn lots of things I don't print. People know I understand some stuff doesn't fall within the public's right to know.

That I won't print something just for sensationalism. That's part of why they give me important information that needs to be told."

"We've agreed," Jack said. "Stop selling."

Eric Dunn took on an expression Jack had often seen on people about to spill the beans—someone else's beans.

"Dorothy Wingate has been a basket case ever since Nora left her office. Somehow you knew that Dot was a patient of Christopher Andujar. What you didn't know, but I figure you suspected, was that she had been blackmailed."

Jack made an open hand gesture. "What we don't know is over what?"

"Here it is. For years Dot has been intimately involved with Philippe Frenet, France's Charge d'Affaires to the United States. She swears only three people knew: Frenet, herself, and Dr. Andujar, whose dead."

Eric relaxed a little, having served up the filet of his message. He closed his lips around the bottle and took another swig.

"Christ, Eric! The woman's the editor of the newspaper your column runs in, that's how she got your agreement not to print the story."

Eric held up his hands. "Cool it, Jack. My column is published in more than one hundred newspapers. If her *Times* dropped my column, her competition has told me they'd pick it up in a New York minute. Dot came to me because I'm her friend."

"Okay. Continue."

"About ten months ago, Dot received copies of photos of her and Frenet engaged in activities that would not fall under the duties of a Charge d'Affaires—even France's. Frenet received a similar package."

"Hell, she's single." Jack shrugged. "A little embarrassment—it passes."

"Frenet is married. And while the French are known for being rather loosey-goosey about sex—or more honest about it, depending on your point of view—his American wife is not. He expects the French government would recall him for embarrassing them in diplomatic circles."

"Tell me about the blackmail."

"Nine months ago they each paid a half a mil, American. They're each worth tons. Dot owns fifty-five percent of the paper. Before his government service, Frenet was the CEO of one of France's largest insurance companies. Still, the blackmailer never came back for more. Go figure. If Dr. Andujar was the blackmailer, his death would explain that. I'm not here to accuse your client's husband, but you have to admit it's a legit question." Then Eric threw up his hands. "I don't know what to believe. There is nothing in Andujar's background that indicates he would get involved in blackmailing his patients, but—"

"But lots that says he would not," Jack interjected. "Besides, if Ms. Wingate really believed Chris was the blackmailer, she wouldn't have let you tell me about it. With him dead, their indiscretion would again be their secret."

"You're right. She doggedly refuses to believe that Dr. Andujar was involved, but she can't figure how else it could've happened. They paid a million clams, but to most blackmailers the first payment is only an appetizer, particularly when the marks have lots more where that came from."

Jack hadn't realized he'd been pacing until his left leg started throbbing. He flexed it a couple of times, then sat sideways on the couch and stretched that leg across the cushion.

"So, Ms. Wingate wants to know if Chris Andujar's the blackmailer? I don't need to tell you, I've already got a client, his widow, who believes her husband was also blackmailed."

Eric got up and drifted over to the window. After a moment he turned. "Of course they'd love their money back. Who wouldn't? But Dot accepts that the money's gone, says Frenet sees it the same. What they really want to know is whether Andujar was the blackmailer. If he was, they can start breathing again because it did end with his death."

It's a legit question, Jack admitted to himself. *First Max raised it, now Eric Dunn. Still, I just refuse to believe it, at least, not yet.*

Eric stood and looked Jack straight on. "Dot understands that if her affair needs to be revealed to bring justice or to stop the blackmailer, then it must be disclosed. She's not happy about that, but she's okay with it. She's also willing to retain you to represent her on this."

"I've already got a client on this matter and don't want a conflict of interest." Jack opened his office door. "Thanks, Eric. Tell Ms. Wingate we'll keep her confidence except for the reason you stated."

Eric put his hand on Jack's shoulder. "One more request, this one from me."

"Yeah?"

"I get first crack at the story when it ends. An exclusive." He raised his eyebrows over a grin that pulled his mustache lopsided.

"You didn't negotiate for that, Eric."

CHAPTER 24

JACK AND NORA started the next morning in MI's case room surrounded by educated guesses. The scenario with the fewest holes went like this: Benny Haviland, the federal fugitive, had been blackmailed into providing the keys to Chris's office. Chris was blackmailed, but didn't commit suicide until after he learned that some of his patients had also been blackmailed. The chink in that reasoning was Jack didn't believe that the blackmailing of his patients would be enough to cause Chris to kill himself.

It all fit, but it was all supposition. Yet somehow Chris Andujar remained the common thread.

"I've got the info on Clark's Janitorial," Max said, standing in the doorway. "The owners are Alan Clark and his wife, Gladys." He slid their pictures across the table.

Jack angled the photos to catch the light. Studied them for a minute, and said, "The Clarks look like Carl Anson and Joan Jensen, two hippies from the sixties. The FBI figures them two, along with Haviland, burgled and blew up a National Guard Armory."

"Whoa," Max said. "Don't tell me—these hippies didn't change the world, right?"

"Not so as I can tell," Jack said.

"The three of them could've been using the janitor service to gain access for their blackmailing," Nora reasoned. "Maybe, later, Benny got cold feet so the other two took him out."

"I've got to go, guys," Max said. "It's my shift at Donny's Club. Listen, when you put more of this together, call me."

"The police had found nothing that indicated Haviland had any big money," Jack said in reply to Nora. "Still, the cops didn't look for hidden assets like offshore accounts. It's also possible that Haviland could have been eliminated simply to fatten Anson's and Jensen's cut from one-third each to one-half each."

Nora branched off in still another direction. "Maybe the blackmailer learned that all three were fugitives and black-mailed all of them? Haviland could have been coming to see us to blow the whistle and get some help. Chris Andujar would have the dirt on his patients, but I doubt all three fugitives would have been his patients. If Chris was the blackmailer, he had a partner. Maybe his gay lover, Troy Engels? Or Tyson? Maybe both of them? They were all buddies: a shrink, a dirty cop, and the CIA's director of black ops. Among the bunch of 'em they could've learned about the three hippie fugitives, and would've known how to run a blackmail game. And how to murder Chris and made it look like a suicide."

Jack found himself nodding in agreement while Nora thought out loud, but in the end he refused to believe that anyone could've gained enough sway over Christopher Andujar to convince him to blackmail his own patients. Still, Nora's thinking was sound based on the sketchy information they had.

Jack didn't like lying to Carol Sebring. She was aces, but he needed to compare the pictures Max had taken of the older

Clarks with the bureau's photos of the younger Anson and Jensen. He had to be absolutely certain.

Like she had the first time, Carol came up to the meet Jack in the lobby of the FBI building.

"I appreciate your doing this again," he told her. "The notes from my last visit got soaked when I was attacked in the alley."

"No problem." She led him back to the same small office he had used during his previous visit. "Sorry to hear about your getting worked over. Still no word on whom or why?" She leaned back against the desk, denting her derriere.

"We may never find out. Thanks again for being so available." He smiled, and sat into the chair gingerly. "Deep bends still tighten my gut."

She took an envelope from under her arm and handed it to Jack. "I forgot to give you this last time—copies of their black and whites." She smiled. "Considering what the fashionable hippie wore in those days, color would have done a lot to jazz up these pictures."

Jack only needed a glance. Alan Clark was definitely the fugitive Carl Anson, although now he had less hair and more flab. *Hey, why should he be immune?*

Also, no doubt, Mrs. Clark was the fugitive Joan Jensen.

On the way back to the office Jack dialed Max's cell phone and set his own in its cradle for hands-free use.

"Howdy, boss. You got anything more on who booby-trapped your car?"

"I don't expect we'll get to the bottom of that until we solve the Andujar case. Is Donny doing anything suspicious?"

"You figure this play school gangster is involved in the blackmailing?"

"What do you think, Max? You've spent a lot of time watching the guy."

"Donny's a punk. He runs hookers and does payoffs and bribes downtown, but he don't have the stones for blackmail and murder. What's your take?"

"The same as yours. What's the punk been up to?"

"He gets home late from his club, spends a couple of hours watching the boob tube and goes to bed. The unboring part is that every couple of days one of the dollies from his club follows him home. No repeats. This guy is living the fantasy life of every American man."

Jack pulled to the curb before entering MI's underground parking where he sometimes lost his cell signal. "Have your crew watch the Clarks for a few days. If they split up, tail Mr. Clark. Keep your tail on Donny, at least for now. If you need more men or overtime, do it. Log their movements the same as with Donny, where, when, and who, with photos of the whos. Anything you need?"

"Nothin' boss. I worked out with Nora how to handle getting my guys paid. You got any comment on that?"

"If it's okay with Nora, I'm fine with it. You're doing a great job, Max. Are the arrangements we made working okay for you?"

"You're living up to your end, boss. If you're happy with me, I'm living up to mine. Maybe tailing the Clarks will give us the break we need. I'll be in touch."

CHAPTER 25

THE TIME HAD come to visit Phoebe Ziegler, the high-demand lap dancer from Donny's Club, who lapped under the name Jena Moves. Jack took Nora along to get her read on Ziegler and to reduce the chances of the dancer claiming Jack got out-of-line.

Nora's research on Phoebe Ziegler indicated she had graduated from high school with academic honors. The police in her hometown reported she had never been in any trouble. Yet in DC she was lap dancing and probably turning tricks.

As he drove Jack kept glancing up the side streets that flowed in to join the main thoroughfare in much the way mountain streams trickle into major rivers. He also kept an eye on the rearview mirror. He never saw the black Escalade or the white Lumina or any other tail car. He couldn't figure why whoever had been having him tailed, had stopped.

Or have they gotten so good that I can't spot them?

The lap dancer's address was on NW Twenty-First Street, just below Florida Avenue. When they turned onto her street, the neighborhood's dogs were busily howling to the percussion of banging garbage cans orchestrated by the city's sanitation workers.

A crepe myrtle sprouting its annual batch of spring leaves stood alone in the small front yard of Phoebe Ziegler's brick row house. The bell didn't work. Jack knocked on the wooden frame of the screen door. Hard. Three times.

After a few minutes he heard someone turning the knob. The door opened narrowly. Jena Moves wouldn't get paid to dance on many laps in the outfit Jack saw through her chained door—a snugly tied, pink terrycloth robe, a sleep-creation hairdo, and no makeup.

"Miss Ziegler?" Nora asked, leaning around to be seen through the crack. "Phoebe Ziegler from Durango, Colorado?"

"Yeah. So?" She ran the words together as if they were two syllables of the same word. She yawned and thumbed a wick of hair back behind her ear. "Do you know what fucking time it is? I work nights."

Jack opened the unlatched screen far enough to wrap his hand around the edge. "We're private investigators. We need your help on a case. It does not involve you directly. Take a minute and call your boss, Donny Andujar. Tell him Jack McCall is asking for your help."

She brought her hand up to hold back her brassy hair, her right breast rising with the effort, and stared at Jack. "May I shut my screen while I call Donny?"

Jack smiled and released his hold on the screen door. She engaged the latch, and her pink slippers disappeared.

After a few minutes she came back and again flipped the latch off the screen. "Come in. This doesn't involve any charges against me, right?"

"None," Jack said as he handed her his card.

She pinched the card with two fingers along the outer edges, bowing it slightly, and looked at it as if it were radioactive.

The young dancer turned and walked further inside. Her pink robe had crusted grayish-tan splotches around her hips and on her butt. A brown throw rug centered the hardwood floor. The room had a faint musty odor Jack couldn't identify. A half full bottle of gin sat on the side table beside its screw cap.

"Miss Ziegler, this is my partner, Nora Burke."

Nora smiled. "Like Jack said, we're not cops. We bring you no trouble."

The lap dancer gnawed at her lip.

"Miss Ziegler," Jack said, "I'll bet you're often treated a certain way because of the notions people have of what a dancer in a club like Donny's must be like."

She emitted a short humorless laugh.

"That happens to us, too. People react to us like we're cops or out to give them a hard time. That's not so. May I tell you why we're here?"

Her eyes darted back and forth between the detectives. She was an attractive woman with a body whose forward thrust had not yet been pulled off course by gravity. Her wholesome look not yet spoiled, but Jack could see hardening taking root around her edges.

He motioned toward a blue fabric couch with a cigarette burn on one cushion. "Could we sit down?"

"Yes. Please. Have a seat." Saying that, she sounded more like the honor student she had been in high school. "I apologize for forgetting my manners. You know, it's just ... well, you kinda caught me off guard. Ya know? Would you like some coffee? I have instant."

"That would be nice," Nora replied.

Phoebe lost the hold on her bathrobe; she grabbed it back, clutched it against her stomach and headed for the kitchen.

Jack looked around the living room. There were no family pictures. The shelves next to the TV held books on art, a few novels, and a college English Lit text. A table bathed in light from the window held a lumpy-looking shape covered with a soiled damp cloth. Whatever was under it would likely be the source of the damp odor.

He heard a microwave oven beep, then the scrape of stirring. After another minute Ms. Ziegler came back carrying a tray with three cups of steaming coffee, a small carton of half-and-half, a bowl of sugar, three spoons, and three square napkins folded half over. She had also put on some lipstick and pulled her brassy hair back into a pony tail. Her face had nicely-spaced features although her mouth was a bit large, her only visual imperfection.

"I hope the coffee's okay." When she sat the tray down, the morning light from the window blinked off her tightly pulled hair. "I'd really like to know why you're here."

Jack surmised she had grown up in a solid middle-class family. She had no streetwalker in her style—at least not yet.

He poured a little cream and stirred while he spoke. "Please call me Jack. Okay if I call you Phoebe?"

Her mouth curled a little. "I don't get called by my real name very often."

"Phoebe, our man was watching at the hotel during your recent tryst with Mayor Molloy. We have pictures of him entering the room and of the two of you in the hallway when the mayor left." He handed her copies of the photos.

Her hand went to her mouth, the first knuckle of her clenched fist white against her teeth. She shook her head with enough force to dislodge the tears welling in her eyes. She wasn't declaring no to anything, just spending the energy of not wanting to accept she had become the way she appeared in the pictures.

"Phoebe," he said, "we aren't trying to cause you any trouble. This is not about you. But I can tell you it will all come out in the end. Donny is cooperating. It would be best if you did too."

"I got nothing to hide." She put her cup down and closed her eyes, tears squeezing out through her lashes. She hid her face in her hands and peaked through her fingers as if they were bars on a private prison.

Nora said, "If you've got nothing to hide, don't hide nothing."

Phoebe's body began to shake, her voice escaping in little more than whispers. "If it's not Donny or I, who are you after?" She put her cup on the table and crossed her arms under the mounds of her breasts. "Oh, my God. Not the mayor?"

"We are not at liberty to say," Nora answered in her gentler way, "not until we get more answers."

Phoebe crossed her legs and tugged the robe up to cover her exposed knee.

She dances naked, yet she's self-conscious about an exposed knee.

She retrieved her coffee, scrunched back into the big chair, and stared into the blackness that filled her cup. After a long moment she looked up, the whites of her eyes revealing her stress. "What do you want to know?"

"It would be political suicide for the mayor to leave his wife for you, so nothing will—"

"I want him to leave me alone," she interrupted, "not leave his wife. He's a pig." The tip of her tongue darted out to wet her lips. "I argue with Donny every time, but he always offers me so much money that I do the mayor again. I hate myself for always giving in."

"May I use your bathroom?" Nora asked.

"Through the curtain. On the right."

Phoebe's eyes watched Nora until Jack spoke to her. "We also know that you have had multiple sexual rendezvous with retired police detective Arthur Tyson, some that included his girlfriend."

"Yes, Mr. McCall, I'm a whore! Okay? There. I said it. Are you satisfied now?" She pressed her eyes with her thumb and index finger, then dropped her hand and spoke in a lower tone. "I sell my body." Through her sobs, she stammered, "Can you imagine a man who farts while he's fucking? Arthur Tyson is a worse animal than the mayor."

Nora came back through the curtain. When Phoebe looked away, Nora gave Jack a short headshake. She had found nothing indicating Phoebe had an addiction to anything.

"Why, Phoebe?" Nora asked. "Why do you do it? Sex is a gift, not a commodity."

Phoebe took in a long, slow breath and let it out the same way. "DC has fabulous sculpture art. I came to see it, to study it, to work while researching schools that taught sculpting." She fussed with the hem on her robe. "I thought I would work a few months while deciding on a school. I waited tables some back home at the Ore House in Durango, so two years ago I took a job at Donny's waiting tables. They provided outfits just big enough to stay on, and the girls taught me how to move and lean in toward the guys to improve my tips. Some of the girls at Donny's kept urging me to do the deed, saying I could make a lot of tax-free cash. It wasn't their fault though. They didn't make my decision; I did."

Phoebe seemed comfortable talking with Nora, so Jack took their cups and went into the kitchen to make fresh coffee. Sometimes you can hear what people are saying between the lines better when you're not also watching them. Her story came out as one she had wanted to tell for a long time, but couldn't say to her family.

"Donny introduced me to one of the regular customers. A harmless older guy. His name is Randolph Harkin. He's a curator at the National Portrait Gallery. Donny knew I loved art and sculpture. On my shift Donny would let me just sit and talk with Mr. Harkin. He was really shy around the girls, but he would relax when I got him talking about art. He was always inviting me to come to the National Portrait Gallery. Finally I went. He gave me a private after-hours tour. No funny stuff. He was a perfect gentleman."

She wedged her hands between her clasped legs, the pink robe pushed down by her fingers.

"We spent hours. He let me look and patiently answered all my questions. It renewed my longing to be a sculptor. I spent a very long time looking at Ferdinand Pettrich's marble bust of Andrew Jackson, our seventh president. Pettrich sculpted Jackson in 1836. It's still as spectacular as the day he finished it. Jackson's hair. The definition in his face. If you're ever there, you must see it."

Nora promised she would.

Jack came back into the room with fresh coffee, just as Phoebe said, "It was the most inspiring evening of my life."

Her long fingers overlapped when she wrapped them around the warm cup Jack handed her. She looked at Nora with moist eyes and spoke through almost unmoving lips.

"I'm not a whore. I don't ... not with just anybody. It started with Harkin, then the mayor, then Tyson. There's been no one else."

She tapped the cup with her red fingernails, then extended her fingers, frowning when she saw the chipped polish. "I never gave a lap dance to anyone before Harkin. The girls keep telling me Donny's is a great place to meet wealthy, important men. One night the bartender gave me a typed note that had been left for me at the bar: 'When Harkin comes in tonight,' the note said, 'give him anything he wants.' Folded inside the note was a thousand in cash! That night I did the deed for money for the first time."

"When was that?" Jack asked.

"A long time ago."

Nora asked, "How long?"

"Well, I'd only been at Donny's about two months—no, less than that. I'd guess twenty months back, around that."

"Who left the note with the thousand dollars?"

"Donny swears he didn't, but I still believe he did. I mean, like, who else? Right? After that first night, Harkin became what the girls called a monther and he paid me. Toward the end he was paying twelve hundred each time."

Jack held up his hand like a traffic cop. "What do you mean 'toward the end?'"

"About two months ago Harkin stopped coming in the club, mid-February, I think."

Jack moved around and sat on the edge of the coffee table close to Phoebe.

"When all this comes out," he said, "the mayor and Tyson have the power and connections to leave you holding the bag. It's time to tell what you know. Why did Donny push you to have sex with Harkin?"

"I don't know what made Harkin special," she said, punctuating each syllable with short, jerky shakes of her head. She wiped her eyes with the end of the dirty robe tie. "I should never have left home."

"Are your folks still alive?" Nora asked. "Are you okay with them?"

"Yeah ... It would just kill my mom if she knew what I was doing." Phoebe sat still. Her eyes fixed on the brown carpet. A truck went by. A fly landed on top the wet cloth over what Jack now realized had to be a sculpture in progress. Then Phoebe continued as if she had not paused. "Mom thinks I work in the office at Donny's. They don't even know what kind of club it is. I love the money, but I hate myself for being weak." She interlaced her fingers and hung her hands over the crown of her head.

"Life is really weird, you know? I used to think of my hometown as dull, now my memories of it seem, I don't know ... safe, I guess." She gave a glimpse of a quirky smile. "In another year I should have enough money to go home and then go through school without having to work part time."

"May I look?" Nora gestured toward the towel-shrouded figurine on the sculpting table.

Phoebe nodded and blushed. "Let me remove the cloth."

Nora gasped and moved aside so Jack could see. The lump turned out to be a clay sculpture of a woman in a ragged dress, gazing heavenward. The face was Phoebe's.

"Oh," Nora breathed, "this is beautiful. Do you have more?"

"I have some at a friend's house. She's a photographer. Do you really like it?"

"You stay with this, girl. You've got talent." Nora glanced at Jack, who retook the lead.

"Phoebe, did you keep the note the bartender gave you?"

"Yes. I'm probably silly, but somehow I figured it might prove something if I ever got ... I don't know. In trouble, I guess." She shrugged. "Do you want to see it?"

"No," Jack said. "I want it. If you ever need me to return it, I will."

"What are you gonna do with it?"

"For starters, I'll find out whether or not the note was from Donny. I'll let you know."

"I guess it won't hurt and I would like to know for real if he sent it. I'll get it."

Phoebe came back into her living room and handed Jack the note. She also brought Polaroids she had taken of several of her other sculpted pieces, the ones she had dropped off to have professionally photographed.

Jack looked at one picture, the sculpted painful expression on the face of dead actor James Dean, and another of a picador driving a lance into the shoulder of a bull. He handed them to Nora. After they complimented her work, Jack startled her back to the present.

"Tell me about Troy Engels."

"Donny says he's a V.I.P. He hoots and ogles the girls. He always comes in alone. We give him verbal foreplay because he sticks twenties in our G's. He's no big deal."

She doesn't know who he is.

Jack took the cup from her hand and set it on the table. "Are you ready to quit? Right now." He tapped the table with the tip of his index finger. "Today."

"What do you mean?"

"Just what I said. Walk away. Don't go in today. Quit. Go home. See your folks. Return to school. Become a sculptor. If you're ever going to do it, why not today?"

Nora scooted down the couch so Phoebe could see her face.

The young lap dancer sat as still as one of her sculpted figurines, then said, "Maybe in another six months."

Nora reached over and put her hand on Phoebe's arm. "This will blow up before six months; we'd like to see you clear of the explosion. You're in a bad life with a bad end. First, you hustled drinks. Then you started stage dancing, next came lap dancing. The number of men you've had sex with for money has grown from one to three. Soon there'll be a fourth, then why not a fourteenth? It's a slippery slope. Get off, or you'll slide lower."

Phoebe's hands were shaking. "You're right. I need to stop what I'm doing. I'll tell Donny no more sex with the mayor. And I'll gladly cut off that pig, Tyson. And if Harkin comes back, him too."

"Phoebe, I meant quit totally. Cold turkey. Leave and go home, then back to school."

If greed could be seen in the eyes, Jack saw it in hers.

"I want to, Mr. McCall, but I don't have enough money. Not yet," her sizeable bosom rose and fell with her animated speech. "I'll only wait tables, stage dance, and do laps. There's good money in lap dancing and most guys don't take that long. I promise you, no more full sex. I will become a sculptor."

They tried to persuade her for another ten minutes; then Phoebe arched her back. "Mr. McCall. Ms. Burke. I appreciate your interest in me and my art, but this is my decision. I'll leave Donny's by the end of this year and I'll stop fucking for money immediately."

The young lady was correct. It was her decision. Jack and Nora exchanged niceties with Phoebe Ziegler and left.

After three blocks, Nora looked at Jack. "The limping, rumpled old man Max saw visiting Donny's club, that was you."

They both laughed.

"That's when you got Phoebe's identity and set Donny up to tell her to cooperate."

Jack nodded.

"Excuse me," Nora said, after removing the grin from her face, "but, well, *dumb* is the word that comes to mind. You went to Donny's from the hospital. In your condition you couldn't have punched your way out of a paper bag."

"I had the angles covered."

"Oh? You had the angles covered? I'll tell you what you had. You had a concussion. What if you'd passed out? What about that angle, Mr. 007?"

He stopped at the light.

"Well? What if you had passed out?"

"How long you know'd me, missy?"

"Damn it. Drop the cute cowboy crap." She put a stern look on her face and crossed her arms, elevating her cleavage, a bra strap teasing his eye. "I've known you the better part of two years," she said. "Now answer my question."

He curled his hand around his wrapped steering wheel and squeezed. "If I could walk, I had to go. Donny didn't expect me."

Jack drove on in silence, figuring she knew he was right.

He knew she was right, too.

CHAPTER 26

AFTER ANOTHER MOSTLY sleepless night watching old movies, and a late call to Nora, Jack didn't call Clark's Janitorial Service until ten in the morning. He gave his name as Walter Bartholomew.

"I've recently acquired two local office buildings," he said, "for which I need a new janitorial service." Gladys Clark quickly agreed that she and her husband Alan would meet Mr. Bartholomew for lunch in two hours.

Jack arrived at the restaurant fifteen minutes early and, after arranging for a quiet rear booth, he called Nora at the office. "I'm sorry I called you so late last night. I didn't realize it was nearly two. You should have told me to take a flying jump and hung up."

"Don't feel like the Lone Ranger. I've had those nights. What old movie did you watch?"

"The only one I remember was *The Big Sleep*, with Humphrey Bogart as Phillip Marlowe. It's a classic."

"Sort of ironic, watching that movie when you couldn't sleep?"

"You got that right. Anything happening there?"

"The typewriter expert should be here any minute. These days he rarely gets calls on typewriters, but the police have used him several times. You know, even if Donny's confession for beating you up and the note Phoebe Ziegler gave us were typed on the same machine, it won't tell us why Donny paid her to get it on with Randolph Harkin."

"After you get the expert's confirmation, I plan to ask Donny that very question."

"I should know in an hour or so."

Jack looked up to see the host coming toward him, menus in hand, with Alan and Gladys Clark trailing close behind.

"They're here, Nora. I'll get back to you."

Gladys, a very large woman, wore an orange sack dress, and moved as if well-chewed caramel had replaced the fluid in her joints. Alan had thin shoulders and a fringe of hair circling his head. He wore black tennis shoes like Bennie Haviland had worn to climb into the dumpster.

Mr. Clark slid in first and moved to the closed end of the booth. His wife sat on the open end and removed a dark leather portfolio that had been substantially hidden under her gigantic arm.

They ordered and, as soon as the waiter had left the table, Jack stepped off the edge of his deception. "You two don't look at all like your pictures."

Mrs. Clark turned toward her husband, her tight brown curls swinging freely around her dumpling shaped face. Alan put his hand on top of his wife's hand and they exchanged glances before he said, "What pictures, Mr. Bartholomew?"

Jack opened a folder and pushed copies of the photos of fugitives Anson and Jensen across the table.

Alan held up the pictures, angled for Gladys to see, and then shoved them back in Jack's direction. "Just who are you, Mr. Bartholomew? And what do you want?"

Jack put his hands flat on the table. "For starters, my name isn't Bartholomew. It's Jack McCall of McCall Investigations.

Thank you for not wasting time with a fruitless attempt at denial." He put the photos back inside the folder.

The fat fingers of Ms. Jensen's hand gathered part of the tablecloth as she crabbed her flat hand back into a fist. She spoke through thin lips, "My husband asked what you wanted, Mr. McCall."

"I'll answer that in a moment. Let's start with what we know. You both are long-sought federal fugitives. The murdered body of your partner in the National Armory job, Benjamin Haviland, got left in a dumpster not far from my office."

She eased out her thick tongue, circled her lips and drew it back.

"I'm not with the police or the FBI," Jack said. "Your cooperation will decide whether I'll benefit most from your help or from the headline: Local PI nabs Federal Fugitives."

Lunch came, Jack had ordered for them, but the Clarks were in no mood to eat. Jack squeezed a lemon wedge into his iced tea and sipped. Then spoke. "Mrs. Clark, I see you brought your portfolio. Open it and prepare a list of every building to which you've had keys within the past three years. Just the names of the buildings will be fine."

She rose from the booth, her doughy feet oozing around the velcro-straps of her sandals. "What if we just tell you to go to hell and walk right out?"

"Your choice, Mrs. Clark, I've got a winner no matter what you decide. Do you prefer I call you Joan or Gladys?"

"Gladys has been my name for a very long time now." She sat back down, the fat rings of her neck and arms clustering like groups of soap bubbles.

Jack gestured toward Carl Anson, "how 'bout you?"

He took off his glasses and rubbed the bridge of his nose. "Alan is now my name. Listen, Mr. McCall, what we did, well, we were ignorant. The Vietnamese War was wrong and racial discrimination was running amuck in America. In the foolish impatience of youth, we felt patriotic. What we did was criminal. We know that now."

"Who killed Benjamin Haviland?"

The married fugitives shared a stolen glance. Alan spoke. "Ben had been a nervous wreck for months before his death."

"We don't know who killed him," Gladys blurted, "or why. It's been driving us crazy. We've hardly slept since Benny was murdered." She put her head on Alan's shoulder. "I think I'm going to be sick, honey." Her face went pale. She closed her eyes.

These two were leftovers from an earlier age, matured hippies who had outgrown their civil disobedience.

"Benny was an equal partner in your crime," Jack said. "Why wasn't he an equal owner in your business?"

Alan Clark laid his glasses on the table. "Benny was a follower. Truth is he would never have gotten involved with the Armory job in '72 if we hadn't pushed him. When Bennie's money ran out he came back to us for a job. Gladys and I had gotten married. We had each other. Ben had no one. He worked hard but had no life. Every Saturday night he would sit, drink, and watch the girls at Donny's Gentlemen's Club. Once a month he would stay after they closed to shampoo their carpets. He did it off the books. We knew he used our equipment. We looked the other way. He traded the shampoo job for free drinks and, every so often, Donny would comp Bennie a lap dance."

Gladys came out of her stupor. "Benny had a pathetic life, and we are partly responsible."

The waiter came over to ask if the food was okay. Neither of them had taken a bite. Jack told him they had experienced a mutual loss and really didn't have an appetite. The lemon slices were still wedged onto the rims of Alan's and Gladys's untouched glasses when the waiter cleared the table.

Gladys looked at Jack. "Benny was so unhappy. I wonder if he felt any relief when he died?"

"When I saw Haviland," Jack said, "he was slouching into the corner of a dumpster with insects eating part of his face. I saw fear, not relief."

"That's morbid." She opened her napkin, put it over her face and began to sob.

Alan spoke while his wife fought to regain her composure. "Bennie lived in constant fear. He feared being arrested by every policeman he saw, even the meter maids. That's partly why he liked working at night. Felt he would be harder to recognize in the dark wearing his stocking cap."

Gladys swiped away a tear moving nearly sideways across her puffy cheek.

"Alan and I decided we would enjoy whatever normal life we could get before someone like you came along and it ended. If what you want from us is a crime, you can just turn us in. Our life of crime is over. What is it you really want from us?"

Jack sipped his tea. "That list. I want that list complete. And the keys to get in each of your buildings, including any pass keys needed for the interior offices, also the procedures for turning off any alarms."

"No," Gladys said. "We told you no criminal activities." Then her husband added, "Turn us in, Mr. McCall and take whatever benefit comes to you from that."

Jack smiled. "I've been testing you. I will likely need some access to your buildings, but not right now. If I do, I assure you it will be to help solve a crime. I'm working a case that involves a tenant in a couple of your buildings. I may need access to their offices."

Thirty minutes later Jack had convinced them that if he needed that access, Alan Clark would search him before he went into the elevator and again when he came back down to the lobby. That way, without knowing which office Jack had visited, Clark would know that nothing had been taken in or out.

Gladys stared into Jack's eyes for a long minute, and then asked, "Is your case about blackmail?" Alan jerked his head toward his wife, his brow furrowed. She reached over and patted the top of his hand.

"It could be," Jack answered. "Why do you ask?"

"About a year and a half ago, in late summer," Alan said, "by courier, we received smaller copies of those pictures you just showed us. The next day a man called demanding two-hundred-fifty-thousand dollars. We were told to leave the money under a bush in the Sculpture Garden in the National Mall. The blackmailer must have been watching us for months, because the bush he described grows near a bench we often sit on during the summer. We—"

"We almost went to the police right then," Gladys said, finishing her husband's point. "But we paid. We had a little more than that left from selling the weapons we took from the National Armory."

"And?"

"And," Alan did a whole-body shrug, "several weeks later he called to assure us we would never hear from him again, and we haven't."

"Describe his voice."

Gladys shuddered as if a cool breeze had found her spine. "He sounded like something from a science fiction movie. Later, in a movie, we saw a guy hold some vibrating gizmo against his neck. The blackmailer sounded like that." Her head flopped sideways against her husband's shoulder.

Jack tilted his head to draw her eyes back to him. "You need to keep working on that list."

"I'm done," she said. "We only do about a dozen." She pushed the pad back toward Jack. "They're all large, and we've had most of them for years. Now you don't get in them, not one, except for the way we agreed. Right?"

"As we agreed." He glanced down at the list and recognized two buildings. The one where Chris had his practice and where he and Nora had gone to met with Chris's pal, Dr. Radnor. Then he returned his attention to the Clarks. "For now, just go back to living your normal lives. Don't change anything. I doubt you'll hear again from the blackmailer. If you do, contact me immediately. You're not prepared to deal with him without help."

The two fugitives left without offering to shake hands.

As Jack walked out, Nora called. The typewriter expert had come and gone. Both notes had been typed on the same machine, an old IBM Selectric. Before hanging up, Jack asked Nora to call Eric Dunn. "He may be able to give us another piece of this puzzle."

CHAPTER 27

ERIC DUNN WALKED into MI with his coat dangling from one finger, draped back over his shoulder. Jack estimated Eric's height at five-nine, but he looked shorter with the coat ending behind his knees.

"Sorry I couldn't get here sooner." He dropped into an oxblood leather chair in Jack's office and shook his head. "It's been a crazy one."

"Two of the usual?" Mary Lou asked after sticking her head through the doorway.

The two men exchanged glances and nodded. Jack said, "Yes. Thank you, Mary Lou."

He turned to Eric. "I want to poke around in Donny Andujar's background."

They paused when Mary Lou came in carrying a tray holding two Coronas with lime slices protruding from their necks. She'd also brought a few napkins, a small knife, the rest of the lime, and an ice bucket chilling a second round. "In case your meeting runs overtime." She grinned.

When the door closed, Jack continued. "We know Donny opened his club about three-and-a-half years ago, no small accomplishment for a man who was then in his early thirties.

I know his folks would not have financed it. What can you tell me about where he got the money? How he learned the business? Stuff like that."

"Some facts," Eric said, "some rumors. Before Donny started his club, he worked for Luke Tittle, a shady character who owned one of the town's swankier lounges, Luke's Place. Tittle opened in the late seventies and operated for decades, until the police shut him down the year before Donny opened his place."

After a deep pull on his beer, the columnist added, "When I worked the crime beat I used to hang out at Luke's."

"Tell me about the joint."

"Luke's was many things, but not a joint. Luke's was one of the swell spots. Only top call brands, no house pours. I expensed mine to the paper." He winked. "A lot of non-arms-length contracts got negotiated in Luke's. My articles referred to Luke's as 'a local hot spot' or some such euphemism. In those days, the customers were waited on by pretty cocktail waitresses wearing pushups under skimpy outfits. Nothing like the nearly nude getups wore these days by the girls at Donny's."

Sam Spade's kinda joint. "What did Donny do for Tittle?"

"He started as a bartender and worked up to assistant manager. He also dealt some cards in Luke's private backroom casino—a playroom for the power brokers who liked to roll the dice and turn a card. Except for coming in as customers, the cops let Luke's backroom operate. That's about it for the facts."

Jack forced the lime down through the neck of his bottle until it dove into the beer, swirled it around a bit and took his first drink.

"What about the rumors?"

Dunn loosened the knot in his tie. "After Donny became an assistant manager, a few high-class hookers started decorating Luke's stools. He limited the girls to one in the daytime and two during evening hours. The girls were not allowed to solicit. They had to be approached."

Eric put his empty on the table and motioned. Jack lifted another out of the ice bucket, wiped the moisture off the outside of the bottle, sliced a fresh lime wedge, jammed it into the neck, and handed it to Eric, who was already busy telling his story the way Jack assumed Eric would dictate a draft for one of his columns.

"Rumors were that Donny ran the girls and split his end with Tittle. Donny was quickly becoming a real up and comer in the local rackets. The story went around that Tittle's silent backers planned to bankroll Donny in his own place. Tittle's specialty would remain serving liquor and gambling, while Donny's new place would serve liquor and girls.

"Then the big twist. New Metro Chief of Police Harry Mandrake ordered a raid that surprised everyone, and arrested Luke Tittle. Two days later, Tittle was out on bail and within hours he was gunned down. End of story."

"Tittle's high-end gambling clientele would've had open accounts," Jack said. "What happened to their markers? And who were Tittle's silent partners?"

"Not even any hints about his partners or, for that matter, whether it was even true that he had partners. After the raid and Tittle's release, our readers had little interest in accounting records. The sexy story became, who gunned the saloon king?"

Jack held up his beer bottle. "Let me change the subject. Tell me about the killing of Tino Sanchez. Could his death be connected with Tittle and his missing records?"

"Don't you recall any of this, Jack? It wasn't all that many years ago."

"Those years I was pretty busy in the Middle East."

Eric nodded before jutting his chin up and stroking his neck. "Sanchez was a big story, but a short one. Chief Mandrake had promoted Sanchez, his longtime partner, to chief of detectives. Luke's Place had been raided and Luke Tittle murdered. Sanchez's life ended like punctuation on the back end of the Tittle story."

"What do you remember?"

"I was the crime beat reporter at the scene. Mandrake and Sanchez had gone out for dinner. Walking into the restaurant, Mandrake spotted some fella wanted for questioning. I don't recall his name. One of Tittle's gunsels, the name won't come to me right now.

"The thug ran with the chief in pursuit. Sanchez, the considerably heavier man, followed with the gap between them widening with each block. The suspect took them on a merry chase before cutting into an alley. When the police backup arrived, Sanchez had been shot dead by the suspect and Mandrake had shot and killed the suspect. Mandrake told what happened and the physical evidence supported his telling. The gun that shot Sanchez was traced back to the suspect. The forensics team found gunpowder residues from the firing on the suspect's hand and his prints on the gun. The review board ruled the shooting righteous."

After Eric Dunn left, Jack called Nora's extension and asked her to join him. He filled her in on what Dunn had told him. Then asked what she remembered from the cop's angle about the raid on Luke's Place and the killings of Luke Tittle and Tino Sanchez.

She took a seat at the end of the couch near the window. "As for Tittle's betting records, the cops who searched Luke's Place and his two homes didn't find them. Chief Mandrake then worked out a deal. Tittle was to give the records to Sanchez the day after he made bail, but Tittle got dead before that meeting."

"What about the killing of Tino Sanchez?"

"An arrest turned bad. Shit happens." Nora kicked off her shoes, snuggled into the corner of the couch, and turned toward Jack. "The shooter was called 'The Counter.' His real name was Terrence Leoni. He was Tittle's accountant, with oversight of the backroom casino. The shooting board ruled Mandrake's killing of Leoni justified." Nora tucked her legs under her. "It was a really juicy story. What makes you curious?"

"It all seems too pat. Luke's place is raided. Tittle is arrested. Tittle is out on bail. Tittle is killed. Tittle's accountant is killed. Tittle's records are never found."

Nora nodded. "It's been years and nothing more has come of it. Whoever ended up with the records may have burned 'em so as not to be tied into Tittle's murder."

"Was Donny at Luke's Place the night it was raided?"

"Don't remember, if I ever knew, but I can find out. Anything else?"

"Nope."

"Then I'm outta here." She smiled at Jack. "What're your plans for tonight?"

"Sleep."

"No old movies?"

"I need to crash."

"Me too. A man I find very interesting called late last night, but I'm hoping he doesn't tonight."

"I bet he won't."

Nora grabbed her purse and when she got to the doorway, she turned back, that half-turn profile that seems to come natural to women.

CHAPTER 28

AT NINE-THIRTY the next morning Nora was back in the doorway to Jack's office. "I stopped to see Chief Mandrake on my way in. To answer the question you asked yesterday, Donny was working at Luke's Place the night the raid went down. The officer in charge of the raid let Donny go without booking him or even naming him in his report. Let's get some coffee."

On the way, Jack asked, "Who was the officer?"

She didn't answer until they had their coffee and were inside the case room. "Tino Sanchez was the officer in charge at the scene. I didn't want Mary Lou to hear me mention her father."

Nora sat down and ran her finger inside the gap above the top button of her bright blue blouse with a stiff white collar, her nail temporarily leaving a thin white trail. "The chief told me he approved Tino releasing Donny and all the employees. The target had been Jake Tittle, not the folks who worked for him."

"What can you tell me about the rumor that Tittle had been paying for protection for his backroom gambling casino?"

"The chief said that was also true. The raid had convinced Tittle that Mandrake was serious about cleaning up gambling, so Tittle was agreeable to a deal with the chief. Tittle admitted arranging police protection through Tyson, who owned a piece of Luke's Place—off the books of course. Tyson had been his bagman, and Tittle promised he'd testify against Tyson.

"The deal included Tittle's records in exchange for the chief's help with the DA's office for immediate bail. Tittle would have gotten bail on that rap anyway; so all the deal meant was bail came a little cheaper. Oh, the chief also told me Tyson could not have killed Tittle because at that time Tyson was in a stakeout on the other side of town."

Jack rolled his eyes. "By the time Tittle was killed, the entire police department, the DA's office, and the court likely knew about the deal for Tittle's records. So anybody with a serious need to stop Tittle from turning over those records could've been the one to drop Tittle on the sidewalk."

Nora slipped her fingers back inside the opening at the top of her blouse. "True enough."

Jack heard her nails rake her skin, and watched the material pouch up to show a flesh-colored bra strap.

"When Tittle got gunned," Nora said, "the chief also lost his witness against Tyson." She gently ran the tip of her tongue between her lips to capture a spot of coffee that lingered in the corner of her mouth. "It took the chief another two years to get enough on Tyson to coerce him into early retirement."

"Yet the chief and Tyson continued, hell, right up until now to play poker together."

"In McCall speak, yep."

"So, all we've got is the chief's hearsay retelling of Tino Sanchez's description of the raid of Luke's Place."

"We got more. The chief let me read Sanchez's handwritten notes from the raid. They contained nothing important the chief hadn't already told me. He let me make copies." Nora pulled a folder from her portfolio and pushed it into the center of the table.

Jack went over to the window and changed the angle of the blinds to soften the glare from the morning sun. "What do you remember from before the raid?"

"I wore a uniform in those days." She shrugged. "The first thing I remember is the chief posting a general raid-mobilizing exercise for that night. This morning he told me only Sanchez knew of his plan to turn that exercise into a real raid on Luke's Place."

Jack tossed his pencil onto the table. "What did Sanchez's file say about search warrants?"

"Warrants were issued for Tittle's home, his vehicles, office, even his summer house on Chesapeake Bay. Nothing. To this day his records are a Jimmy Hoffa." She pointed toward the file she had pushed to the middle of the table. "It's all in there. Read it for yourself."

Jack used his fingers to clothespin his nose. "The whole thing smells. Tittle's records that disappeared would've shown payoffs to politicians and gambling IOUs from the rich and powerful. The federal fugitives were not blackmailed over gambling debts, and we've got nothing that suggests Chris Andujar had a gambling problem, but I'm betting there are folks out there who were, and, you know what, we may know one of them."

CHAPTER 29

MAX FOUND THE door to MI's office unlocked; Mary Lou was gone from the reception desk. He called out. No one answered. Mary Lou hadn't seemed the type who would just go to lunch and leave the door unlocked. He knocked on the closed door to MI's private case room. No answer.

He locked the office door and walked down the hall toward the restrooms. After a few steps he heard the sound of a distant scuffle. Near the stairwell he heard a muffled cry. He flung open the door to see Mary Lou cowering in the far corner of the landing.

A bulky biker spun around, a wad of keys on a chain rattling against his hip. His head had been shaved, including his eyebrows, giving him the look of a bleached bowling ball. He wore a sleeveless denim jacket with the gang name Hellseekers monogrammed on the back.

"What the hell you want, old man?" the thug growled, raising the back of his hand.

"Whatever the doings between you and your wench here surely ain't no concern of mine," Max said. "I just like taking the stairs. I don't trust them elevators. You ever walk for health? No, course you wouldn't, you're not an old man like me." He leaned forward and rubbed his lower back. "I'll just skedaddle on down to the street. I'll try to hurry, but I don't move so good no more, not since that gawl-danged arthritis got in me knees. You under—"

"Shut up you old fart, and get your ass back through the door you came in. Now!"

"Just hold your horses, Laddie," Max replied, dripping the brogue. "I hope you ain't one of them young ruffians who thinks being ugly and smelly makes it okay to be ill-mannered?"

A switchblade appeared in the biker's hand; Max heard the click of the release that blossomed its blade.

"Fuck you old man. Now get your ass outta here. I won't tell you again."

Max leaned into the corner beside the door, crossing one leg over the other. "Does your dear sainted mother know she carries the shame of her son growing into the kind of slimeball who would beat this wee lass?" Max's leather jacket creaked when he crossed his arms. "Tis a crying shame. Sure as I am that you'll be prayin' for her forgiveness this Sund'y morn."

Mary Lou started to rise. Max motioned to her. "You stay where you are, Little Missy. The air don't smell so rotten down low in a room, and the smell will be leaving soon."

"I'm gonna cut you Old Man, and leave you here bleeding next to this bitch."

"I wouldn't be trying it, Mr. Smelly. You see, I know a lot about you, while you know nothing 'bout me, other than I'm old and slow, and better smelling than you."

The biker's eyes gave the early warning Max had been angling for. The instant the biker lunged, Max's front leg, on which he had no weight, whipped out to greet the hooligan's groin. The biker doubled over.

Max grabbed the man's forearm and smashed it against the railing. The biker's arm made a nasty cracking sound, followed by the clanging of his switchblade as it tumbled down the corrugated metal stairs toward the floor below. From in close Max used his elbow in a short, compact swing that found his attacker's nose. The Hellseeker tumbled down the stairs to the next landing, his face slamming against the wall.

Mary Lou, who had a cut lip and a little puffiness under her right eye, was shivering from fear. He extended his hand. "C-mere, Darlin'."

"Oh, Max. I was afraid for you."

"Missy, do you have your office key with you?"

"Huh? What?"

He put his hands on her shoulders and spoke slowly. "Do you have your office key?"

"Yes."

"Then you get on back. Wrap some ice in a towel and put it on your eye and lip. I need to stay here and chat with our friend. He should be waking in a moment or two."

Mary Lou spoke around jerky gasps. "He demanded I give him Donny's confession. I told him I don't work the cases. That I didn't know anything about any confession." She touched her lip and winced.

"Go along now, Missy." He put his hand under her elbow to move her toward the door. "I'll be with ya in a jiff."

Max went down to the landing on which the biker, dazed from slamming into the wall, was just coming around. Max lifted the edge of the biker's denim jacket and removed a gun. Then took a seat two steps up from the landing. A moment later the hooligan moaned and rolled partway over. His face had been lying in a pool of blood from his broken nose.

Max stretched out his leg and placed the crepe sole of his Chukka boot on the biker's neck.

"Now let's drop the cute talk, you sonofabitch. Keep your hands behind you and turn over the rest of the way. Nice and slow. Now." The biker turned. "Open your mouth," Max said. "And don't you be getting no blood on my new Chukkas."

Turning without the use of his hands, the biker smeared the shoulder of his sleeveless jacket through the blood, but he didn't open his mouth.

Max held the stair rail for support and leaned closer. "It's always nice to use someone else's gun, that way it traces back to the victim, not the shooter." He slid the barrel back and forth along one side of the biker's nose while he counted: one, two.

"Don't shoot you crazy old man. It's open. It's open."

"Shame on ya, Mr. Smelly. Had ya been that cooperative before, this calamity never woulda befallen ya. Here I go for-gettin' I was gonna drop the brogue." Max slid the barrel into the man's mouth. "Now I want ya to be reaching around to unfasten the chain that's attached to your wallet."

"That's ullshit, old man," the biker said, unable to pro-nounce the "b" with his lips around the muzzle.

"No problem. I'll just jerk until your belt loop tears. But then don't you be blaming me none if this here gun of yours goes off."

The biker reached around with his left hand and unhooked the chain.

"Turn back and put your nose against the wall."

"But I'm bleeding."

"Yes, you are. The real question being, are you going to be bleeding more?"

The biker obeyed while Max sat on the stair and looked through his wallet. It was stuffed with cash.

"Your license shows your real handle is George Rockton. Why'd you tell me your name was Mr. Smelly?"

From against the wall the biker's voice sounded tinny and distant. "I didn't. You used that name."

"You should be thanking me then, Mr. Rockton. I've made you aware of a failin' in your social graces. If you let your eyebrows grow and bathe more often, I be thinking you'd find more favor from the lasses, and without having to abuse them. There I go again, slipping in and out of me brogue. My shrink tells me stress is the cause of me doing that. Now I want you to roll back over so you can see my eyes, the windows into my black Irish soul."

Rockton rolled.

Max tapped his barrel on the biker's chin. He opened his mouth again, beads of sweat dotting his forehead.

"Most of the men I've kilt were finer men than you'll ever be, men guilty of nothing mor'n being loyal soldiers for the British occupying army. Their deaths helped only Irish folk. Killing the likes of you would help the whole world. Did you know there were Irishmen fighting with General Custer at the Little Big Horn? Aye. There ain't never been an army worth its salt that didn't count at least one Irishman in its ranks."

Max withdrew his gun barrel just far enough to let the biker use his tongue when he spoke, his lips kissing the end of the barrel with each word.

"Please don't take my cash. It's all I got."

"Please, you be saying. Now the man says please. Don't you be worrying none about your cash. If'n you flunk my quiz, well, they don't take cash where you'll be headin'. My blasted arthritis is kicking up, so I can't be staying in this position long. I need some information you have, and if I don't get it you're right soon be a Hellseeker, like it says across your back."

"What do you want to know?" Rockton said, his words sputtering a bit in the nose blood flowing across the corner of his mouth.

"What do your friends call ya?"

"Rock."

"Well I ain't your friend, Rock, so I'll still be calling you Smelly." Max moved his gun to under the biker's chin. "When did Donny Andujar order you to come get his confession?"

"Donny didn't send me." A run of sweat cut a trail through the red smeared along the side of his face.

"No good, Mr. Smelly. How else would you be knowing about his confession? No more lies. Me arthritis is paining something awful, and I ain't never been no patient man."

"Donny told us, but he didn't tell me to come after it." His whisker stubble darkened the cleft in his chin. "Wait a minute, how do you know about Donny Andujar?"

Max thrust the gun barrel hard into the biker's soft neck wattle. "I'll be asking the questions. Why do you care that McCall has Donny's confession?"

"Donny told me and his bodyguard, I don't know his name, and some guy we all call Blink that McCall made Donny identify us as the ones who beat him up. I didn't want the confession out there with my name on it."

"Okay. Your idea and Donny approved it."

"No! Donny told us not to do it; that's why I came alone. I quit Donny and I'm heading outta town. That's why all my cash is in my wallet. Let me go and you'll never see me again." His eyes pleaded along with his voice. "I promise."

"Mr. Smelly, if I ever lay me eyes on ya agin or hear tell of you makin' contact, even bein' within view of that little lassie, your nose will be covered with falling dirt."

"My stuff's on my hog. I'll be outta DC before the sun goes down."

"You be on your way, then. I'll be covering you when you pass your shank on the below landin'. Leave it there. I'll be holding onto it and this here gun to plant at the scene of a crime in the event you ever bother that lass agin."

Max slid his hand along the railing as he backed up four stairs to clear more space between them. The dazed biker stood and used the back of his hand to wipe the wet blood from his lips, then licked his hand as though he couldn't afford to give up the protein. He looked at Max with a confused expression of curiosity and fear, cradled his right forearm in his left hand, and staggered down the stairs. Max could tell the arm wasn't broken, likely just torn up inside.

CHAPTER 30

GEORGE ROCKTON LIFTED the ringing cell phone from the pouch on his Harley. "Rock here. Who are you?"

"You know who this is. I need a job done."

"No way. I'm splitting town right now."

"Then you could use some traveling money. I'll double the fee I paid you last time."

Rockton slowed his motorcycle and moved into the right lane. "Haviland was twenty-five large, you offering fifty?"

"Yes, fifty, but you'll have to work fast. I'll leave the money for you in the same place as last time. You can pick it up four hours after it's done."

"This being my last job for you, how do I know I'll get paid? We'll need to meet for this payment."

"No. I keep my word, Mr. Rockton. This job is about my eliminating an enemy, not about making a new one."

Rockton angled his front tire toward the next off ramp. "If the cops catch you, they'll send you to jail. If you try to stiff me, I'll find you and send you to hell."

"You'll be paid," the caller said.

"Fuck it. Why not. I was just thinking about stopping to see a skirt before I split. You got a deal. Who's the target?"

"Don't get your love life in the way of my business."

"Don't tell me how to do my job. Who is it?"

"Jack McCall. You know the name?"

"Sure. I'll take care of my business tonight and McCall tomorrow, then I'm gone. Agreed?"

"No later than tomorrow."

"It could be tonight if I can find him after I make my stop. Then I'm moving on."

"I'll pay an extra ten if it's done tonight."

Jack and Nora entered the National Portrait Gallery of the Smithsonian for their appointment with the Gallery's Assistant Director and Head Portrait Curator, Randolph Harkin II.

The gallery, located in the old Patent Office Building at Eighth and F Streets NW, had many of its pieces out on a tour and most of the gallery closed for a major renovation.

After asking for Harkin, they sat down. Someone had gone to a considerable effort to gain sway over Harkin. Then something profound had occurred to end his involvement with Jena Moves. Nora's research indicated that Harkin was not a wealthy man. That begged the question, what interest could the blackmailer have in Harkin other than his access to art?

It seemed only a minute before the receptionist said, Curator Harkin is on his way up.

Had Harkin been a woman he could have been described as petite, but there was no such word for a man. His thin hair featured a precise part just above his left ear and a comb-over top.

"May we go somewhere private?" Jack asked the plain man.

Harkin led them down a long hall before making a sharp left into a small conference room. "There's a pot of coffee and a pitcher of water on the credenza." He gestured. "Please help yourselves."

Jack walked partway to the credenza, and then stopped. "Sit down, Director Harkin." Then Jack softened his voice, "May I get you something?"

"Ah, coffee, please. Black is fine. If you will, I prefer Curator to Director. I'm an assistant director but head portrait curator, so that is the more appropriate title. When you called, you said you needed some advice about art for a case you're working?"

Nora cleared her throat and euphemistically stepped into the shallow water. "Curator Harkin, wouldn't it be difficult to fool people? I mean people who know art? Wouldn't they be able to spot a forgery from across the room?"

Harkin's face crowded with confusion. "You'd think so, but not if the copy is good. Over the years the art world has been taken in by some rather audacious forgeries. Would you care to hear a few fascinating stories?"

Jack set a cup of black coffee in front of Harkin. "Sure. Please."

"Hans van Meegeren, a Dutch painter, was arrested after World War II and charged with treason. The Dutch government claimed he sold a national treasure in the form of a Vermeer painting to Germany's Field Marshall Hermann Göering. Meegeren defended himself against treason by proving in court he had not stolen the Vermeer, but painted a copy for Göering. The court found Meegeren not guilty of treason, but convicted him of forgery."

Nora laughed politely; Jack remained stone faced.

"How can that be done?" Jack asked. "I mean, over time aren't there changes in canvases, paints, even the frames themselves?"

"Definitely. However the true copyists—the French call them *maîtres copistes*, master copyists—artificially age canvases, and even match paint thicknesses and the resins for the paints. They make brushes as they were made at the time the true artist painted the original. They use old wood for the frames, even boring the frames to create fake worm holes."

"That's amazing," Nora said. "But Field Marshall Göering was not an art expert. Can true experts be similarly fooled?"

"In 1935, the Museum of Modern Art in New York City held a Van Gogh exhibition. A college prankster molded a piece of beef, displayed it in a velvet-lined box, and attached a label that read: 'The ear that Vincent van Gogh cut off and sent to his mistress, a French prostitute, December 24, 1888.' The prankster smuggled his supplemental exhibit into the museum, where it became the hit of the show. Not even the museum staff realized it didn't belong."

Harkin tittered then settled back in his chair and crossed his legs. "So, what can I do for you two? I'm sure you came to learn more than a couple of history's great art hoodwinks."

Jack looked at Nora.

"Curator Harkin," she began, "we would like your opinion on the feasibility of the following: A master criminal has proof of an illicit relationship between a museum curator and a beautiful young woman, and he uses it to blackmail the curator into committing a crime. Let us say swapping art forgeries for real works of art, or something like that."

Harkin sat stiffly, his eyes not blinking.

Nora picked up her pencil and opened her note pad.

"What about it, Harkin?" Jack asked with a sharper edge to his voice. "Is it feasible a young, nubile lap dancer, one who knew about art and sculpture, could compromise someone such as you?" Jack held Harkin's eyes with his gaze while shaping his lips into a knowing half smile.

Nora laid down her pencil and gave Harkin's fear a softer landing. "Naturally, the curator would not have been involved in the premeditation of the crime. He would have been duped, a victim of sorts, himself."

She rolled her chair back a little as Jack added, "Seduced. Figuratively. Literally."

Jack watched Harkin as he drew in his receding chin as if trying to pull his mouth down into his neck. Harkin was cornered and bright enough to know it.

"It would be best if you finished the story," Jack said.

Nora drove in the last nail. "Jena Moves has already told us her side of it."

Harkin stared into his coffee, probably wishing it was a dark pool into which he could dive and disappear. Then he told a rerun of the story Jack and Nora had heard from Phoebe Ziegler.

"Why did you stop seeing the lap dancer?" Jack asked.

Harkin stretched his mouth as if yawning, but he wasn't. "It was like you said, Mr. McCall. The blackmailer had a video of us—Jena and me. It even had sound. I could not believe some of the noises I had made. I come from an old-fashioned Baptist family. This is very hard to talk about."

"Too late for that."

Harkin looked down. "He forced me into giving him four original national treasures, portraits of former presidents, and substituting forgeries."

"How long ago?"

"Mid February."

Nora looked up from her pad. "Tell us about his voice?"

"It was tinny. He had camouflaged it with one of those voice box enhancers, or whatever they're called."

"I fail to see why all this coerced you into criminal behavior," Nora said. "You're single, and the young woman is an adult. So what if it came out?"

"In your world, perhaps it would be so. Not in my world, Ms. Burke. I am very active in my church where I have often spoken against libidinous behavior. On a professional level the people who support my position as portrait curator, and on a broader level the National Portrait Gallery itself, are above reproach. Had this come out, I would have been fired and unable to secure meaningful employment with another museum. In short, it would have ended my life."

"You have referred to master copyists and forgers. Is there a difference?" Jack asked.

"Oh, my, yes." He nodded vigorously. "A copyist is an artist with masterful skill but perhaps lacking in creativity. He uses his great craft to copy famous works of art, including the signatures of the original artists. The copyist also adds his own signature and the date he made his copy on the back of the canvas. He sells his reproductions to buyers who know they are getting copies. A forger does essentially the same thing as the copyist, except that the forger does not add his signature to the back of the canvas, and he sells it without disclosing it is a copy."

"Did the backs of the replacement paintings you received include signatures disclosing the names of the copyists?" Jack asked.

"It appears they were once there, Mr. McCall." He quivered as if surprised by a cool breeze. "But chemicals had been used to obliterate those signatures."

"Then would it be accurate to refer to them as forgeries?"

"Yes. But by the blackmailer, not by the copyist or so it would seem."

Nora put down her notepad. "A capable crime lab could probably raise the name."

Jack looked sideways at his partner. "Let's not get ahead of ourselves. If we pursue that effort now, the story will undoubtedly get out, as will Mr. Harkin's role as an accessory." He pointed at Harkin. "You'd be arrested and, worse yet, the blackmailer might destroy the originals."

Harkin put his thumbs inside his fists.

"Curator Harkin," Nora asked, "are you suggesting the blackmailer paid a legitimate master copyist to reproduce these four presidential portraits? Then obliterated the signatures of the copyist from the backs, converting them into forgeries?"

"That would be my guess, Ms. Burke." Harkin sat motionlessly with his stare fixed on his thumb-socketed fists.

"Harkin." Jack said, speaking sharply enough to make the man look up. "Isn't it also possible that the blemishes on the backs of the canvases could have been from reusing the back side of old canvases from the right historical period? That would mean the obliterated signature on the back could have been the artist of that canvas's original picture or perhaps some other painter when the canvas had been previously used. If so we could be looking for a forger and not a copyist."

"That is also possible, but in my view less likely." He ran his hand over his head mussing the strands of his comb-over.

"Are the forgeries here on display?" Nora asked, again making notes.

Harkin sat forward. "Yes. I keep thinking they will be spotted by the very next person who looks at them." Then he sagged back into his chair. "The truth is they're very good."

"Do you know copyists capable of making such forgeries?"

"There are many fine copyists," Harkin shrugged, "however, only a few are capable of reproducing portraits that were painted over such a span of years."

"Why would that be?" Nora asked.

"Few copyists have reason to learn how to reproduce paints and brushes as they evolved over a lengthy period of years, not to mention the skill to emulate the subtle changes in style."

After giving the curator some time, Jack asked, "What happened to the originals?"

"You don't think he told me, do you?" Then he sighed. "I have no idea."

"Where did you and the blackmailer swap the originals for the forgeries?" Nora asked.

Harkin ran his fingers across the bottom of his small round chin, looked down and began.

"One night I came home and the forgeries were in my house. In my home! Then a call came telling me to switch them and to leave the originals in the back of my car. Leave national treasures in my car—it was crazy! He had me drive to the Four Seasons Hotel and leave the keys on top of the left rear tire. Then I was told to go into the hotel restaurant and not come out for an hour. That was the longest hour of my life. When I returned, the originals were gone and he had left the videotapes of Miss Jena and me."

"Since then?" Jack and Nora asked, in near duet, before Jack added, "Do you still have the videotapes he returned?"

"I've had no contact since. As for the tapes, I burned them. I'm still afraid every time my phone rings ... every time I walk into my home at night. This may sound insane, but when I walk past those pictures I feel the eyes of those presidents are upon me." He finished with his arms on the table in front of him, his fists still strangling his thumbs.

"How would the copyist know how to make exact dupli-cates without first having the originals?"

"Excellent transparencies of famous paintings are avail-able. Any copyist could choose from a wide variety of sources."

"The National Portrait Gallery collects portraits of distin-guished Americans, not just presidents," Nora observed. "Yet the blackmailer demanded only presidential portraits. Is that correct?"

"Yes. Four presidents. McKinley, Lincoln, Garfield, and JFK. Lincoln and Kennedy are among the more popular, but Garfield and McKinley? I mean, why not George Washington and FDR, or Teddy Roosevelt and Ronald Reagan? Those four are all much more popular than Garfield and McKinley."

"Those four were assassinated during their presidencies."

"Of course! I should have realized that, Mr. McCall. American history was never my best subject. But why would he choose the dead presidents?"

"I have no idea." Jack shrugged.

"Mr. Harkin, certainly you knew this would all come out sooner or later."

Harkin hung his head. "I thought about running, but to where? I don't know how to be a fugitive from the law. I lack the funds to run to some third-world country and buy protec-tion. I guess it's time for me to go to jail."

"If it's any consolation," Nora said, "Jena Moves did not know you were being filmed. She didn't know you were going to be blackmailed."

"Thank you for that, Ms. Burke. Still, in the final analy-sis, her interest was the money, not me. I was an old fool act-ing out a fantasy."

"You're not the world's first fool," Jack said, "and you won't be its last."

Harkin's body language read surrender. "Is this when you take me to the police?"

"First, we'd like to recover the portraits. That would help the National Gallery, and could make things go easier for you at trial. Will you help us?"

"I've told you everything I know." He wiped his eyes. "How can I be of further assistance?"

"By saying nothing," Nora answered. "By going on with your job as you have."

He sat silently. Then nodded.

"Take us on a tour," Jack said, rolling his chair back. "Show us the gallery. Point out the fakes, but refer to them as if they're the real deal."

Harkin led them out of the small conference room and around a corner. "This is our Hall of Presidents. Here you will find the portrait of every American president, with one exception. William Jefferson Clinton wanted his likeness to be a sculpted bust rather than a painted portrait."

Harkin pointed out the first fake as if it were real, saying, "On your left is the famous Lincoln portrait painted in 1887 by George Healy."

They walked a little farther before Harkin stopped to point out the Garfield portrait painted by the Norwegian Ole Peter in 1881. Jack could sense the reverence Harkin felt for the art. The gallery had been his life.

A few minutes later, Harkin said, "This is the McKinley portrait. And over here," he pointed, "President Kennedy, painted by William Draper in 1966."

They continued looking to avoid a pattern as to which art pieces had been their real interest. Nora asked him to show them the Pettrich sculpture of Andy Jackson.

"That was Jena's favorite," Harkin said. "That piece is not part of the Hall of Presidents. There, Jackson is an oil as are all the presidents except, as I described, Clinton."

A little later they entered Harkin's office. He shut the door and turned toward them. "If you believe it will help recover the paintings, I'll continue my charade." He sighed faintly. "Every time one of my staff speaks to me, I expect they've come to tell me the forgeries have been discovered. In a strange way, now that someone else knows, I feel some relief."

Jack shook the curator's hand. "If you carry out the role we've agreed to, we'll testify as to the help you gave us and the nation should we recover the portraits."

"Thank you, Mr. McCall. Ms. Burke."

"Mr. Harkin," Nora said, "we need you to spend tonight making an exhaustive list of every portrait painter and every copyist who, in your opinion, has the skill to duplicate those four originals. Do not differentiate between the ones you think might be guilty and those you feel could not be. Just as you were, other honest men can be corrupted."

"And give us whatever you can on their whereabouts," Jack added.

"I'll call you as soon as it's finished." He seemed energized by the task.

"If we are to recover the portraits, we need to find the blackmailer. Our best bet to find his trail is through identifying the copyist or forger." Jack poked his finger against Harkin's chest with each of his last three words. "That's your job."

As Jack and Nora walked out, they heard Harkin's quivering voice behind them. "If you recover the portraits, can we just exchange them back into the gallery so no one will ever know?"

CHAPTER 31

JACK AND NORA walked into their office to see Mary Lou sitting at her desk. Her clothes were disheveled; she held an ice bag against her face.

"What happened?" Nora asked, rushing to their young receptionist.

"Some guy from a motorcycle gang beat me up." Then Mary Lou told them about Max being "unbelievably heroic," as she put it.

"He has such a relaxing way about him. He got me laughing and I forgot the hurt." Her eyes sparkled from within her darkening cheeks. "I just love him."

Nora headed for her office.

"What did Max say to get you laughing?" Jack asked.

"He asked me if I knew the difference between a Harley and a Hoover. When I said, I didn't, he said, 'The position of the dirt bag.'" Mary Lou winced when her laugh spread her fat lip.

When Nora returned, Jack said, "I'm gonna go see Donny. That biker is one of his gang."

"Cool your jets." Nora put her hand on Jack's shoulder. "I just called Max. He had a nice chat with the biker. Donny had no part in it. The biker has left town and will not be back. His name is Rockton. Max kept his gun and his knife with his prints. So, before you go off half-cocked, talk to Max."

"I'll call him right now."

"I left him on hold. I figured you might want to talk with him."

Jack went into his office and poked the lit button on his phone.

"How's she doing?" Max asked.

"She's more shook up than hurt. Thanks to you."

"Should I have called it in? Had Metro come get the guy?"

"Why didn't you?"

"The cops would learn Rockton came to get Donny's confession. Suggs would then get in your face about your not telling him you knew it was Donny and his goons who worked you over. There could only be one end of that road: We'd have to put our case aside because Suggs would reopen his investigation into the death of Chris Andujar."

"You did right, Max. Metro had the case and let go of it. It's ours now and we're not about to give it back."

Jack rejoined Nora and Mary Lou.

"After I talked with Max, I called the chief to tell him what happened and that you were all right. I told him the best the biker could be charged with is simple assault, and that Max ran the guy out of town. You cannot tell your Uncle Harry about the biker demanding Donny's confession, that's confidential to our case. Tell him you don't know anything about why the biker had come here. That all you know is he roughed you up, maybe to deliver a message to me. You understand? I know this won't be easy for you to do, but we told you when you started with us that you would on occasion be privy to information you must keep confidential. This is important." Mary Lou nodded. "Now, would you like to go home?"

"I'm fine, Jack. Really. I want you guys to solve this case. Stop worrying about me."

"We'll be in the back if you need us." He motioned for Nora to follow him.

"Troy Engels finally returned my call, right after I hung up with Chief Mandrake." Jack scooted his backside onto the tabletop, leaving his feet dangling just above the floor. "I asked him why he'd faked being nervous enough to stutter at our open house while asking me to keep Tyson away from him."

"I've been curious about that ever since we learned that Tyson and Engels were poker buddies," Nora said. "What did he tell you?"

"I quote: 'Jack, you know I'm just a frustrated old spook who misses field ops; all us guys marooned on a desk are the same way. Every now and then I get in a playful mood and act out a practice scenario. I figured if I could fool a top op like you, I still had it. I apologize if my little playacting caused you any difficulty.'"

"That's a crock. What about his affair with Chris Andujar? Did you confront him about that?"

"No."

"Why not?"

"Over his years with the CIA Engels has been a top covert operative. He wrote several of the Agency's training manuals. He still runs their mock interrogation classes. He heads up deep operations that never see the light of day, including several for which I led field operations. My asking that would have told Engels we know he had a gay relationship with Chris and he would not have given me anything in return. Advantage, Engels."

"You've said you doubt the intelligence community knows that Engels is gay. Instead of Andujar being blackmailed and committing suicide, he might have told Engels he was coming out of the closet? If so, Engels may have bumped off Andujar to keep him quiet."

"Possibly, but not likely. Engels could have leveraged Chris into silence without killing him, and I can't see Chris wanting to come out of the closet. It would have crushed his wife and ruined whatever modicum of a relationship he had with his son. No. Both Engels and Chris would want that kept a secret. That scenario also doesn't explain Andujar's missing quarter mil. Besides, if Engels had killed Chris he could have arranged for him to simply disappear—like Jimmy Hoffa."

Nora's body language told him she knew Jack had it right.

Jack then suggested a more likely set up: Haviland got the blackmailer into Chris's office to get the goods on some of his patients, and later into Donny's Club to tape Harkin with Jena Moves.

"But Chris's files were only coded," Nora retorted. "The blackmailer would have the goods on people without knowing who they were."

Jack nodded, and then said, "The blackmailer had film taken in Donny's club for leverage over Harkin. Maybe they used surveillance equipment in Chris's office."

Jack dialed his phone and called Clarence Drummond, the former CIA surveillance expert who had a few days earlier took countersurveillance measures in the home of Chris's former receptionist, Agnes Fuller. Drummy agreed to join Jack tonight to perform a sweep of Chris's office, and while they were at it, the office of Chris's pal, Dr. Radnor. Access courtesy of Clark's janitorial service.

CHAPTER 32

ALAN CLARK WAS clearly skittish when Jack and Drummy approached the back door of the office building in which Chris Andujar had rented space for his practice. Clark's cleaning crew had left, leaving the building empty except for the three of them.

Jack did not introduce Drummy to Carl Anson, alias Alan Clark who kept looking at Drummy, clearly wondering who he was and why he was with Jack.

After beseeching Jack to be as quick as possible, Clark gave Jack a master key and waited in the lobby.

Andujar's office had already been picked clean by Goodwill Industries. Nothing remained but an unreliable florescent ceiling light with a periodic flicker and a constant hum from its defective ballast.

Drummy gave Chris's office a fast sweep using equipment capable of detecting virtually any radio-frequency eavesdropping device made, including those used by government intelligence and law enforcement agencies.

"Ain't nothing here, Jack. If anything ever was, it'd be long gone by now anyway. No installer wants his equipment found in the office of a dead doc the cops booked as a suicide."

Jack began repacking the equipment while Drummy used a handheld xenon lamp in combination with infrared and ultraviolet filtration to search for an indication that bugs had been hidden in the baseboards, drapery cornices, walls, or ceiling panels.

Suddenly, Drummy snapped his fingers and pointed to a faint image of a forearm print on the wall just below the acoustical drop ceiling. He climbed the ladder and slid a two-by-four foot ceiling panel to the side.

"I got scratches here on the support grid. The recorder was likely right here."

Drummy lowered the acoustical panel. Jack took it and examined the pinhole in the white side of the panel. Drummy then pointed at a small channel bored into its soft unpainted surface.

"See that? A tiny camera was used to provide pictures as well as sound. The guy's equipment was crap, very dated, but it'd do the job."

"Would the filming be constant?"

"I doubt it. More likely it all started with a voice activated recorder, after that the camera would take pictures at preset intervals. The audio is the more significant part of the surveillance. The periodic pictures did the job of eliminating any doubt as to the identity of the person speaking."

What they found would fit the known blackmailing of Chris's patient, the newspaper magnate, Dorothy Wingate, and her beau, Philippe Frenet. It could also support Jack's theory that another of Chris's patients, Allison Trowbridge, had been blackmailed, but they had not yet established that extortion had actually occurred.

Alan Clark was pacing in the lobby when they came out of the elevator. Jack offered to let Clark look through Drummy's equipment case.

"Let's just get out of here," Clark said excitedly. "The other building should be clear by the time we get there. I just want this night to end."

Twenty-five minutes later Alan Clark locked the three of them inside the building where Jack and Nora had been a few days before to interview Dr. Radnor. Clark collapsed into one of the lobby chair.

Jack and Drummy got off the elevator on the floor below Dr. Radnor's office and walked up one flight of stairs. Radnor's office was close to the size of Chris's, only Radnor was still in practice so his office had furnishings, phones, and cable television service.

Drummy used the same equipment and process he had used in Andujar's office. He also used a Time Domain Reflectometer on Radnor's telephone and data cable. He found no signs of bugs in position, but found similar markings above one of the acoustical panels in the ceiling. From the top of the ladder, he shined a bore scope into a hole he had found behind the smoke detector.

"There's a scrap of wire left inside. The kind commonly used for RF recorders, not smoke detectors."

With Chris Andujar dead, removing the surveillance equipment from his office made sense. But why remove the equipment from Radnor's active practice? Is the blackmailer being cautious enough to limit the number of marks he obtains from a single source? It would seem he got the goods on Dorothy Wingate and her lover, along with whatever he had held over Allison Trowbridge from the bug in Chris's office. But, at least so far, they had no knowledge of any patient of Dr. Radnor being extorted. When they confirmed Trowbridge had been blackmailed, they would know the *how*.

Jack and Drummy took the stairs down to the floor below, and were nearing the elevator when Jack paused at a door with small white block letters: The Office of Dr. John Karros. Medical doctors often put their specialty under their name. Dr. Karros had not.

"Drummy?" Jack raised his eyebrows.

"Why not?" Drummy said. "Could be another shrink?"

"Our blackmailer may be limiting how many marks he'll take from one source, and it looks like his specialty may be using psychiatrists to find his targets. If Karros is a shrink, with him being in the same building," Jack shrugged, "I would, wouldn't you?"

Drummy nodded, and said, "The convenience of a double hitter might have been too good to pass up. Only take us a minute to find out."

Doctor Karros's lobby materials indicated he was, in fact, a psychiatrist. Drummy unpacked his equipment to sweep Karros's office.

"I should go touch base with Clark," Jack said, "he's probably jumping out of skin."

When Jack came out of the elevator, Clark rushed up waiving his hands frantically. "Where's the other fella?" He pulled a handkerchief from his back pocket and wiped the top of his partly bald head.

"Relax, Alan. You and your people are in this building for hours every night. Keep your lunch bag open as if you're taking a break. I entered my number into your cell phone. If anyone comes in the building, they'll need a key. If that happens, hit redial and my phone'll ring. Then hang up. We'll be ready to play the role of two of your janitors."

"If what I'm doing gets out—you should be done by now. This is taking too long." Clark ran the blue hankie over his head again, then across the back of his neck.

"We'll be another twenty minutes. Should anything happen, just call my cell number and we'll adjust. Relax. Finish your sandwich. The sooner I get back up there, the sooner we'll be back down."

Jack stepped into the elevator, giving Alan the peace sign from the hippie era.

"Man. I haven't seen that in a long time."

"That's the attitude. Be cool." The elevator door closed on Jack's reassuring smile. He got off the elevator two floors below Karros's office and walked up the stairwell. If Clark had watched the lobby elevator panel, he wanted him to remember the wrong floor.

When Jack entered Karros's office, Drummy held his finger to his lips. "I hit a hot one," he whispered. "A voice-activated recorder set up to take a single picture on activation and again every few minutes. My equipment picked up the infrared bloom from the optical device. I erased our visit."

Drummy had already packed his equipment; they eased out into the hall and relocked the door.

"Maybe," Drummy reasoned, "this is a fresh set-up. Your blackmailer is still soliciting new customers." He paused. "Then again, if the blackmailer used Clark's supervisor, Bennie Haviland, to get in, maybe events dictated that he kill Haviland before he could get this equipment out. Maybe Haviland was coming to see you? No, no, that can't be. The equipment would have been here long enough to fill the tape, and very little of it has been used. This set up's pretty new. And you know what really seems screwy?"

"What?" asked Jack.

"From what you've told me your blackmailer is smarter than the average bear, so why is he using this old stuff? I mean he's got no capacity for remote viewing or retrieval?"

"I've got no answer. Not yet," Jack replied, "any other observations?"

"Sloppy workmanship." Drummy shook his head. "Whoever installed this junk knew how. It's just sloppy—except for wiping everything down so he'd leave no fingerprints."

"If he's removing his prints, what makes it sloppy?"

"He left wire cuttings, just like at the first two offices. A careful technician would've removed everything." He patted Jack twice on the shoulder. "We'd better get downstairs."

Clark was waiting with his nose nearly against the elevator doors. "Tell me you're done. That we can get out of here."

"We can leave. But I want you to remember our talk about keeping quiet about tonight's activities." Clark again ran his hanky over his brow. He and his wife had a lifetime of keeping their own secret, so Jack figured they'd keep this one too.

On the way to Drummy's house, Jack said, "Are you available tomorrow?"

"I can be."

"Come by MI in the morning. Let's find out if our blackmailer has somehow bugged our office. The building doesn't use Clark's janitorial, but the blackmailer may have leverage with more than one janitor service. I also want you to check my house and Nora's apartment."

CHAPTER 33

JACK NEARLY RAN the red light at Pennsylvania Avenue when he heard the radio newsflash:

> *Shots fired at the residence of a Miss Phoebe Ziegler. An unidentified woman is dead. Police are at the scene. More at eleven.*

Jack had already dropped Drummy off at his home. He spun a U-turn and headed for Phoebe's apartment about a dozen blocks to the north. While he drove, he dialed.

"Harkin? Jack McCall. I came by your place earlier. Where were you?" Jack hadn't stopped to see Harkin, but he wanted to read Harkin's reaction.

"You must have gone to the wrong house. I've been right here since I got home from work. Ask Ms. Burke. She's called twice to check on my progress on the list of copyists. It's finished. What's this about, Mr. McCall?"

"You haven't had the news on? Have you been alone?"

"Yes, alone. No, I have not watched the news. I've been working on this list and digging up addresses. What's going on?"

"Jena has been murdered. I don't know anything more than that."

"Oh, my God." Harkin audibly sucked back a sob. "Poor Jena."

The tires on Jack's Concorde screeched as he dropped from fifty miles an hour to a dead stop along the curb a few houses from the small cluster of units where Phoebe lived, had lived. The area in front of her place was bedlam. Cop cars were scattered like an impromptu meeting of drunks.

"Stay put, Harkin. Talk to no one. Our deal remains the same."

"I can't keep up this charade now." He was crying openly.

"Her real name was Phoebe Ziegler. Did you murder Phoebe?"

"What! Of course not. I couldn't hurt—"

"Then our focus remains on the portraits. You took your pleasure. Now you suck it up and carry your load."

Jack approached the property while uniformed officers dispersed the neighborhood crowd. A bullet-riddled body lay along the curb, a dead hand snagged on the foot peddle of a black and chrome Harley Davidson, Road King. One of the uniformed officers put up his hand when Jack walked toward the house. He stopped. "Who's in charge?"

"Sergeant Paul Suggs, Major Case Squad."

"Sergeant Suggs." Jack hollered toward the house. "Yo. Sergeant Suggs."

Two uniform officers were off to the side talking with two detectives. Like all modern cities, DC investigated every officer shooting. The two uniforms were likely the shooters, the suits tonight's edition of the department's shooting team. Right then, two other guys with cameras wandered out onto the porch.

"She could've danced on my lap anytime," one of them said.

"Your lap and my face." The other replied. They both laughed.

"Shut your mouths, you sons-a-bitches," Jack screamed over the uniform's shoulder. "Or come over here and I'll shut 'em for you."

"Now hold on buddy," the uniform blocking Jack's forward motion said. "If you knew Ms. Ziegler, the sergeant will want to talk with you."

"Yeah. I knew her." Jack said to answer the officer. Then he called out again. "Suggs. Sergeant Suggs. It's Jack McCall."

Suggs came out the front door and down the sidewalk toward him. When he got close, Jack could hear his left shoe squeak with each stride.

"Good evening, Mr. McCall," Suggs said. Then he turned toward the porch. "You two mugs are here to shoot pictures, not to shit out of your damn face holes."

Suggs took Jack's arm and led him away. "You knew this woman?"

"Nora and I met Ms. Ziegler through her employer, Sara Andujar's son, Donny Andujar." Jack started around Suggs, toward the apartment. "How did she die?"

The sergeant slid over to stay in front of Jack and then loosened his tie. "Jack. I can't let you on this scene. Forensics just arrived and the M.E.'s not here yet. At the Haviland scene, Chief Mandrake invited you in. I can't take on that decision, not at a homicide scene. The dead guy hanging on the bike was put down by the cops first on the scene. The shooting team is over there interviewing the shooters." He motioned with his head. "We haven't identified the dead guy."

Jack stepped back and took a deep breath. "I believe you'll find that crud is George Rockton, a bouncer at Donny's Club where Ms. Ziegler danced under the name, Jena Moves. Now you give. How was she killed?"

"Looks like strangulation. We found her naked. I'm guessing the dead guy's the killer, but that isn't established. The station got a call from a neighbor who heard fighting and screaming. We had a car in the area. They got here in minutes. Rockton, if that's his name, fired on them and made a break for his motorcycle. The officers put him down. Were these two lovers?"

"I don't know. I just know they both worked at Donny's club. I don't think they were an item. The other girls at Donny's would know."

"Tell me about her," Suggs asked, "other than where she worked?"

"She still seemed like a good kid, not all hard yet. She came to DC to study sculpting. She was saving her money to go to school. She invited Nora and me over to see one of her pieces."

"You seem ... upset by her death."

"Nora and I tried to talk her into leaving Donny's and returning to school right away. I should've ... I don't know, convinced her somehow. Tried harder."

"Don't put this in your pocket, Jack. It doesn't fit. She was a big girl—well, big enough to make her own decisions. She made them and they went bad."

"Thanks, Paul. She didn't have enough to be a burglary target. What does it look like? A rape and murder? Torture for information? What's your gut on this?"

"We can't rule out a botched burglary, but I doubt it, there just ain't much he could haul away on his motorcycle. It appears they had sex. From what I saw before you called me out, it wasn't consensual. I'm expecting the M.E. to get here any minute. We'll know more after she's done."

Suggs took Jack by the arm and got him walking toward his car. "From the multiple marks on her neck, the rash like spots on her skin, and the hemorrhages in her eyes, the perp repeated near-strangulations. Or, maybe she's one of them sicko gaspers. Or maybe he got off that way. He was a mean prick though, I can tell you that." Suggs paused a moment, then went melancholy. "Things have certainly changed over my years on the force. Whatever happened to the days when if you wanted someone dead, you just pumped 'em full of lead? Brutality has become a growth industry. Maybe I've just gotten too old for this job."

Jack couldn't tell Suggs about Phoebe's relationship with Harkin. The slim chance that he could find the presidential portraits would drop to zero if that story broke.

"What was used to strangle her?"

"It looks like a dirty robe tie. I was about to look for a matching robe when you started hollering."

"Was it pink terrycloth?"

"Yeah."

"It's her robe all right. You should find it inside. If she's like most people, it's probably on a hook behind the bathroom door."

"Gee thanks, Sherlock." Suggs rolled his eyes. "You must be a topnotch PI."

"Listen, Suggs, I don't need your attitude. I was just trying to help." Then Jack tried again to move around the sergeant.

Suggs moved over again, keeping Jack from reaching the porch. "Okay, Jack. I didn't realize you knew her all that well."

"I didn't. I already told you. I only saw her that once. She struck me as a sweet kid. Nora felt the girl had real sculpting talent. If you haven't found her work yet, you will. Please take in any of her sculpted pieces. I'm going to hire an attorney to pursue getting them released to Ms. Ziegler mother. Would you do that, Paul?"

"Sure."

The story Jack had told Suggs danced around the whole truth and nothing but the truth, but he needed to stop the questions about how and why he got to know the victim.

Jack thought as Suggs continued to walk with him toward his car. *The blackmailer might have killed Phoebe as part of sweeping his trail clean, if he figured I didn't know about Randolph Harkin. Still, he had to know that killing Phoebe would lead the cops to Donny's club where they would learn that for over a year she had a once-a-month date with a guy named Harkin. No. It made no sense for the blackmailer to kick up that dust. He'd let it lay. If, on the other hand, he knew I talked to Phoebe, he'd figure I knew about Harkin and that I'd be able to squeeze that soft little man to find out about the swapping of the portraits. Either way, killing Phoebe would only turn up the heat on him. Given this bastard's penchant for caution, if he hasn't already sold the real paintings, he'll squirrel them away while things cool.*

Suggs opened Jack's car door. "Get out of here, Jack. Go home. Nothing else you can do here. I'm sorry about all this."

"Hey, Paul, you're finally calling me Jack."

"Fuck you, McCall, and the horse you rode in on."

CHAPTER 34

JACK MET DRUMMY at seven in the morning. By eight the security expert had found no evidence of surveillance equipment in MI, and had left Jack's office to sweep his home and Nora's apartment. After he left, Jack and Nora went into their case room to discuss the death of Phoebe Ziegler, but Paul Suggs had summarized it best: "The choices had been Phoebe's. She made 'em. They went bad."

Nora looked up from the papers in front of her. "I stopped at the National Portrait Gallery. Harkin's there. He's wrung out but holding up. Here's his list of copyists."

Jack slid the chair between them back toward the wall and rolled close enough to see the list. Nora's perfume was soft and attracting. "How many are there?"

"Eleven in the U.S.," she said. "I think we're on solid ground assuming the copyist is in the U.S. That would avoid the problems associated with getting the phony paintings in through customs and the real ones out. Diplomatic immunity might be the weak link in that assumption but we've had no reason to think in that direction."

"What's the geographic distribution?"

"Three in the D.C./Virginia/Maryland area and three in New York City, the other five are in the Midwest and far west."

An hour later they had identified three trails they needed to get on fast: finding the forger, baiting the blackmailer through the surveillance equipment in the office of Dr. John Karros, and getting in Art Tyson's face. They had nothing that fit tight on Tyson, but his car matched with the car they saw outside Sarah Andujar's house. Chris Andujar's receptionist was his girlfriend. He had owned a silent piece of Luke Title's Place and the accounting records missing from Luke's could explain Allison Trowbridge being blackmailed. Yeah. They had a fourth trail: finding out if Allison had been blackmailed and over what.

Nora would contact each of the artists by phone. She would also finagle an appointment as a new patient with Dr. Karros. For that she'd need to develop a story ripe enough to give the listening blackmailer a reason to shake her down.

Jack spotted the name on a half-opened second floor window overlooking Eighteenth Street: *A. Tyson, Private Investigator.* The building was across from Joey's, a neighborhood watering hole in the Adams Morgan district in northwest DC.

Jack stepped inside the one-room office to see Tyson sitting behind a desk butted up against the side wall, a cold, mostly-smoked cigar wedged between his fat fingers. His thin plastered down hair could have been mistaken for a grease smudge if not for the gray streaking through the smear. A waste basket sat in the corner on the dirty green vinyl floor, the area around it littered with spent wooden matches, snapped in two.

So it was Tyson parked outside Sarah Andujar's home.

Tyson looked up, a crooked grin on his face pushing his hammered-in nose off center. He held a phone in one hand, and brought the hand surrounding the blunt cigar to his face, a keep-quiet finger touching his lips.

Jack leaned against the wall and imagined how Dashiell Hammett, the creator of Sam Spade, might have written the description of Tyson's office: In the dark, quiet gut of the night the room was cast in pink light from the pulsing energy of the neon sign over Joey's Bar. The cold room lacked a family portrait or even one of those free cheesecake shots that come inside when you buy a cheap frame. Tyson's desk was home to a phone, a lamp with a green plastic shade, and the rest of the mess that wasn't balanced on top the file cabinet or stacked on the dirty beige visitor's chair. Spade couldn't tell if the tarnished spittoon next to the desk was a functional accessory, or merely a period piece for ambience. On the floor—

Jack's thoughts were interrupted when Tyson hung up the phone. "Hello, Artie," he said. "I wasn't sure I'd catch you in this early."

"Early? Shit. This is the back end of yesterday. I work nights. Sleep afternoons." He thrust his chin forward like a fighting cock. "What do you want?"

"You invited me to come see you. Promised to explain the ins and outs of being a DC snoop dick, if I recall your phrase." Jack's attempt to match Tyson's smirk failed.

Tyson reached in a bottom drawer and brought out a bottle of whiskey grasped by the neck. On the return trip, his hand brought up two stubby glasses decorated with smudges; his index finger deep inside one, his wide thumb getting personal with the second. He poured a big gulp into each. Then stared at Jack like a dim bulb stares from the far end of a dark hallway.

"Quit fencing, McCall," Tyson said. "That's not what brung ya. You're uptown. Me, I'm skidsville. I know it. What the hell you want?" Tyson picked up the index-finger glass, inclined it toward Jack and chugged its contents in one swallow. Jack left the wide-thumb glass sitting.

Jack had learned the word *gumshoe* for private investigators watching detective movies from the forties. He couldn't recall ever having used it before, but gumshoe fit Tyson and his rumpled office. Still, Tyson had been right. They were sniffing each other like a couple of circling dogs.

"Okay, Artie. Here's a part of it. We know you were a silent partner for Tittle and his bag man for protec—"

"An old rumor," he bellowed. "Ancient history. Get to the point, McCall. Spit it out." He illustrated "spit it out" by squirting a dark stringy clump of tobacco juice into the spittoon next to his desk. Thus, answering one question: the spittoon was an accessory and not noir deco.

"For curiosity's sake, tell me one thing?"

"If I can, sure," Tyson said, "one PI to another." Tyson made a noise that sounded half snuff and half snort.

Jack hadn't been invited to sit, but he did after picking up the files from the dirty beige chair and stacking them on top of some cameras and recording equipment on the floor along the wall.

A cockroach scampered out of one of the folders when Jack started to pick them up off the desk. Tyson hammered the roach with the flat of his hand and swept the twitching remains off his palm and into the spittoon, then wiped his hand on his pants. Then he returned his attention to Jack. "So ask. I ain't got all day." Then he shrugged, picked up the thumb glass and took its contents in a single swallow.

"At my open house you went to speak with Mayor Molloy. Almost the moment you got to him, he started shaking his head. To what was he saying no?"

"Hell, who knows. I'd had a few that night to celebrate your opening. I don't even remember speaking to Molloy. I ain't exactly in the mayor's inner circle."

"You mean your poker games with the mayor aren't on his social calendar?"

Tyson's squint pouched his cheeks up to smear the bottom edge of his glasses. He again spat at his spittoon. "Well, aren't you Sam Fuckin' Spade."

Jack considered that a compliment, but Tyson had gotten the middle name wrong.

He decided not to ask Tyson if he had been outside Sarah Andujar's house that first morning. He wouldn't get anything out of Tyson unless he had him by the short hairs, and he didn't. Not yet.

Jack stood.

Tyson stood also, his belly closing the desk's partially opened pencil drawer. He hacked up a mouth wad and fired it at the spittoon. This time he missed. The two men stood temporarily mesmerized by the green slime slithering down the side of the desk.

"You got more to say, McCall?" Tyson asked after sitting back down.

"That's it for now, Artie. That is, unless you wanna talk about why Donny Andujar was so eager to get Jena Moves on her back with Randolph Harkin?"

Tyson's smirk disappeared. He refilled the void with a hard, blank look. Then he laughed. "Donny runs whores. The whole town knows it. I've been in there enough to know that Jena Moves had what it took from her hips to her lips. He prob'ly just wanted another working mattress-back. Now, if that's all, I got to be excusing myself."

Jack decided to skip shaking Tyson's roach-crusted hand. "Thanks, Artie. You were thoughtful enough to visit my office. I wanted to repay the courtesy. I'll see you around."

Jack had turned his back and taken the two steps necessary to reach for the knob when he heard a chair screech hard and hit the wall. He spun around.

"Interesting interrogation, McCall. Me, an ex-copper versus you, ex-king-shit spook." The vein in Tyson's temple twitched to its own rhythm. "I put four killers in the ground and another dozen in the can, and the city threw me out like I was garbage."

Tyson used the back of his hand to wipe away a stringy white substance that had bunched up at the corner of his mouth.

Jack moved closer, Tyson's desk standing as a demilitarized zone. "I guess some of us just get the breaks, Artie. I'm leaving now, unless you have something else you wanna say."

Tyson hacked again and leaned toward his spittoon, then swung his head around and spit whatever he had brought up onto Jack's face.

Jack wiped his face with his hand, wiped his hand on his shirt, and wiped Tyson's grin with his fist. The fat gumshoe went down like a puppet without strings.

The surveillance equipment stacked in the corner beside the room's one file cabinet was the same kind that had been installed in the office of Dr. Karros.

Jack left Arthur Tyson, Private Investigator, after dumping the contents of his spittoon over him from grin to groin.

CHAPTER 35

JACK STOPPED AT home, tore off his shirt, threw it away, took a quick shower, and changed into a fresh pair of slacks and a shirt he had just picked up at the cleaners. He was meeting Max for lunch. While sliding his feet into a pair of black loafers, Drummy called.

"Your place was clean, but I hit the jackpot at Nora's. There was a wireless near her living room phone and another in the bedroom. The conversations pass to a CD in a micro recorder hidden in some rocks out front so he can swap it out without having to get inside her place."

"That doesn't sound like the kind of stuff you found at Dr. Karros's."

"For sure, this equipment is up to date. The CD will hold a ton."

"Anyway to trace it?"

"I'm still here; you want it out?"

Jack rubbed his chin. "We have to assume it was put there by the blackmailer. What's your guess on why the equipment is more state-of-the-art than what we found in Karros's office?"

"The easy answer is two different installers; but this kind of work isn't usually a team sport. One thing that is certain, the guy who would use what's here wouldn't be caught dead using the junk in the doctors' offices. The two may not be related. This one could be a curious lover. Is Nora dating anyone in the business?"

"Not that I know of. Let's leave it in place. Since Benny Haviland was killed, maybe the blackmailer got a new electronics man. Then again, Haviland could have planted the bugs making a new installer necessary. Maybe his loot from the blackmailings let him upgrade. We could guess all day. Whoever it is, he'll be eager to keep up with what's on it. I'll alert Nora. Maybe we can use it to flush him out. There are some trees in front of her place. Can you set up a camera so we can see whoever comes for it?"

"Piece of cake. And I'll bring you a remote that will let Nora check from inside the house to see if any pictures have been taken."

The restaurant where Jack was meeting Max had a counter with round stools and a dozen or so booths covered with red checkered oilcloths. The menu featured sandwiches named after Hollywood stars. The place was a throwback to the days when if it wasn't cooked on a grill, it came out of a deep fryer, so the food tasted great. Every time Jack drove by, the place was packed with people breathing grease and treating their mouths to a good time.

Jack ordered his usual, the Humphrey Bogart. Max's choice, a hotdog named the George Hamilton. They both backed up their sandwiches with a Killian Red Ale. He brought Max current on the investigation before saying, "You made quite an impression on Mary Lou. Thanks for handling the biker."

"You've seen his type, boss, loud and nasty disguised as tough."

"I'm just glad you came by when you did."

"You know, if I'd have called in Metro for the assault on Mary Lou, Phoebe Ziegler might still be alive."

"Max, you know better than to armchair quarterback these things. Hell, I could say the same. If I had given Suggs Donny's confession that named George Rockton as one of his goons that beat me up, Rockton might've been arrested. In either event, the biker would have been out on bail fast and might well have still raped and murdered Phoebe Ziegler. This thinking also assumes the blackmailer had no other muscle than Rockton, and we don't know that either."

"That's good rationalizing, boss, but still—"

"Still nothing," Jack said sharply. "The bottom line is we had an investigation underway regarding Dr. Chris Andujar. We knew of no credible threat to Phoebe, hell, no threat whatsoever. Rockton chose to commit a crime. No one is at fault for that but Rockton."

The waitress, wearing a checkerboard apron that matched the oilcloths on the tables, brought them their orders. Max raised his Killian Red. "Here's to confusion for all the enemies of the Irish."

Jack raised his glass and they each took a drink.

"Okay, boss. I don't figure you're bribing me with this here George Hamilton just to talk about Mr. Smelly?"

"You're right," Jack said through a big grin. "I need to know about Mayor Patrick Molloy. Family background. Real stuff, without the public polish. The mayor's Irish and you're Scottish and Irish. You once told me that your families came here when you two were boys. You okay with my asking?"

"When we was kids the mayor and me was real chums, but for the past twenty-five years he's acted like he never knew me. I got no grudge, but I got no problem telling you what I know. It's all ancient history though."

Max, not a guy for those fancy mustards, lathered his dog in plain yellow, sprinkled on onions, and suffocated it with pickle relish. Max looked up. "What? A man has to eat his greens." He winked and took a first bite.

"Ancient history is exactly what I'm after," Jack said. "I need a peak at the real guy."

"My family and Patrick Molloy's family left Chicago for DC on my ninth birthday. Patrick was a few months younger than me—still is fer that matter. Before we was born, Patrick's daddy, Sean Molloy, and my pa, Alastair Logan, met in Chicago where they both worked for the Irish racketeer Dion O'Banion. In the beginning they both drove beer trucks. My pa stayed a driver, saying he had to provide for his family and that the silliness of prohibition made it okay to deliver for a bootlegger. Sean Molloy, the way my pa told me, let his ambitions reshape his sense of right and wrong, and over time Sean moved up in O'Banion's mob from driver to enforcer to all-around hooligan."

Max paused to take the second bite of his George Hamilton. By the length left, Jack estimated that for Max a hot dog took three bites. When the waitress came by, Max, busy chewing, hand signaled for another Hamilton dog.

Jack picked up the second half of his Bogey, a dill rye sandwich made with meat loaf cooked with cut up carrots and mixed-in cheese and layered with slices of bread-and-butter pickles. Along with the sandwich the place served pan-fried, diced new potatoes that Max explained in South Ireland were called English Queens.

"Wasn't O'Banion the competing bootlegger Al Capone had gunned down in a flower shop?"

"That'd be O'Banion." Max's second dog arrived and he set to dressing it while he talked. "In the mid-twenties, three killers, probably out-of-town talent so they wouldn't be recognized, walked into O'Banion's flower shop like they was customers. One guy shook O'Banion's hand to keep him from drawing his piece while the other two pumped O'Banion full of lead. After that, our papas went to work for Bugs Moran, a half Irishman who took over O'Banion's mob.

"In twenty-nine, Capone came after Moran by engineering what the press called the St. Valentine's Day Massacre. They killed off a bunch of his boys but missed Moran, who wasn't at the scene. It finished Moran as a big shot though. Patrick's daddy, Sean, got killed in a gun fight in '42. Patrick, still a wee lad, never remembered his pa. My pa kept on as Bugs Moran's chauffeur until Moran left Chicago for Ohio. That's when we all came to DC. My pa died about fifteen years ago; the doc labeled it natural causes."

Jack moved his sandwich back from his mouth.

"I've seen pictures of Mayor Molloy with an old man identified as his father. Is he a stepfather?"

Max talked around bite one of dog two. "That'd be Patrick's uncle, Liam, his pa's younger brother. The mayor and his momma came to live with Liam after Sean went down for the count in Chi-town. Liam's old; he must be, I don't know, ninety maybe. He's a good man. He's raised Patrick as his own. To Patrick and the world his uncle is his papa."

Max inserted bite two of dog two while Jack asked, "Why did your families pick DC?"

Jack waited while Max chewed and washed the bite down with a gulp of his red ale.

"The mayor's ma picked DC 'cause Liam lived here and he would take 'em in, that simple. As for my folks, my ma wanted my pa out of the rackets. DC got 'im away from the Irish hooligans in both Chicago and New York."

Jack dropped his napkin in his plate and pushed it aside. "Is your mother still alive?"

"No," Max said with his eyes shut. "Momma, God rest her soul, was the last of the adults in my family to be born and raised in the land of our ancestors. She grew up in Ireland and then lived in Scotland with my pa before they came to the States. I have no brothers or sisters, and my Colleen could not carry a child." His voice got distant. "We talked about adopting, but never got it done. I don't expect to be procreating— how's that for a big word—at my age, so, unless I got a relative the family never spoke about, I'm the last of the Logans."

"The last and the best." Jack raised his glass. "Answer this one from your gut. Could the mayor be involved in blackmail and murder, or is he just another politician cutting deals that dance back and forth across the law line?"

Max used his finger to wipe mustard from his upper lip. "Don't rightly know." He looked at his finger. "The Patrick I knew would want no part of it, but the man may not be the boy." He licked the mustard from his finger. "Boss, can I ask you something?"

"Sure."

"We got lots of folks auditioning for the role of blackmailer. I figure you're trying Tyson, Engels, and Donny on for size, and from what you're asking, maybe even Mayor Molloy. I mean no disrespect, but have you considered that Dr. Christopher Andujar could have been involved?" Max put up his hand. "I know the man meant a lot to you, but it's a valid question."

Jack picked up and nibbled the corner of the sandwich crust he had left on his plate. "Oh, it's valid, Max. I keep asking myself that very question and I just can't figure him being guilty."

Max raised his eyebrows. "You got anything more than emotion working here?"

"Yeah. I think so. If Chris was guilty, why commit suicide? At the time of his death the blackmailings were working like a well-oiled machine." Jack shrugged. "For him to be guilty he would have needed cohorts because somebody had to kill Haviland after Chris was dead."

"So he had accomplices."

"Damn it, there are just some people you know would not be involved in blackmail and murder. I've only known you a short while, but if someone asked me if Max Logan could be involved in a serious crime, I'd know you could not. Aren't there some people you just know that about? People on whom you'd bet it all?"

Max grinned. "If you're that sure about Dr. Andujar, boss, then I'll stand with you. What about Agnes Fuller? She had access to Chris's patient files and she has been in bed with Tyson. Literally. Still is, apparently. One of Chris Andujar's patients may have told him about being blackmailed over something that patient had only told Chris. Folks tell deep, dark shit to their shrinks. Chris might've reasoned it had to have been his secretary and set a trap, caught her and made her tell him what was going on. The shame of it might have driven him to commit suicide—or perhaps drove Tyson to murder Chris and the others to further cover his tracks."

Max poked a finger at Jack. "It would work pretty much the same if we substitute Donny Andujar for Ms. Fuller. The punk coulda finagled a copy of the key to his pa's office. If Dr. Andujar found out his son was blackmailing his patients that could explain Andujar's suicide. Now, in spite of all this, I still hold the opinion I told you the other day: Donny lacks the stones. So, I find myself coming back around to Ms. Fuller and her lover, Arthur Tyson. As for Haviland and the other two fugitives, while Tyson was with Metro, he was the Fed's contact man on warrants. That means Tyson could have located Haviland and agreed to not arrest him in return for getting inside Chris Andujar's office. The same thing could apply for them other shrinks."

"You've been giving this a lot of thought, Max."

"Ain't you heard, boss, the mind's a terrible thing to waste. 'Sides, I need something to chew on while sitting stakeouts at Donny's Club. I'm telling you, the how remains a guess, but Tyson's square in the middle of this thing. I just know it."

CHAPTER 36

JACK FOUND DONNY Andujar in a back booth. One of his nubile dancers sat across from him, her naked legs crossed, her translucent spiked heels revealing red painted toes.

"Hi, Donny. No, no, don't get up. Finish your food. We can talk right here, if the lady will excuse herself."

Donny leaned against the wall at the end of the booth and put his legs up across the bench seat as the dancer took hers down. "If I don't eat by five," he said, "we get too busy and I end up going hungry." Sticking out from under his Levi's was today's selection of squaretoed boots: black, polished snakeskin with scuffed toes. He took off his NBA Washington Wizards' cap, and looked at the dancer who still stood at the end of the booth. "Go powder your nose, honey. You're up in a few minutes."

Jack slid into the booth on the side she had vacated. The seat was still warm.

"Sorry to hear about Phoebe Ziegler buying it. The cops left here about an hour ago."

Jack could smell Donny's too-spicy aftershave. "I'm surprised they didn't arrest you."

"Shit, McCall, I had nothing to do with Phoebe getting offed. Thanks to you she would only do laps, but we would have gotten her on her back again. Once these broads round their heels for money, they never stop. Hey, it's the American dream—earn lots of dough doing work you enjoy."

"You're a good man, Charlie Brown."

"Don't preach me, McCall." He pushed the sleeves on his tan shirt higher on his forearms. "It takes all kinds. Phoebe Ziegler was Jena Moves, not some artsy-fartsy broad. She just hadn't quite come to grips with who she was. Now, enough about that, what brings you here?"

Donny had gotten part of it right. Preaching wasn't Jack's work. "Which of your girls will be the Mayor Molloy replacement for Jena Moves?"

Donny put his fork down. "You know about that?"

"Yep."

"We've been encouraging His Honor to let the girls ... try out. Competition's good right? Sweet Connie, the one with me when you came in, is penciled in to be the first applicant." Donny's shoulders shook while he chuckled at his own sick wit. "The mayor likes the girl-next-door look and there aren't too many of those in this business. Can I get you a beer? Something to eat?"

Jack had eaten with Max, but a shared meal aided conversation. He glanced at the menu and pointed to the all-American meal: a burger, fries, and the house cola.

When Donny held a lever on somebody, he expected them to play ball. Holding Donny's confession meant Jack held the lever, so it was Donny's turn to play ball.

"Phoebe Ziegler told me she first got on her back with a harmless, meek-and-mild guy. That you pushed her to do it even left her a note with a thou as payment. What made that guy so important?"

In other words, did you know about the art heist?

Donny spread his palms and grinned. "We make a bit extra when one of the girls satisfies a customer. Jena didn't just have a bitching bod, she had the face. The innocence. So we wanted to get her started. Call it my contribution to upward mobility in America. She told me about that note; I didn't leave it."

They stopped talking when Sweet Connie brought Jack's meal. The skimpy food-service outfit she wore put more in front of Jack than just the burger he had ordered.

"Do you know why we call her Sweet Connie?" Donny asked after she had left.

"Nope," Jack replied, with contrived curiosity.

"She's the color of semisweet chocolate. At first that's what we called her—Semisweet Connie—over time it got shortened."

"Phoebe gave me the note," Jack said, bringing the conversation back to his reason for being there. "The experts tell us it and your confession, which I watched you type, were both prepared on that old IBM in your office. So, let's try it again. Why did you push Phoebe toward the meek guy?"

Donny motioned downward with his hands and lowered his voice. "All right. All right. Keep your voice down. The other girls don't need that kind of persuasion. But they'd love the dough. Okay. Sure. We paid her. The mayor's always wanting to fuck Dorothy from Kansas—without her dog Toto." He laughed again, enjoying his self-entertainment.

"Give."

"Don't you have any sense of humor, McCall?"

While he chewed, Jack rotated his hand for get-on-with-it.

"I didn't have Dorothy from Kansas. The closest piece I had was Phoebe from Colorado, so we needed to get her going. We just figured meek and mild would be perfect for her first money fuck."

Jack took a bite of his burger and watched Sweet Connie peel off her server's uniform before stepping onto the raised stage. It was her turn to display her terpsichorean talents.

"Twice you've referred to 'we.' Did you end up with Tittle's partners after the cops shut his joint?" Jack held up a french fry. "A warning before you answer: I got a good idea of what names you should be giving me here, so don't try to foul this one off. Who's the we?"

The men playing pool stopped when Connie walked over to the pole on the stage, pulled herself upside down, and held her position by wrapping a leg around the pole. Her stiletto heels were long enough to each hold four skewered marshmallows. When she began to move down the pole, a guy sitting against the stage stopped his beer pitcher in midair, and then slowly lowered it in a cadence matching her slide.

Jack cleared his throat and willed his eyes from the stage. "Donny, I've been keeping my end of our bargain but," he tapped the end of his finger on the table and then raised it to point directly at Donny. "If you try shitting me now, our deal's history."

There's a saying for the critical point in negotiations: The next person who speaks loses, so Jack stayed busy eating one greasy fry after another while staring at Donny. He wasn't about to ignore the wisdom of America's top salespeople.

"Art Tyson. He's a partner, off the books."

Jack stayed stoic. "Good start. Continue." The salesperson's creed had worked once, so Jack dragged a long fry through the puddle of catsup on his plate and waited. The bar delivered another drink before Donny spoke again.

"Troy Engels. Christ, McCall," he contorted his face, "don't make that an issue. I can't stand the fag fuck, but I can't handle heat from the Feds. Engels owned a piece of Tittle's. He came with Tyson. They each hold fifteen percent."

"So that's why Engels keeps his ear to the ground for anything that might affect your club?"

"Yeah. I never blackmailed him over the pictures of him and Dad. He doesn't even know I got 'em. Had them. You got 'em now."

"You don't know how lucky you are you didn't try extorting Assistant Director Engels. He would have had you for lunch and spit out the seeds. Who else has a piece?"

Sweet Connie strolled to the end of the stage nearest Jack, locked her eyes on him and, to the words of the wonderful Cole Porter song, *Love for Sale*, executed a couple of bumps and grinds that would have sent any normal woman to a chiropractor. After that her hips took a well-earned rest while her hands traveled up her thighs and over her breasts.

Donny lowered his gaze and shrugged. "I don't know the identity of the third guy. Engels says he doesn't even know. Tyson and Engels own thirty percent, I have fifty-five. Someone else holds the other fifteen. Only Tyson knows. He distributes that investor's cut along with the payoff money. I'm not blowing smoke here. The mayor's a guess. I don't know."

Jack let Donny foul off that pitch and came back with another: "Now that you've told me about Tyson and Engels, I'll give you one chance to revise your answer about who wanted Ms. Ziegler to seduce Randolph Harkin."

"Tyson pushed it. His exact words were, 'Jena has half your regulars pounding their puds.'" Donny used one hand in a pumping motion. "Tyson kept saying, 'Push Jena at old-man Harkin, the guy's a pipsqueak from some art joint, and Jena digs art. Get her on her back once and we've got a new cash register with legs.' If Tyson had another reason, he never told me."

"And she fit the mayor's criteria," Jack said, "the non bimbo girl next door."

"Yeah. The mayor likes to pretend it's something other than a bought piece of tail. Sweet Connie is pretty clean cut, but she's an air-head next to Jena. Truth is, I miss Jena. I never even got my turn."

"You're a good man, Donny, sentimental and all. When's the last time you saw your mother?"

Connie had finished her stage duties and was wiggling back into her server's outfit when she caught a signal from Donny to bring another beer.

"I went over for dinner last night ... You know that she still hasn't cleaned out Dad's bedroom. His clothes are still in the closet." He rolled his eyes. "That whole scene is really weird, man."

"Give your mother some time. She has to get used to your dad being gone before she can put him out of the house emotionally."

"I'm telling you, McCall, my mother emasculated daddy to the point he turned fag. Did everything but cut off his balls."

Jack frowned, but let the comment go. "Tyson was Tittle's bag man. Now he does it for you, but he's been off the police force for years. What good is Tyson to you now?"

"Tyson still knows the older cops and with their help he meets the younger ones." Donny turned his palm up and rubbed his thumb across his finger tips. "He says it's actually easier to pass the green without being on the force. And, like at Tittle's, Tyson's the front man for the phantom investor."

Jack thought top sales professionals called his next move a presumptive close. "Let's go to your office. I want to look at your payoff book."

"No can do, Mr. M." Donny exchanged his under and upper boots as if he were flipping one of his burgers. "Don't have a book. Luke Tittle kept records of payoffs and IOUs.

It got him killed. Tyson keeps it all in his head. I don't even know who gets the cash. That's our deal. It gives Tyson his power. I give the dough to Tyson and the authorities leave us alone, so he's making it happen."

Sweet Connie couldn't stop doting on Donny. This time she came to clear away the dishes and offer more drinks. Jack waved her off. Donny watched as she walked over and bent down to put the dirty dishes into the tray under the end of the bar. Her hair, sprayed as hard as a football helmet, moved as one unit.

"She's Tyson's favorite. But his girlfriend, some wrinkled old prune, I don't know her name, preferred Jena for their threesomes. Tyson saves Sweet Connie for when he wants to go one-on-one."

"Donny, have you considered that Sweet Connie may be spying for Tyson? She seems very interested in what we're saying, and their one-on-ones would provide cover when she reports to him."

Sweet Connie put another beer down in front of Donny. He ran the back of his fingers up and down the stubble on his cheek, perhaps considering Sweet Connie in a new light.

"What about you?" Jack asked. "You staying in this racket?"

"The money's great and my partners would be pissed if I bailed. Someday I'll move on. But not as long as the law leaves me alone."

"I'll bet Luke Tittle felt that same way."

Sergeant Suggs called the moment Jack walked through MI's door. His preliminary analysis of Phoebe Ziegler's death had been, as he put it, "right on the money." The M.E. reported she had been partially strangled several times before being killed. Phoebe had also engaged in forced sex before she died, and the tests confirmed it had been the biker, Rockton. Cause of death: asphyxiation.

A fancy word for having the life choked out of you.

Jack stuck his head into Nora's office to tell her about Suggs's call. She told him he had just missed a call from Eric Dunn. "He said to tell you Dorothy Wingate has had no more contact from the blackmailer."

Jack went back to his office. A few minutes later he heard Nora's footsteps. Then she swept through his doorway, eyes wide, strawberry-blond hair bouncing. Her arms were filled with department store boxes.

"Have you thought anymore," he asked, "about our using that tap on your phone to pull this guy out of hiding?"

She put the boxes on one of the chairs. "I don't see how we can force anything there. I mean, you could call me and we could discuss something that might encourage him to stick his head out far enough for us to chop it off. But it would be hard to properly time the trap we set because we don't know when he'll next come to pick up his recording CD. Drummy's camera will eventually give us his picture or somebody who works for him. Then again, this guy's pretty cautious so he could decide that hearing my doings might not be important enough to risk being seen, but why would he set it up if he wasn't going to come get it. So, as you can see, on that angle he's in control, not us. I will tell you that having listening devices inside my house cramps my style a little," she wiggled her hips, "but business before pleasure. Now, an angle we control is my going to see Dr. Karros to dangle a big payoff in front of the blackmailer."

Jack agreed.

Nora started opening the boxes before asking, "Would you like to see the new outfit I got for my appointment with Dr. Karros?"

"Sure," Jack said after she had already yanked the taped tissue paper free and folded it back.

"A friend is going to help me with my hair. We're going for that just got out of a passionate-bed look. I'm using the name Candice Robson—my friends call me Candy."

"How'd you pick that name?"

"It makes me sound kinda like a centerfold babe, don't you think?" She grinned.

Jack smiled but kept his thoughts to himself.

Nora held the dress just below her bust while dangling a new pair of patent leather, open-toed high-heeled shoes from the fingers of her other hand. The dress had a high bottom and a low top. "I'll paint my toenails after my hair's done." She put down the shoes and held up a matching handbag. "All business expenses, of course."

"Of course," Jack replied, with a gentle shake of his head.

She laid the dress across the open box and modeled a shiny black hat with a wide brim. Then she held up a Beretta Tomcat, thirty-two caliber pistol, saying, "And no modern girl's outfit is complete without a pretty-woman gun."

After Nora left his office Jack tried to picture how she would look dolled up as Candy Robson—no doubt more stimulating than Sweet Connie.

CHAPTER 37

NORA PLUMPED UP her breasts using her fingertips, checked to be sure her pretty-woman gun didn't bulge her soft fabric purse, popped a piece of gum in her mouth, tossed her head back to capture a little attitude, and opened the door to the office of John Karros, Doctor of Psychiatry.

The receptionist sat behind her desk in a sleeveless dress, eating from a bowl of what looked to be plain yogurt sprinkled with crushed Oreos—a health food and pig-out meal rolled into one. Despite her unusual eating habits, she was a solid woman with bodybuilder biceps. She picked up her intercom line.

"Ms. Candice Robson is here for your ten-thirty, doctor."

A moment later, a door opened off to the side of the receptionist's desk. "I'm Dr. Karros. Please come in, Ms. Robson." He held the door open causing her to turn slightly to move past him. He appeared to be in his mid-forties and was fashionably dressed with a splash of expensive cologne.

She sensed his eyes on her fanny as she walked deeper into his office.

"Please take a seat, wherever you'll be comfortable."

Nora chose a chair not visually blocked by his desk. Dr. Karros took the chair across from her and crossed his legs, taking a moment to straighten the crease in his pleated taupe trouser leg.

"My receptionist tells me you called yesterday and got an appointment for this morning. Why don't you begin by telling me why we had to meet so quickly?"

Nora took two chews on her gum and wriggled in her chair; the doctor watched the jiggle in her abundant cleavage. "Well, Dr. Karros, I'm from Jackson Hole. That's the Jackson Hole in Wyoming. I come to DC once a year, and also the Big Apple, that's New York City, once a year. I tell the folks back home the trips are about visiting museums and historic buildings, but the truth is I come to kick up my heels and have a good time."

"Were you born in Jackson Hole?"

"Oh, gosh, no. My folk's place, where I was born, was a little dirt-water town outside Jackson Hole, so tiny you'd miss it if you blinked driving through. I met my old man in the local tavern where I worked and he drank. My husband, a much older man than me, died a few years ago. Anyways, he left me about four million in bonds and cash. I always envied them rich folks living in the Hole, so I moved into town and started getting involved in civic stuff."

"I see."

She crossed her legs. "I'm a single woman now. Well, actually a widow." She stood, put her hands on her hips, and turned in a tight circle being careful to keep the brim of her hat between her face and the camera position Jack had described. "I can't wear no outfits like this back home. You like it?"

"It's very nice, Ms. Robson." He smiled. "But how does all this bring you to me?"

Nora leaned forward as she retook her seat. "Well, Doctor, you help folks with their thinking, don't you? I mean, folks who are troubled by somethin' in their past, things that's keeping them awake nights. Stuff like that. Right?"

"You could say it that way. Yes."

"Good. Now, I can't be talking about this to nobody in Jackson Hole. I head back there in a few days. Anyways, that's why I needed your help right now. Today."

"Then we should get started. Be assured whatever you say is confidential."

"It's like this." She put her hands flat on her lap, letting her thumbs circle down the inside line of her thighs. "Four days ago I was driving down some street. I don't remember the name of the street, not sure I ever knew it. Anyways, some old lady just comes out in front of me. I mean like right in front of me. In the middle of the block, not in no crosswalk where she shoulda been. Anyways, I hit her. That is, my car hit her."

"Was she all right?"

"I didn't stick around, but I doubt it. I felt the bumps. My car went all the way over her. It scared me so I kept going. There were people around who coulda done anything I coulda done. The papers said she died."

"What have you done since?"

"I had my friend's car steam-cleaned; I forgot to tell ya, I was driving his car, not my rental." She crossed her arms below her breasts and shuddered; he watched. "I feel like a criminal, Dr. Karros, and it weren't my fault. She shoulda been in the crosswalk."

Karros uncrossed his legs, this time without concern for the creases in his trousers.

Nora put her fingers to her lips and stretched her chewing gum out from her teeth that held the other end. "The article in the paper said she was eighty-two and had that Alzheimer thing. So the old lady probably didn't know what happened anyways." Nora shrugged dismissively. "I mean, if my mind went, I doubt I'd wanna live. Heck, she just mighta been glad it happened. Anyways, that's what I need you to do. Make it get out of my head." Nora ended her statement with a perfunctory nod.

Dr. Karros's eyes widened. "It doesn't work like that, Ms. Robson. Have you considered talking to the police?"

"Lord no." She popped her gum. "If that old woman's family were to find out I had a healthy chunk of change, they'd sue me and take it all. Then how would I live? I ain't going back to hustling drinks. I mean, it's not like I meant to hit the old broad. Besides, like I said, she shoulda been in the crosswalk." Nora hung her head and waited for Karros to ask more.

He ran his fingertips through the hair above his ear. "Where were you coming from when you hit her?"

"Now that's a bit embarrassing to talk about."

"Everything you say is confidential. It might help me figure how I can help you."

"Well, okay. I was out the night before partying some. You understand. I spent the night in a hotel, don't remember which one. I was with some other folks. I got us the penthouse. We stayed up almost all night. When I came to, everyone had split. Don't you go misunderstanding now. I was always faithful to my old man. But now he's gone, so what's the harm in me having some real fun a couple of weeks a year when I get outta Jackson Hole?"

She pursed her lips, then continued. "Anyways, in the mornin' I headed back to where I'm staying with a friend. A man friend. He don't like me giving out his name or nothing, so you gotta use this here cell phone number." She snapped open her purse, slid a piece of paper part way out, and read him the number.

"I believe my receptionist has your number."

"Oh, yeah. I forgot. So, whatdaya think? Can you give me a pill? Maybe a shot. Or one of them exercise things they do in the horror movies? Hypnotize me. Something?"

Dr. Karros closed his eyes for a moment. "What you're feeling isn't a symptom that a pill can stop. What's keeping you awake is your inner voice telling you to take responsibility for your part in what happened."

Nora made a tisking sound with her tongue against the roof of her mouth. "Didn't you hear me, Doc? It'd cost me big time. I can't be taking that chance. I mean, the old lady weren't no healthy mother with young'ns to raise. Her life was about over anyways."

They sat looking at each other until Nora suddenly stood and huffed. "Dr. Karros, I'm disappointed. Truly, I am. I thought you was reputable. I mean, the yellow pages says you are. I'll never come back or send any of my friends." She reached for the doorknob and then turned back. "That confidential thing still goes, right?"

"Right."

She stomped out, wagging her behind.

CHAPTER 38

"JACK, SOME GUY named Dean Trowbridge is on hold," Mary Lou said. "He's angry, yelling and demanding to speak with you. He claims he's Allison Trowbridge's father."

Allison Trowbridge was the patient of Chris Andujar Nora had called on without being expected. Jack had been guessing Ms. Trowbridge may have been blackmailed over an IOU from Luke Tittle's casino. If he had that right, it would establish that Tittle's records had not been lost.

"Mr. Trowbridge. Jack McCall. How may I be of help?" Nora had stepped in Jack's office when she heard Mary Lou say the name Trowbridge.

His voice sounded like a load of gravel sliding off the back of a truck. "Mr. McCall, do you know who I am?"

"Mr. Dean Trowbridge, father of Allison Trowbridge. At least that's the name you gave when you called. Who are you?"

"I am Dean Trowbridge, a member of the board of directors of First International Bancorp and a major owner of real estate in and around the District of Columbia."

"Mark me down as impressed, Mr. Trowbridge, if that's who you are. Now, what can I do for you?" Jack wanted to stick a pin in the stuffed shirt, but decided it would be best to first learn whether Trowbridge would admit or deny Jack's suspicion.

"One of your detectives came to my daughter Allison's home a few days ago. I demand you leave her alone."

"Listen. First off, I don't know you are Dean Trowbridge. Until I do, I'll not discuss this with you. If you are who you say and this is important to you, come down here and show your identification. Then we'll talk. If you are Allison's father, you know what I'm saying is for her protection. Anyone could claim to be you on the phone." Jack put his hand over the mouthpiece and said, "Let's find out how concerned he is."

"I'm not used to being spoken to in that manner, Mr. McCall." Jack moved the phone from his ear when Trowbridge raised his voice. "I've been an advisor to the last three presidents."

"Then call one of them, but if you wish to talk with me, you have my conditions. Call back when you're ready to meet them." Jack hung up confident the passion he had heard over the phone would not allow Trowbridge to let the matter drop.

Max, who had walked in just before Jack hung up, said, "A progress report, boss. The owners of Clark's Janitorial go to and from work. Other than that, they've gone out to dinner and a movie. Donny's routine remains the same. He works, and every few days a different one of his dancers waltzes him home." Max groaned gleefully. "This fellow has captured the real meaning of being an equal opportunity employer. I gave Nora all the written reports and the time sheets for my crew, and the pictures we've taken. I don't believe there's anything there that would interest you. Do we keep it up?" He unscrewed the cap off a bottle of spring water and took a drink.

"Keep it up on Donny. Drop the Clarks and put that manpower on Art Tyson. He'll be more adept at spotting a tail. If we're lucky, he's arrogant enough not to notice. And be sure to use men who are not chummy with Tyson."

Mary Lou stuck her head through the door. "Mr. Trowbridge is back on the phone."

Jack put the call on a speaker phone. "Mr. Trowbridge, when would you like to come in?"

"If you'll send a car, I'll come now. I don't appreciate your style, Mr. McCall, but your point regarding whether or not I am Dean Trowbridge is valid."

"Thank you for that, sir, but we don't have cars and drivers to pick people up. You'll have to get here on your own."

"I don't drive myself and I won't ride in a common taxi. My chauffeur has my limo in for servicing. It's urgent that we talk."

Max signaled that he would go.

"I'll send Max Logan," Jack said. "Mr. Logan is a detective in our firm. He is not a chauffeur, so don't expect him to kowtow."

"I will even open the door to his automobile myself, Mr. McCall. I'll be ready in two hours. I gave my address to your receptionist. Is that agreeable?"

"Mr. Logan will ask for your identification after you get in his car, before he begins to drive." Jack looked up at Max and grinned. "Mr. Logan will be there in two hours."

"Trowbridge is here, boss," Max said. "I put him in the small conference room up front. I ain't never seen a man more full of himself than this jerk-off. Like you suggested, I let him open the car door himself. He pushed it open with the side of his hand, as though doing so would somehow soil him. On the way here he ran his mouth about why he's a blue-blooded American."

"Describe him."

"Had a face lift—too few wrinkles and no eye bags, white hair, trimmed eyebrows, brown eyes, and Clark Kent glasses. I'd put him at six feet with a drinker's gut, and tiny everywhere else. Hands are heavily arthritic. He's wearing a black custom-made suit, and a white shirt with black accessories. And he's as nervous as a blind cat in a room full of rocking chairs."

"Socks?"

"Now, you're testing me, boss. They was gray. He holds 'em up with them little garter belts for men. When we got here, I surprised him by opening his door. He flashed 'em when he stepped out."

Jack grinned and motioned for Max to take a seat. "I think his daughter's been blackmailed over IOUs to Luke Tittle. Were you familiar with Luke's Place?"

"As a cop and a time or two as a customer, they poured my favorite Irish."

"Give me an overview of his joint."

"Weren't no joint."

Eric Dunn had made that same point.

"Luke's Place was one of the Beltway's fanciest. He also ran a small, classy backroom casino offering roulette, craps, and blackjack every night. Tuesdays and Fridays featured high-stakes poker. No slots. Only serious, well-heeled gamblers walked the red carpet into Tittle's backroom."

"The police give him trouble?"

"Nope. Luke's had a reputation for being safe for the wealthy with the weakness. The fix was in. We never raided the place until after Harry Mandrake became chief."

Jack put his hand on Max's shoulder. "Come in with me. I'd like your read on this guy's story."

"And yank his chain by having the driver sit in."

Jack laughed. "That too. This guy's used to having his own way, so let's keep him a little off balance. We need to establish that he's not in charge."

"Like you done on the phone."

Jack nodded as they walked out of his office.

Mr. Trowbridge was holding his hat when Jack and Max entered, an unlit cigarette moving in the corner of his mouth like a fishing bobber in a choppy lake. He gave Jack the up-and-down look as if he were about to recommend a new haberdasher.

"Are you Jack McCall?"

"Yes. How do you do, Mr. Trowbridge."

"Your man here wouldn't let me smoke in his car. You mind?" He jutted out his jaw that held the white cylinder between his bleached teeth.

"Our office is nonsmoking."

Trowbridge jerked the cigarette from his lips and stuffed it into a silver case he took from his inside pocket.

Jack made a dismissive hand gesture. "I apologize for all this ID stuff. I had to be certain before discussing your daughter."

Trowbridge glared at Jack and cleared his throat. "May we speak in private?"

"This is as private as it gets. I need a witness as to who said what. Mr. Logan stays."

With that Max stepped over and offered to take Trowbridge's coat. The older man unbuttoned the front and turned with the familiar grace of one accustomed to having others remove his coat. "Please be careful," he said, "the coat's imported cashmere. I bought it last spring in London."

"I'll hang it on this here coat tree." Max pointed the hanger. "Would that be all right, sir?"

"Yes. Thank you, my good man."

Trowbridge made himself comfortable in a swivel chair, turning it just far enough to angle his back toward Max. He rested his elbows on the arms of the chair and intertwined his gnarly fingers.

"As much as it pains me to admit it, Mr. McCall, you were right. You had no way of knowing that I was *the* Dean Trowbridge." He cleared his throat and firmly pushed his glasses tight against his face. "I will not permit you to tape this conversation. I'm here to demand you cease harassing my daughter."

Jack sat still for a moment before saying, "Our meeting is not being taped. Mr. Trowbridge, you're a successful man. I respect your accomplishments, but knock off the demanding. That style doesn't work here."

The two men stared at one another until the old man looked down. Jack took on a presumptive air to cover what was in large part a guess. "We know you paid off when Allison was blackmailed for her activities in Luke Tittle's place a few years back. It is not our intent to disclose any of that to anyone. We need you to tell us what you know about the blackmailer and how it went down."

"Mr. McCall, do I have your assurance this will remain confidential?"

"Yes, unless I need to tell the authorities to prevent others from being blackmailed, or to catch and convict the blackmailer."

Trowbridge took off his glasses, rubbed his eyes and put the glasses back on. "All right," he said. "On the conditions you stated. In the event you release what I am about to tell you without it being necessary, I will sue you, sir. As for Mr. Logan here, he's of no consequence. I can have a dozen people, all with better pedigrees, swear I was somewhere else at whatever time you claim I was here. My driver is right this moment parked outside a building where I am having that meeting with that dozen people; and he will so swear. Do we understand each other, Mr. McCall?" Trowbridge took on the look of a coyote secreted near a rabbit hole.

Jack decided to let Trowbridge have his little king-of-hill feeling. The man might be more open feeling that he had gained some measure of protection over what he was about to say.

"You are a businessman of considerable success," Jack began. "You've sat in on a lifetime of important meetings and negotiations where you had to hear what was said by voice and body language, even nuances. I want you to draw on those skills when recalling your talks with the blackmailer. Tell me what he said and what you heard without him saying it. Okay?"

"All right."

Trowbridge spread his fingers before laying the flats of his hands on the conference table and looking into Jack's eyes. "As you've implied, Allison gambled in Tittle's backroom. She drank heavily and lost heavily. She didn't know how to do either, but, well, young people often rebel through such behavior, don't they?"

"Some. What's relevant is that Allison did."

Trowbridge frowned. "The blackmailer called on my private line in the study of my home, a number I had given to only a few in my inner circle. He said he held Allison's markers totaling a quarter of a million. He demanded payment or he would turn them over to the press." Trowbridge coughed up something, and then swallowed. "I paid. He returned the IOUs."

"Come now, Mr. Trowbridge. We both know Tittle would not publicly acknowledge his illegal activities, but, even if he did, the press would have written it as the gangster Tittle taking advantage of an impetuous young woman. You're a wealthy and savvy man. From what you've told me, you would not have paid the blackmailer."

The lines in Trowbridge's face leaked sweat. He swiped at a bead running down his cheek and again pushed his black-rimmed glasses tight against his face.

"There were also some pictures of Allison ... being com-promised by Tittle and some of his cronies. I paid to get back her IOUs and those damnable pictures." He pulled off his glasses, tossed them onto the table, and irritably swiped his damp eyes.

"Did you get them?"

"Yes. I thank the blackmailer for being a man of his word and for his respectful manner. I'd also like to thank whoever killed that bastard Luke Tittle."

"Tell me what your daughter told you about that night. As precisely as you remember."

"She said. 'I got wasted.' She kept losing at the table and they kept bringing her drinks. After she had lost more than she realized, Tittle told her if she didn't do what he demanded, he'd come to me. She didn't know what to do; she did what Tittle told her. After she told me that, she got up, ran for her bedroom, and slammed the door. A few minutes later I heard her regurgitate into the water closet."

"You mean throw up in the toilet?" Max asked.

"Yes, Mr. Logan, if you insist on being tawdry." Trowbridge shifted in his chair, recrossed his legs and then ran the flat of his hand down the front of his shirt.

"Okay," Jack said, "let's get back to what happened. Tell me about his voice."

"He spoke with a lisp the first time. But he used proper grammar and was well mannered."

"The first time? You heard from him again?"

"Yes and I immediately presumed he was calling for more money."

"Wasn't he?"

"No."

"Then why?"

"To tell me I could pick up the IOUs and those execrable pictures in the same place I had left what he referred to as 'your contribution.' It was no such thing; I assure you. It was an illegal exaction. Then the scoundrel laughed and said, 'You don't think I'm honorable enough to keep my word? As I promised, you will never hear from me again.'"

"And you haven't?"

"Not a word."

"Tell me more about his voice? He had a lisp, and—"

"He did not have a lisp. He spoke as if he did during the first call. During his second call he dropped the fake lisp. Instead he held one of those units against his throat that allows people with damaged voice boxes to speak through the aid of vibrations. The only common element during the two calls was that he remained well mannered."

"Put a timeline on these events?"

"The blackmailer's initial call was a year and a half ago. That's when I first learned of Allison's, shall we say, unladylike behavior. About nine months ago the cur called the second time for the purpose I explained a moment ago. That long wait was excruciating, but we had no alternative but to sit tight. To his credit, the blackmailer kept his word."

"Any other contact?"

"None."

"Do you still have the pictures so we can identify the men?"

"I burned those horrid pictures in my fireplace, then I scooped up the ashes and, as Mr. Logan would describe the activity, flushed them down the toilet." He touched his mouth and ran his tongue across his lips.

"What about the IOUs?"

"I disposed of them in the same manner."

"Mr. Trowbridge," Max said, "did you pay before or after Allison started her sessions with Dr. Andujar?"

"Before."

"Are you certain of that sequence?" Jack asked.

"Yes. For quite some time Allison insisted she could deal with it alone, but she became a recluse. A week after we recovered the pictures, I convinced her to see Dr. Andujar."

Jack looked at Max, who nodded slightly. Tittle's records had somehow gotten into the hands of the blackmailer. And the blackmailer had not learned about Allison through her sessions with Chris Andujar.

"How did you select Dr. Andujar?" Max asked.

"I got his name from a friend."

"Who?" Max asked.

"Dorothy Wingate. She had gone to Andujar for years. Swore by him."

Jack came back into the conversation. "Is there anything else we should know?"

"I've told you everything, Mr. McCall. I should be going now."

"Mr. Logan will drive you back to where he picked you up."

Max held up Mr. Trowbridge's imported cashmere coat.

Nora dashed into Jack's office. "I've been waiting for you to get free."

"Wassup?"

"I've found the forger," she exclaimed, bouncing up and down on her toes.

Jack watched her bounce a moment longer before asking, "How long are you going to keep me in suspense?"

"Herman Flood, he's one of the portrait painters on Harkin's list. He lives and paints in New York City, in Manhattan. I told him I was the wife of the unnamed man who bought his paintings of Lincoln, Garfield, McKinley, and Kennedy. He freely confirmed painting them."

"What else?" Jack asked while watching her shift her legs to a sort of parade rest stance, tightening her skirt across her thighs.

"Nothing else. At that point I quit talking. I didn't want to risk saying something that wouldn't match up. I said we were the Millers, and we needed portraits of our directors to hang in the boardroom. We have an appointment for tomorrow morning at eight in his studio. I made our reservations at the Novatel Hotel in Manhattan. I figured we'd drive; it's about four-hours. I also made dinner reservations at Gallagher's Steak House, next door to the hotel."

Nora sauntered over, sat on the edge of Jack's desk and put a hand on her exposed knee. Then she gave what Jack assumed was a glimpse of the persona she had used during her meeting with Dr. Karros.

"Ms. Candy Robson from Jackson Hole would like you to take her to dinner in the Big Apple."

CHAPTER 39

ON THE WAY up in the elevator at the hotel in Manhattan, Jack again asked Nora if Drummy's camera outside her place had taken a picture of anyone coming to retrieve the recorder.

"No. I'm as anxious as you are, but so far, nothing. If the guy only knew about my salacious behavior, he'd have been there already." She rolled her eyes and smiled. "I'll check again as soon as we get back."

"If there's still nothing," Jack replied, "I'll have Drummy check the remote and the camera to be sure they're working."

When the elevator doors opened Nora turned to face Jack. "Candy will need a few minutes to get ready for dinner. She'll buzz you."

Jack rode up to his floor and went into his room. He wasn't sure what to expect from Nora as Candy Robson. One minute he was filled with hopes, even fantasies, and in the next minute crowded by reservations. Nora was his partner.

After a while, he called his office.

"McCall Investigations. Mary Lou speaking."

"It's Jack, anything shaking?" A moment later he heard a knock. "Hold on, Mary Lou, I think Nora's at the door." He put his hand over the mouthpiece. "Come in. It's unlocked."

"Hi there, big boy. My name's Candy Robson and I'm looking for a handsome hunk to take me to dinner."

She looked ravishing. He kept his hand over the mouthpiece and held the phone out. "I'm checking in with Mary Lou."

Nora walked over and stood in front of him and shimmied her shoulders, leaned in, and kissed the exposed side of his neck. He inhaled her perfume. His mouth inches from her cleavage.

He had forgotten the phone when Mary Lou startled him. "Nothing's happening here. Anything shaking there?" He mumbled something, then Mary Lou said, "Now you and Nora find some time for fun while you're in the Big Apple. You know, all work and no play."

"If you need us," Jack said, "you know the number. If you need someone fast, Max is on standby."

Jack hung up the phone. "Now stop that. Behave yourself."

Nora stopped.

"Who told you to stop?"

"Why you did, and tonight I'm yours to command."

She leaned in and kissed his neck again, then put her arms around his shoulders, her cleavage coming even closer to his face.

Jack hadn't been with a woman since Rachel died and his body was sending him past due notices, yet he was swamped by the feeling he would be cheating on his deceased wife.

"Stop!" He said too loudly and felt embarrassed. "We're ... we're going to be late for dinner."

In the elevator, Nora told Jack about the steakhouse. "Gallagher's has been here for, I don't know, a hundred years or something. The place was started by one of the Ziegfield girls named Gallagher. The walls are filled with autographed pictures of celebrities from Mayor Jimmy Walker, Mickey Mantle, and John Barrymore to the big names of today. And the food's great."

After being seated, they ordered martinis. Then reviewed their plan for handling the forger they would see in the morning. After chatting through dinner, he signed the credit voucher for their meal and emptied the second bottle of wine into their glasses.

Nora moved her glass and, without taking her eyes off Jack, crossed her arms below her breasts, making them rise even farther above her low-cut neckline. Then she reached out and put her hand on top of his. "Jack, we've been dancing around this long enough, and I've had enough to drink to say what's on my mind. Will you listen?"

"Yes."

Their faces were as close as possible, allowing for the disinterested table that stood between them.

"Rachel saved my life," Nora began, "neither of us will ever forget her. No one can ever replace her, but we both know Rachel would not want you to live without love." She stood and held out her hand. He took it and they left.

Jack unlocked the door to his hotel room and held it open. After they were inside, Nora closed the door and turned to face him. She approached him slowly, until she was standing right before him. Leisurely, she traced the curve of his neck with her fingers. She went up onto her tiptoes to have her lips trail over his ear, his cheek, and onto his mouth, teasing him with the tip of her tongue. Their lips met in all their glory. The kiss was not gentle, but hungry. A kiss crowded with promises. The air clouded with intimate feelings.

She backed away a few feet and turned slowly. "You haven't told me how you like me as Candy Robson?"

Jack sat in the chair off to the side of the bed, still uncertain how he felt about what was about to occur. "I like Nora Burke, but you do look delicious in that Candy dress."

She moved to other side of the bed, and slowly took off the dress. Beneath it she wore a red and black, satin and lace bustier with a see-through panty to match. Then there were her stockings. The back-seam, thigh-high nylons looked delicious on her. She walked around the bed dragging her dress beside her and dropped it on the floor next to his chair. She lowered her head and kissed him, a lingering wet kiss.

He reached up and put his hands on her.

After a few minutes, Nora stepped back, put one foot up on the bed, and slowly peeled off one of her nylons crowned by smooth white flesh, and draped it over the lamp on the dresser. Then she removed and draped the second stocking, casting the room in muted grayish light.

"Close your eyes," she said.

He could hear her moving about, but could not tell what she was doing.

"Open your eyes."

She was in bed, leaning into several pillows propped against the headboard, her reddish-blond hair outlining the side of her face. "Come over here," she said, patting the open sheets beside her.

On the way he passed the bustier and panties she had draped overtop the nylons, easing the grayish light into a soft pink. The top sheet covered the lower half of her body except for one exposed leg, her arms extended along the sides of her breasts. Her nipples awakened.

CHAPTER 40

HERMAN FLOOD'S STUDIO loft was atop an old
industrial building across from the Hudson River. The lobby
windows revealed hand-wiped smears wherever the sun
struck the glass. The wood paneled walls around the bank
of elevators wore dust the way peaches wore fuzz. Jack and
Nora stepped into an elevator which greeted them with an
indecipherable groan. Jack lowered its rough-hewn wood-
slatted door, and pressed the hard white button below a
hand-printed label that read: loft. When they stepped out at
the top, the deep-throated horn of a river barge hollered a
message understood by others who spoke boat.

The loft's hardwood floors were covered with row after
row of paintings leaning against high walls. The entire room
was awash in the brightness that poured through windows on
two sides and a peaked industrial skylight. One row of paintings was fronted by a colorful rendering of the city's night
lights reflecting off the river. Across from that a wonderful
capturing of the skyline of Manhattan, but mostly the room
was filled with portraits. A few of famous people, the rest
unknowns, older, weathered faces with lines like road maps
that foreshadowed their journeys, lessons learned, and pains
survived.

Herman Flood's painting skills far exceeded his selling skills.

Flood was older than sixty. He had small hands but a strong shake. He wore frail wire-framed glasses, a blue New York Giants T-shirt and a pair of jeans; both streaked with blotches of paint. His unruly white gossamer hair tossed like a salad of colors from his artist's palette.

The old man's warm smile towered over him as he shook hands with Nora. "How do you do, Mrs. Miller? I enjoyed speaking with you on the phone. Hello, Mr. Miller." He nodded slightly. "It's kind of you both to visit my studio. If you wish, look at my paintings. When you're finished, you can tell me about the portraits you want done."

"Your talent is obvious," Jack said. "May we sit over there?" He pointed toward a small couch and chair near the window.

Flood rushed ahead to remove two blank canvases from the couch and an open box of paints that sat on the small table; the box's loose flaps extending like ears listening in four directions.

"I have some sodas in the back. Would either of you like one?"

"Our names are not Miller, Mr. Flood," Jack began, ignoring the invitation. "This is Nora Burke. My name is Jack McCall. We're from McCall Investigations in Washington, D.C."

Flood's body sagged, and his face spoke confusion.

"You painted copies of four presidents from the originals that hung in the National Portrait Gallery. Your paintings have been swapped for those originals."

"Good Lord." Flood's eyes, rimmed by concentric wrinkles, flitted from Jack to Nora, then back to Jack. The artist put his hands to his face and mumbled through his fingers. "I didn't know. Maybe I suspected some at first ... Maybe I didn't want to know." He lowered his hands. "No. I did not know. I've had opportunities, plenty. I could have been wealthy." He gestured around. "Instead I live alone, an obscure painter, painting to live because I live to paint. It's what I do. It's who I am. But I'm a copyist, not a forger."

He sagged deeper into the chair, his hands again covering his face.

Nora pulled a little pointy paper cup free from the dispenser next to a large bottle of water and filled the cup. She touched Flood's slumping shoulder; he took the cup and drank.

"I've painted all my life. Now my work ends up being used as forgeries." He lowered his eyes.

Jack sat forward. "Mr. Flood, we aren't the police. In our eyes you're a victim, just like the National Portrait Gallery. We want you to help us find the criminal who conned you and stole four of America's art treasures."

"I'll help any way I can, but I must be guilty of something."

"Gullibility, for certain," Jack said. "But at times we've all been bitten by that bug. You are a painter, a master copyist, lied to by a master criminal. It's true you wanted the fee. The criminal counted on that."

"Wait a minute. My signatures were on the backs of the canvases. Isn't that how you found me?"

"Your signatures had been chemically removed."

He rubbed his arms as if he were cold. "I can't return the fee. I've used it to pay debts."

"Would you like another cup of water?"

"No, thank you, Mrs. Miller. Forgive me, Ms. Burke."

He got up and walked a path worn in the wooden floor planks by countless past walks by himself and those who had occupied the loft for decades before. When he reached the far side of the room, he gazed down into the river.

Jack went to him and spoke softly. "This is no longer about you. It's about finding the criminal. It's about recovering the portraits." He paused, hoping his comment had taken root. Then said, "Tell us about when he contacted you."

Flood paced as he talked. "The first call came about eighteen months ago. We discussed the assignment. The next morning I found an envelope under my door stuffed with fifty thousand dollars, half the agreed fee. He even threw in extra to cover the costs of the portrait transparencies I would need."

"Didn't the whole thing seem odd?" Nora asked.

"Sure. It seemed odd; it was odd. And I let him know that the next time he called. But the way he explained it, made it seem okay."

Jack, still standing by the window, asked, "What date did you find the envelope under your door?"

Flood reached onto a shelf behind him and picked up a black appointment book. He rambled on about the bills he had paid with the money while flipping the pages.

"The man told me about the limits of cash you can deposit into a bank without having to complete forms, and that I should keep most of it in cash. Ah, here they are. I got the first half of the fee on September sixteenth, the year before last. I made a few deposits from the seventeenth through the twenty-fifth, in several different accounts, and held the rest in cash."

"How did the caller explain the need for secrecy?"

"He told me right off that it was an odd assignment." Flood went to the water cooler and leaned his crossed arms over the top of the bottle. "He said his client was a wealthy businessman from the Middle East who loved America and did a lot of business with us. That some of the radical Islamist elements in his country were starting to accuse him of being too close to America."

Flood pulled free another cup, filled it with water, and drank it down. "The caller explained the portraits were of the four American presidents who had been assassinated in office. The Middle Eastern businessman planned to hang them in his palace. Then, when the radicals came, he could make incendiary statements. The only good American president is a dead president, like that. He'd then remind the extremists that he donated a part of his profits to help fund Islamic fundamentalism. It was all for show, he explained, so they would not see him as an American sympathizer."

"The good financier of terrorism," Jack snarled.

Flood raised his hands. "I didn't do it to aid terrorists. I'm just a simple painter." As if a puppeteer had relaxed the strings, his arms fell limp to his sides.

Jack had seen many American soldiers killed with weapons paid for by Middle Eastern businessmen who financed the terrorists while claiming to be moderates themselves. Entire governments in that part of the world played that game.

"What else?" Nora asked.

"The man would not give his name. We could not meet. He would make all payments in cash." Flood's face turned ashen. "It was weird. I grant you that, but it was plausible ... Wasn't it? He came through with the rest of the money."

"I'm not going to judge you." Jack said, in an unconvincing tone.

Nora took the lead to give Jack a moment to chill out. "Tell us about how you gave him the paintings and how you received the other half of your fee?"

Flood crushed the empty paper cup he still held. "I agreed to be finished in sixteen months. Believe me that was a breakneck pace. The paint must be layered and time is needed to let the paint age at several points in the process. He called this past January to confirm I was on schedule."

"Were you?" asked Nora.

"Yes." Flood said, continuing to squeeze the crumpled cup as if it were a hand-exercise ball. "We agreed I would deliver them on February sixteenth. He told me to cover my paintings in white paper and put them in the back of my van. I was to park at the Ritz Carlton on the Avenue of the Americas, just south of Central Park. He said, 'In hotel parking lots, people take things in and out of the backs of vehicles all the time. You will not raise anyone's attention if you do it exactly the way I'm telling you.'

"I was to park away from the hotel building, near other parked cars, but in a spot where the spaces on each side were empty. 'Get a duplicate key to your van,' he said, 'and lock all the doors. Put the original key on top of the right front tire and keep the duplicate key with you.'"

"Then what"

"He told me to walk south until I got to the Museum of Modern Art. I was to go inside for an hour and then walk back to my van. He promised to leave my other fifty thousand under the front seat. He made me repeat all his instructions about the hotel, the keys, and the museum."

"And he had left the rest of your fee?" Nora asked.

"Just as he promised. I remember taking a deep breath. If he had been a crook, he would have taken my paintings and not paid me. Wouldn't he? So, I figured his bizarre story had been true."

"Or he considered that you might call the cops, and his plan to substitute the forgeries for the originals would be scuttled. He couldn't cheat you without cheating himself."

"I didn't think of it that way, Mr. McCall. I didn't know he planned to swap them and steal the originals. I saw the rest of the money as validating the whole thing had been on the up and up." Flood tossed his balled up cup at the corner waste basket. It bounced off the wall and rolled under a chair. He came back and sat on the couch, turning to Nora. "You must not have had any trouble finding me. There are only a couple of other copyists capable of duplicating the artists' differing styles as well as being knowledgeable about the methods of trompe l'oeil."

"What?" Nora asked.

"Trompe l'oeil is the art of visual deception. It includes things such as creating the appearance of the cracks that time leaves in paint, and boring fake worm holes in frames. I did all that. I even oven-baked the copies to make them indistinguishable from the originals without thorough scientific examination."

"What else can you tell us about the man who hired you?" Jack asked, not caring about the technical art mumbo jumbo.

"Nothing." Flood raised his eyebrows. "The man had his paintings. I had my fee."

CHAPTER 41

COURTESY OF THE rising sun and New York's tall buildings, Jack drove out of Manhattan through alternating blasts of warm sun and cool shadows.

After a few nervous glances he looked right at Nora. "About last night—"

"It was good for me. How about you?"

"That's not what I meant. I mean—"

"Jack. You're an attractive man, and I'm a woman who claims the same rights men have enjoyed for eternity. It was clear you were struggling with your growing desires, and we're partners so we're supposed to help each other, right?"

"I don't think that falls within partnership duties."

"Hey, Jack. I wanted you. It's that simple. Helping you get over the hump and have sex again after losing Rachel was just an extra. Said plain, you had to be horny and I didn't want you falling into the wrong hands. Look. I'm not reading anything else into it. Okay?"

"I don't know what to say," Jack replied. "Thanks for the help. It was great. You're a gorgeous woman and a wonderful lover. All of that, but I don't want it to affect us working together. You know?"

Nora reached over and gently kneaded the short hair at the back of Jack's neck. "It won't, not unless you go and start getting silly about it. Look. Nothing has changed. Let's agree it was just a one-night stand."

The hum of cars reverberated as he drove through the Holland Tunnel. Coming out the other side, he asked, "Is that how you see last night?"

Right then the ringer on her Candy Robson phone played its melody. Nora answered and listened for a moment, then enunciated through silent lips, "It's the blackmailer," before speaking into the phone. "I'm driving, gimme a minute to pull over."

Jack stopped the car. She tilted the phone so they could both hear.

"Listen up, Candy Robson, you'll wanna hear this."

Jack heard Nora's taped voice give the details of a real hit and run killing that Nora had found in the police reports. He then heard her confess Candy Robson's guilt, her negligence, her heavy drinking prior to it, and to having fled the scene. Her words also showed a lack of concern for anything other than preserving her cash. In short, she had been a grade-A blackmail target. Jack gave her a thumbs-up for her performance.

"My God!" Nora shouted in Candy's ditsy voice. "That quack doctor promised me everything was confidential. How'd you find out? And just who in the blooming hell are you?"

"Shut the fuck up and listen good. I'm only gonna say this once. I want one million bucks, half in hundreds, the other half in fifties. No sequential bills. No new money. Put it in a black fabric sports bag and—"

"I don't got that kind of money." Nora said in the uneducated style of Candy Robson.

"Listen, rich bitch, that tape has the whole story. You didn't care about the old broad you flattened. You married your old man for his money and then fucked him to death, so cut the bullshit or I'll demand two million. Don't worry. You got plenty left."

"I've seen movies about blackmail. You'll never stop. You'll keep coming back for more."

"Quit whining. You gave up your options when you drove off after running down that old lady. You'll only pay me once. I won't come after you again."

"You leave me little choice. Where do I put my money?"

"Listen up. I won't repeat these instructions."

She and Jack pressed their heads together. Jack held the phone. Nora poised to take notes.

"You got tomorrah, Friday, to get the cash. On Sunday, put the bag with the mil in your trunk. At eleven A.M. sharp, park your car at the National Cathedral. It's way out Massachusetts Avenue. Take Wisconsin and turn just before the Episcopal Church House. Turn left at the parking sign and drive two-thirds of the way down. Angle-park on the left side near the tree with the black leaves. You'll see six cement steps leading up to a small grass area on the south side of the Cathedral."

"Slow down," Nora told the blackmailer, "I ain't no secretary."

The man waited a beat. "Do not arrive before eleven. It's now 6:04. I'll wait while you set your watch to that time; do it now." He paused, and then went on. "Follow the stone path that'll be ahead of you to the left, not the brick path that angles right. Continue past a small pool to an open-air fountain enclosed on three sides by a block wall. Face the fountain. Step onto the bench to your left and drop the bag over the wall." He paused again.

"Return to your car, but don't leave. From there, walk past your car to the long set of steps on your left. Walk up those fifty-one steps, cross the street, and continue up the stairs on the other side. That will take you to the south portal of the Cathedral. Enter. Stay one hour. Then leave by the northwest door. Walk back around to your car and go home to Jackson Hole. If you never return to DC, you'll never hear from me again. But if you return, ever, your pals in Wyoming will be going to your funeral.

"You'll be watched all the time. My gunman will have you in his scope. If you don't follow these orders to the letter, you're fucking dead. If you bring anyone with you or call the cops, I'll know, and this tape on which you confessed running down the lady will find its way to the same cops you talked to."

Before the sun rose Friday, Jack took Max and drove onto the grounds of the National Cathedral. Drummy had gone by to pick up Nora so he could check the remote and camera at her house before joining them at the cathedral. There still had been no pictures taken, but the equipment all checked out to be in proper working order.

The cathedral has a grandness crafted by past geniuses who, working without computers, had molded majesty into block and concrete.

The blackmailer would not be loitering at the cathedral two days before the payoff. Still, they all had dressed like tourists, wore hats, and carried cameras. They took lots of pictures to camouflage the ones they really wanted, the route Nora had been ordered to follow; the possible positions from where the blackmailer might watch; and the various paths he might take to and from the payoff drop.

Two hours later, back at MI, they spread out those photographs, discussed their alternatives and finalized their plan. Drummy would arrive very early to set up cameras to cover Nora's approach, the fountain entrance and interior, as well as the possible directions from which the blackmailer might approach the drop. Drummy would then stay out of sight in an unmarked van in the parking lot that Nora would drive through. A tire on his van would be punctured to explain its presence in the lot.

Jack would take a position in the tree on the south rim of a grassy area about the size of a football field. From there he could watch the entrance to the fountain room where Nora would leave the payoff.

Max would hide near the entrance to the fountain in an area thick with shrubs fronted by a sign identifying them as English Boxwood.

They were as ready as possible and their excitement was palpable. Tomorrow should be the day for which they had been waiting, the day during which they would stop accumulating questions and start compiling answers. Maybe, hopefully, the day they would meet the blackmailer.

Before leaving Jack called Mr. Trowbridge and also Alan Clark to confirm the blackmailer had not, once given, called them to change the location or time they were to leave their payoffs. He hadn't. Hopefully, the blackmailer would not do so this time either.

CHAPTER 42

THE BACKS OF Sarah Andujar's hands were bandaged, her lower arms heavily scratched, some having scabbed over.

"Hello, Jack. Hello, Nora. Thank you for coming. I am eager to hear your progress report."

"What happened?" Nora asked looking at Sarah.

"Oh, it is nothing, more embarrassing than anything." She led them toward the back.

Jack and Nora stopped and stood still as soon as they stepped down into the sun room. Sarah's prized rose bushes had all been hacked off. Jack gently put his hands on the old woman's shoulders. "Sarah, is that how you hurt your hands and arms?"

"Oh, all right; I'll tell you. I kept seeing Christopher standing out there among the roses. I called to him but he did not answer. He always seemed just beyond where I was so I kept cutting. I know it sounds crazy, but I just lost it. I had no idea what I was I doing until I found myself sitting in that garden chair, exhausted, with my pruning shears on my lap and my wonderful rose bushes all over the ground."

"Have you seen a doctor?" Nora asked.

Sarah shook her head. "I put ointment on the cuts and scratches and bandages. It's not as bad as it looks; they're healing well."

"I believe Nora was referring to a psychiatrist," Jack said, "perhaps Dr. Radnor? Your husband trusted him."

"Odd as it may sound, despite my husband being a psychiatrist, I do not believe in it."

Sarah shooed her guests into the study while she went into the kitchen to get them all some refreshments. A few minutes later she wheeled in a serving cart with a pot of coffee, a pitcher of hot tea, and a tray of buttered croissants. She acted as if they had just arrived and the garden issue had never been discussed.

"Thank you for coming. I am pleased you have made enough progress to warrant giving me a report."

Jack and Nora sat in two Eisenhower chairs with peach colored cushions while Sarah poured coffee for Jack and, assuming Nora would want tea, poured the two of them a cup. Then she sat in a chair across from her guests.

"I hope we didn't give you false hopes," Nora began. "We believe in giving our clients progress reports even if there is no progress. In this case, we've had some, but only in a general way."

"Please tell me."

Jack sat forward. "You were right. We know, or are very sure, Chris was blackmailed. As of yet we cannot say by whom or over what."

Sarah stared at Jack. "Is there anything else?"

"Other people have also been blackmailed."

"Others?" She squeezed a lemon wedge over her tea, hard enough that some of the spray touched a few of the unbandaged scratches on her arm, causing her to grimace.

"We can't say who," Jack said, "but yes there were others."

"I can imagine their misery." She stirred her tea, tamped the spoon on her napkin and rested it on her saucer.

"Frankly, some deserve your sympathy." Nora smiled thinly. "Some don't."

Jack blew on his coffee and took a first sip. "We'll know more before we're done."

"Are you going to catch this bastard?" The widow blushed. "I apologize for that word."

"I'd've used a stronger word," said Nora.

"We'll catch the bastard," Jack answered. "No guarantee, but we expect to. You need to treat what we've told you like a national security secret."

"I understand."

"This study is a grand room." Jack got up and wandered over to look at an array of framed credentials and awards. "Chris's accomplishments as a psychiatrist are quite impressive."

"Thank you. I was very proud ... I still am proud. I never spend much time in this study. Now I sit here a lot." She ran her hands along the yellow padded arm rests of the Madison chair she had chosen to sit in. "This was his room." She looked at the urn on the mantle. "I believe he is pleased I chose it as his final place of rest. Do not think me silly, but I believe his spirit is still in this room. That belief gives me comfort."

Jack stepped to the side wall and looked at a collage of pictures of Chris and Sarah with Donny at various ages over the years. The other pictures featured Chris with Chief Mandrake, Mayor Molloy, and Arthur Tyson playing poker, golfing, fishing, and barbequing. A few others were of Chris at professional conferences with others from his profession.

"He had a nice group of friends along with a great wife and a son. He died a wealthy man."

Sarah smiled wistfully. "I like to think of him that way. As you see, there are a lot of pictures. That is why I didn't need the ones from his office. Please, again accept my apology for speaking harshly when you were thoughtful enough to offer to bring them to me."

"I've forgotten all about that, so why don't you."

"Who's this fellow here?" Nora asked, pointing to a man in a photo at a barbeque in the Andujar backyard.

"That's Father Timothy Michaels, our priest for many years. Some years ago he transferred to Boston and was shot dead a short time later. They never caught the man."

"Man?" Jack repeated. "How did they confirm the shooter was a man?"

"I just assumed, I guess. I do not associate ladies with acts of violence. Father Tim was a fine priest. It can be a sad world when these things happen."

"Yes, ma'am," Nora said. "But there's a lot of good out there as well."

"And the media spends far too little time on the good," Sarah said.

"Amen to that," Nora added, by now also looking at the pictures. "There's Dr. Radnor. We met with him."

"Most of them have been Chris's friends since they were teens. My husband loved them all, called them his rogues' gallery." She frowned as she pointed at a familiar face. "That Arthur Tyson is a coarse man. I never really cared for him, but my husband felt he kept the others from getting stuffy. My Christopher always saw the good in everyone."

"What are these flowers?" Nora asked. "They have such a deep red outside color with vibrant yellow centers."

Sarah joined Nora at the plant stand near the hall door. "That's a trumpet honeysuckle. They are graceful flowers. The yellow matches the fabric on the chair I sat in. I buy them in the plaza as a cut flower whenever I tire of the varieties I grow. They have a long vase life—even longer if you put a penny in the water."

Jack took advantage of their position near the door. "Sarah, we need to be going. When we're finished, we'll bring out a final report and go over it with you."

Sergeant Suggs called while Jack and Nora were driving back to the office.

"McCall, I just finished talking with the other dancers and some old walrus over at Donny's Club; the girls called her Gypsy. You were right. Rockton was a bouncer there, and like you said, he had the hots for Phoebe Ziegler. The girls say she wouldn't give him a tumble. Looks like he decided to take what he wanted. I also found out that Ms. Ziegler had for several months been seeing a man this Gypsy described as a distinguished middle-aged nerd. If the girls knew his name, they wouldn't give it up, but I've got a solid description. The guy has since stopped coming in. You got any idea who that might be?"

Jack paused long enough for Suggs to come on the prod. "Are you holding out on me, McCall?"

"Where are you, Sergeant?"

"I'm a coupla miles from the ROC on Indiana. After I turn in my report, my next stop is home to have a beer and watch a movie in bed—anything but a detective story—and then my first good night's sleep this week. You got any objection?"

"Sergeant, I'm afraid you won't be watching that movie. Nora and I will meet you at the Regional Command Center in less than an hour. If our hunch is right, we'll bring you the middle-aged nerd."

Jack made a U-turn and headed for the home of Randolph Harkin.

At the moment the police had no reason to link the death of Christopher Andujar with the killing of Donny Andujar's lap dancer Phoebe Ziegler, but he could not hold off Suggs any longer. Jack also realized that once Suggs began to grill Randolph Harkin that he would learn about the art heist at the National Portrait Gallery. And he already knew that Phoebe had been employed by Chris Andujar's son.

By the time Jack arrived at Harkin's home he had decided how he would *wall off* Harkin and the art heist from the death of Christopher Andujar. Jack would tell Sergeant Suggs that he and Nora had met Phoebe while visiting Donny Andujar as part of helping Sarah Andujar, and that Phoebe had invited them to see her sculpting work. While at Phoebe's home, they cautioned her about the potential problems of her activities at Donny's club. That after Phoebe told them about her relationship with Harkin, they had gone to see Harkin to ask that he discontinue his association with Phoebe.

Suggs would begin by interrogating Harkin and, in no time, Harkin would be talking about how tapes of him with Phoebe were used to gain his help in an art swap at the National Portrait Gallery. But Harkin had no knowledge of Chris Andujar, so his confession to Suggs would not draw in Chris's death and Jack's belief that Chris had also been blackmailed. That should allow Suggs to learn about the art heist while being kept in the dark about the blackmailing of Christopher Andujar.

Forty minutes later, Jack and Nora delivered Randolph Harkin to Suggs at Metro's Major Case Squad ROC where over the next couple of hours, things played out just as Jack had expected they would. Jack and Nora also gave Suggs separate written statements covering their visits with Harkin and with Herman Flood, the painter of what became the forgeries.

Harkin would at least be charged with grand larceny for the theft of the four presidential portraits. "I'll need to ask Chief Mandrake," Suggs said, "whether this is a local or federal beef, given the paintings were stolen from the National Portrait Gallery and them being pitchers of the presidents and all."

CHAPTER 43

"STILL NO PICTURES at your place?" Jack asked as soon as he saw Nora the next morning.

"I checked before leaving home." Nora shook her head. "Maybe the guy's taken the money he's gotten already and headed for the border?"

"Maybe he's had a heart attack," Jack said, "or been hit by a bus or found Jesus, but absent those possibilities he hasn't pulled the plug."

"Not without Candy Robson's million, you mean."

Jack nodded. "If he doesn't come for your black bag, we'll know something big has happened. Until then, the game's on. We play it out."

Max came in and made two cups of hot spiced tea. "I hope the saints will forgive an Irishman for drinking tea. Mary Lou fixed me one of these yesterday and I'm hooked. I'll be with ya in a jiffy. I wanna take one of these up to her."

Jack had asked Max to come in so he could keep the retired homicide cop connected to the big picture. After bringing him current on the copyist Herman Flood and the arrest of Curator Harkin, he asked Max what he could add to Nora's recollections about the death of Mary Lou's daddy.

"Nothing, but I got an observation."

"Let's hear it."

"The death of Tittle, his bookkeeper Leoni, and Chief of Detectives Sanchez cut the ties to Tittle. My gut's screaming that whoever holds Tittle's records is our blackmailer."

Jack and Nora nodded their agreement.

Thirty minutes later they still had nothing fresh. Nora and Max left.

Jack stood next to the window, his mind drifting to Rachel and thoughts of apologizing for being unfaithful, but instead he felt a sense of relief wash over him. He couldn't explain it, but he knew Rachel had released him from his grief.

Mary Lou snapped him back to the here-and-now when she buzzed. "My uncle called. He's on his way up. He wants to take me to lunch. Do you need me for anything before we leave?"

"Let me chat with your uncle for a minute before you go. Tell me when he arrives."

"He just walked in. I've already shooed him toward your office."

Mandrake leaned into Jack's office. "I'm told you wanted to talk with me?"

"Hi, Chief. Can you give me a couple of minutes before you two go to lunch?"

"Sure."

"What's the jurisdiction on the Harkin arrest?"

The chief unbuttoned his coat and took a seat. "The FBI is assisting, but it's a local beef."

"What are you going to do with Harkin? He's no real crook. A rush of hormones dragged him into something he had no idea how to handle."

"After discussions with the Smithsonian and the FBI, we decided to continue working Harkin the way you set it up. I authorized no arrest record and a paperless release to keep it away from the media. Harkin agreed to continue as if nothing has happened. It stretches the rules, but if he was going to skip he'd already be gone. Like you, we came down on the side of trying to recover the portraits. We're keeping him under surveillance."

"This whole case has been weird," Jack said. "I need to tell you something else because I don't wish to give the impression we're holding back anything your department should know."

The chief took off his cap and waited for Jack to speak.

"We've located Carl Anson and Joan Jensen, two federal fugitives suspected in the burglary and destruction of a National Guard Armory in the seventies."

"Why you telling me and not the Feds?"

"A valid question, Chief, they are federal fugitives. At the same time, they could be connected to your Haviland murder investigation. I tripped over them while looking into Chris's death."

Mandrake sat down and rested his cap on his knee. "Have you got anything that supports your belief that Chris didn't commit suicide?"

"No. We believe Sergeant Suggs is right on that. Chris committed suicide. However, we think Sarah is right that, at least in part, he took his own life because he was being blackmailed."

Mandrake shook his head. "I can't agree. I think that's all part of Sarah's denial. You got anything solid?" He absentmindedly ran a finger across his bushy eyebrows which appeared to have been recently trimmed.

"There's the money that Sarah claimed Chris had in their bank box. Then again, Sarah found the box empty, and she had never actually seen the money."

"That's not much," the chief said. "I've known Chris since we were kids. I can't imagine there being anything in his life that could rise to the level of blackmail material." He grinned. "We called him the town square."

"We haven't told Sarah, but we're sure Chris had come to realize his gayness. Is that a word? Maybe I should have said bisexualness. Then I'm not so sure that's a word either."

The chief looked up and chuckled, then reached out and squared the paper napkin in front of him along the straight edge of the small table sitting in front of Jack's desk.

"Even if Chris was gay, and I doubt that, it doesn't prove he was blackmailed. And I wouldn't mention that to Sarah. She's turn-of-the-century. It would crush her."

Jack nodded. "There's more, all circumstantial. Our security expert found markings that suggest a recording device had been mounted in Chris's office. The janitor service for his building is the one for which Benny Haviland worked as a supervisor. Haviland frequently shampooed the carpets at Donny Andujar's club, where the pictures were taken of Harkin and Phoebe Ziegler. That service is owned by Alan and Gladys Clark, the aliases for Carl Anson and Joan Jensen. All these overlays can't be coincidental."

The chief raised his brows. "Whoa, big fella. You got a lot hooked to that caboose. Circumstantial evidence can get very persuasive when you string enough of it together. But you've told me nothing the district attorney could use to indict anyone beyond the stolen portraits and nothing that ties to Chris's death. You got any physical evidence other than scratches where you say some surveillance equipment had been positioned, without knowing by whom?"

"Not a thing. I just wanted to bring you current seeing that some of this is on the edge of your department's investigation of the Haviland murder."

"I appreciate it. Anything else?"

"No. The Clarks are aware I know they're Anson and Jensen. I'll have them surrender to the Bureau within the next couple of days."

"Be careful, Jack. Unlike curator Harkin, those two know how to run and hide. If they do, the Feds could see you as an accessory for not having turned them in." He again finger-combed his eyebrows using both hands on both brows. "And I know now, so that also applies to me. How long you figuring to wait?"

"You're right. I'll do it tomorrow morning, here at my office. I'll set it up with the Bureau. Thanks for helping me talk it through. Enjoy your lunch with Mary Lou. By the way, you were right we're very pleased with her work and her personality."

The chief smiled. "She's a sweetheart, no doubt about that. Give my thanks to Max Logan. Mary Lou told me what he did. She's very taken with Max. So, what comes next?"

"We're going to see someone soon who we think will open another door. I'll get with you after it plays out."

CHAPTER 44

JACK AND NORA turned up a private cement driveway, stopping near a high iron gate. He rolled his window down and spoke to a gardener trimming a pyrachantha that grew off to one side, its orange-red berries dotting every branch.

"I'd like to see Dean Trowbridge."

"He's in a rotten mood, Mister," the gardener said. "If I was you, I'd come back later."

"Most people are in a bad mood when I'm with 'em."

"You an undertaker?" A gold tooth peeked out from inside the gardener's smile.

Jack laughed. "No. He's expecting me, though."

"Pull up to that there post." He pointed. "And hit the button on the box. They'll answer from up on the hill."

Jack moved forward and engaged the speaker. "Jack McCall and Nora Burke. We have a meeting with Mr. Trowbridge."

"You're expected," the box replied. "Are you and Ms Burke alone?"

"Yes."

The gate divided in the center and quietly rolled to each side of a paver driveway bordered by precisely trimmed, knee-high hedges backed by large trees with landscape lights set into the crotch of the lowest major branch of each tree.

Jack had convinced Trowbridge to let them talk with his daughter. Allison was an adult, but Jack wanted to avoid the risk her father might convince her to clam up. The two men had agreed the meeting would be at Trowbridge's home with him present, and that Nora could come after Jack suggested Allison might be more comfortable with another woman in the room.

As they neared the top of the hill, Nora pointed out a five-car garage topped by what appeared to be servants' quarters. Jack entered a circular drive, stopping under a high roof supported by four stone pillars. Two steps of matching stone led to a slate-floored portico and an oversized wood door inset with stained glass.

A well-dressed young man with a roman nose opened the car door on Nora's side. "Good afternoon, Ms. Burke," he said, then stooped and looked over at Jack. "Leave your car, Mr. McCall. I'll have it parked."

Nora got out.

"I prefer to park myself," Jack told the young attendant, "and keep my keys."

The man pointed toward an open parking area just beyond the circle. "Over there, Mr. McCall, with your hood to the low wall, please."

Jack parked where the young man had pointed. Over the landscape wall he saw a large swimming pool. The lotion on three young women in small bathing suits glistened in the sun. A much older man, with a deeply tanned body bisected by a tiny white Speedo, stood among the ladies. A second man silently floated in the pool, his belly bobbing above the water.

A dainty front door buzzer produced a deep gong. A moment later the door opened in the hand of a nondescript houseman wearing dark slacks with a polo shirt inscribed The House of Trowbridge. The height of the doorstep brought the houseman's forehead to Jack's chin. He stepped inside and found Nora adorning the end of a fainting chair in the entrance hall.

"Mr. Trowbridge wishes for you and Ms. Burke to join him in his study," the houseman said, "this way, please." He led them through a large arch and down a wide hallway to a set of double doors crowned with an alabaster chambranle. He knocked, opened both doors and stepped back, adding a slight bow.

The large study was rimmed with floor-to-ceiling bookcases fronted by a sliding ladder. Trowbridge looked up from behind a mahogany desk with an inset leather writing surface. The hard corners of the desk were softened by three books standing upright between two black elephant bookends studded with authentic ivory tusks. Trowbridge, his fingernails buffed to a shine, took a long draw on a cigarette, tilted his head back and blew smoke toward the ceiling.

"I'll be with you in a minute, Mr. McCall."

Trowbridge stubbed out his cigarette, picked up a large-bowled, pre lit pipe and, after a few masturbatory strokes along its hard shaft, put it in his mouth. Next, he poured two fingers of liquor, scotch according to the little pewter tag on the decanter, he held it up to the light, swirled it, and sipped. "Ahhhhhhhh." His voice a rasp file scaring old wood.

He balanced his still-burning pipe in a tray and extended an open box of cigars toward Jack. "It's okay if you smoke here, Mr. McCall. This time we're on my turf."

"No thank you. I don't smoke."

Trowbridge shrugged. "Allison has been informed of your arrival. She'll join us soon." He stood wearing a cream-colored v-neck sweater that creased neatly just above where it hugged his black slacks, and came around the desk as silently as a night creature on the prowl.

"This is quite a house, Mr. Trowbridge."

"A bit extravagant I admit, but I call it home." He turned, picked up his pipe, took a puff, and blew a redundant message: this is my house and I'll smoke if I want to. The behavior lacked only a childish *yan, yan, yan.*

"That's an unusual painting over your desk," Jack said, trying to woo Trowbridge away from his fixation on his right to smoke.

"That's an original Bosch, one of only, I believe, seven of his paintings that he signed. Not many people like his work, but I find it captivating. His work focused on the temptations of evil and the lure of lust. Notice the owls? In the Middle Ages owls were considered evil? They were looked upon as the guardians of the entrances to hell, very different from our modern depiction of owls as symbols of wisdom."

Living alone had over time apparently turned Trowbridge's home into a portmanteau in which he gathered and indulged his varied vices.

"You know a lot about art?"

"I know a lot about making money, Mr. McCall, but I know something about nearly everything."

Trowbridge's grandstanding was interrupted when a nervous young woman entered the room. Going for the look of purity, Allison had worn her blonde hair down with a slight flip, white slacks, and a white silk blouse, slightly shadowed by the outline of her bra.

"Mr. McCall, Ms. Burke," Trowbridge said in a voice roughened by a lifetime of tobacco and hard liquor, "My daughter, Allison."

The young woman sat alone on a white couch. Her red lips the only thing of color in the white and blonde vision.

"I have a few friends waiting," Trowbridge said. "I've fully apprised Allison of our previous discussion. You may start knowing that she is up to speed."

You jerk. This is not one of your board meetings.

Nora ignored Trowbridge's statement and skimmed the surface of what she guessed about Allison's horrid night upstairs at Tittle's place. While Nora spoke, Allison's face turned ash gray.

At one point the old man started to open his mouth, probably to challenge the need for Nora's recap, but instead kept turning his cigar without taking it from his mouth.

"Allison," Jack asked, "have any of your friends who also hung out in Luke's Place been blackmailed?"

Trowbridge stopped turning his cigar.

Allison started fussing with her hands. "Only a couple of my friends hung out there. I won't give you their names. One, a man, gambled with only cash. One of my girlfriends used IOUs as I did ... She ran away. I don't know why."

"Can you put a date on that?"

"I don't remember exactly, but nearly two years ago." She clasped her hands in her lap.

"About the time you were blackmailed?" asked Nora.

Her lower lip quivered, "A little before."

Jack leaned forward. "Have you heard from this friend since?"

"No."

"Do you know if she's alive?" Nora asked in her easy way.

Allison clamped her palms onto her thighs, her knuckles white. "I see her brother sometimes. He hears from her by phone. I've asked him if he knows where she is—not to tell me where, but just does he know. I saw him yesterday, he said, 'Sissy keeps saying I can't come home yet.'"

Jack looked toward Trowbridge. "Let's step out in the hall so Nora and Allison can talk woman to woman?"

"Mr. McCall, I could not advise my daugh—"

"Daddy. I'll be fine with Ms. Burke. Please wait with Mr. McCall."

Jack sat outside the door in a ornate wooden chair with massive eighteenth-century rococo carvings bumpy against his back. Trowbridge, his teeth clamped tightly on the pipe he had switched back to before leaving his desk, walked down the hall and turned the corner toward the front door. Jack noticed the paintings hanging in the hallway outside Trowbridge's study included portraits of Napoleon, Stalin, and Churchill.

"I'm glad we're alone," Nora said, after Jack shut the door. "Men don't always appreciate a woman's point of view on this kind of stuff." She moved to the couch near, but not too near, Allison and described with more specificity what she believed Allison had endured upstairs at Tittle's.

"That's essentially correct, Ms. Burke," Allison said, embellished by nervous twitches in her hands.

"Please call me Nora. Why did you say 'essentially correct,' instead of just saying correct?"

Allison flicked an imaginary spot from the front of her white slacks and again clasped her hands. "I knew the identity of two of the men, and I saw the face of the third, a younger man whose name I never knew." She licked her lips and wiped her eyes. "I'm sorry. It's just, well, not easy to talk about getting smashed and being coerced into giving head to three men."

Nora reached over and held Allison's hand.

The younger woman took a deep, slow breath. "Two of them were Tittle and his accountant. I knew him as Terry."

"Terrence Leoni?"

"I think that's right."

"What about the younger one, the one whose face you recognized?"

"He was one of Tittle's managers." Furrowing her brow, she added, "I'm not even sure I'd recognize him again. When I was upstairs doing ... well, I just stared at his squaretoed boots."

"Anything else you remember?"

She closed her eyes and slowly shook her head. "I don't want to remember. I want to forget."

"You may never forget. Accept that you were the victim of an assault. You have no reason to feel guilty. Sex is a joy. Don't let this mess up sex for you." Nora squeezed her hand and they shared a dry, humorless smile. "Did you start seeing Dr. Andujar before or after the blackmailing?"

"Oh, long after."

"What about the blackmailer?"

"Only Daddy had contact with him."

"Did you ever talk to Dr. Andujar about that night at Tittle's? The men you remembered?"

"Yes," Allison nodded, "but not for a long while. Finally I told Dr. Andujar it was Tittle and the man I knew as Terry and the younger guy in the squaretoed boots."

"When was that?"

"My last session with Dr. Andujar, the week before he died."

Allison's head came up suddenly and she grew more animated. "Dr. Andujar was great, just fabulous. He helped me regain my self-respect. I took his death very hard. He had been my anchor ... That sounded selfish, didn't it?" She blinked, a tear escaping her right eye. "I just meant—"

"I understand what you meant. You've been very brave. I promise you we will not tell your father any part of what you have told me." Nora stood and put a hand on Allison's shoulder. "I'm not a psychiatrist, but if you ever feel like talking, girl stuff you know, call me."

CHAPTER 45

NORA'S CALL STARTED Jack's morning. "No," she said, "Drummy's camera has still not taken any pictures in front of my place. Now get your mind clear. Dress rehearsals are over. Today we find out who's at the bottom of the barrel." She hung up without waiting for him to reply.

Almost immediately, Jack's phone rang again. This time the caller was Drummy. His cameras on the cathedral grounds were set. He had punctured one of the van's tires and told the cathedral office his van would be out of their lot no later than two that afternoon.

Nora would wear jeans and a loose-fitting sweatshirt. And because the possibility existed that the blackmailer might know Nora as Nora, she had also planned to wear a broad-brimmed hat and sunglasses. She would carry her Candy phone, whose number only the blackmailer had. Jack and the others would have their cells on vibration. If Nora's phone rang, they would all hear it and know the call was from the blackmailer.

The wild card remained that the blackmailer could call and order Nora to a different drop, but he had not done so with any of the known prior marks. Instead, he had carefully selected the locations for each of the payoffs. The specificity of his instructions to Nora, made it likely he would not change the location this time either.

The forecast for a crisp Sunday morning was holding. The dry, still yellowed spring grass would not show Jack's tracks.

By eight-thirty he had gotten tolerably comfortable on a big limb of the large tree that bordered the grassy area across from the fountain. He leaned to one side to ease the pressure on his still sore ribs. The tree had a cooperating canopy that would allow him to see Nora all the way from her car to the fountain, as well as watch her all the way back to her car.

He eased a branch aside and peered down over the toes of the black running shoes he wore below his jeans and forest-green turtleneck. The gentle morning breeze busily tossed a few leaves, while others dashed across the grass with each sudden gust. At nine he stared at the spot where Max was supposed to step out briefly.

Max was carrying his Glock 17 that came standard with a 17-cartridge magazine. Jack and Nora each carried a .9mm Beretta 92FS. Jack was hoping that none of them would need their guns. He didn't want a Sunday morning shootout on the grounds of the National Cathedral.

Max stepped out. So far, everything seemed to be running on schedule.

A moment later, an old dark Plymouth coupe swung out around Drummy's van. By leaving the van in plain sight Jack figured it would be less threatening. He was counting on the expectation of a million-dollar payoff being enough of a lure to prevent even the most cautious of criminals from driving away, even if something didn't look just right. The old Plymouth drove through the parking lot and out of sight.

In the distance, several tourists carrying cameras were snapping pictures of the grounds designed like an old European monastery, while others retreated into the parking lot to capture a full view of the soaring cathedral against the backdrop of the clear blue sky.

Jack's watch pulsed against his wrist—fifteen minutes to touchdown.

Right then, an old farmer in overalls and a sweat-soiled straw hat stepped out of the gazebo in the Bishop's Garden, a slight limp in his left leg. The man's hat prevented Jack from seeing more than his lower cheek and chin. The low morning sun glistened off his gray unshaven stubble. The farmer wandered aimlessly until he reached the grassy area near Jack's tree. There, he sat on a bench with a view of the fountain.

Damn.

The interloper took his camera case from around his neck, opened it, and used the bench to install a new roll of film. Jack heard the click when the farmer twisted his wrist to seat a zoom lens. The farmer stood, turned, and snapped several pictures of the cathedral. Then he limped down one of the paths pausing here and there to take shots of some of the bushes, including the signs showing their botanical names.

Jack peeked through the branches to see Nora pull her rental car into the lot, then drive around Drummy's disabled van. Just as the blackmailer had instructed, she parked in front of the tree with the blackish leaves. The date and time stamp on Drummy's photos would establish her arrival.

Nora's trunk lid popped free just before she stepped out of her car with a camera dangling from around her neck, the strap comforted between her breasts. She tugged down her view-blocking sunhat, reset her dark glasses, and moved to the back of the car where she lifted the black bag from the trunk. After climbing the five stairs to the lower grassy area, she turned and used her remote to lock her car.

Nora started down the walkway, looking nervous as Candy Robson would be. When she reached the walled fountain area, she stepped inside the relatively small enclosure and looked out to be sure no one was in a position to watch her.

Through his binoculars, Jack watched Nora step up onto the bench to her left and rise onto her toes, the line of her calf muscles flexing as she hefted the bag over the wall. She walked out of the fountain enclosure with her head down, continued for a distance and then turned down the path that would take her back on the course dictated by the blackmailer.

Two minutes later the farmer came back into view, limped in the direction of the fountain, and went inside the walled area. Jack quickly rotated his binoculars in time to see Nora climb the last few stairs and enter the cathedral. Then back to see the farmer take out his camera and snap two pictures of the fountain.

After another minute, the farmer came out of the fountain room, looked both ways, and quickly stepped around the north side of the wall enclosing the fountain, disappearing into the bushes. He had been out of sight only seconds when he reappeared holding Nora's black bag by its hand grip, the shoulder strap dangling close to the ground. He casually strolled to one of the benches near Max's position. When he bent down and reached for the zipper, Max stepped into the clear.

"Freeze," Max said.

The farmer let go of the zipper bag and stood slowly, raising his hands.

The farmer could be some shill the blackmailer hired to pick up the bag.

When Jack dropped the last few feet down from the tree, he heard Max's command: "On your knees." The farmer obeyed without favoring his gimpy leg.

The limp had been a ruse. Maybe he is the blackmailer.

Max put handcuffs on the farmer who jerked against the restraints and finally, after thrashing about, gave up.

"Hello, Blackmailer," Jack said from behind, "I see you're eager to look at the million."

"There ain't no million, is there McCall?"

Jack knocked the farmer's straw hat off and looked down at a blank face reminiscent of a fish with a hook firmly set in the corner of its mouth. "Tyson! Why am I not surprised?"

"What's in the bag, McCall? Not no million bucks, right?"

"No, Mr. Tyson. Or is it yes? Yes, there's no million dollars, but maybe you'll get a million years for blackmail and murder."

Tyson twisted on his knees to face Jack. "I ain't killed nobody. You got me on attempted blackmail. That's it. I'll do the time standing on my head. Fuck you, and you too, Max. You're scum to turn on a fellow cop."

"You're no cop," Max bellowed. "When you were, you disgraced the department. I'll enjoy coming to your trial, wouldn't miss it." He turned to Jack. "Boss, you think you can arrange for me to throw the switch? I'd like to watch his ugly mug while the electricity slams through his shaved head, the smoke rising from his burning brain."

"Go to hell, Max. Your melodramatic shit won't work on me. There's no death penalty in DC, and nothing I've done is a capital crime in any jurisdiction."

Drummy had moved closer, taking pictures as he approached to show they were not abusing Tyson.

"Listen, damn it. This is my only attempted blackmail. I tell you I ain't killed nobody. Have a heart you guys."

"Have a heart?" Max snorted. "I'm more sentimental about the bacteria living in my toilet. You want me to call Metro, Jack?"

Jack liked the thought of Tyson rotting in a cell just for being an all-around crud, but not just yet. He jammed Tyson's straw hat back on his head. Interrogating Tyson offered their best chance to find the real blackmailer.

CHAPTER 46

JACK AND MAX herded the handcuffed Tyson into the elevator and brought him up to MI's office. Drummy had left from the cathedral for his workshop to develop his pictures. Nora had rushed back ahead of the others to change her outfit, so Tyson would not learn that Candy Robson was not a real person.

Jack twisted the thin plastic rods that rotated to close the Venetian blinds over the windows in the conference room; then he called for Tyson to be brought in. Max shoved a spare straight-backed chair near the table and sat Tyson down so the chair back would be between his cuffed hands and his body.

Tyson violently twisted his head, the force dislodging his dirty straw hat. It fell to the floor. Max kicked it toward the wall. Jack stood waiting across from Tyson on the other side of the table. After Tyson had exhausted his spare energy, Jack spoke.

"Arthur Tyson, this interview is being recorded and filmed." For the record Jack stated the date, time, and their location. "Mr. Tyson, you are not under arrest. In fact, we have no authority to arrest anyone other than as a citizen's arrest, which we are not exercising at this time. We deny any responsibility to Mirandize you. You may refuse to answer any or all of our questions. At any time, upon your request we will cease our questions and call the Metropolitan Police Department of the District of Columbia to report you black-mailed our client Candice Robson. I anticipate the police will arrest you at that time, but that will be their call. As a retired career police officer you understand the dynamics of that process and your attendant rights."

Tyson squirmed hard enough to rattle the handcuffs against the chair.

"When you were a cop," Jack said, "you had a history of excessive force. You are handcuffed to protect us from that. These handcuffs are not intended to intimidate you or create the impression you must answer our questions. In addition to myself, Jack McCall, a DC licensed private investigator, and Nora Burke, a DC licensed private investigator, both partners in McCall Investigations, Max Logan, a retired DC homicide detective employed by McCall Investigations, is present. Arthur Tyson, are the terms of this interview agreeable to you, or would you prefer we contact the police department and all wait in silence for their arrival?"

Tyson grimaced and nodded before he spoke, "Okay. I'll talk with you so you'll see this beef is bogus. As for the Robson broad, I'm betting she's been pinched for hooking. If I'm wrong, I'll shave my balls and paint 'em pink."

Jack glanced at Nora who was fighting back a smile.

"In the event you are not aware," Jack said, "McCall Investigations is looking into the death of Dr. Christopher Andujar, which the Metropolitan Police Department has ruled a suicide. In the course of our investigation we have come to learn the following: You were a bag man for Luke Tittle. You disbursed bribe monies on behalf of Mr. Tittle to insulate the illegal activities of Mr. Tittle's business, known as

Luke's Place, from the lawful activities of both the DC police and various regulatory agencies. You owned a fifteen percent interest in Luke's Place. We have a witness who will testify to this fact. You now function in that same capacity in the employ of Donny Andujar with respect to protecting the illegal activities of his business, known as Donny's Gentlemen's Club. We have a witness who will testify that you own fifteen percent of Donny's club.

"During your years as a police detective, you maintained Metro's files on old federal fugitive warrants. Benny Haviland, one such federal fugitive, worked as a supervisor for the Clark Janitorial Service. As such he had after-hours access to Donny's club, and also the buildings in which the following psychiatrists had offices: Dr. Christopher Andujar, deceased, Dr. Phillip Radnor, and Dr. John Karros, whose patients included MI's client, Candice Robson."

"Except for Robson I got nothing to do with none of that."

Jack continued. "The curator of a major art gallery has been blackmailed into switching forged paintings for works of art. The leverage over the curator included photographs of him having sex with a lap dancer at Donny's club. Available witnesses include the forger of the paintings, the curator at the gallery, and Donny Andujar. We allege that the murdered Benny Haviland gave you access to install that camera. Said lap dancer has also been murdered. Donny Andujar will testify that you pushed him to get that specific lap dancer to have sex with that curator."

Tyson's body language indicated he was getting the picture. All of it pointed to him.

"We have other prominent locals, patients of the deceased Dr. Andujar, who are ready to testify they were blackmailed about issues they discussed only with Dr. Andujar. We believe it can be proven that Benny Haviland got you into Andujar's office where you illegally installed surveillance equipment. Dr. Andujar's patients were blackmailed for a total of one-and-a-quarter million dollars.

"Dr. Andujar had private treatment sessions with Dr. Radnor, in whose office we also found indications you had installed surveillance equipment. We are confident the equipment used for this and these other instances of illegal surveillance will tie to equipment the police will find in your office. Before his death Dr. Andujar paid a quarter of a million dollars. That blackmailing contributed to the death of Dr. Andujar. Two federal fugitives are ready to testify they were also blackmailed."

Perspiration worked its way down Tyson's grainy skin to spill into the deep crevices along each side of his nose. The trail of sweat followed those creases until it flowed in at the corner of his mouth. Annoyed by the sensation, Tyson swung his head fiercely. The sweat flew from his face.

"I believe that the police, using the information we've uncovered, can establish that you illegally installed surveillance equipment in the office of Doctor of Psychiatry John Karros that led to your attempt to blackmail one of his patients, our client, Ms. Candice Robson, for one million dollars."

"I swear, other than that Robson thing I didn't shake down nobody, and I didn't rub out Haviland or hire Rockton to kill the whore."

"You just blackmailed Robson. Is that what you're saying?"
"Yeah."
"How did you get the dirt on Candice Robson?"
"Like you said, I bugged her shrink's office."
"Dr. Karros?"
"Yeah."

"Come on, Tyson. You expect anybody to believe that you bugged Dr. Karros's office, but that you didn't bug the office of Doctor Radnor who is in the same building? Also Dr. Andujar's building for which Benny Haviland also had keys. The equipment in your own office will smash that lie."

"Okay. I bugged them too. But the real blackmailer made me do it. I just put the recorders in the offices. I don't know nothin' else."

Tyson twisted his head to the side and wiped the coagulated saliva from the corner of his mouth onto the shoulder of his denim shirt.

Max spoke for the first time. "You're an ex-cop, Tyson. How many years you think you're gonna do for all this?"

Tyson again jerked his head, his flailing hair flipping perspiration into the air.

When he didn't answer, Max prodded him again. "I got no sympathy for you, Arthur—how many years?"

Tyson just sat there with sweat dripping from his nose onto the thighs of his overalls.

Max slammed the flat of his hand on the table. "Right, Artie, the number of years won't matter. These charges will get you into a prison where there'll be lots of your old friends. Fellows you worked over when you carried a badge. Fellows you sent up, who hold a grudge."

Except for a tic just left of his mouth, Tyson's posture hid his being alive. Then he blurted, "I can't go in one of them prisons," his voice beginning to crack.

"Tyson." Jack said sharply. "Intelligence work has taught me that justice comes in lots of forms. Some are unconventional, but still effective."

Tyson hunched forward and then turned his head to each side, using his hunched shoulders to wipe the sweat from his cheeks. "If I cooperate," he said. "If I help you solve them other blackmailings and murders, can you get the charges against me knocked down to just Robson, with any time served to be in minimum security?"

"Artie," Jack said, "you know I can neither control nor speak for Metro or the D.A.'s office. If what you're saying is true and you help slam the cell door on the blackmailer and murderer, at the least you'd be free of those charges. I would also agree to use my influence with Ms. Robson. I may be able to get her to ask the D.A. to drop that charge."

Tyson sat erectly. "Yeah. That's the only real charge against me. Robson lost no money. Maybe a few nights sleep, but hell, that's nothing. Right?"

"I want to ask you more questions, Mr. Tyson, but before I do, let's go back over the terms for this interview. At your instruction I will call Metro to come here. If you wish I will stop asking questions and you may at any time refuse to answer any or all questions."

"Yeah. Yeah. What I'm saying I'm saying of my own free will. I wanna cooperate. So ask. Go on for Christ's sake. Ask."

CHAPTER 47

JACK TURNED TO Nora. "Please get Mr. Tyson a towel from our washroom. Max, remove the handcuffs." While Max moved around behind Tyson, Jack said, "Tell us if you need to go to the head. Otherwise, don't get out of that chair."

Tyson nodded. "Sure. Okay." He rubbed his wrists and watched Nora walk back in.

She threw the towel at him. He caught it, grinned at her, and wiped his face. During this brief break, a let's-get-it-done attitude had replaced Tyson's tough-guy act.

"So ask."

"How have you sustained your standard of living over the years? Oh, before you answer, I want to again remind you this is being recorded and filmed."

"No way, McCall," Tyson raised his hands above his shoulders, stretching from side to side. "I'm here to talk about the blackmailer. I ain't about to rat on myself."

Jack was pleased by Tyson's reply, it had confirmed he understood his right not to answer, and that Jack would respect his decision.

"Then tell us about the blackmailer."

"He paid me to put the bugs in the offices of them shrinks."

"Andujar. Radnor. Karros. And Donny Andujar's club?"

"Not Karros, but, yeah ... the rest of 'em." He swabbed his neck with the towel before adding, "Nobody else."

Max and Nora had glanced at Jack when Tyson split out Karros, but Jack shook his head. He would let that pass for now.

"Lemme tell you something else." Tyson looked at Max, then Nora and finally, Jack, his silence building suspense. "You know as well as me the big risk in blackmail, like in kidnapping, is picking up the dough. I took that risk." He shook his head. "I hope you nail the sonofabitch."

Max pulled out the chair next to him and put his foot on the seat. "That brings us to the big question, Artie, who's the blackmailer?"

Tyson shrugged. "Search me. He gave me instructions by phone. He was always reminding me I didn't know his identity, and that I would die if I took one dollar more than my cut." Tyson looked up and pleaded, "I just picked up the loot a coupla times. Not from all them pigeons you mentioned. I took my end and left the rest at a drop like he told me. I don't know who he is. That's how he kept me in line."

"Which payoffs did you pick up?" Jack held up his right hand, his index finger pointing toward the ceiling. "And Artie, I have solid information on this, so don't try to stroke me."

Tyson spread his hands as if he were a TV evangelist. "I never got told names, but I picked up a payoff of one million. I shoulda just grabbed that one and kept going. I also picked up a half mil and a quarter. That's it. You say the quarter was Chris Andujar. I never knew that. Chris was an okay guy. I got no clue why I was told to force Donny into pushing Jena Moves to spread her legs for that pipsqueak, and I can't help you on Jena gettin' bumped off. The word is the biker did it for his own reasons. This town's full of hookers, so we got one less. No big deal."

Jack clenched his fists and leaned closer, his knuckles pressing white against the table. "You didn't even know her name, you bastard. It was Phoebe Ziegler, a young woman with a mother and a future."

Max put a firm hand on Jack's shoulder and took over questioning Tyson. "How do you know the blackmailer knocked off Haviland?"

"He told me." Jack sat down while Tyson embellished his answer. "He kept telling me he'd plug me too if I didn't do exactly what he told me every step of the way. And Jack, I'm sorry. I didn't know you had a thing for Jena. Hey, but get in line. Guys all over town were walking with stiffies every time they saw that broad."

Jack wanted to slug the soured ex-cop, but he fought down the urge. He was not about to hand Tyson a defense that he had been beaten and intimidated.

"You knew Benjamin Haviland." Jack made it sound like a statement of fact, not a question.

"Yeah," Tyson freely admitted. "A good while back the blackmailer told me to meet a guy who would get me in Chris's office. That guy was Benny."

"How did you pass the surveillance tapes to the black-mailer?" Jack asked.

"Benny handled all that. I showed him how to put in new tapes and take out the full ones. He did it during his visits to the buildings as janitorial supervisor. The only thing Benny ever told me was that he left the tapes at drops like he was told. One time he said he was ordered to go behind the building and give them to some guy on a motorcycle. My guess is that was the same biker who iced Jena."

"Did Benny know the blackmailer's identity?" Max asked.

"I asked him once and Benny got all freaky. 'Listen, man,' he said, 'I don't know and I don't wanna know.'" Tyson snorted. "In his college days Benny was one of them smart-ass, I'll-save-the-earth hippies. That bum never even made it to fly-speck on the ass of the earth."

Jack looked at him askance. "Artie, you've taken calls from this guy for a long time. You can't tell us you don't know his identity."

"What name did the blackmailer use to refer to himself?" Nora asked.

Max tagged on, "What did he sound like?"

"He sounded different all the time," Tyson said while bobbing and weaving his head to add a visual illustration. "Sometimes muffled, sometimes with one of those vibrator gizmos against his neck, and other times he just whispered. Sometimes he sounded like Donald Duck. About once a week he'd call me while I was in a restaurant, to remind me his guys were always watching me."

Tyson spread the towel open and held it using both hands, covering his face.

"A name!" Nora barked. "What name did he give you?"

Tyson slid the sweat-soaked towel up his face and over the top, his straight damp hair matting to his head. "Moriarty! Okay? He called himself Moriarty. And every time that looney tune said 'Moriarty,' he chuckled. I'm telling ya, this asshole is fuckin' wacko. I only went along 'cause he threatened to shoot my ass."

He's working on his defense again.

"And the money was good, right Artie?" Nora asked in a disgusted tone.

"Moriarty was the name of Sherlock Holmes's archenemy," Jack said.

"I know that," Tyson protested. "I tried reading Sherlock Holmes once, but it was too old-fashioned. I don't know why the blackmailer picked that name ... Can Nora get me a dry towel?"

Jack stood up. "I'll get it." Jack went into the washroom off the conference room, dropped the sweat-soaked towel into the trash and washed his hands. When he returned, he slid a clean towel across the table to Tyson who grabbed it and again started talking.

"The blackmailer once said, 'Holmes often prevented Moriarty from getting the loot, but Holmes could never catch Moriarty.'" Tyson ran the fresh towel over his forehead and neck before continuing. "Then the guy said, 'I'll top Moriarty. I'll get away with my spoils.' ... I'm telling you, he's one weird motherfucker. This is the only guy who's ever scared me, and I ain't never even met him."

"You said he told you he killed Benny Haviland?" Nora asked.

"He bragged about it. Said, 'Benny disobeyed my orders.' He warned me not to do the same or I'd end up lying next to Benny." Tyson snuffed loudly and cleared his throat. "Moriarty told me half his gang used to tail Benny and the other half me. Now they was all watching me. And I'm here to tell you, those guys were good. I'll give 'em that. I never saw nobody."

Jack brought it together. "We can tie you directly or indirectly to the blackmailing of eight people and several deaths. Do you want us to have the cops come now, or do you wish to keep talking with us?"

"I'm talking, ain't I? Hell, the only guy I know ain't Moriarty is you, Jack. If you was, I'd already be dead."

"Why did you remove the electronic surveillance equipment from Donny's Club and from the offices of Andujar and Radnor, but not from Dr. Karros?"

"After Moriarty silenced Benny, he ordered me to remove my equipment from Donny's club and Radnor's office. I had already cleared out Andujar's office right after Chris took himself out. Moriarty told me I should toss the equipment and the keys to them buildings into the Potomac. I kept the equipment. Maybe I shoulda done what he said."

Tyson had stopped just answering questions; he was now telling his story.

"Benny got gunned when Moriarty no longer needed him. I knew that once I removed the electronics, he'd no longer need me. Things were getting hot and the cops knew nothing about nothing. The heat was coming from you, Jack. Enough heat that Moriarty was pulling the plug. He wanted to get away from you. I wanted to get away from him.

"The same night I took my gear outta Radnor's office; I stuck it in Karros's. Both them shrinks are in that same building and they both see lots of rich patients, and being a cop taught me rich folks usually got more skeletons in their closets than the lowlifes. I figured even if Moriarty's guys were watching me, they'd be outside the building with no way of knowing I had bugged Karros to get the goods on one of his nut jobs. Just my luck it turned out to be your client, the Robson broad."

"Where did Moriarty have you leave the payoffs?" Jack asked.

"He kept changing it. One time a lockbox in Union Station, another time in an airport locker, then under the bench in a try-on room at a department store. Like that. Always public so I had no solid chance to spot him. There ain't nothing there for you to follow. He's smart and careful."

Tyson looped the towel around his neck and clung to the ends with his elbows down and continued spilling his story. "With Candy Robson's mil, I'd be long gone. Moriarty would never find me. That's my only blackmail job. The rest is a little B&E, illegal surveillance, and money pickups. I doubt the D.A.'ll buy into accessory to murder."

"Bottom line," Jack said, "if we don't catch this Moriarty, maybe he doesn't exist. Maybe the jury will see your entire Moriarty story as bull."

Tyson yanked the ends of the towel hard enough to snap his head back. "Jesus. Jack. I didn't snuff Benny. I got a solid alibi for my time the afternoon Benny got wasted. Me and Agnes Fuller were doing a threesome with Semisweet Connie from Donny's Club. Them two'll tell you. They'll testify for me."

"Arthur. Arthur. It's not my call. The only way I can help you is to catch Moriarty. Will you help me do that?"

"What the hell I been doing here? I don't know anything else. Gimme a break."

"You haven't come clean yet; I can't help you yet."

"I wear size fifty-two pants. What the hell else you wanna know? Tell me, so I can tell you. Christ all mighty."

Jack smiled. "You and Engels are fifteen-percent silent partners in Donny's Club, just like you were for Tittle. The third investor with the same percentage gets his cut through you. Who is it?"

"Some rich, politically connected local snob. Name's Dean Trowbridge. The bastard thinks his shit don't stink, but the sonofabitch was not too pure to take his cut—not to lily white for that." Tyson said while rubbing the inside tips of his index and middle finger with the pad of his thumb.

When Tyson looked down, Jack glanced quickly at Nora and Max, who were also trying not to show their surprise from hearing the reference to Allison's father.

"Did Trowbridge know he had been a silent partner with Tittle?" Jack asked.

"That dickhead didn't wanna know from nothing. Just as long as I brought him his bag of bills each month, he never asked. He got the dough and got to keep feeling superior." Tyson finished with a snort of disgust. Then he wiped his nose with the back of his hand.

"Why," Nora asked, "why would a wealthy respected man like Trowbridge invest through a crooked cop? Come on, Artie, that's bull."

"It's not bull! Them white collar guys might look, talk, and smell better than two-bit smash-and-grabbers, but they're still crooks through and through. No matter how much they got, they always want more, particularly that asshole Trowbridge."

Nora came back at Tyson. "That doesn't explain why a rich crook like Trowbridge, if he is one, would invest through you."

"Years ago I covered up a thing involving that jerkoff and a couple hookers. He was afraid that if it got out his rep would be mud. I let him go and held onto the evidence. Later, when I needed money to invest in Tittle's Place, I went to Trowbridge to remind him he owed me. He came across on condition I get a piece for him too, but he didn't wanna know what the investment was. When I needed dough for a slice of Donny's club, I tapped Trowbridge again. Only that time he was eager. Why not, after the fat tax-free profits I'd brought him from his end of Tittle's place?"

Jack slid a yellow pad across to Tyson, followed by a pen. "Write a list of the people in the Metro PD, City Hall, and the Feds to whom you've delivered payoffs for Tittle, Donny, or both. The amount each got, how often, and for how long."

Sweat beaded on Tyson's forehead. "Christ, I can't do that." He ran his sleeve under his nose, then across his forehead. "They gunned Tittle. They'll kill me too. You was with the Feds, Jack. Can you get me in the witness protection program? If I stay here, I won't make it to trial."

"It's all up to you, Arthur. If you don't want to provide that information, just say so. But think about this: Until you ID them they'll be trying to prevent you from talking. Once you've named them, their identities are out. They'll be into damage control. It's your decision though. If you don't want to do the list we'll call Metro and you can take it from there with them."

Tyson sat staring at the pad, turning the pen in a tight circle with his fingers.

CHAPTER 48

TYSON'S LIST OF payoffs included several detectives assigned to Metro vice, and some liquor and health department people, but Mayor Patrick Molloy and Chief of Police Harry Mandrake were not on his list.

While Tyson had been writing his list, Jack had called the two federal fugitives, Carl Anson and Joan Jensen, a.k.a. Mr. and Mrs. Clark, owners of Clark's Janitorial. They professed no desire to again become fugitives. They agreed to come to MI at ten-thirty the next morning, Monday, knowing they would be taken into custody by the Federal Bureau of Investigation. As a precaution Jack had Max take his guys off watching Tyson, and put them onto the Clarks.

Next, Jack called Suggs and requested that he come to MI and pick up Tyson. The Sergeant was none too happy about the call for this had been the first Sunday he had taken off in over a month. But after Jack filled him in, Suggs agreed to come right over.

While Jack had been talking with Suggs, he saw a note Mary Lou had left on his desk late Friday. The mayor's office had called requesting that Jack meet with Mayor Molloy on Monday at two.

Twenty minutes later Sergeant Suggs walked in with three uniformed officers and took Tyson into custody. Jack gave Suggs the bribe list along with the tape and film of his interview of Tyson. Jack retained copies.

Mayor Molloy was behind his desk when Jack arrived the next day. His shirt open through the first two buttons, a small cross nesting in the gray hair on his upper chest.

"Hello, Jack."

"Hello, Your Honor."

"Last Friday, Chief Mandrake told me you'd brought in Curator Harkin for aiding and abetting in an art switch at the National Portrait Gallery. Then yesterday, I heard you asked Metro to come to your office to pick up Arthur Tyson for blackmail and murder. Now, this morning, the media has reported the FBI picked up two federal fugitives at your office. Your business is certainly booming."

Jack smiled. "It has been busy, Mr. Mayor, but I don't think Tyson is the end of that story."

The mayor pinched the loose skin of his neck between his fingers, and then pulled outward before releasing it to find its own way back. "Oh! There's more?"

"Yes, Sir. Tyson is guilty of accessory to blackmail, possibly even to murder, but he's not the main man. As I understand it, for now, Tyson is being held only on the charges he admitted to in our interview. The blackmailings are not yet official police cases because the victims, other than Harkin, have yet to admit they were blackmailed. The two fugitives the Feds picked up agreed to cooperate about their being blackmailed. I expect there are quite a few others, but I doubt most of them will ever step forward."

"Why not?"

"The blackmailer demanded payment only once from each victim, so when they were not blackmailed again, and having paid to protect their secrets, those victims will continue to keep quiet."

The mayor tilted back in his desk chair, "Sounds logical, diabolical actually."

"Mr. Mayor, why did you want to see me?"

Molloy furrowed his brow and leaned forward. "Let me get straight to it. I've heard you've been making certain inquiries about my activities. Why?"

"May I be candid?"

"I'd prefer that."

They waited while his secretary brought in a carafe of coffee and two cups on a tray with cream and sugar. She offered to pour. The mayor waved her out. She shut the door.

"MI never set out to look into your activities, Mr. Mayor. We were looking into the death of Dr. Christopher Andujar. Toward that end we tailed his son Donny. That led us to the hotel where Donny delivered one of his lap dancers to a room occupied by you. The pictures my staff took include you and the young lady in the hall outside the room. That lap dancer, you knew her as Jena Moves, was Phoebe Ziegler, the young woman murdered a few days ago."

"Holy Moly." The mayor lowered his head while he dropped two sugar cubes into his cup and added cream. "I knew of the Ziegler murder, but didn't realize she and Jena was the same woman."

Jack looked directly into the mayor's eyes. "Have you been blackmailed?"

"No. I have not." His stare stayed on Jack while he first squeezed, then stroked his chin. "What made you think I had?"

"Curator Harkin was blackmailed after being videotaped having sex with the same woman. And mayors are folks criminals would love to have the goods on. Why'd you let yourself get involved with Donny and his lap dancer?"

The mayor tucked his lips inside his mouth and released them with a slight popping sound. "Mine is a common ailment, a foolish old man with an appetite for beautiful young women. Not children. Young women." He stood, walked around his desk, and sat on the corner closest to Jack. "Give it to me straight. Will all this come out? If the press or my opponents get it, you know I'm cooked."

"Mr. Mayor, I happen to think you're doing a solid job. I'm not aware of anything that indicates you participated in these murders and blackmailings. If I learn otherwise, I'll call the press myself. Still, as you've acknowledged, you have not conducted your personal life in a proper manner."

The mayor nodded slowly.

"I want to ask you a question I didn't ask Tyson because I realized you would not want it in his taped interview. I respectfully insist you answer it now. When Tyson came over to you at my firm's open house, you emphatically shook your head no. To what were you saying no?"

"Arthur got me in the corner and with his drunken breath started pumping me to accept one of Donny's other girls. I'd already heard it more often than I cared to, so I cut him off. I knew why he wanted me to accept someone other than Jena. I guess I should say Phoebe. I never knew her real name. When I asked, Phoebe told me Donny was paying her to be with me. She planned to return to school in a year and needed the money. I have already put a stop to that whole thing by refusing any of Donny's other girls. I knew it had to stop."

The mayor looked over and, even though they were alone, lowered his voice. "Will all this go public?"

Jack gave his who-knows gesture. "You were not mentioned in our interview of Tyson. As long as I have no knowledge that you are guilty of anything other than infidelity, a personal—not societal—crime, I don't plan to do or say anything."

"Donny's bribes and his fraudulent liquor license application," the mayor said, "where he stated he owned one-hundred percent of his club will be enough to assure he'll lose that license."

"You can expect," Jack said, "that Donny will try threatening you in order to hold onto his license. And it's even more likely that Tyson will pressure you for influence with the D.A."

Mayor Molloy sipped his coffee, his thumb through the handle with his fingers around the cup. He blinked rapidly before again revisiting his worst fear. "Should my affair with a murdered lap dancer go public, my marriage is over, along with my position as mayor. Still, having sex with consenting adults is not a crime. If anyone tries to blackmail me, I'll tell them to go to hell."

"Future events will confirm whether or not you keep that pledge."

"I've already promised myself that." He stood, shook Jack's hand, and asked, "Is there anything I can do to show my appreciation?"

"Keep doing your job and keep your pants zipped."

On his way to police headquarters on Indiana Avenue, Jack stopped to buy a new pocket knife, then at a bank to pick up some paper rolls for coins, and finally to a grocery store for some of those plastic bags that zip closed at the top. Then he called Dean Trowbridge.

"What do you want McCall?" The old man's voice sounded like he had a mouthful of pebbles.

"Just wanted you to hear it from me, Trowbridge."

"Hear what?" His coarse voice adding impatience.

Jack turned left and shifted his cell to his other hand. "As you probably know from the news, last night at my office Arthur Tyson surrendered himself to the Metropolitan Police Department. What the media hasn't yet learned is that in his confession Tyson disclosed he handled some investments for you."

"That's a lie." His voice quivered. "I don't even know this Arthur Tyson."

"Your worst nightmare has turned real. One of those investments made you a silent partner in Donny's Gentlemen's Club, and before that a part owner of Luke's Place."

The other end of the line went quiet. "There's no way to prove that." Jack heard him sigh, then say, "I didn't know."

"Yeah. Sure. A minute ago you didn't even know Tyson. How does it feel knowing you helped put in business the people who defiled your daughter? That your greedy pursuit of more and more money helped make what happened to Allison possible."

"I'm sure you're enjoying this, McCall." His voice cracked. "Did you call just to gloat?"

"No."

"Then why?"

"Your role in all this will come out in the trials that will follow. Your daughter will learn you helped bankroll Luke Tittle's place. The only decision you control is whether Allison hears of your involvement from you or through the media. You told me she once begged you to forgive her indiscretion. It's now time for you to beg her to forgive your greed. Bottom line: this is about Allison, not about you. Handle it right, you blue-blooded bastard."

CHAPTER 49

JACK WALKED INTO Metro P.D. headquarters a few minutes early for his appointment with Chief Mandrake. The front desk called the chief's secretary who approved McCall coming straight back to the chief's office.

"Hello, Jack. You've certainly been keeping my department busy the last couple of days." The chief reached across his desk.

Jack shook his hand, adding his left on top of the chief's right. "Oops, I'm sorry, Chief, I scratched you."

"No problem."

"We're close to wrapping up our inquiry into the death of Chris Andujar. I wanted to bring you current."

The chief took Jack's coat and hung it on the coat tree in the corner, then steadied the swing of the wooden hanger that held his own coat suspended from one of the other hooks.

"First you found an art forgery," the chief said. "Then two Federal fugitives, and now you've nailed Arthur Tyson for murder and blackmail. You've been a busy boy."

Mandrake slipped a pink phone message memo, the only item on his desk, under the padded edge of his desk blotter. "Is all this stuff connected to Chris's death?"

"In a way, may I?" Jack motioned toward the coffee pot on the side table.

"Of course, I should have offered."

"Chris's death was a loose thread. Once I pulled it everything started to unravel."

The chief frowned. "Tyson was a bad cop, but I'd be lying if I didn't admit to mixed emotions. Along with Mary Lou's daddy, the three of us joined the force together, went through the academy together, lots of memories."

Jack rested his cup on a coaster on the small table between the two straight back chairs that fronted the chief's desk; he sat in one of them.

The chief got up to refill his own cup. "Arthur and I agreed long ago that we would not let our different paths be divisive among our common friends. I increasingly found that pretense a strain. To be candid, I'm relieved it's over." He added cream and sugar, stirred, licked the spoon, and set it to blot on a napkin next to the pot, then returned to the chair behind his desk.

"I believe," Jack said, "the story Tyson told in my office was, for the most part, true."

"I've listened to that tape. You surely don't believe that malarkey about a blackmailer who calls himself Moriarty?" Mandrake chuckled. "That's a bit too melodramatic for me."

"Things just don't add up to Tyson being the blackmailer," Jack said, shaking his head.

"What sort of things?"

"First off, Tyson's just not smart enough. The art forgery job is the work of a renaissance crook. That's outside Tyson's Neanderthal mind. Tyson's smash-and-grab, not finesse. His story about Moriarty, he's not capable of thinking that up ahead of time, and the man's wholly incapable of ad-libbing it during interrogation. Tyson's brawn not brains."

"I have to agree with that. At the academy, Tino and I were always helping Arthur with his studies."

"Sherlock Holmes never caught his Moriarty." Jack grinned. "Maybe that'll be my fate too—not catching my Moriarty."

"Okay, for the moment," the chief said, "let's assume there is a Moriarty, and Tyson is not him. You got anything saying who is?"

"Some stuff, but its flimsy. I don't want to keep you."

"If it isn't Tyson, this modern Moriarty is still out there." The chief straightened the lay of his black service tie. "I told the desk to hold my calls. Maybe together we can find another thread to pull."

"I was hoping you'd offer. I've been turning all this every which way but loose for so long that I'm afraid it's become a hopeless snarl. Last week, you helped me reason out how to proceed with surrendering the federal fugitives; I hoped you might offer to do that again. A fresh mind can do wonders."

The chief opened a desk drawer and removed a lined yellow pad. Then he leaned forward and pulled the pencil out of a writing set rooted in a purple crystal geode sitting at the front of his desk. "Shoot."

"Well," Jack began, "our newest client, the one Tyson admits trying to blackmail, told me the blackmailer swore and talked rough. The other marks described the blackmailer as well spoken. Moriarty would be well mannered. He would enjoy pushing emotional buttons to satisfy his feeling of intellectual superiority. Tyson is a ruffian who would enjoy scaring his victims viscerally. The way I see it, we've got two blackmailers, and I've only caught the minnow."

"An interesting theory. Do you figure Tyson or this possible other blackmailer murdered Chris?"

"I think Suggs got that right. Moriarty blackmailed his marks only once and Chris had already paid. Chris didn't have to commit suicide."

"Then why did he?"

"Like the others, Chris had expected to be blackmailed again and again. Right about then he also learned his son was involved in the sexual abuse of a young woman. In the end, Chris was out of money and full of shame."

"What else have you got which points away from Tyson?" Mandrake asked as he repeatedly slid the pink phone memo out and back under the edge of the blotter.

"Tyson said Haviland passed on to Moriarty the tape of Jena having sex with Harkin. The way that one went down, Moriarty handled it without Tyson. And Tyson says he has a solid alibi for the night Benny Haviland was killed. So it would appear Moriarty shot Haviland, or paid the biker Rockton, or somebody else to do it."

"Something you may not know," the chief said, "while Tyson was still with the department, his duties included keeping track of old federal warrants, so the trail on the three fugitives does lead back to him."

Jack shook his head. "Your department didn't get pictures of the fugitives until a year after Tyson left the force, but even if Tyson had found the fugitives without the pictures while he was one of your detectives, it would mean he waited a long time before blackmailing them. Tyson doesn't impress me as either patient or meticulous."

Jack couldn't say it because of his commitment to the mayor, but Tyson also knew about the mayor's affair with Jena Moves, and Tyson would have blackmailed the mayor immediately.

"Tyson used his own voice to call our client, Candy Robson. To the contrary, Moriarty used various means to disguise his voice when speaking to all the other marks." Jack walked over and put his empty cup down on the tray on the side table while he continued spelling it out for the chief. "We interviewed one mark blackmailed for the repayment of IOUs given to Luke Tittle. I think there are more of those victims out there, but the one is enough to tell us that Moriarty has Tittle's records."

Chief Mandrake's face showed surprise.

"You had Tittle set up to give his records to Tino Sanchez," Jack went on, "but Tittle got gunned down. Then Sanchez was killed a few days later. Did he ever actually ever take possession of Tittle's books?"

"No. Tino would have told me." Mandrake raised his large eyebrows "Hell, Tino would have given the records to me. It had to have gone down like it says in the record."

"After being paid, Moriarty returned some of the IOUs Tittle was holding, so Moriarty had to have them."

The chief opened a desk drawer and got a hard candy. It stuck in its plastic wrap, so he held it to his mouth and used his tongue and lips to pull it free before saying, "Could Donny Andujar be Moriarty? If Chris learned his son was a blackmailer in addition to the sexual assault you spoke of, that would go further to explain Chris committing suicide." The chief reached into the same drawer, and tossed a candy to Jack.

Jack caught the piece of candy unwrapped it and put it in his mouth. "I thought that for a while. Donny had worked for Tittle. But to learn about the fugitives he would have needed connections in your department after Tyson left the force. In the end, Donny lacks too much to be Moriarty."

"What about Engels?" Mandrake asked. "He's got all the skills."

"You're right about that; Engels could carry it off. I really considered him, even wondered if Chris might have been in it with him. Chris could have provided the marks and Engels could have run the games. But I couldn't get past two strong reasons for eliminating Engels."

"Which are?"

"Engels would not have shaken down Chris, his own lover, for being gay like him. It would have been too close to home." Jack slid forward on his hard chair and stretched his legs out in front of himself.

The chief folded the phone message in half lengthwise, and then ran his fingernail along the crease to firm the fold. "You said two reasons?"

"Oh, yes. There are lots of ways the CIA's deputy director of covert ops could get crooked cash. Much more cash than he would through these blackmailings, and with more control and less traceability."

The chief reversed the fold on the phone message, flattening it back to full size. "So, then, who in the hell is Moriarty?"

CHAPTER 50

"MORIARTY COULD BE anyone." Jack grinned. "Hell, Chief, you could be Moriarty."

Chief Mandrake tilted back in his chair and clapped. "You've solved the case, Jack."

When they had stopped laughing, Jack said, "You're retiring this summer to the island nation of Vanuatu, a country with no criminal extradition treaty with the U.S."

The chief stopped laughing and expelled a sarcastic snort.

Jack's grin narrowed. "It's an interesting coincidence that both Mandrake and Moriarty start with the letter "M" and both names have eight letters, a little inside humor, Chief?"

Jack took out his new pocket knife, opened the small blade, and cleaned under the fingernail he had used to scratch the back of Mandrake's hand when they shook. Mandrake sat quiet and watched Jack put the residue from under his nail and also the pocketknife in one of the paper coin rounds he had stopped and gotten at the bank, and then put the coin wrap into one of the plastic bags. Jack wasn't sure he had scratched Mandrake hard enough for effective DNA evidence, so the chief couldn't be sure either.

Jack casually reached forward and picked up Mandrake's candy wrapper, and dropped it inside a second plastic bag.

"I know the date," Jack said, "and the exact time Moriarty was in New York to pay Herman Flood the first fifty thousand, and the date he returned to take possession of the four portraits and pay Flood the balance of his fee. You won't be able to account for those hours."

Jack got up and walked to the side table where he picked up the spoon the chief had licked and the napkin on which the spoon had blotted, putting them in a third evidence bag.

Jack sat back down, looked at the chief, and smiled knowingly. "You're Moriarty. You blackmailed one of your lifelong friends, Chris Andujar, and it led to his suicide. You blackmailed Anson and Jensen, Harkin, Wingate and her French lover, and Allison Trowbridge. I have no doubts there are others we haven't found. You blackmailed Haviland into helping you and then murdered him, or possibly paid Rockton to kill him as well as Phoebe Ziegler.

"When you told me of the death of Mary Lou's mom, deep sadness came over you. She was much more than your friend's wife, wasn't she?"

Mandrake's tongue darted out, moistening his lips. "You're full of shit, McCall."

"Mary Lou is your daughter, not your Goddaughter." Jack held up the three bags of prospective DNA evidence. "You know how this works. Mary Lou has locks of her mother's hair and also of Tino's. When she showed me her locket, I could see the follicles on Tino's hair. In a short time the world will know Mary Lou is really your daughter."

Mandrake raised his eyebrows, inhaling deeply. "All her life I've longed to say it out loud. Say it for someone else to hear, my daughter, Mary Lou Mandrake. That felt good, but it should never again be said. Mary Lou has a loving memory of her mother. Let's not soil that. And she cherishes the image of the father she knows, Tino Sanchez. Let her remember her parents as she does. It will comfort her when she learns her Uncle Harry is Moriarty."

The only decent spot left in his blackened heart is his love for his secret daughter.

"You know what's coming," Jack said, making it seem as inevitable as daylight follows darkness. "The D.A. will charge you with multiple counts of murder. The whole story will be told and retold in the tabloids: chief of police blackmails citizens, and has a secret daughter."

Jack rubbed his hands together. "You killed Tino Sanchez after he got the IOUs from Tittle. It's likely you also killed Tittle after he gave Sanchez those records, then killed Leoni to cover your murder of Tino Sanchez."

Mandrake started to interrupt, then put his arms on his desk, wrinkling the pink phone memo. He looked at Jack, his face twisting into a surrendering smile. "How did you first know?"

"At first, I didn't know. More like I didn't want to know. But little things kept pointing your way. I kept shaking them off but, in the end, you were the only one with links to Tittle's records, the know-how to control Tyson, and the instincts to pick up on Chris's hidden sexual orientation. You had the access to learn the identity of the three federal fugitives. You were at the scene when Tino Sanchez was killed. The entire report on his and Leoni's death came from one unimpeachable source, the chief of police, you."

Chief Mandrake smiled the way one does at an inside joke. "I had Rockton set up to do one final job, to kill you. After somehow you discovered the surprise I had left under your car. Then I was going to take Rockton out, but my officers, unknowingly, did it for me. His fate was sealed when he touched Mary Lou. Rockton shot Haviland on my order, but I had nothing to do with the biker killing Phoebe Ziegler.

That was his thing, but so what, this city will never run out of whores." He gestured dismissively.

"Go to hell, Moriarty."

"Hah," the chief bellowed. "There is no hell. A man reproduces and dies with no more grandeur than a pulled weed."

"Moriarty was smart," Jack said. "He was careful, patient, and detail-conscious. So are you. In the end you were the only one to whom I could draw connecting lines from all the victims, the blackmailer's traits, and the related events. The only part I couldn't figure, still can't, is why. You're one of America's most highly respected police chiefs."

The centers of Mandrake's eyes went dark like lusterless black thumbtacks inserted to hold up his face.

"All my life I believed in the system. I fought for principle. Believed in God. In the Catholic Church. I believed that good would prevail. After cancer took my wife in her prime, I could no longer believe in myths and blind faith. In the years following my fling with Mary Lou's mother, I came to realize that my wife was one of God's finest, yet He took her while leaving the scum I dealt with every day. Then Father Michaels sexually assaulted my ... my daughter."

His eyebrows moved downward, leading his forehead lower. "The church gave Father Michaels a transfer, a slap on the wrist. What was true for the rest of the world was even true of the holy Catholic and Apostolic Church. The church only cared about getting their dirt under the rug before Sunday collections started dropping. Principle didn't mean shit. Money. Only money. The rest was a mirage. That's when I knew the truth. There is only one real choice for each of us—prey or predator. That day I became a predator."

He laughed derisively. "Justice and goodness. To protect and serve. So much horseshit. I decided to get mine and live the high life."

Mandrake again reached for his candy drawer.

Jack moved forward, sliding his fingers under the overhang on the chief's desk, palms up, ready to flip the desk. But Mandrake's hand came out grasping only another hard candy. He unwrapped it and put it in his mouth. "Hey, Jack, you want another wrapper?" He laughed and massaged his temple, then went silent. When he looked back up, water had welled in his eyes. "I loved Tino Sanchez. He just wouldn't let go of his belief in heaven and hell."

Except for the caricature effect of his massive eyebrows, the chief's face wasn't an unusual face. A bit aged. A bit homely, but certainly not a face anyone would see as patently evil.

"I'll do anything to spare Mary Lou."

"It's too late, Chief."

Mandrake smiled in the friendly way he always had before. "I still hold the IOU you gave me at your open house. I imagine it wouldn't cover you forgetting about my being Moriarty?"

Jack slowly shook his head.

Mandrake swiveled his chair around and picked up a picture from the credenza behind him, a photo from his swearing-in as chief of police. He laid it flat on his desk and, true to his fastidious nature, lined the frame up with the top edge of his blotter.

"Jack, you're a man who likes to pay his debts." Mandrake took off his badge and laid it on top of the picture. "Give me ten minutes to straighten my things and we'll call it square."

He got up and walked to the coat rack, put on his coat, looped the hanger back on the tree, steadied the swing, and fastened the buttons. "Please wait in the chair just outside. I can't get out except past you." He put his hand on Jack's shoulder. "I'll stamp your IOU paid for ten minutes."

Evil had rotted the man from the inside, leaving only a light-skinned veneer over his private hell, and a desperate desire to protect his daughter.

"Where are the four presidential portraits?" Jack asked.

"At my home. That was the only time I went for anything but cash, and it turned sour. I had an Iranian buyer set up who could get the portraits out under diplomatic protection. While I was returning from getting them from Flood in New York, the man was called back to Iran. He disappeared without a trace ... Ten minutes. Please."

Jack understood why the chief wanted the time, but he had not decided whether to agree. He had seen men on the battlefield give up their lives for their comrades, while others made the same choice to avoid capture, or to not return home a disabled burden to their families. The chief wanted to save his daughter the pain of learning that he was her real father, and that he had killed the man she lovingly remembered as her father. He also wanted to spare her the humiliation of the inevitable long and very public trial.

Jack stood up and walked to the door. With his hand on the knob, he turned back. "Ten minutes, Chief, not eleven."

Jack fixed his eyes on the wall clock across from the chair just outside the chief's office. Each time the second hand completed a full sweep the minute hand jerked forward. The fourth jerk seemed to tug the minute hand too far. The fifth jerk seemed a little short, as if making up for the longer fourth jerk. The process repeated again and again.

Sweep. Jerk. Sweep. Jerk.

Six minutes. Seven.

Jack felt his grip tighten on the cold metal arms of the chair.

Eight minutes. Nine.

The instant the second hand swept past twelve for the tenth time, Jack felt the wall vibrate and heard a sound he had heard all too often in his life.

Sergeant Suggs and another detective came running toward him, their guns held with the muzzles up. Suggs went into his chief's office high, the other detective low. Jack followed.

The side of Chief Mandrake's face rested on the desk blotter, a pool of his blood discoloring the wrinkled pink phone message. His right hand, in an unnatural position, still clutched his police pistol. The chief's left hand had flopped sideways to rest against the spacebar on his keyboard, sending the cursor on an endless line-after-line journey across the screen.

The scene reminded Jack of the police picture taken of Chris's destroyed face collapsed on the desk in his study. The Andujar case had come full circle.

Suggs lifted his chief's sleeve. The cursor halted. Then Suggs slid free the yellow legal pad with its red-soaked edge. He held it at an angle so Jack could read with him.

I'm Moriarty. Tyson told the truth in his interview at the office of Jack McCall. I killed Tittle after Tino Sanchez received Tittle's records. I got Sanchez to keep quiet about getting Tittle's records by convincing him it might help us if the killer believed the records were still out there somewhere. Sanchez insisted later that the records be booked as evidence. I told him of my blackmail scheme and begged him to go along. He refused, so I killed Tino Sanchez, the father of Mary Lou Sanchez, and the best cop I ever knew. The best man I ever knew. I paid Rockton to kill Haviland whom I had blackmailed to gain entry into various offices in buildings cleaned by his employer.

At the bottom and onto the next page he had listed the location of the four presidential portraits, Tittle's records, and the banks with the account numbers where the funds the marks had paid would be found. He had also listed the insurance carrier for his life policy and stated that Mary Lou, his goddaughter, was the sole beneficiary.

Mandrake had not admitted killing Father Michaels in Boston. He could not without leading the authorities to discover that Mary Lou was his daughter.

Jack reread one part, silently: "I killed Tino Sanchez, the father of Mary Lou Sanchez." Mandrake was again telling Jack to let Mary Lou keep the papa who lived in her heart.

Meticulous to the end, the statement was signed, Harold Mandrake, Former Chief of Police, District of Columbia, Metropolitan Police Department.

CHAPTER 51

JACK WALKED OUT of Metro after promising Suggs he would return in two hours to give him a statement regarding his meeting with Chief Mandrake. The place was bedlam. The cops could use the two hours.

The truth is never cruel, only the act about which the truth is being told. Still, that truth could only bring Mary Lou pain. He would discuss his decision with Max and Nora, but he would not tell the police. Chief Mandrake had been right; the fact that he was Mary Lou's birth father did not need to be in the public domain.

When Jack got back to MI, Nora and Mary Lou were talking.

"Nora. Mary Lou. Please go into my office." It must have been something about his demeanor for neither of them said or asked anything. They just got up and went into his office.

He put the phones on hold, locked the door and joined Nora and Mary Lou who were sitting together on the couch. He took the younger woman's hand.

"There's no easy way to tell you this honey. Your Uncle Harry is dead. He shot himself."

Mary Lou denied what she had heard, then went into Nora's arms and sobbed and talked. She compared her Uncle Harry's death to the loss of Tino Sanchez, the man she believed to be her father. When she asked what happened, Jack told them the whole story, leaving out that Mandrake was her birth father. Some day, he would tell Mary Lou the rest of it. After life had put more of a crust on her, and after she had digested the pain that Uncle Harry had been the modern Moriarty.

Before heading back to Metro, Jack called Max and filled him in. Then he said, "Drop the tail on Donny Andujar and come cover the office. Nora's going to take Mary Lou to my home. They'll both stay with me for a few days."

Mandrake had indirectly confirmed Jack's theory. There were still members of his blackmail club they had not identified. The total of the money listed on the chief's confession was close to double the amounts paid by the victims Jack had uncovered.

Donny's business would be shut, and he might serve some time. Jack would speak to the FBI on behalf of the Clarks. They had been decent citizens for decades, and the case might not have been solved without their cooperation, certainly not as quickly. He doubted any charges would be filed against the copyist, Herman Flood, who had been both gullible and culpable, but not truly criminal. Perhaps Allison Trowbridge's girlfriend, who had run away, would now come home.

While driving Jack called Sarah Andujar from his car, hoping to reach her before she heard anything. Moriarty was already the lead story, limited to the often used teaser: details on the late news.

"Hello, Jack." Her gentle voice sounded loving.

"Our investigation is complete."

He drove another block before she spoke. "Tell me."

"I need to spend some time at the police department, it might stretch into hours. I'll come by around eight and tell you all about it. But you were correct, Chris had been black-mailed. The blackmailer was Harry Mandrake."

He heard her gasp. "Are you certain?"

"No doubts. He confessed before committing suicide."

"My God. First my Christopher. Now Harry."

"Are you okay?"

Sarah sniffled. "I'm okay. Thank you for telling me."

"I'll see you around eight."

Her voice stopped him before he hit the *end* button. "Jack!"

"Yes?"

"What—" He heard her take a deep breath. "What did Harry blackmail my husband over?"

"We'll talk about that tonight."

"I won't be hearing it on the news, will I?"

"No. I'll see you at eight." He hung up just as he pulled into the lot at Metro PD.

Jack sat in one of six chairs in a mid-sized Metro conference room. The out-of-the-way room was never used for case suspects because it had no two-way mirror and, Jack guessed, no listening mechanism. The air was a bit musty and the rectangular table had more places with scratches than places without. The other chairs were occupied by Mayor Molloy, the police commissioner, Metro's deputy chief of police, its chief of detectives, and Sergeant Paul Suggs, the first officer on the case that had started it all, the suicide of Dr. Christopher Andujar.

The police commissioner spoke first. "There will be no minutes and this meeting will not be taped or recorded. When this meeting finishes we will discuss the timing and content of a public statement."

During the meeting, Jack picked up whiffs of the usual police department odors: sweat, the supposedly forbidden tobacco and a new one, the odor of cordite that had been moving through the building's air ducts since Chief Mandrake discharged his sidearm.

The official reason for the mayor's attendance was that Jack's statement addressed the criminal conduct of DC's dead chief of police, but Jack knew the mayor was also there to learn if his involvement with Phoebe Ziegler might come out.

The meeting started with Jack telling how his suspicions had begun, how they grew, and the content of his meeting with Mandrake. The meeting ended at seven-fifteen. On the way out of Metro Jack saw detectives and uniformed officers huddled in small groups, talking in hushed voices.

"What will Mandrake's death mean for the department?" The question's hidden meaning: how will this impact me? Another he overheard was, "Chief Mandrake was a good dude. I heard they're going to make Deputy Asshole our new chief," and on and on.

Mayor Molloy suddenly appeared from a side hallway. He grabbed Jack's sleeve and tugged him inside an empty office. "You knew about the chief when you were in my office, didn't you?"

"Mr. Mayor, I had a strong suspicion, but I would not discredit the chief by mentioning it to anyone. I wasn't absolutely certain until Mandrake confessed."

Molloy continually glanced in one direction or another, even though the two of them were alone. "The chief could have had a million character witnesses," Molloy said. "Why didn't he fight it?"

"Who knows," Jack said. "Perhaps he felt the money and portraits would eventually be found. Perhaps he feared going to jail as an ex-cop or the shame of losing his reputation. Perhaps his conscience finally overwhelmed him, or he just didn't want to go through the legal process and all he knew that it entailed. We may never know, Mr. Mayor."

"Still, if the story gets out—"

Jack cut him off. "It's over, Mr. Mayor. Mandrake confessed. He's dead. He told us where to find the presidential portraits, Tittle's records, and the money. I expect Tittle's records will combine with Tyson's confession about payoffs to give you a solid picture of police and city corruption over the past five to ten years. All in all, Mayor, that's a pretty good haul."

CHAPTER 52

JACK ARRIVED AT Sarah Andujar's home a few minutes after eight. The porch light was off. His shadow from the streetlight led him until he caught up with it on the porch. The door was ajar. No lights were on inside except for a stiletto from the streetlight that had sliced through the slightly parted drapes. He pushed the door a little farther and eased in sideways.

"Sarah? It's Jack."

She didn't answer.

He opened the hall door into the garage. Her car was there; the hood was cool to the touch. A faint light was coming from Chris's bedroom next to the study. He looked in. A small lamp was lit on the nightstand next to the bed. The comforter and sheet had been folded back on an angle. The room was empty, the adjoining bath dark. He went upstairs. Sarah's bedroom was dark, her bed made.

The outside temperature was mild so he went to see if she had fallen asleep on the sun porch. She hadn't. When he stepped back into the kitchen, he saw a note, with today's date, attached to the refrigerator with a little magnet in the shape of a red rose.

"Chris, I went to visit a neighbor. I'll be with you soon."

Sarah had spoken of Chris's spirit being in the house. Still, Jack had no idea Sarah felt the presence of her dead husband to the point that she would leave him notes.

As he turned to leave the kitchen, he glanced into the backyard softly lit from the circular dome lights along the brick walkway. Her slaughtered roses were still strewn around the yard. The cuttings, now dried enough to lay much flatter to the ground, revealed that the American Red Beauty, the rose bush Sarah had gotten from her mother's garden, stood proud, the only rose bush she had cut down.

Jack stood staring at the decimated garden. Then he ran to his car.

The speedometer needle surged upward, the engine straining to respond to the demand from his foot.

Troy Engels lived on Jefferson Street, a few blocks from the Andujar home. While Jack had worked for the agency, he had once been in Engels's home. Cornering on two wheels left little time for thought, but he tried to recall the floor plan of the house he needed to reach before it was too late.

Engels had been Jack's control for two of his early covert counterterrorism missions. Jack would never like Troy Engles, but Engels had not been involved in the blackmailings or murders, so Jack didn't like the sudden thought that had spurred him to action.

The fountain near Engels's front door slurped and gurgled while throwing water into the air, then catching it a moment later in its own circular pool. Jack barely heard his knock over the action of the fountain. He looked through the glass in the narrow relight next to the door. He saw no one. He tried the door. It was unlocked.

Engels is a security freak. He would lock his door.

For the second time in less than an hour he cautiously moved into a private residence, this time the residence of the deputy director of the Central Intelligence Agency. His Beretta 92FS held just above his shoulder.

The living room lamp was lit, still the scene felt foreboding. Except for a few shadows, the darkened kitchen held no surprises. A Land Rover was parked in the garage. The hood cold.

A faint line of light brightened the narrow space beneath a closed door at the far end of the hall. He headed that way, checking the guests' bathroom and the laundry room as he passed them.

He pressed himself against the wall, aimed his 9mm at the center of the doorway, reached out with his left hand and eased the door open far enough to be sure no one stood behind it. He entered the master bedroom and pushed open the door to the connected bath to find the source of the light: a nightlight plugged in next to the sink.

The CIA's director of covert operations sleeps with a nightlight. Doesn't that beat all?

By the time Jack returned to the bedroom, his eyes had adjusted enough to reveal an outline on the bed, the outline of a man. As he drew closer, Jack recognized the man. Engels was naked. He was dead.

Jack checked the walk-in closet before turning on the lamp.

A bullet had tunneled through Engels's wrinkled forehead. Blood that had first pooled in his right eye socket had spilled over to trail down his cheek, creating a jagged red shadow on one side of his head.

A gun rested hard on the nightstand. The shooter had needed both hands for what had come next. Engels's genitals had been severed and stuffed into his mouth. There was no blood spray outward onto the sheet. His heart had stopped before the violent amputation.

Within the intelligence community Engels was known as a man of extraordinary achievement. He had crawled out of the squalor of his birthplace into the inner circle of his nation's intelligence operations. In Jack's opinion there were times when Engels had been overzealous. Times when he had used people as pawns in his black-ops chess games. Still, Engels hadn't deserved to die so ugly. No one did.

Back in the living room, Jack took out his cell to call Sergeant Suggs before it dawned on him that he was in Virginia—outside Suggs's jurisdiction.

He heard the shrill sound of wind fighting through a crack. The noise led him to the rear sliding glass door which had been left open less than an inch. To avoid smudging any prints, he stretched as high as he could, wedged his fingers into the crack and slid the door over far enough to let him out to the rear patio.

"Sarah?" he whispered as he stepped outside. "It's Jack ... Sarah."

She did not answer. She was lying in the cold on a chaise lounge. As he stepped toward her, he kicked something, her pruning shears still sticky with sap from her roses, and blood from Troy Engels's genitals.

Sarah had not cut down her roses looking for Chris; she had used the roses to symbolically castrate her unfaithful husband, and now she had done the same thing, literally, to her husband's lover.

The scratches from the thorns of her roses would no longer itch; her scabs would no longer draw tight. Sarah Andujar was dead.

A bloody kitchen knife had fallen to the deck next to her frail body. The cuts were so deep that her right hand extending beyond the arm of a chaise lounge, elbow-up, appeared to hinge at the wrist. Her blood had flowed within an expansion joint in the decking and into the pool, further darkening the unlit water.

He fought off the impulse to shut her eyes; nothing should be changed before the authorities arrived.

Whap. Whap.

An envelope, anchored by a heavy glass candle holder, flapping in a sudden breeze busily slapped the top of a wire-mesh patio table. A shaky hand had written on its face: To Be Opened by Jack McCall. He sat on the stationary end of the diving board.

Dear Jack:

I have slain the beast. You are undoubtedly wondering why.

I told you and the police I went to bed the night of Christopher's death and found him the next morning. I lied. That night when I got home from my book club I found Christopher, holding his gun, sitting in his study. He was crying. He told me he had paid our life savings to a blackmailer who threatened to reveal that he had taken his heart from me and given it to Troy Engels. He told me he did not wish to disgrace me further. He begged me. "I can't do this without your help." He put the gun against his temple and pleaded. You knew Christopher as, everyone thought of him, a man's man, but he was soft inside. I slid my finger over his, over the trigger. He looked at me and nodded his head. I squeezed with him, or maybe I squeezed alone. I am no longer certain. I hired you with the desperate hope you would find that Engels had been the blackmailer and that you would recover our money.

Now I won't need it.

Donny stayed with me a few nights right after his father's death. One night after Donny thought I had gone to sleep, I heard him talking on the phone to Engels about his being a silent investor in Donny's disgraceful club. So Engels had also contributed to the decay of my son.

I wanted Engels to be the blackmailer so I could see him in jail. That cannot be so, now, I'll see him in hell.

Sarah Andujar

Jack realized then there had been clues he had not seen or perhaps had not wanted to see. When he and Nora had visited Sarah to give their first progress report, he had looked at pictures hanging in Chris's study. None of the pictures of Chris with his friends included Troy Engels. When he told Sarah he had the pictures Nora had salvaged from Chris's office, Sarah had lost it for a moment, gotten angry and insisted they be thrown away. The pictures Chris had kept in his office all included Engels. That clue had been there. Subtle perhaps, but there and he had failed to see it.

The latest hint had come less than an hour ago, when Sarah asked, "I won't be hearing on the evening news why

Harry Mandrake blackmailed my Christopher, will I?" She had been afraid Chris's relationship with Engels would become common knowledge. In the end, she could not face that her husband was gay.

Jack went inside and called a number he would always know, the twenty-four/seven secure line that rang directly into Engels's department at the CIA.

"This is Jack McCall. Troy Engels is dead. His death is not the result of any terrorist or foreign activity. He's at home. You know the address. I'll come by Monday morning to be debriefed ... No, I will not talk to the control officer on duty. Tell him if I'm bothered before Monday I'll suffer a massive loss of memory."

Jack hung up without waiting for a reply. He unknotted his tie, leaving the two ends trailing unevenly down his shirt, and headed for his car.

When Jack turned onto George Mason, he dialed his cell phone. This was scoop time in the newspaper business.

"Eric Dunn."

"Eric. Jack McCall."

"Jack. It's frigging late."

"You wanted the scoop. Get out your pencil."

Jack told the columnist about the blackmailer who called himself Moriarty, a longtime good cop whose heart had rotted. Next he told Eric about the dirty ex-cop and scummy PI, Arthur Tyson. He also told the fascinating story of the heist at the National Portrait Gallery, and how that connected to Donny Andujar's club and the death of Phoebe Ziegler. Lastly, he spoke of the payoffs and Tittle's records.

He omitted the deaths of Troy Engels and Sarah Andujar. He'd leave the CIA to decide how to spin their deaths.

He ended with the story of the blue-blooded investor, Dean Trowbridge, another of America's growing number of amoral, I-can't-get-enough money grabbers.

Then Jack hung up without saying anything more.

Not even goodbye, take care, or I'll see ya around.

EPILOGUE

FOR THE PAST week, the stories of blackmailings, murders, and indiscretions had unsettled the nation's capital, but like a pail of water left to sit after having been stirred, things had settled back to calm. Well, DC's brand of calm anyway.

On Monday Jack had gone to the CIA as promised and told his story. By the end of the week the agency had loudly praised Engels and quietly closed their file on his death. A separate story told of the sad suicide of Sarah Andujar, a widow who could not survive the grief of having lost her husband a few months earlier, when he too had taken his own life.

The Friday evening sun would set in a little over an hour. Jack decided he would watch it go down from his balcony while sipping a little Maker's Mark, and use the solitude to tuck his memories of Rachel into a warm private corner of his mind where he could visit her, while otherwise letting her go.

Tomorrow morning he was taking Roy to ride a big dump truck. In the afternoon the boy was going to a friend's house for a sleepover, and Jack had a date with Roy's mother, Janet.

He cracked the bedroom door to let in some fresh air, turned on his gas log fireplace, and settled down at the small desk in his bedroom. The time had come to prepare his final report to Sarah.

Dear Sarah:

My real assignment was not identifying Moriarty, but finding out what happened to your husband. Chris and the mysterious Troy Engels died for two primary reasons. They lacked the courage to live their sexual orientation, and together they shattered your fantasy life.

Chris might have coped with the blackmailing, but he was devastated when he learned Donny had sexually assaulted his patient Allison Trowbridge. Then you stepped in and helped pull the trigger. I can't guess what the final outcome will be for Donny and, frankly, I don't care.

You had met Mary Lou Sanchez. I expect she will rise above the twin catastrophes of the murder of the father she knew, Tino Sanchez, the good cop, and the suicide of Harry Mandrake, her birth father, the bad cop.

True to eternal history, the members of each generation must perish or survive, despite the sins of their parents who never meant them harm. In the end, life is a series of choices. These young people will make theirs as we made ours.

In the final analysis, justice is a perfect concept we struggle to apply to imperfect people and circumstance.

McCall Investigations, Inc.

Jack McCall

Jack crumpled his report to Sarah, and tossed it in the fireplace.

The End

NOTE TO READERS

It is for you that I write so I would love to hear from you now that you have finishing reading the story. I can be reached by email at david@davidbishopbooks.com, please no attachments. For those of you who write or who aspire to write I encourage you to write, rewrite, and write again until your prose live on the pages the way it lives in your mind. If you have found errors of fact or location, I would like to hear about them. As for any errors you might imagine in spelling or punctuation or capitalization, please let me rest in peace. There are many conventions and styles with regard to these matters, and I often have characters speak incorrectly intentionally, for that is how I envision that character would speak. I will reply to all emails that respect these requests. And with your email address, I will send you announcements for my upcoming novels. Thank you for reading this story. I'd love to hear from you.

With appreciation,
David Bishop

P.S. I have two, maybe three other writing projects in mind for release this year. *The Original Alibi,* and possibly a collection of short stories. I may also get another novel finished: *Empty Promises.* These are working titles and may be revised. To stay current on these endeavors and other announcements, please visit my website from time to time or stay in touch with me through email, Facebook or Twitter.

www.davidbishopbooks.com
david@davidbishopbooks.com
facebookcom/davidbishopbooks
twitter.com/davidbishop7

An excerpt from David Bishop's next novel, *The Original Alibi*, begins on the following page. For a list of David's other novels and their release dates, please see the front of this book.

The Original Alibi

A Matt Kile Mystery

by

David Bishop

PROLOGUE

"I BELIEVE THAT'S your cell phone, dear." The woman's husband said.

"Hello, Mrs. Clark," said a voice into her ear. "I see you are enjoying your first evening walk on the beach with your new puppy. How lovely. Have you and Mr. Clark named the pooch?"

"Who is this?"

"It doesn't matter. What matters is that you stay on the line after what is about to happen, happens."

"What are you talking about?" Mrs. Clark demands, "Who are you?"

Right then the leash Mrs. Clark held went limp, their white poodle falling to the sand. "Bobby, what happened? Snookie is, I don't know, she's just . . . down." Mrs. Clark held her cell phone as if she no longer knew she had it in her hand.

Bobby, her husband bent down, his knees displacing the sand next to Snookie. "She's dead, Mel. I think Snookie's been shot."

Melinda Clark began to bounce on her toes, her hands waving spasmodically. She dropped her phone onto the beach,

i

bent down to Snookie and began to cry. She went to her husband; he held her.

Several minutes later, Bobby Clark picked up his wife's cell phone, shook off the sand, and started to close the top when he heard a loud voice. He held the phone to his ear. "Hello?"

"I've been waiting. Sorry about Snookie. It was necessary. You should know I took no pleasure in it."

"Did you do this?" Mr. Clark asked. "Who the hell are you?"

"To your left, near the partially burnt log I've left a box for you to use to take Snookie home. It's the right size. The inside has a soft new towel. It should do nicely."

"You shot Snookie? Why?"

"Take Snookie home and bury her in your yard. You will hear from me. In the meantime, be glad you were not walking your newest grandson, Bobby, named after you, I presume. Your wife sometimes walks the little tike on a leash just as she today walked Snookie. I will know if you say anything about this, to anyone. If you do, Bobby Junior will be my next target."

"But what do you want? Why us?"

"All that will be made clear. Do not fret needlessly. There will be no more violence if you do as you've been told. What will be required of you will not be difficult. It will not cost you any money. And it will be painless, if you follow orders. We'll talk soon."

The phone went dead.

THE ORIGINAL ALIBI
CHAPTER 1

ELEVEN YEARS LATER:

"Don't forget boss, we got a ten o'clock appointment. Its eight now," Axel said, as he handed me the morning paper, and put down a tray holding a glass of fresh-squeezed orange juice and a buttered English muffin.

It was pleasant enough sitting on the balcony, a little chilly but that's why they make robes.

Axel started working for me only a few days ago, but we'd known each other for years in a very different setting. We were cellmates during my four years in state prison. I looked up. "Isn't that my shirt you're wearing?"

"Yeah."

"And my belt, why are you wearing my belt?"

"You wouldn't want your pants to fall down, would you, boss?"

"No, of course I wouldn't. And before you set up any more of these appointments, let me remind you I write mysteries. I don't handle cases in real life."

"You was a homicide dick and a good one from what I hear. And you got a PI license."

"I just wanted to prove I could get one after the governor pardoned me. I'm a writer now, end of story."

"Aren't you cold out here, boss?" Axel wrapped his arms around himself, gripping his biceps. "You wanna go inside?"

"It's a little nippy, but I'll stick for a while. But I do wish they made robes in various lengths. No reason they can't." I'd been six-three since the eleventh grade but over the years robes keep getting shorter. Probably for the same reason two-by-fours are no longer two-inches-by-four-inches.

I helped Axel's parole along with the promise of a job. He had been inside for thirty years, during which he became as sweet a senior citizen as you'll ever know. A half a million dollar payroll had been taken by a lone gunman, without violence. The jury had found Axel guilty. Axel had never changed his claim of innocence, but he had sometimes winked at me when the subject came up. It was likely why they held onto Axel while letting out younger hardasses because of the overpopulation of prisons. So I did what I could to grease the wheels.

In these first few days, his duties included trips to the dry cleaners and doing the home laundry. Unfortunately, we wore the same size clothes, or near enough for Axel who was an even six feet. For each wearing, he hand-altered my slacks by rolling up the pant legs. He also adjusted for our different waist sizes. I wore size thirty-eight and, I'm guessing, his waist size at thirty-six, maybe thirty-four. My guess was based on his having my belt cinched up two notches tighter, which meant there would now be his and mine cinch marks in the leather.

"Boss, you remember that movie where Jack Nicholson's character said, 'never waste a boner and never trust a fart. Well, that man was a prophet." Then Axel rushed inside. The Bucket List was a wonderful movie but I didn't like him quoting that line while he was wearing my slacks. I settled back and looked at the paper with an eye out for Axel's return.

A few minutes later, Axel came back out. I felt some relief as he was still wearing the same pair of my pants. "You helped save Clarice Talmadge," he said, as if he had never left the conversation. "I kept up with that story before you got me sprung."

I looked over at a gull that was circling past the balcony just off the railing. "I didn't get you sprung. The parole board was about to release you anyway. You'd been in long enough. I just tossed a job offer in the mix. That's all."

"That's what tipped the scales." Axel looked over at the gull that squawked while making its third pass.

I knew why the gulls, there were three now, were squawking. Axel sometimes threw pieces of bread out over the rail and he hadn't this morning. This was why feeding the birds was against the building policy. I'd have to speak to him about it, but for now I couldn't deny him the kind of small pleasures he had been denied for decades.

"You got out because you were no longer a threat to society, maybe to my wardrobe, but not to society."

"Well, that don't change the brilliant way you saved Clarice Talmadge's ass and, from what I've seen in the hallway, hers is an ass I'm glad you saved."

"Clarice was different. She was a neighbor and a friend accused of killing her husband, Garson. I just handled the investigation for her defense attorney."

"This case'll be different too, boss," he said while picking up the coffee carafe.

"How many times I gotta tell you to stop calling me boss? It's not necessary."

"Seems right to me, after all I work for you."

"You can't call me Matt, but you can wear my pants?" I held up my empty cup.

"Now you got it, boss." He filled my cup.

"The appointment, fill me in."

Axel took a seat and poured himself a little coffee. "Not much yet to tell. This guy, Franklin's his name, Reginald Franklin III, how's that for a handle, he's an attorney with a client who needs your help. He freely admitted his client specified Matthew Kile as the investigator he wanted. Admitting that up front told me that money's not an issue. I told him it would be a grand for this morning, just to talk to you and see if you'll handle the case. He understands that money's gone whether or not you join up. He didn't quibble. He's bringing the check."

I expected Axel would be around during the Franklin meeting. Axel didn't really have a set schedule. If I needed him, I told him and he'd be there. Otherwise, he came and went as he pleased and when he wasn't around I shifted for myself. I think Axel saw himself as my Kato or Dr. Watson or some such character. If I could have my choice, I'd prefer him as Archie Goodwin, the able assistant of Nero Wolfe, but then I would fail in comparison to Wolfe. My waistline was likely only half of Wolfe's girth, not to mention my falling well short of his genius.

"So what do you have going today?" I asked.

"After our meeting with Franklin, I've got a few errands then I'll have lunch with the fellas at Mackie's. Don't worry, boss, Franklin won't know I'm around unless you call for me."

"You think Franklin could be the real client?"

"No way, he's fronting for someone. I could tell by his voice. He wasn't uptight. He did tell me it was some old case the cops have tossed aside. The dude's a smoker too, so get him out on the balcony if he tries to light up. A pipe, I think. I could hear him inhale and bite down on the stem."

After thirty years in the big house, as Axel still called prison, he had mastered reading the tone and pace of people's voices. He can read body language or faces, cons or bulls. All the old timers could do it, at least the ones with an ample helping of brains and judgment.

"The odds say I won't take it."

"Why not? You've about done up the book you was working on. And, hey, a grand's nothing to sneeze at. You know?"

THE ORIGINAL ALIBI
CHAPTER TWO

IT WAS THE eighteenth of December, when I parked my new Ford Expedition in the turnaround in front of the home of General Whittaker, the client of the attorney, Reginald Franklin III. His home, an elegant place that looked to be about six thousand square feet, located south of Long Beach, backed up to the Pacific Ocean. The door was opened by a man about fifty in a white shirt with a starched collar, the rest of his dress being black. His pants were hitched up closer to his neck than his navel. His ears reached out from his head like they were expected to catch balls rather than words.

He looked me up and down without disclosing the impression he gleaned from having done so. "Good evening, Mr. Kile. You're expected." Seeing my surprise at being recognized, he added, "Your picture is on the dust covers of your books. My name is Charles, Mr. Kile."

Few people called them dust covers any longer so Charles was a reader and, apparently, one not yet converted to reading eBooks.

"Please follow me." Charles was an average sized man in his late fifties. He looked fit and confident in his ability to do his job. He led me into a wide junction in the hallway, next to a wonderfully decorated Christmas tree, tall enough to grace both the ground floor and the second story which was open overhead. "Please wait here, Mr. Kile, while I let the general know you've arrived. Some slight noise or movement caused me to step beyond the tree and look up the stairwell to my left.

From the balcony, a nubile woman wearing a black something that aggressively fell within the category of lingerie, said, "You must be Mr. Kile." It wasn't a question. Not the way she said it.

I smiled and nodded. Having always believed that seeing a woman in skimpy lingerie meant, at the very least, that the relationship automatically advanced to a first name basis, I said, "Call me, Matt." We exchanged smiles only they weren't equal. Hers was framed in red and had a gloss that reflected the top light on the Christmas tree.

"Well, Matt," she said, "Charles sat a tray on the side table when he went to answer the door. Would you be a sweetheart and finish bringing it up?" She added, "Please," while leaning her forearms on the banister. At least I assumed her forearms were on the banister. I wanted to be a good sweetheart so I picked up the tray which held one glass and a decanter of something you and I would both guess was alcoholic and started up the stairs.

"This is a lovely home," I said after advancing a short distance.

"Yes it is. During the general's career, toward the end when he was a member of the joint chiefs, this home entertained two U.S. presidents and one pope."

"With you wearing a much different outfit, I'm sure."

"I was living with my mother then," she said, "and a little young during those years to wear something like this." She stood straight, bust out, and turned slowly to be certain I had fully grasped, figuratively speaking of course, the composition of "something like this." I actually preferred her adorning the banister, but if that sounded like a complaint, it lacked substance. I had come not expecting to see anyone more attractive than a long-retired general.

I was ten steps from her when Charles silently arrived beside me and took the tray. I stopped, wishing that Charles had waited for me at the bottom of the stairs.

"The General will see you now, Mr. Kile. Please follow me back downstairs to the study."

As we turned, she revealed her platform heels and red toenails by coming down the stairs far enough to take the tray. She was old enough to realize that platform heels and skimpy lingerie went together like me and a warm feeling. Had I worn a hat I would have held in front myself as she came closer. She and I exchanged one of those smiles that meant the kinds of things that smilers in such situations are never sure about. Then I switched my attention to not tripping and rolling down the stairs.

Over my shoulder, she said, "I hope we can continue getting acquainted some other time." I held the railing and turned to see her again displayed on the banister.

"I'd like that," I said. Then I followed Charles down the stairs, well, I did after wishing I might one day be reincarnated as a banister, but not just any banister, her banister.

"Matt." I turned back and looked up at her. "Ditch the tie. You can do better." Then she turned her head, tossing her blond hair across her shoulders, and she was gone.

"Charles, who was the lady?"

"Karen Whittaker, sir, the general's daughter. She's thirty-five, in case you're curious about that. The general was a late poppa." His tone did not disclose disapproval, but I did detect a slight shake of his head.

"Why, Charles, I understood it was bad form to talk about a woman's age."

"Yes, sir. But not Karen. She's proud of being thirty-five and looking twenty-five. She works at it. Hard." We shared those brief looks that men share. I'd explain, but the guys would kick me out of the club because they would know some ladies would read this.

General Whittaker rose from his chair, slowly, but agilely for his age. His body was now slighter than it looked in pictures of him from his robust years, yet he still had a military posture. A burgundy colored jacket, not exactly a smoking jacket, but not a sport coat either, covered a long-sleeved khaki shirt. The jacket tailored to expose a matching measure of shirt cuff on each of his arms, which were thin enough that the garment hung as cleanly as it would on a store mannequin. He was well dressed and neat except for a crop of white hair freely growing from his ears. His wrists were frail. The skin on the backs of hands, mottled. Still, his handshake remained mildly firm, yet cool to the touch.

"Mr. Kile," he said, "as you stated in one of your books, I like people better than principles, and people without principles best of all. And from what I've learned you should be one of my favorites. And I like your tie, but you didn't need to wear one on my account."

So far I had learned that my ties were a matter that could divide families. I agreed with the general, I liked the tie, but I doubted I would ever wear it again. Women who show cleavage don't fully realize the power they possess and please don't tell 'em.

"Are you married, Mr. Kile?"

"Once."

"Divorced?"

I nodded without hiding my irritation at his questions. "Too bad."

"My ex-wife would disagree with you."

"Kids?"

"With due respect, General, that's enough of that. This isn't a lonely hearts meeting."

He smiled the kind that said he didn't do it much.

"Before we get started I want to return the check your attorney, Mr. Franklin, gave me yesterday." I put it on his desk. "I can't help you with your case."

He left the check lying there and flicked his wrist a few times as if shooing a fly. I took this as an invitation to sit down; I did. After looking at his pocket watch, likely the one the articles reported he had carried since his youth, he said, "You are on time; I like that, sir."

His study was as elegant as the rest of the house, though decidedly more masculine. A massive mahogany desk sat between us, a wall of glass behind him showing off the Pacific Ocean like it flowed simply to grace his home. The moon glazing the night fog sitting on the horizon gave the sheen of a protective coating. The way the sky looked, we might have another hour of good visibility, depending on the wind. The light in the study had been designed to be soft and indirect. According to that daily column in the newspaper that announces the ages of people they figure the rest of us care to know, the general was eighty-seven. One of the articles on him that I read before coming said he suffered from chronic uveitis, an inflammation of the eye. The condition would explain the subdued lighting.

The sidewall of the general's study closest to his desk was mostly bookcases, with some wall area left for photos from his career; the wall on the other side crowded with more photos and plaques. One four-shelf bookcase held only VCR tapes.

He noticed my looking and said, "Family events mostly, I've had the older ones originally in film converted."

"I wish I had done more of that. My early family life is mostly in still pictures, but I've got a ton of those."

"Mr. Kile, if you won't help me, why in tarnation did you come?"

"You're a great American, General Whitaker. It would be disrespectful not to tell you in person."

"Call me, General. Everybody does, even my daughter. As long as you were kind enough to come, before you leave please do me two favors?" Not used to being opposed, he went on without waiting for my answer. "The first, you should find decidedly easy. Drink a Tullamore Dew on crushed ice with a lemon twist." He picked up a handheld bell and rang it. Charles came through the door instantly with a pewter tray centered by a short frosted glass, apparently filled with the Irish whiskey of my ancestors.

The reports said the general could no longer drink himself, but enjoyed watching others imbibe. If he liked them, he felt he was drinking with them. If he didn't like them, well, they didn't get offered the drink in the first place.

The general gave the impression that being eccentric could be a lot of fun. Of course you had to be somewhat wealthy to be eccentric. If one is poor and unconventional in manner and deed, one is simply considered a bit nutty.

"You said two things, General?"

"That I did. While sipping your Dew, read this letter. It is addressed to you. You will notice it is not opened. The letter is from one of my dearest friends, yours too, Mr. Barton Cowen.

I took the letter gingerly between two fingertips and held it for a moment, feeling like a mouse eyeing trapped cheese. Barton Cowen was the father and husband of the family killed by the thug I shot dead on the courthouse steps to earn my four years inside with Axel. Bart came to see me every week while he relentlessly inspired public opinion until the governor's office granted my pardon. Like the mouse, I could not turn from the trap.

When I finished reading Bart's request that I help the general, I sat motionless, looking, I suspect, like an envelope without a name or address on its face. But I knew I had no real choice.

"General, tell me about the case."

"The older I become," he said, "the more impressed I am with what a man is, rather than what he seems. And I like who you are."

"Were it not for Mr. Cowen I would have spent three more years as a guest of the state, and then walked out as an ex-con rather than a pardoned man. But you knew that, General. You knew I could not refuse you after reading this letter." I dropped it onto his desk.

"What I knew, Mr. Kile . . . may I call you Matt?"

"I'd prefer you did, General. Please go on."

"What I knew, Matt, was that you were intrigued. Perhaps it was my reputation mixing with your curiosity. Perhaps from the stories you wished to learn if I would offer you a drink. Then it may have simply been that you are divorced and hoped to meet my celebrated daughter."

"Hmmmm."

"And what does that mean?"

"It means, hmmmm. But to revise and extend my remarks as you regularly heard members of congress say during your years as a member of the Joint Chiefs of Staff, "I had the pleasure of meeting your daughter on the way in. She is a lovely woman."

"Nicely said. A man predisposed to be a fighting man, learns to do so. A woman predisposed to being a seductress hones her skills similarly. Both arts designed to control the man before them. My daughter is not an excessively promiscuous woman, but, like her mother, she enjoys men and is an unapologetic tease."

I recalled a quote from Count Tallyrand, *In order to avoid being called a flirt, she always yielded easily.*

The tone in which the general spoke about his daughter, suggested he was not stressed in the slightest by his daughter's choices or personality. I also guessed he liked the style of woman she had grown to be, or so it seemed from his reference to her mother.

"But, yes," he said, picking back up with what he had been saying before discussing his daughter. "I expected you would come. From your history, I knew you felt a responsibility to set things right. Tell me, Matt, what is your opinion on firing squads?"

"Well, general, they do get the job done. Of course, there are no appeals so one must be certain of the guilt of the person put against the wall."

"You were sure when you took out that crud on the courthouse steps, eleven years ago."

"Yes, general. I was. He deserved it. Now whether it did more good than harm I can't really say."

"That disgusting fellow would have killed more people. Destroyed more families. What you did was the right thing, sir."

"I do think that general. Yes, I do. Still, it hurt those I love, confused their lives. I didn't really think about that part of it when I should have."

"Now don't slide back, Matt. America has become too much of a nambi-pambi society. We need more swift justice. There is a certain discipline society surrendered when we gave up the get-it-done effectiveness of firing squads and public hangings. As for my situation, I knew you were the right man when I read of your helping your houseman, Axel, get his parole. You're a smart, tough guy with a heart and that's exactly what I need."

"What I need is another one of these." I held up my glass. "Then I'd like enough details to determine if I can help. I understand it's an old case."

It has been said that the world has seven deadly sins. I have an eighth: curiosity.

The general rang the bell, and again Charles magically appeared with a tray balanced on his hand, the new glass as frosty as the first. The general's troops had been trained and strategically positioned. I thought my coming was to show respect to a famous retired general. Instead, his welcome was similar to how Sitting Bull had invited General George Armstrong Custer into the Valley of the Big Horn.

"I am no longer able to project my orders as I once could," he said, raising the bell, his smallest finger restraining the clapper. "I know this bell appears aristocratic, but it is unfortunately, necessary. Charles understands, don't you Charles."

Charles nodded, then stood tall and asked, "Will there be anything else, General?"

"Nothing, Charles. As always thank you for your attentiveness and efficiency. Oh, there is something else. Mr. Kile will be looking into that ugly matter some years back involving my grandson, Eddie. His work will require that he learn a great deal about each of us and the goings on within this family. You are to cooperate fully. Answer his questions whatever they may be. And run interference as necessary to gain him access to the individuals and firms that serve this family. We shall trust Mr. Kile's discretion."

"As you wish, General." A slight bow, then Charles closed the door to the study.

"You were correct," he began, "it is an old case. Eleven years, tomorrow, to be exact. Late that night, my grandson Eddie's fiancée, Ileana Corrigan, was murdered. She was expecting my great grandson, a tragedy. I doubt you recall the case; it happened during your first year in prison."

"Tell me about Eddie's parents."

"Eddie's father, Ben . . . Benjamin, my son, was forty-five when he was killed in Desert Storm. That engagement did not kill many of our boys, but it did my son. His mother, my wife Grace, died from breast cancer when Ben was twenty-four; that was in '70. Eddie was born to Ben and his wife, Emily, in '79, so Eddie was twelve when his father was killed. Emily never enjoyed motherhood. Without Ben she wanted to leave. I gave her some money, she signed what my attorneys put in front of her and Eddie came to live with me. Truth was Eddie had been with me whenever Ben was overseas, which was about half the time. Emily would take off until Ben came back, so I have largely raised Eddie with the help of Charles who has also been a great help with Karen."

"I'm sorry for your losses, General."

"Yes. Well. We all have our troubles. But let's get back to the matter at hand. Sergeant Matthew Fidgery was the homicide detective who handled the murder of Ileana. I understand you and he are great pals."

General Whittaker had launched his attack against Fort Kile with a letter from the one man I could never fully repay, and then closed his entrapment with a reference to the case being one of Fidge's unsolved. In between he served Tullamore Dew, and likely arranged for his daughter to extend her, what shall I say, enticing welcome to the family Whittaker. I felt like the deer tied across the hood of a pickup truck. And I didn't yet know jack about the case.

The general smiled. If tonight had been a chess game, this would be the point where I would lean forward and tip over my king. But I had no king to tip over. Instead, I illustrated my capitulation by leaning forward and picking up the check for the thousand dollars.

Like Axel had said, a grand's nothing to sneeze at.